Unexpectedly Bookish

ELISE KENNEDY

I

CONTENT WARNINGS

See the end of the book for content warnings.

Also by Elise Kennedy

***Love in Fairwick Falls* Novels**

Accidentally in Bloom (Rose & Gray)

Wallflower in Bloom (Violet & Jack)

Conveniently in Bloom (Lily & Nash)

Unexpectedly Bookish (Pearl & Reed)

Falling at the Barre (Olivia & Luca)

Forever in Bloom (Allison & Wells)

***Cozy Nights in Vermont* Novellas**

Fall Inn Love

Falling in Vermont

***Only One Cozy Bed* Novellas**

Pumpkin Spice & Pour-overs

Apple Cider & Subterfuge

Hot Cocoa & Mistletoe

Snowed In & Snuggle Weather

***Jingle Bell Springs* Novellas**

The Grump in Jingle Bell Springs

For the
Women Who Rage

*May your hellfire spirit find
the one who burns for you.*

Chapter One

REED

R eed Berry was in *love*.

It wasn't with a woman, though.

Or a man, or a car, or a wristwatch, or a new flavor of syrup for his coffee.

He was in love with a one-hundred-year-old crumbling former library in Fairwick Falls, Pennsylvania.

He caressed the curved walls that were in desperate need of patching. His eyes devoured flawless stained-glass transoms, somehow still standing after decades of neglect.

He fell to his knees at the mint-condition, wide, circular reference desk. The deep walnut finish, the built-in card catalog drawers, with a circular opening wide enough to sit in.

It called like a siren on the edge of the sea, begging him closer.

Am I getting half-hard for a card catalog?

Jesus, I am *a nerd.*

He'd already drafted blueprints for his dream bookstore. This space would slot perfectly into his plans.

The front doors were ornately carved wood with a small stone column on either side. The entryway had mistreated marble floors with a starburst design, and gave way to dark wooden floors.

The ceiling was vaulted high, and bits of decorative plaster-work. Bright light from the afternoon sun shone in the second story windows. Dust motes swirled in the air, sparkling in the sunbeams. A small second story overlooked the open space below, creating a U-shape with plenty of room for book tables or shelves on each side.

Brass rails and deep shelves that would be perfect for displays lined the back wall of the building.

She's gorgeous.

"Wow." He ran his hand through his hair, ruffling it.

"Yeah," the commercial real estate agent sighed. "You'll need a lot of work to get this up and running. I mean, take out that huge wooden desk–"

"No," he said quickly. "No, that's the perfect thing for this space. It's exactly what it needs."

He already felt protective.

"Shoot." The agent held up her phone. "I need to take this. You okay to poke around?"

"Yep," Reed said, already distracted with all of the architectural details, still somehow miraculously intact.

In the quest to find the perfect building for his bookshop, Reed had looked in every major city in Pennsylvania. Finally, he'd tried Fairwick Falls since his best friend had moved here a year ago.

Cute shops lined the town square. A diner, a flower shop, a local hardware store, and a trendy-looking restaurant were only steps away.

This was *exactly* the kind of town that could support an independent bookstore. One that could live up to the dream he and his step-grandfather had shared.

Converting this into a bookshop would be his last project as an interior architect before he hung up his T-square and became a full-time bookshop owner. He couldn't imagine a better send-off for his career than reimagining this place.

Should he restore the defunct fireplace with original dark turquoise tile around it? He was debating whether to use it for a display or to restore it when his phone dinged.

LUCA

stopping by in 2. k?

REED

Yes!!!!

LUCA

k

His best friend was a man of few words.

Reed tended to ramble and have big ideas while Luca was quiet and down-to-earth—a details guy.

Reed *should* have been a details guy, given that his livelihood as an architect required him to be exacting. That was exactly why he had to leave.

He'd always felt like a round peg in too square of a hole.

He walked over creaking wood floors covered in papers and trash. Tall shelves held a brass railing, perfect for a rolling book ladder.

He laughed. *It's too perfect.*

Something scurried from one pile of trash to another. *Okay, almost perfect.*

But I can work with this.

The heavy front door opened, scraping against the marble, and the hulking frame of his life-long best friend appeared.

Reed grabbed Luca in a bear hug.

"Where's the tornado?" Reed asked.

Luca slapped his back hard. "Field trip with her Girl Scout

troop. Brought some company though," Luca said, throwing a thumb over his shoulder.

Pearl, Luca's younger sister, sauntered through the door with her head buried in her phone, her thumbs flying over her screen.

Reed's stomach dropped.

It had been approximately nine and a half years since Reed had last seen her in person—Pearl Bishop, the subject of all his high school fantasies, and his best friend's little sister.

They'd all grown up together, with her just a year younger than him and Luca. Reed had watched her go from stoner guy to stoner girl and back to stoner guy, never stopping at his own nerdy, straight-A station.

Luca would send photos of family holidays, and Reed remembered every single one with Pearl in it.

His eyes had hungrily traced every detail in the photos, filing them away like a meticulous hoarder.

Every curve, every pout. They lived rent-free in his head, on a constant shuffle of attraction.

Nothing could compare though to seeing her in person.

Her porcelain skin and doll-like face were delicate, in beautiful contrast with her piercings and dark makeup. Her pouty lips were painted a jet black, and she had thick dark eyelashes, with piercings on her eyebrows and septum.

Round cheeks, an elegant neck, her permanent scowl etched between her eyebrows, and curves all made his heart skip a beat.

Tattoos flowed into a full patchwork sleeve on her arm. She wore skin-tight black jeans that hugged her thick hips, ass, and thighs. She'd ripped an old band t-shirt and rolled the sleeves, cutting the front to make it a deep V-neck. Her tattooed cleavage peeked out.

She's so goddamn hot I can't breathe.

He'd been a little (okay, a lot) in love with her in high school but figured he'd romanticized the past.

He hadn't.

She glanced up from her phone and did a double take. He waved and flashed a bright smile, trying to mask the dizziness at seeing her.

Pearl had always made him nervous. She said exactly what she thought, whether or not people wanted to hear it.

"You got hot." She frowned as if she'd said, *You're covered in bird shit.*

She went back to her phone with an exasperated look.

Why do I love that so much?

"Been a long time, Pearl."

He'd hit his last real growth spurt after high school, so he probably looked different. He'd been so busy in college and grad school that Luca had always come to visit him. Last year, he and AB had celebrated her fifth birthday in Philly and they'd all had a blast.

Pearl pocketed her phone with a sigh and crossed her arms, looking unimpressed. "So...you're moving here?"

"If I can buy this place. Isn't it great?"

"I do love dead birds," she said flatly, pointing a long, sharp nail at a suspicious-looking mound of feathers in the corner.

Goosebumps covered his arms at her eyebrow raised in challenge. Her black hair was glossy in the sun, and a shine in her hair winked at him as she cocked her head.

His mouth went dry.

Shit, she is distractingly hot.

"What do you think?" Reed asked Luca, trying to keep himself from drooling at Pearl.

Luca flexed his considerable arms as he crossed them. "This is a lot of work, man. Sure you're up for it?"

"I've seen every commercial bookshop space in the state of Pennsylvania. This space has *it*—that indefinable star quality."

"The splatter from recent murders?" Pearl said, lifting a suspicious-looking tarp with her foot.

Fair, that pile of ooze looks murdery.

Luca shook his head at Pearl with a chastising look. "Sorry, she's no help. This building's been empty since we moved here, so you'll have some negotiating room."

"It's at the top of my price range, but it includes the apartment in the back. If I scrape my savings together, I could make it happen. I want to start right away, maybe even launch this fall," Reed said, getting excited.

His dream was at his doorstep after hoping for so long. *I'll be able to quit the job I hate and make something amazing.*

"AB keeps talking about beating you at Connect Four again," Luca said with a soft smile. "It'd be great to be in the same town after so long. Right?" His pointed look at Pearl made her roll her eyes.

"Just what this cute-ass town needs. Another cute-ass store." Pearl pocketed her phone and shrugged. "Everyone's in each other's business. You'll love it, since you're a freak who loves people."

"Aww, you still remember," Reed said, smiling warmly despite her teasing.

"You're a fucking ray of sunshine in human form. It's hard to forget," Pearl said, waving a hand in his general direction. "I'm gonna go pick up AB from Girl Scouts while you ladies gossip."

Pearl turned on her heel and walked out the door without further comment.

The door slammed behind her, and Luca rolled his eyes, letting out a long-suffering sigh. "That's her being nice."

"I remember," Reed said, sighing over the view of her leaving the building.

"When would you move in?" Luca asked.

"In a month, maybe? I need to quit my job, pack up. I could probably get the keys to this place by then."

A smile glowed on Luca's face. "AB is gonna flip when I tell her. I gotta get back to the body shop, but let me know if you need anything."

They hugged, and as Luca left, Reed went back to dreaming about his new love.

His *bookshop*.

He could practically smell the books already. People would mill through the stacks, sit in cozy chairs. Kids would run to the amazing children's section full of bright picture books, with stuffed animals lining the bookcases.

Maybe there could be a weekly story time.

He'd have community events and author signings. *Poetry readings, too. If those are still a thing.*

He couldn't wait to tell ImpossiblyBookish he was finally taking the leap and starting his dream project. She didn't know it was a bookshop yet. He'd keep that part to himself until he was certain it would be perfect.

It *had* to be perfect when he told her.

He'd met her in a book discussion app and connected over a mutual hatred of Hemingway and love of all things pop fiction.

Every day for the past four months, she'd been the best parts of his day. And a few memorable nights, as things had gone from bantering, to flirty, to very X-rated.

He didn't know what she looked like, but their easy conversation was more than enough for him to find her endlessly alluring.

Pretty much his dream woman.

Too bad she lived in Denver.

But today? His eyes scanned the building full of promise.

This just might be the best part of my year.

The real estate agent came back inside. As she was about to

open her mouth, Reed did the most rash thing he'd ever done in his life—his mouth leapt before his mind could keep up.

"I'll take it."

HEMINGWAY_CANSUCKIT

I'm quitting my job today

IMPOSSIBLYBOOKISH

CONGRATS AND FUCK THE MAN

welcome to the 'i'd rather slit open my stomach
and rip out my liver than work for a fucking
suit' club

B Y O A R M

HEMINGWAY_CANSUCKIT

Bring my own …artisanal rabbit meatballs?

Ancient romance manuscript?

Animatronic raccoon miniature?

Also I don't think that's where your liver is.

You'd die before you could even rip it out.

IMPOSSIBLYBOOKISH

see? so metal.

Bring Your Own Anarchist Reading Materials

we meet every tuesday at 3:17pm.

HEMINGWAY_CANSUCKIT

Nothing I love more than a punctual anarchist.

Alas, if only I could fly to Denver for a 3:17
meeting

IMPOSSIBLYBOOKISH

i'd bring breakfast themed snacks just for you.

HEMINGWAY_CANSUCKIT

Noam Chomsky *and* cinnamon rolls??

You know the way to my heart

Thanks for the support.

I'm nervous to do my own thing

IMPOSSIBLYBOOKISH

i know, hemingway.

hence my distraction techniques.

if you need more distraction tonight, you know
who to message.

HEMINGWAY_CANSUCKIT

Can't wait, Bookish.

It's a date

Chapter Two

PEARL

One month later

Knitting needle?

No, no.

Not painful enough.

Rusty hacksaw, maybe?

Pearl idly thought about how to disembowel the man in front of her who'd berated Violet, her sweetest of sweet peach bosses at Bloom, for the past two minutes.

Pearl was usually behind the wheel of the Bloom delivery van, but today she was just a customer, waiting to pick up her special-order balloons for her niece's birthday.

The man pointed a finger at Violet. "I overpaid for an expensive Boston fern four months ago and it's dead now."

Violet's smile wobbled with nerves. "I'm so sorry, I know how hard it is to lose a plant—"

"So where's my refund?" the man sneered, leaning across the counter.

Pearl growled.

Extra rusty, dull hacksaw it is.

Pearl rifled through her enormous purse searching for her wallet so her hands didn't wrap around the guy's throat.

Keys, AB's EpiPen, a book, lotion, another book, black nail polish, book, broken granola bar, headphones... ah, wallet. Always at the fucking bottom.

She stuck her arm in the long satchel, disappearing like Mary Poppins into the never-ending bag.

Violet pushed her curls behind her ears. "Our store policy only covers thirty days after purchase. I'm happy to show you what fertilizer—"

"As if I'd buy anything here again," the man said, puffing his chest. "You need to hire a man who knows what he's doing and dress properly." He gestured to Violet's crop top, where a band of skin was barely visible. "No one wants to see a fat tummy when they shop, little girl."

Violet's mouth fell open in outrage.

Pearl saw red. Her hand was instantly fisted in the man's shirt, getting in his face. "The *fuck* did you just say to her?"

The man flinched, startled.

Pearl already stuck out in the cute-ass town of Fairwick Falls with her demon sex tattoos, facial piercings, and fishnets. Might as well use it to her advantage.

She pointed a long, sharp black nail at Violet as she twisted her fist in the man's shirt, pulling him closer. "That woman is a fucking gorgeous angel, you rat-faced turd. Violet is too nice to throw you out, but it would be my *pleasure* to drag you out by the *four hairs* clinging to your greasy bald spot."

"Pearl," Violet said, giving her a warning look.

"Whatever," the man said, stepping back now, but Pearl saw the fear in his eyes. *Ha.*

"I'm takin' these, and writing you a review." He swiped a

pecan bar and cookie from the checkout counter where local snacks were sold.

The man tore open the bar and took a bite as he took photos of the store and started typing.

Violet blew out a breath. "It's fine. Leave him be." She gave Pearl a tired smile as she rang up Pearl's order. "I'll get AB's balloons. They came in today."

Pearl looked at her bank app as she waited for Violet to come back with them.

There was just enough in her checking account to cover five balloons *and* buy groceries. Her niece was turning six today, but five would have to be enough.

She gulped.

Ah hell. *Who am I kidding?*

Who needed groceries when your favorite tiny human was obsessed with unicorns?

Lily walked down from her studio above the store. "Hey, Pearl. You excited for the party this evening? Nash said—"

A noise clattered behind them.

The asshole man lay on the floor clutching his throat, flowers and chocolate bars scattered around him from crashing into a display.

"Were there nuts in those?" he croaked, looking at the wrapper in his hand as he coughed.

Pearl snorted. "Nuts in the *pecan* bar? Yeah, genius." *He's probably faking it for an insurance scam.*

She was unfortunately all too familiar with what a real allergic reaction looked like.

"Allergic," he coughed out.

No one moved in the store as everyone stared in shock.

His face turned red and gasped for air.

Annnnnd that's what a real allergic reaction looks like.

She groaned, already seeing how the next five minutes of her life were going to go.

Fuuuuck me.

"You." She pointed at Lily. "Call 9-1-1. You"—she pointed to a woman browsing in the store—"check his phone and see if he has a contact to call."

Pearl kneeled beside the piece of shit clutching his throat. "Got an EpiPen?"

He shook his head. "Think I'd be…like this…if I did?" he said, gasping.

"Well, *I* have an EpiPen, smartass." Pearl's eyes gleamed as she saw him register that his life was in her hands.

That she could let him just…wither away.

Tempting, honestly.

But alas, a glimmer of a soul sparked under her cold, dead heart.

She started feeling in her purse for the EpiPen and smirked, raising an eyebrow. "I can watch your ugly, misogynistic face turn purple"—he gasped for breath beside her—"*oooor* I can be nice. But you've gotta Venmo me seven hundred dollars. This shit's expensive when you don't have insurance."

The man nodded, panic in his eyes.

"And apologize to Violet." Pearl pointed to Violet, who stood in shock with a handful of unicorn balloons.

The man coughed and nodded with fear. His face was turning an alarming shade of purple. "S—s—sorry."

Pearl reached deeper in her purse. "*And* tell her she's really pretty."

"Pearl, come on!" Lily said, talking with 911.

"I'm trying! Jesus fuck me in the eardrum," she muttered, peering in the bag. "Why did I think carrying a five gallon bucket bag was a good idea?"

Her hand landed on it. *Finally.*

"Okay, this is going to hurt," Pearl said, uncapping it. "Mostly because I don't like you."

She stabbed his thigh with the EpiPen way harder than necessary.

But he was mean to Violet, so whatever.

Payback's a bitch, and so am I.

The man gasped as the epinephrine took hold and his face de-purpled.

Pearl pulled up the payment app on her phone, but the man just leaned over, gasping. She patted his back. "C'mon, assface, get your phone out. That EpiPen isn't gonna pay for itself."

EMTs burst through the door.

A uniformed woman ran in with a bag, and a man pulled a gurney behind her. "Luckily, we were next door eating lunch," the EMT said as she knelt beside the gasping asshat.

Pearl got to her feet, panicking. "But—"

They swept the man onto the gurney and out the door before Pearl could even form a coherent plea.

The store was quiet again.

"I, um, threw in a sixth balloon," Violet said with a pained smile and handed Pearl the bright balloons.

She officially had six balloons, no money, and now no seven-hundred-dollar EpiPen for AB.

Fuck!

PEARL POPPED pink bubbles with her gum in frustration, attempting to concentrate on her pulpy 70's sci-fi novel.

She leaned against her car in the kindergarten pickup line, the heel of her Doc Martens thumping on her car door. Six unicorn balloons were stuffed in the back seat.

Giving up on the book, she tossed it through the open window of her car. She couldn't concentrate, and the hot purple alien women deserved her focus.

Today was a fucking big day. It was the last day of school, AB's birthday, and the two-year-anniversary party at Bloom *that I have to fucking go to*. Then they'd do birthday fun stuff with AB until they all crashed on a sugar high from the over-the-top birthday cake she'd made for AB.

She knew who would make her feel better.

IMPOSSIBLY_BOOKISH

i stabbed someone to life today

HEMINGWAY_CANSUCKIT

Am I your accomplice now?

Knowing you stabbed someone?

IMPOSSIBLY_BOOKISH

stabbed to LIFE

plus, it was a consensual stabbing

HEMINGWAY_CANSUCKIT

Kinky

Pearl snorted. Hemingway_CanSuckIt was the only person who'd kept her going the last few months.

He was her favorite person to talk to, to be distracted by, to dream about. They shared an overlapping taste in books, the same dark, ironic sense of humor, and dreams of running away from it all.

HEMINGWAY_CANSUCKIT

Are you okay? I saw the crazy storms in Denver.

When she'd learned he also lived in Pennsylvania, Pearl had told a *teensy* lie so she didn't get murdered in her sleep, saying she lived in Colorado.

As a printer salesperson.

No one had follow-up questions on printer sales; plus, it was more impressive than "Girl who works gig jobs with no benefits so she can fuck off when she pleases and make time for her brother and feral, perfect niece."

Once their chats had gotten steamy, he'd offered to exchange phone numbers, but her phone number was *also* a Pennsylvania number.

She'd thought about getting a burner phone, but then she'd have to carry two phones and that just felt crazy.

When her cheap vibrator broke during one of their X-rated chats and she didn't have the thirty dollars to replace it, Hemingway had offered to buy her one.

They'd both gotten off to the idea of her using something he'd bought her.

She'd found a mail-forwarding service in Denver, and lo and behold, a week later she'd had a state-of-the-art vibrator in hand. It suctioned, it buzzed, it bounced, and it was huge. Literal perfection.

He'd passed the not-a-creeper test a handful of times now, but still.

She was in too deep.

IMPOSSIBLYBOOKISH

ya, on the road in Kansas, sellin those printers

She loved the anonymity of it all. She could just be a woman who liked books, not a generally disliked poor fuck-up with anger issues and weird interests who was stuck living a shitty, small life.

The moms in the pickup line sneered at the booming tortured voices screaming from the windows of her beat-up Nissan. Her car stereo blasted a screamy, death-metal cover of *Let It Go*, and, frankly, it fucking slapped.

Peering over her sunglasses, she slowly rolled up her middle finger with a long, black, coffin-shaped nail, eager for this to be the last school pickup for three months. She helped her brother by picking up AB every day and couldn't wait to not see those judgy bitches for three months.

AB's birthday just happened to coincide with the last day of school, so her feral little niece would probably be a feral little monster today.

I can't wait.

An old-timey bell rang, and kids streamed out the school doors. A tall-for-her-age girl with a too-big lavender backpack covered in unicorns pushed her way through. "AP! AP! AP!"

"AB! AB! AB!" Pearl shouted back. AB couldn't say "Aunt Pearl" when she was little. All she'd gotten out was "AP," so Pearl had called her AB instead of Annabelle.

Both nicknames had stuck.

"It's my birthday!" AB launched herself at Pearl's thighs.

Pearl wrapped her arms around the best thing in her life. "Well damn, good thing I got unicorn balloons, huh?"

AB screamed when she saw. A thrash-metal chorus of *Friend Like Me* had started, and they head-banged outside the car.

Pearl didn't give a shit if she'd spent her last fifty dollars on silly birthday balloons or people thought she was an unfit aunt; this was what sixth birthdays were all about.

"C'mon, nugget. Let's get you to Girl Scouts."

"And then I get my birthday cake?" AB asked as Pearl buckled her into her booster seat.

"Yep, your dad and I have to go do this boring work thing, and then I'll pick you up and we will have a unicorn extravaganza."

Pearl very specifically forgot to mention a certain someone

would be staying at their house tonight. She didn't want to hear AB go on and on and fucking *on* about how fun he was.

The guy Pearl couldn't stop thinking about since she'd seen him last month.

Reed Berry, her brother's best friend and a giant pain in her ass.

Chapter Three

REED

Reed clutched the gold key in his hand and stared lovingly at the bookshop on the Fairwick Falls town square.

It's somehow gotten more magical in my four weeks away.

Now it was his, and he couldn't wait to get started.

He'd spent the last four weeks furiously packing, researching, and preparing for the first day of being a bookshop owner. He couldn't wait to finally get started.

But first, he needed to grab the spare key to Luca's place where he'd be crashing tonight.

LUCA

You comin to Bloom still for a house key?

REED

Be there in 2!!

Luca was unveiling a custom van he'd designed for the business owners of a flower shop where Pearl worked part-time.

He couldn't imagine the black-is-my-favorite-color goth

queen among all the pretty florals, but he'd take any glimpses he could get of her as he stopped by to pick up his key.

Reed crossed the street to the bustling flower shop where bright floral arrangements were interspersed with houseplants and gifts. The floral scent immediately put him at ease.

He easily found Pearl in the party crowd, given how she stuck out. It was one of his favorite things about her, always had been. She was unapologetically herself.

She waved with little enthusiasm as she walked to him. He bit his lip, trying to keep the goosebumps at bay. She was curvy, and the way she settled into her hips as she walked had been the star in his every tenth-grade fantasy. Every curve on her body swayed, and he had to squeeze his eyes shut to keep it together.

My pants are too thin for this.

"Hey," Pearl said, looking bored. Pearl turned toward the group of people around her. "Um, guys, this is Luca's best friend, Reed."

"I hope you brought some booze!" a tipsy blonde called. "Because the good stuff just ran out." She turned to him, but her smile fell.

Reed waved with a bright smile, but the crowd's faces started to fall one by one.

He glanced at his shirt. *Do I have a stain or something?*

A tall brunette in the crowd stared at him as if she'd seen a ghost. The champagne flute in her hand slipped, hit the ground, and shattered into a million pieces.

The music stopped. Everything came to a standstill.

"How old are you?" the tall brunette blurted out.

This is a weird town. He quirked an eyebrow. "Um, twenty-seven. Almost twenty-eight," he clarified.

The room let out a sigh of relief.

What the hell is going on?

Maybe Fairwick Falls was a bad idea.

Too bad he was now financially tied to a building five hundred feet away.

"Why do you care how old he is?" Pearl asked with a heavy scowl.

"Um, because..." One of the women faltered, trying to explain.

"Well," a reedy voice called out from the crowd, belonging to an older woman in a neon orange tracksuit.

"You look like our dead dad," the drunk blonde shouted out.

Oh.

Shit.

Twenty minutes later, Reed sat with Luca and the three owners of the flower shop. They were sisters, and they stared at him as if he was a ghost.

He'd wanted to meet other business owners in town, but this was admittedly a weird first step.

Reed smiled weakly, still perplexed. He adjusted his glasses. "I, um...I'm sorry if I made you feel uncomfortable and ruined your thing."

"Oh, don't worry about that. Thank you for chatting with us. We know this is a little odd," said the woman with thick, curly hair holding a baby.

Violet, I think, is her name.

"Do you have any family in the area?" the tall brunette, Rose, asked.

He glanced at Luca who shrugged. *Some moral support backup you are, my dude.*

"I don't know," Reed said honestly. "My mom isn't from the US and my biological dad was a mystery. Just a weekend fling. She married my stepdad who's great and adopted me, but, you know. I'm not, um..." he trailed off, not sure what to share.

His mom said she'd looked for his biological dad but had turned up empty. She'd only had a name, and they'd met in passing at a popular tourist destination.

"Our mom died when we were kids, and our dad died unexpectedly a couple years ago," Violet said. "We don't have any cousins on either side of our family, and if there was even a chance..."

"You're about three years younger than me, so it would have been after our mom died," Lily, the tipsy blonde, said.

Rose handed him an old, worn picture. "We've kept this behind the counter since we re-opened the shop two years ago."

Reed jumped, nerve endings on alert.

He was in the photo.

The photo was at least twenty years old and featured a man who looked exactly like him with three girls surrounding him.

His pulse pounded. He'd never had any inclination to search for his biological dad. He was just happy to be part of the Berry *we-don't-do-steps-in-this-family* family. They'd treated him like their own since he was six years old.

He'd decided a long time ago he didn't need anybody else.

The man staring back in the picture had the same heart-shaped face, same eyes, same shock of auburn hair, same *everything* that Reed saw in the mirror every morning.

His heart pounded in his chest.

"Are you from around here?" Lily, asked.

"Um, a few counties over. Luca, Pearl, and I grew up in West Hickory."

"Wild," Lily said, hiccuping a little.

"So what, you think he could be like...related to you?" Luca said, eyebrow cocked.

"It's probably just a coincidence. It's very flattering, though, that you think we could be related or something. Like a long-lost cousin," Reed said.

He didn't dare ask what their father's name was.

He was afraid of the answer.

"Do you think your mom might still remember him?" Rose asked. "Our dad mentioned a fling in passing once I was an adult."

She looked haunted for some reason.

"Rose, we're pressuring him," Violet said with a kind look at him.

"Well." Rose shrugged defensively.

The baby in Violet's lap started to cry. "Frank needs to be nursed. Excuse me."

Reed's skin prickled in full-body goosebumps. "Frank is the baby's name?"

"Named after our dad," Violet said as she went down the stairs.

He gulped, feeling dizzy. "I could ask my mom if she remembers his name, maybe."

Lies. You know what his name is.

He held up his phone. "Do you mind if I take a picture of it?"

"Please," Rose said.

He took a photo of the old picture and handed it back.

Reed wanted to put them at ease. "I'm sorry for ruining your party. It's been great meeting you, even if we just end up being neighbors. I bought the building across the square, actually. Turning it into a bookstore."

Lily jolted up. "A bookstore? Oh my gosh, Vi is going to pee her pants."

"A bookstore?!" Violet shrieked below.

They chuckled, the weird tension having released in the room.

Lily clapped her hands excitedly. "Come by anytime you

want to talk. I designed this whole store, and I've been itching to get my hands on that building."

His heart contracted a little.

It was nice to have met a few people in this new, weird town he was moving to, even if they probably weren't related.

Frank is a common enough name, right?

Yes, he'd happily come back to Bloom to buy plants for his bookshop, but he couldn't imagine he'd have any connection beyond that to the owners.

I mean, what would the chances be?

IMPOSSIBLY_BOOKISH

i'm gonna kill janice

i swear to god, if she sends another @everyone message about tagging decorum, i will light this whole app on fire

and i dunno, mail her a dead dove or something

okay not a real dead dove, because…sad.

but a VERY real likeness

HEMINGWAY_CANSUCKIT

It's a book app for chrissakes. Her mod power has gone to her head.

Did you see the four paragraph explanation she posted about the misuse of lie and lay?

IMPOSSIBLY_BOOKISH

yes

it made me want to lie/lay in oncoming traffic

HEMINGWAY_CANSUCKIT

Why do that, when there are so many more comfortable places to lie/lay?

IMPOSSIBLY_BOOKISH

like on top of you? 😊

HEMINGWAY_CANSUCKIT

On top of me, under me, next to me. I'm not picky

Just as long as it's with you, Bookish.

Chapter Four

PEARL

On the way home from picking up AB, Pearl's mind drifted away from the bananas scene at the Bloom party. She'd yelled, "Sorry, gotta go be an amazing aunt" and *noped* the hell out of there.

Luca and Reed could figure out the drama with her bosses at Bloom. She had dreams to dream.

Just like every Tuesday evening on the way back from Girl Scouts, Pearl drove past the building she'd stared lovingly at for so long.

A glass-front bakery stood empty, just waiting for somebody to rent it.

A secret part of her *desperately* wanted to be that person.

AB had been deathly allergic to wheat since she was a baby, and Pearl had carried an EpiPen with her ever since. Pearl didn't want her to miss quintessential childhood foods like Wonder Bread, Twinkies, and birthday cake, so she'd become an expert gluten-free baker in the last five and a half years.

It turned out to be the *one* thing she was actually good at.

Pearl dreamed about opening a bakery, making a shit ton of money, and then throwing AB the biggest, best parties ever.

Because her allergy was so life-threatening and she was still so young, AB couldn't go to sleepovers and birthday parties. She had to sit in a special spot in the lunchroom. AB was a sweet kid who was easy to like, but Pearl knew it had to be hard to feel that different.

Pearl looked in the rearview mirror. AB happily flopped her legs back and forth, surrounded by her bright balloons. She deserved the fucking world, and Pearl was going to make sure she never felt left out.

But the hustle life of running your own business? That wasn't really Pearl's vibe. She could barely scrape together gas money, let alone cobble together the five thousand dollars for rent, down payment, insurance, equipment, and security deposit for a bakery.

It's just a stupid pipe dream.

And I'm stupid for even wanting it.

Pearl pulled onto the street of their little rental house that she, her brother Luca, and AB shared.

"Maybe the crows brought me something. I told them it was my birthday," AB whispered to herself as Pearl parked. "I wonder where Beulah is."

"Probably putting in overtime at the fart factory." This razor sharp wit caused AB to double over with laughter as she got out of the car.

Beulah, their evil hag of a neighbor, had been a pain in their ass since they'd moved in two years ago, even calling Child Services after she saw AB running barefoot in the yard last summer. Pretty much every government service that could be called *had* been called on them, so Pearl always gave Beulah's house a double finger salute.

"The crows left me a doll head!" AB squealed.

Pearl had moved in to help Luca after his fiancée, AB's mom, had died. They were just kids themselves and couldn't afford fun activities. So every place they'd lived, she and AB had trained the crows. In return, they'd bring little bits of trash, pennies, and, on occasion, special objects like a creepy doll head.

"Look, they poked its eyes out," AB yelled as she held it with glee. "Creepy."

"So creepy," Pearl said with encouragement as she unlocked the door.

"I'm gonna get my unicorn sweatshirt!" AB screamed as she ran through the kitchen, throwing her backpack down.

The last seven months had been nothing but unicorns. Unicorn bedsheets, unicorn shows, unicorn shirts, unicorn folders, and AB had requested a unicorn cake where she could see the inside of a unicorn.

Pearl's little goth heart had nearly exploded with pride at the creepy-ass request.

Luca walked in as Pearl got out the unicorn cake she'd worked on for fucking *hours*.

"Look at this rainbow barf masterpiece." She pushed the four-layered, rainbow icing cake onto the kitchen table. She'd even given it an upside-down ice cream cone for the horn, iced with lavender swirls.

"Looks amazing," Luca said placidly as he tossed his boots in the mudroom. "What'd you use this time?"

"Major-eleven-allergen-free flour, applesauce, hopes, dreams, and some dirt probably." She shrugged as Luca chuckled.

She loved seeing her brother smile after years of his empty, sad eyes.

Pearl snapped photos of her masterpiece. She'd really nailed the eye-meltingly bright icing this time.

Luca poured a glass of tap water. "Ever hear back from the owners of the bakery?"

Pearl's stomach fell again. "I heard them *laughing* as I told them how much money I had for rent. I need to find another part-time job now that the hellspawn Montgomery twins don't need babysitting anymore."

Luca scrubbed at his hands with a special soap to get mechanic grime off. "I'll float you a loan. Just tell me how much."

Pearl shook her head no. She couldn't fuck up his and AB's life. "I'm not built to run a business. Customers have to *like* you. You can't yell at them, and flipping them off is generally frowned upon. Plus, you need your cash for gas and road-trip snacks."

Luca and AB would be leaving tomorrow on a two-month trip to Florida to visit AB's maternal grandparents.

"We can talk about it anytime you want," Luca said, drying his hands. He'd founded his own successful body shop with hardly anything right out of high school.

"Knock, knock," a deep, warm, cheerful voice called from the front door.

"Noooo," Pearl groaned, not wanting him to intrude on their birthday fun with AB. "Can't he come back when we're all asleep?"

Luca pointed at her. "Be nice. It's just for tonight."

"There's...there's not enough cake for him," she said, staring at the enormous cake.

"Hope it's okay I let myself in." Reed tossed his duffle bag down. The bright happiness in Reed's face with his warm smile and chiseled jawline punched her in the stomach.

Pearl had picked her jaw off the floor when she'd seen him last month. He'd gone off to college looking like a never-going-to-bloom twelve-year-old. He'd largely remained a mystery she didn't think much about since then.

Now, standing in their kitchen, he looked like a dude bro who'd have opinions on polo or boating, with his muscular frame, golden tan, cut jawline, and expensive-looking clothes.

His smile was warm as he talked with Luca, and she licked her lips, thinking about his sculpted mouth. A few freckles were sprinkled on his cheeks, and his thick auburn hair was just long enough to brush the top of his eyebrows.

Even worse, there were still shadows of the nerdy kid she'd known. Glasses, an academic look with his button-up shirt and sweater vest—*Fucking sweater vest!*—over his muscles and broad shoulders.

The combination made her off-kilter. Dizzy. Confused.

A little horny.

Apparently there was such a thing as being *too* hot. It was weird and unsettling, like watching a dog walk on its hind legs for too long.

You couldn't trust it, all that hotness. She didn't *like* this feeling, being offset and not entirely in control.

Give her someone snarky, someone suspicious. Someone like Hemingway_CanSuckIt.

"Hey," she said to him finally.

Reed's smile widened as he looked past her.

"Did you make that? That's amazing." He set his backpack on top of his bag.

"Hey." She poked his shoulder. "Go wash your hands in case you have any wheat on you." Pearl pointed to the sink.

She was on edge from having used her EpiPen earlier that morning.

Luca stared at her and mouthed, *Fucking be nice.*

Pearl gave him the universal head wiggle for *I* was *being fucking nice, dickhead.*

"So," Pearl sighed, feigning disinterest. "You're staying in Fairwick Falls now, or what?"

See? I can be so nice, Pearl's eyes said as she squinted at her brother.

Reed nodded as he scrubbed his hands. "I'm looking for

temporary apartments. I need to find something until the apartment above the bookstore is ready."

"You know what?" Luca said, pointing from Reed to Pearl. "Why don't you stay here while AB and I are gone this summer—"

"But I was going to walk around naked," Pearl whined.

Reed hit his head on the cabinet above the sink, startled by something.

"And," Luca continued, ignoring her, "use your rent money to hire her for the bookstore. You'd get it running faster. Plus, Pearl is looking for another part-time job. She knows books, and you're launching a bookstore. Easy, right?"

Luca looked at her smugly.

A face perfect for smothering in his sleep tonight. "Traitor," Pearl muttered under her breath.

Reed dried his hands and adjusted his glasses, thinking. "It'd be nice to have the extra help. I could probably open this summer if it wasn't only me doing it all."

"What would I even do?" She scoffed. She wasn't getting anyone coffee.

"Whatever I need done, I guess," Reed said with a bright smile. "You'd be like my assistant. All the hours you'd want."

Pearl's stomach twisted. She did need to replace the EpiPen for when AB was back. Her handful of hours at Bloom weren't enough to cover it and living expenses.

And she needed more cash for the life she wanted. Her own apartment, a new car.

An allergen-free bakery.

Could she actually build a nest egg for all her dreams if she had a job with more hours?

"I'll think about it," Pearl said, her eyes connecting with Reed's briefly.

Reed's smile made her skin buzz as he nodded back. "I'd be

lucky to have your help. So, where's the birthday girl?" he yelled louder.

"Uncle Reed!" AB screamed as she ran into the kitchen. They did a complicated series of hand gestures, arm flaps, butt wiggles, stepping around each other like chickens, and then ended with making a horn on their heads and whinnying.

Pearl scowled.

Sonofabitch. He *gets a secret handshake?*

"Happy birthday, Anna the Bell-Breaker!" Reed pointed to AB, pretending to be aghast. "Did you know she left a *big crack* in the Liberty Bell when she was in Philly?"

"It was there when I got there." AB giggled.

Turns out the combo of very hot man and dorky dad energy was *devastatingly* adorable.

Her ovaries were practically panting. This had to stop right fucking now. *Heel, girls. Heel!*

"Is it time for cake yet?" AB yelled. The unicorn horn on her sweatshirt bounced from her excitement.

"Oh, shoot, your birthday present is outside." Reed jogged out and came back holding the largest goddamned stuffed unicorn Pearl had ever seen, barely able to push it through the door. "I heard somebody liked unicorns in this house."

AB screamed with excitement so high, the windows could have shattered.

Pearl mentally facepalmed.

Who needed balloons when you had a stuffed sparkly unicorn the size of a fucking Holstein?

Luca lit the birthday candles. "Come on, blow out your candles, Annabelle." His usually stern expression looked like a melted puddle of ice cream as he stared at his daughter.

She jumped off the cow-sized plushie and ran laps around the kitchen before stopping at the cake with six multi-color candles on it. She closed her eyes tight and blew out all six candles.

"Okay, you ready?" Pearl held a knife, ready to cut the cake.

"Did you do it?" The bloodlust in AB's little eyes made her proud.

"What do *you* think, kid?" Pearl cut a slice out of the cake, causing the gluten-free gummy worms and multi-colored goo she'd layered into the cake to spill out.

"Ew, it's so grooooooss. It looks like unicorn blood. I love it!" AB's arms wrapped around Pearl, whose stone-cold bitchy heart melted into her own pool of black ice cream.

AB stabbed a piece and took a bite. "It tastes like…"

"Candy rainbow barf explosions?" Pearl suggested.

"Yeah! Uncle Reed." AB turned quickly. "Wanna see my doll heads the crows brought me?"

"…Yes," Reed said slowly, taken aback, but tried to meet AB's enthusiasm.

AB threw open the sliding glass door to the backyard.

"I wish we could do a real birthday party." Luca sighed as they watched AB and Reed run around the backyard. "Maybe next year."

Pearl lightly punched his arm, wanting to knock sense into him. "You saved for a big Disney trip. She won't remember some snot-nosed kid at her birthday party in ten years. She's going to remember riding all the scary roller coasters with her dad."

Luca shuddered. "God, I hope she doesn't want to do roller coasters. You're sure you don't want to come with?"

"Wuss." Pearl bumped her hip against his with a smile. She was so fucking proud of him. After how shitty their parents had been, he'd managed to be the best dad ever to AB. "Nah, you guys need bonding time."

And I need to make some cash.

Luca's eyebrows knitted together. "It's not a problem if he stays here, right? Sorry, I should have asked first."

"I'm pissed about your scheming." Pearl stuck her tongue out. "But it's fine. He's a good guy, and perfectly harmless." *Despite the hotness.* "Like a sentient mannequin with no downstairs parts."

"It'd mean a lot to me if you tried to be friendly. He'll be around a lot now," Luca said.

She sighed. "If I must."

She twisted her traitorous lips to keep them from smiling as Reed jumped like a possessed sock puppet while AB blasted him with her bubble gun.

Psst, do you see how cute he looks? her ovaries whispered, swooning.

Shut up, shut up!

AB ran up the patio stairs and yanked open the sliding glass door, panting. "AP, I hit Reed with my bubble gun and blasted all the toxic mascaras outta him."

"Toxic *masculinities*. Good job, nugget," Pearl said, squatting down. "Now, show him your self-defense class moves. He'll love it."

AB took off.

Luca gave her a *what the fuck* look. "Self-defense class?"

"It's what we call watching *Miss Congeniality*."

AB stomped on Reed's foot, elbowed him in the stomach, and bit his hand. Pearl doubled over, weeping from laughter. She was so proud.

Yes, she could handle Reed being her roommate and potential boss. She wasn't the least bit tempted by all that happy hotness.

That hasn't always been the case, though, she admitted the buried secret.

No one else on earth knew that the hot, nerdy man had origi-nally been the sweet, nerdy boy who'd been her very first kiss.

IMPOSSIBLYBOOKISH

so i just finished a bodice ripper from the 90s
that was…

…beat for beat…

The Count of Monte Cristo

HEMINGWAY_CANSUCKIT

Bookish. Dearest. Darling.

It's 2 in the morning in Pennsylvania

IMPOSSIBLYBOOKISH

sorry for waking you up

go to sleep!

HEMINGWAY_CANSUCKIT

Well now I can't stop thinking about the ghost of
Alexandre Dumas possessing an innocent writer
with a perm and feather bangs.

Getting women horny while they drank Frescas

And ate Snackwells

And watched…uh…Dallas?

IMPOSSIBLYBOOKISH

the nineties were more

horny women, snackwells, and

9-oh-2-1-oh

HEMINGWAY_CANSUCKIT

yet another fantastic haiku

IMPOSSIBLYBOOKISH

::waves like a princess to the adoring crowd::

i'm just saying

i would have read classic books sooner had they been wrapped in this horny-flavored cheese.

HEMINGWAY_CANSUCKIT

So, what classic should be next?

Pour some horny-flavored cheese on me

IMPOSSIBLYBOOKISH

it was the best of cocks,

it was the worst of cocks

HEMINGWAY_CANSUCKIT

To be on top,

Or not to be on top

That is the question

IMPOSSIBLYBOOKISH

it is a truth universally acknowledged,

that a single woman in possession of a good rack

must be in want of some tit fucking

HEMINGWAY_CANSUCKIT

That sounds like a personal truth, B

Rather than universal

IMPOSSIBLYBOOKISH

my boobs are pretty great

and it might be a BIT of a personal truth

i do love a good tit fuck.

mine are sort of perfect for it.

HEMINGWAY_CANSUCKIT

Jesus. I'm trying to go to sleep here.

Can't do our thing tonight.

> IMPOSSIBLYBOOKISH
>
> okay fine. night!

HEMINGWAY_CANSUCKIT

….

Jesus bookish.

I'm fucking HARD now.

Your fault.

> IMPOSSIBLYBOOKISH
>
> ::flutters eyelashes::
>
> hope this close up helps you sleep.
>
> {photo loading}

HEMINGWAY_CANSUCKIT

Holy fuck

I

cn't brate.

breathe*

Your cleavage is…

Holy fuck.

your breasts are …

Bookish.

I don't think there are words in the English language.

Lickable? Perfection? Resplendent?

IMPOSSIBLYBOOKISH

it's the only part of me that doesn't have an identifiable mark, so i thought i'd give you a treat.

sweet dreams.

HEMINGWAY_CANSUCKIT

You're evil

IMPOSSIBLYBOOKISH

evil AND horny

HEMINGWAY_CANSUCKIT

Fine. We can do the thing.

Give me 2 minutes

Such a brat.

IMPOSSIBLYBOOKISH

you love it

HEMINGWAY_CANSUCKIT

God, I really fucking do.

…You want your tits fucked tonight, gorgeous?

IMPOSSIBLYBOOKISH

yes please 🖤

HEMINGWAY_CANSUCKIT

Kneel on the edge of your bed

IMPOSSIBLYBOOKISH

what do i get if i do?

HEMINGWAY_CANSUCKIT

SUCH a brat.

Fine.

A pic of my cock weeping for you

You've already made a mess of me.

IMPOSSIBLYBOOKISH

fuck. yes.

i've always wondered what it looked like.

okay, i'm on my knees

for you and you only h

HEMINGWAY_CANSUCKIT

{picture loading}

IMPOSSIBLYBOOKISH

whoaaaaaaa

hemingway.

hon. that's a fucking huge cock.

i adore you but come on.

i want to see yours

not some internet porn guy.

send me the real thing

please?

HEMINGWAY_CANSUCKIT

I don't think I've ever laughed so much while
also this hard.

That's me, B

IMPOSSIBLYBOOKISH

prove it.

give me the finger in the next photo

HEMINGWAY_CANSUCKIT

I thought you preferred three fingers

IMPOSSIBLYBOOKISH

fine, three please.

HEMINGWAY_CANSUCKIT

Fine.

{picture loading}

Uh.....

Bookish?

IMPOSSIBLYBOOKISH

brb finding a custom wallpaper site so I can stare at this on my ceiling every day.

that's a porn cock, h.

thick and long

HEMINGWAY_CANSUCKIT

About the size of the vibrator I sent

Tried to match it

IMPOSSIBLYBOOKISH

no waaaaaaaaaaaaay

fuuuuck me

how did you not tell me this?

holy shit that's so hot

can't use it right now. roommates will hear.

HEMINGWAY_CANSUCKIT

I'd start with your huge, perfect tits. Squeezing them. Sucking on them.

Run my tongue between them and get lost in them

Fuck I love heavy tits like yours.

Your skin is like ivory and those fucking veins on them...

I want to lick them. Trace every one with my
tongue up to your throat.

Bite your shoulder.

IMPOSSIBLYBOOKISH

yessss

HEMINGWAY_CANSUCKIT

Can't stop thinking about them.

Shove my face in them, scrape my teeth along
the curves.

Show me how wet your panties are

IMPOSSIBLYBOOKISH

can't

not wearing any

HEMINGWAY_CANSUCKIT

Christ.

Spread your thighs when you kneel.

Get the vibrator but don't turn it on

IMPOSSIBLYBOOKISH

okay

HEMINGWAY_CANSUCKIT

I'd cup you

Would you soak my hand?

IMPOSSIBLYBOOKISH

yessss

fuck

my hand is covered in it

HEMINGWAY_CANSUCKIT

Rub it between your tits

Get it all.

IMPOSSIBLYBOOKISH

jesus

this is so hot. it's so slick when i grab them.

HEMINGWAY_CANSUCKIT

Do it again, I want you covered in your scent
for me.

I'd lick a valley, wanting to taste you

Then I'd squeeze your tits together tight, and
fuck straight up, slow and hard, popping
between them

Rubbing the head of my cock right at the top
again and again.

Shove the vibrator between your tits.

Feel good?

IMPOSSIBLYBOOKISH

oh my god

yes. big and heavy.

i need to come so bad

HEMINGWAY_CANSUCKIT

You'd rub your clit, teasing it while I fuck your
perfect breasts

Squeezing them together

Pulsing up in them harder and harder

Slick

Tease your clit for me B

IMPOSSIBLYBOOKISH

my pussy is so wet, that its loud

HEMINGWAY_CANSUCKIT

Don't care. Rub harder.

Goddamn I want to fuck your tits so badly

IMPOSSIBLYBOOKISH

i'm gonna come….

where are you gonna come on me?

HEMINGWAY_CANSUCKIT

Oh I think you know Bookish

IMPOSSIBLYBOOKISH

say it

HEMINGWAY_CANSUCKIT

Fuck. Can't last.

Too hot. Feels too good.

As I'm about to come I'd shove your mouth
down on my cock

Like you like it

IMPOSSIBLYBOOKISH

Y-

es

I'm about tocomefukkkk

HEMINGWAY_CANSUCKIT

Fucking into your mouth as

I come

Flooding it down your throat

fuccck me

comming

IMPOSSIBLYBOOKISH

holy shit, i came so hard i had to bite my hand to keep from screaming.

that was so hot.

i wish i could be there right now

...

hemingway?

did i kill you with my tits?

HEMINGWAY_CANSUCKIT

Almost

Jesus.

I am an absolute mess

And you are perfection

IMPOSSIBLYBOOKISH

thank you

HEMINGWAY_CANSUCKIT

Any time.

Alexandre Dumas's ghost would be so proud right now

Chapter Five

REED

good morning 🖤

That fucking black heart emoji always made him happy.

Reed fought a dopey grin in the early morning light despite the pain in his back. He'd slept on Luca's torture chamber couch last night.

How long had it been since he'd had somebody wish him good morning? The simple act of being thought of first thing shot straight to his heart.

And his cock, remembering last night.

HEMINGWAY_CANSUCKIT

I was thinking about you, too.

Wondering if you were one of those morning readers.

Good morning, by the way. 

IMPOSSIBLYBOOKISH

WHO THE FUCK READS IN THE MORNING?

HEMINGWAY_CANSUCKIT

Sociopaths, I think.

IMPOSSIBLYBOOKISH

like for fun? they read when they could be
sleeping?

HEMINGWAY_CANSUCKIT

I'm glad we're on the same page.

Sometimes I think about this fictional cottage by
the sea I would live in, in an ideal world where I
would wake up late, be lazy, drink coffee. Maybe
I'd read in the morning then.

I'd have a personalized trolley of tea there
for you.

IMPOSSIBLYBOOKISH

ooo, my own tea trolley

HEMINGWAY_CANSUCKIT

And I think there'd have to be a fireplace.

Crucial for those windy ocean days.

But here he was setting up his bookstore in a very landlocked
state, but she didn't need to know that.

IMPOSSIBLYBOOKISH

are you a cuddler?

you seem like a cuddler

His heart leapt in his throat. He *yearned* for cuddling. It had
been years. Literal goddamn years.

HEMINGWAY_CANSUCKIT

I'm an expert cuddler.

Black belt and everything.

if i ever doubted you were a man, it's been
cleared up right now.

only a man could make cuddling competitive

He burst out laughing into his arm, not wanting to wake anyone in Luca and Pearl's house. AB was still asleep upstairs.

HEMINGWAY_CANSUCKIT

Guilty as charged.

IMPOSSIBLYBOOKISH

alright, talk me through what expert cuddling
looks like because, to be honest, i'm on the
fence

Oh god. It'd been ages since he'd been close enough to anybody to cuddle. He closed his eyes, picturing...who?

Bookish? The photo from the night before was the first time he'd seen any part of her. It had only been a close-up of the line of her cleavage.

He pictured someone with an otherworldly quality to her. It seemed like Bookish didn't fit in like he didn't fit in. Maybe they would fit together.

HEMINGWAY_CANSUCKIT

My back is against the couch with my leg
extended

And you - or anyone who needs a cuddle

IMPOSSIBLYBOOKISH

anyone, huh?

HEMINGWAY_CANSUCKIT

Okay, not just anyone.

They'd settle back against me.

He sighed, thinking of the pleasure of having a constant weight pressed against his chest, quieting the noise in his head. If he could figure out how to wear a weighted blanket at all times, it would solve a lot of his problems.

HEMINGWAY_CANSUCKIT

A light blanket would be drawn over your legs to keep you warm, or I might hook one leg over yours.

IMPOSSIBLYBOOKISH

sir, this is a cuddling expedition, not the second base express

HEMINGWAY_CANSUCKIT

You would lie with your head on my chest, arm hooked around my waist.

I'd fold you into my chest, letting my arms surround you.

I'd have one hand for reading and one hand playing with your hair.

Stroking it out of your face as you read your own book or I read Walden aloud.

IMPOSSIBLYBOOKISH

reading aloud and playing with my HAIR?

jesus fucking

CHRIST

alright, i take it back.

you do have a black belt.

~

PEARL

Pearl stood barefoot in the yard as Luca backed out onto the alley drive.

Don't cry, don't cry.

Reed stood beside her as they waved Luca and AB off on their adventure. "Your memories are going to be magical! You'll have the best time ever!" he called.

"Say hi to Belle for me. Tell that bitch I want her library!" Pearl yelled, her stupid throat catching with emotion.

AB waved back, her little hand poking out from Luca's SUV.

"You old softy," Reed muttered under his breath as he waved like a goofy maniac.

"I'm hard as fuck," Pearl said, surreptitiously wiping a tear from her eye. "It's just been a long time since I've been away from them"—a catch hissed in her throat—"and you know what? You're stupid."

She *had* actually looked forward to spending two glorious months alone doing torrid things all over the house.

Now she had a hot man, who was somehow hotter than he'd been last month, living with her.

"Come on, daywalker. Let's get you out of the sun." He spun her by the shoulders toward the house. Her shoulders were already starting to burn.

She hated that he remembered.

"Hey," a weaseling, metal-grinder voice called from the next yard over. The voice sounded like a carburetor was going bad and perhaps a small animal was trapped inside it.

Beulah, the human equivalent of a poison tree frog, and her stupid giant hat peeked out from her manicured rose bush. "Get your piece of trash duct tape car off my property line."

"It's on the *road,* and barely one inch in front of your house, you blind old cavefish," Pearl said, flipping her the bird as she stomped up the back patio steps.

"Get a job!" Beulah yelled.

"Only if it's digging your grave, crypt keeper!" Pearl yelled back as Reed gently maneuvered her in through the back door.

"Is it wise to upset the finicky old neighbor?" Reed asked as Pearl stomped past him.

"That's the tip of the iceberg with Beulah Spurgeon."

He grimaced. "God, it sounds like you're barfing when you say that."

"That's also how I feel when I look at her." Pearl opened the cabinets to angry snack.

Shit, she'd forgotten to go to the grocery store again. With the lingering balance of a whole two dollars in her bank account, she'd have to snack on dry ramen. The rest of the birthday cake was in the freezer for when AB got back from their trip.

Reed pointed toward the front door. "I need to bring in the rest of my boxes..."

Pearl stared at him with narrowed eyes.

"...And I guess I will be getting them myself. That's okay, I need the exercise," he said, cheerfully whistling as he pushed open the screen door. He jogged to his shiny, certified pre-owned sedan that sat in stark contrast next to her hunk of dented gray metal literally held together with duct tape.

Beulah was mean, but she was accurate.

Pearl threw her head back and groaned. Fuck, she was gonna have to work for that man.

He was going to be so fucking cheerful, it would make her teeth hurt. Like when she'd snorted Sweet'N Low in ninth grade on a dare and had coughed puffs of sweetness for days.

But she *also* really wanted scrambled eggs and hash browns at Pop's diner instead of lukewarm ramen. So, sacrifices would have to be made.

She'd never wanted to work for the man—or *any* man, to be frank—but she needed to be there for AB. She wanted a future, maybe even growing beyond her fuck-around phase she'd been in for the last ten years.

Punk is doing what you want, right?

Maybe it *could* be punk to get your shit together.

Reed opened the door with his foot as he carried in two suitcases and two boxes. His shirt strained against the muscles of his toned and tan arms.

Quality biceps. The kind that dipped and curved into other muscles with a vein running over them.

She couldn't stop *staring* at them. She felt like a cartoon wolf about to shout *awooga.*

"Pearl? Which room?" he said and caught her ogling him.

Fuck.

"Down the hall on the right, and stay the fuck out of my room."

"Boundaries are important!" he called over his shoulder.

God, she couldn't even faze him. At least she usually got a reaction out of people when she poked and prodded. Reed "The Whistler" Berry took it all in stride.

He was going to be insufferable when she agreed to be his assistant.

I mean, books aren't so bad, right? She spent her money recklessly on three things: tattoos, piercings, and books. She had stacks and stacks of old, weathered paperbacks in her room.

A bookstore could maybe even be fun?

Reed jogged through the house and out the door with a smile and his hair flopping. He was like an actual goddamn golden retriever, auburn hair flopping in the breeze and his tongue lolling with happy excitement, unaware of the horrors of being a human.

Before she could slurp another ramen noodle, Reed bounced back in with an arm full of boxes, including rolled-up blueprints.

"I thought we could go to the building since I have the keys, scope it out, see if it's your jam..."

My jam?

"...and then maybe have a roommate movie and pizza night. What do you say?" His glasses had slid down his nose, and he pushed them up with his arm, unfazed by the heavy boxes he was holding and the utter disinterest on her face.

She couldn't tell him tonight. He'd be absolutely insufferable.

The words *trust fall* would probably come up.

"I have deliveries today to make for Bloom and then three dogs to walk."

His face fell a little. She might have missed it had she not seen it regularly as a kid.

"Sure," he said, shrugging, a happy smile back on his face. "I'm going to work at the bookstore all day today and tomorrow, so, you know...stop by whenever and we can talk about the thing. Or *not* doing the thing. Or just hang out, or eat gluten-free pizza, or, you know...whatever."

Her stone-cold black heart squeezed a little bit for the nice guy who was trying his best.

But then he started fucking whistling again as he jaunted back to his borrowed bedroom.

Pearl pulled out her phone and swiped to her conversation with Hemingway_CanSuckIt.

IMPOSSIBLY_BOOKISH

you wouldn't believe the morning i've had.

the summer is already ruined, everything is terrible

> my new roommate is driving me up the fucking
> wall, and all I can think about is the very purple
> amazing friend that is now too loud to use when
> my roommate is home. Ugh!

She washed her dishes and teacup in the sink. Maybe someday she'd have an apartment with a dishwasher.

Her phone lit up. She kept it on silent, like any normal person.

HEMINGWAY_CANSUCKIT

Your roommate sounds awful

Especially because of the whole giant purple
vibrator part.

I thought about that this morning in the shower.

Even though I'd love to repeat it, mostly I wish
you lived in a place that made you happy.

Pearl's heart clutched. No one in her life talked to her this way. Genuine, and open.

HEMINGWAY_CANSUCKIT

I'm always here if you need to vent. Or blow off a
little steam. 😏

IMPOSSIBLY_BOOKISH

tempting, but alas. work calls.

HEMINGWAY_CANSUCKIT

Already? Isn't it like 7 am there?

Shit. She forgot she was supposed to be in Denver.

IMPOSSIBLY_BOOKISH

yeah, early meeting today…

HEMINGWAY_CANSUCKIT

Good luck. You'll do great

She didn't have a big meeting. Her day wasn't even really that important in the grand scheme of things.

But she decided to pretend as if she needed it and chose to take his good luck to heart.

Maybe it would turn things around for her.

Chapter Six

REED

"And then we went into za public *sauna* and your dad yelped at all za naked people's fiddly bits."

Reed rested his forehead on the cool brick outside his bookshop, wishing he hadn't just heard his mother say *fiddly bits.*

"*Mom.*"

It was nearing hour two of his mom's monologue, and he desperately wanted to see how construction was going inside the shop.

"Oh, don't be so American," she chastised. His mom was originally from Sweden, and her warm, slightly accented voice always felt like a cozy sweater. She and his dad had moved to Europe a few months ago after his dad had retired. "So, how's work?"

He hadn't told them about the bookshop yet. He would.

Someday.

When it's successful.

"Oh, you know, just, um..." What could he tell her that was true? "...work has been busy. I'm launching a new project. Leading it."

Not a lie, technically.

"We're very proud," she said, as a factual statement with little emotion. *Ah, the Swedes.* "Dad wants to say hi."

"Heya, Chip!" His dad yelled into the phone far too loudly. His dad had always gotten a kick out of people saying Reed was a "chip off the old block," following in his architecture footsteps.

His dad was athletic and charming, and a renowned architect—pretty much the opposite of Reed. So, he'd pretended to like architecture as a kid so they'd have something to bond over. He'd spent a lifetime trying to live up to the high expectations of Ralph Berry's celebrated architecture career.

"You're leading a project?" his dad asked.

"Yep, it's a big one," Reed said, his eyes zeroed in on the front door of the bookshop.

This place needs a name, he thought idly.

"That's the spirit." His dad sounded so proud that it broke Reed's heart a little. "With the hours you're putting in, in a year or two, you could be a manager in a boutique firm. Your grandpa would be so proud."

Reed was a third-generation architect. He'd felt like a real member of the Berry family when he'd decided to become an architect in fourth grade

The fact that he'd hated it had been his long-held secret.

"Thanks, Dad." The guilt roiling in his stomach was a physical thing, like the garlic aftermath of a heavy Italian dinner.

You are lying to your parents fully knowing they would not approve. They'd point out your failed ventures after high school, after college, and the single day of your ill-fated Groundhog Day food truck.

He just didn't want to fail.

He couldn't let his grandpa down, the one person who had been a dreamer like him, and the reason he could even afford to buy the building in the first place. When he'd passed, he'd left

Reed an unexpected inheritance with one direction: "For your dreams."

This was his one shot to make something that was really *him*.

"All right, it's time for our *fika*. That means coffee break," his dad said with excitement.

As Reed said goodbye, the flower shop across the town square caught his eye.

What if the Parkers' dad *was* his biological father? Did it change anything?

What would one even do *with three sisters?*

And why the hell did they have to be right across from the store he was forever financially tied to?

The nerves in his stomach eased as he walked through the door, distracted by the thwack of hammers. Construction crews had been working nonstop since he'd gotten the keys.

"Bert, my favorite contractor." Reed stuck up his hand for a high five.

The older man in his sixties sighed and gave him a half-hearted high five.

Reed turned around for a backwards low five.

"I'm not doin' the secret handshake." Bert tucked a pencil behind his ear and went back to the blueprints.

"Oh, come on. It'll be our thing." Reed shot finger guns at him to loosen him up.

"Not gonna happen," Bert said with a chuckle.

"I'll wear you down," Reed said with happy confidence. "But, while I have you, I *did* have a new idea."

Bert dropped his head at the news. He whistled over the noise of the construction. "Everybody, take five!"

Reed pulled out his new blueprint, and it unfurled to the floor.

"Make that ten," Bert called over his shoulder, frowning. "Look, kid, this is the third change you've made in three days.

Why don't you sit on this and we'll come back in a year and discuss it."

Reed swiped away empty coffee cups on the makeshift sawhorse table. "Because I realized what was missing. We have a perfect kids' section. We have this gorgeous checkout counter, but we don't have…?" He wiggled his eyebrows in excitement, waiting for Bert to finish his sentence.

"…A big check with more money?" Bert asked.

"A nook! A big reading nook." Reed smacked his sketch for effect.

"A nook?" Bert echoed, scratching his head.

"See, the nook will be inset on the stage."

"The *stage*?" Bert echoed with exasperation.

"Of course, for poetry readings, performances. Can't be the center of the community without a stage. You're gonna *love* the vision once you spend some time with the blueprints." Reed patted Bert's shoulder.

Jangling keys sounded, and a curvy shadow stood in the open doorway, surrounded by sunlight.

Reed gulped. She looked like a demon coming to collect his immortal soul.

A really hot demon.

Pearl wore a tight-fitting t-shirt knotted high on her soft, curvy stomach. Her black shorts were high-waisted and flowed to mid-thigh with a flounce. She wore torn fishnet tights underneath, a fashion choice Reed had always appreciated.

"Give me a minute, Bert. Use your imagination. Think positively!"

"I'll sprinkle some friggin' pixie dust on it," Bert grumbled, staring at the blueprints.

Reed jogged to Pearl. "Hey, roomie."

She pushed her black sunglasses up to her jet-black hair that complemented her porcelain skin. It was like she'd been destined to become a goth queen.

She blinked and slowly swallowed her iced tea.

He *knew* Pearl. She wasn't trying to be sexy but goddamn if he didn't follow every movement—every flick, every glance, every move of her throat. He could write a dissertation on her thighs, her hands, her nails, the round apple of her cheeks.

She'd been his biggest crush in high school and had been so unattainable it was laughable. They'd been roommates for a couple of days, but he still hadn't gotten used to seeing her.

"I'm in," she said flatly.

He clapped his hands. "I knew it! We're gonna be a dream team. This is going to be amazing. Should we get matching shirts? Maybe we should get *lanyards*."

She glared. "*No* lanyards."

"No, you're right. We don't have the final logo yet. This is very exciting." He did everything he could not to bounce in place. "To get started, we could do a daily 8 AM status meeting. Maybe do team-building exercises like trust falls—"

"I'm out." She spun around.

"Okay, okay." He jumped in front of her. "No trust falls."

Her eyes narrowed.

"...And no 8 AM status meetings," he conceded. "How about I make a list, and then you work on it from nine to five?"

"How about I do the list whenever I want?" She sucked the straw of her pink iced tea. The pink contrasted with her black nails, her black lips, her everything—and thoroughly distracted him.

Is it wise to hire a woman this hot? Wait, what am I saying. He mentally slapped himself. *Be a professional.*

"I trust you, of course. I just want to work together as much as possible so you get the vision. Here." He motioned her inside. "Let me talk you through it first."

He rolled out his most recent sketches on the makeshift sawhorse table. He'd sketched out what the bookstore would look like from the front door, unable to rest last night until it was perfect.

"Here's the indie and local authors display, and the best-sellers," he said, pointing to displays surrounding the circular staircase to the second floor. "Last night I made space for a reading nook. It'll go with the stage where we can have events."

"We?" Her eyebrow raised in suspicion.

"There's no I in team, Pearl."

Pearl rolled her eyes at him. "There's no *we* in it either. What's that?" Pearl pointed to the huge circle above the nook.

"A new, huge window, so we'll get west-facing sun in the evening. Then at night, we'll have inset lights to offset the flying book installation." He swore he saw a smile ghost across her face.

"You'll have flying books?"

"It's an art installation. I think it's important to create a wonder-filled vibe. That's the whole point of this place. Make some magic."

Her eyes scoured the sketch, all business now. "And this?" Her long nail pointed to the sketch with the back entrance.

"Those are bathrooms people can get to from the outside. There aren't many public access bathrooms in town, and...I don't know." He shrugged, scratching the back of his head as he stood up. "I just thought it was the right thing to do. There's the genre fiction bookcases, the treehouse-themed kids' section, and of course, a rolling book ladder that will run the first floor of the building."

A high-pitched *eep* sounded beside him. Pearl bit her lip, but a smile cracked through.

"Was that *excitement*, Pearl Bishop?" *God, she looks adorable when her eyes dance like that.*

"What?" She scowled instantly. "I smile all the time. Don't be ridiculous. Your ideas are, like…" She sighed. "They're very good," she said finally, as if admitting a deep secret.

Pearl never lied. It was what he appreciated about her the most. You always knew where you stood with her.

Her fingers traced his drawings, and he felt the caress land somewhere deep in his soul.

She likes it.

He could burst with happiness that someone saw his vision. He rolled his lips together, savoring the feeling of someone *seeing* him.

"I wanted something beautiful and functional. This is my last architecture project. Then all that's left is to open it and then, I don't know, maybe find somebody and raise a family?" He shrugged. "Or I guess be with my actual family that's here."

"*No.*" She gasped as her eyes went wide. "The Parkers—"

He put a finger to his mouth. The crew walked back in from their break. "I'm not sure how I feel about it. You can't tell anybody."

Pearl's eyes went wide. "But this is *huge.* They're always talking about not having a big family, how they miss their dad. This would be a big deal to them."

"Which is why I don't want to get anyone's hopes up."

Pearl fiddled with her keys, nodding and suddenly quiet. "Well, they're like, very *nice.*" She grimaced, as if it pained her to say it. "I'd murder anybody who looked at them sideways. Almost did, actually."

She *was* a softy. He leaned on the table, willing his body not to be drawn to hers. "Big words coming from our lady of eternal darkness. You don't like anybody."

Me included.

She leveled a gaze at him, chewing on her lip. "I don't know if you've noticed, but I stick out here. We moved here last year because the school in Elliotsville wouldn't accommodate AB's food allergy."

"Bastards," Reed commiserated.

"Exactly." Her bottom lip pouted, and Reed so desperately wanted to bite it.

Nope, stop that. You're coworkers now. She's your assistant and you'll pay her, so you can't ogle her.

"I looked for jobs everywhere, but when you look like me, old farts don't hire you. The Parkers have never treated me differently than anyone else. It's been nice to be...accepted. Anyway." She shook out her hair, looking embarrassed to have said too much. "Give me a list and I'll start on it when I'm free."

"Why don't you compile a list of books to order and used bookstores we could scour. Oh, and furniture. Oh! And decor," he interrupted himself, clapping his hands, remembering his other to-do list. "And I should show you the rest of the plans."

He turned 180 degrees looking for them and then around one more time.

A firm hand yanked his bicep, halting him. Her hand was warm, sizzling on his skin and the heat melted into his bones. He looked into her big hazel eyes.

"You're only paying me to do one thing at a time, so let's start with just one," she said, making too much sense. "Plus, I can't start until Monday. I have a full dog sitting, walking, boarding, and bathing day today, and then a twelve-hour shift tomorrow working a catering gig for two weddings."

He nodded. "Okay. But then you're mine?"

She blinked rapidly, looking caught off guard.

Shit.

He adjusted his glasses. "I—uh, I mean, you're mine until I'm done with you."

Fuck. Not better.

Pearl cocked her head. "Uh..."

"Shit. I-I mean, not like that," he stuttered and bent over to catch his breath. "You won't be with anybody else—Sorry! You won't be *working* with anyone else. You can *be* with whomever you want."

He pressed his hands under his glasses, mortified. "And I will pay you for your time because you'll work for me in a strictly professional capacity."

Awkward silence hung between them.

"This is a terrible idea. You and me," she said.

"Yep." He nodded, still not looking at her as his fingers pressed his eyes.

"Can't wait," Pearl said flatly and spun on her heel toward the door.

He sighed as she walked away, letting his eyes trace her thighs and ass one last time. *She's not technically my assistant yet,* he told his conscience.

What a whirlwind of a life he'd walked into.

Possibly three sisters and a woman who hated him that he couldn't get enough of.

~

HEMINGWAY_CANSUCKIT

So, what printer should I get?

IMPOSSIBLYBOOKISH

fuck if i know

HEMINGWAY_CANSUCKIT

Don't you sell them?

What would a small business need

IMPOSSIBLYBOOKISH

right.

yes

i super do

but i focus more on industrial printers.

like, ones with lasers.

HEMINGWAY_CANSUCKIT

Industrial lasers?

IMPOSSIBLYBOOKISH

just find one on sale

ANYWHO

change of subject

did you see the rage-y discussion in the
romantasy channel?

HEMINGWAY_CANSUCKIT

So many feelings about fairies

IMPOSSIBLYBOOKISH

i kind of get it.

people are protective over their fantasies.

i'd kill for some winged shadow daddy to sweep
me away from this mortal coil

HEMINGWAY_CANSUCKIT

Damn. And me without wings.

IMPOSSIBLYBOOKISH

you're kind of a fantasy h

sometimes i think about if life were different and
we'd have just met

that's the fantasy i have

HEMINGWAY_CANSUCKIT

I probably would have bumped into you at a
bookstore

Apologized of course, immediately.

I'd have asked for your favorite book.

And bought it for you.

Or asked if I could buy you a cup of tea.

IMPOSSIBLYBOOKISH

not coffee?

HEMINGWAY_CANSUCKIT

I would never.

Somehow I'd know you preferred tea.

IMPOSSIBLYBOOKISH

what section you think?

HEMINGWAY_CANSUCKIT

Poetry, of course

What type of poetry would you pick up there?

IMPOSSIBLYBOOKISH

A crostic poems were always my favorite

N ot any other type of poem

A s the reader's eye moves down the first
column

L ike it makes its own word

S eated in the bookstore with you

E lated, that's what I'd be. ....uhh

X ylophone

HEMINGWAY_CANSUCKIT

Naughty acrostic poems, got it.

IMPOSSIBLYBOOKISH

see? you get me

HEMINGWAY_CANSUCKIT

You're my fantasy too, B

Probably a romantasy, now that I think about it

If you're a dream, I hope I never wake up

IMPOSSIBLYBOOKISH

if this is a dream, could you try to sprout some
wings?

HEMINGWAY_CANSUCKIT

Anything for you.

Chapter Seven

PEARL

Pearl swirled cranberry juice and cornstarch together on her cheap saucepan. This was her second try making edible fake blood. She'd woken up early with a vision for a Halloween party she'd throw for AB this fall and needed to get it right.

She moved the whisk slowly in the bubbling, pink mixture. If it boiled, it'd be ruined. She savored the stillness of being the only one at home, as Reed had a tendency to jog back and forth.

He'd gone out for an early morning run, the freak.

They'd officially start working together tomorrow.

It *probably* wouldn't be a disaster.

Anthrax raged in the background over her phone speakers. Thrash metal hit a sweet spot in her brain when she was tired. As her playlist switched to a Megadeath hit, a loud beeping sounded outside, like a recycling truck.

But it's Sunday. She peeked out the kitchen window.

A large tow truck was backing up to her car, and Beulah, in her ogre-esque glory in a faded silk robe and cigarette in her mouth, stood there with a smirk and measuring tape.

Hatred and spite fueled Pearl's speed as she grabbed her keys and dashed out the door.

"Two inches this time." Beulah smirked. "So your car is being towed."

"No the fuck it's not," Pearl screamed.

A greasy-looking man with thinning hair and a stained undershirt slowly got out of the tow truck.

"There is no property line on the road, *Barf-lah*. People can park wherever the fuck they want." She towered over Beulah's tiny, toad-like height.

The heavy metal drag of towing chains sounded as the man moved to hook up her car. She didn't have the money to get un-towed, and the guy looked like he just wanted to be paid.

"Jesus fucking Christ on a Christmas fucking cracker." Pearl dug in her pocket for her keys. "Fine. I'm moving it."

"Told you I don't fuck around," Beulah snarled in her garbling, weaselly voice.

"Wish you'd fuck off the top of a tall building," Pearl called over her shoulder.

She slammed her body into the driver's seat, hit the keys of the ignition *just* so, and the car turned on with a sputter.

She'd backed up a solid foot, just to be safe.

Beulah hobbled back inside. She took great pride in her front landscaping and ugly-ass concrete gnomes. Pearl had made a game of hiding the stupid things.

To date, Pearl's greatest achievement was Beulah sliding all the way into her own trash can, feet dangling out like a cartoon character, trying to grab the concrete gnomes inside.

Oh shit, the cranberry juice.

Pearl dashed back into the kitchen and sure enough, the mixture had started to bubble and turn sticky.

Still looks like blood though, even if the consistency is fucked.

Then Pearl got an amazingly *awful* idea.

With happy abandon that made one frolic in a spring meadow, she skipped out the door and threw the fake blood all over Beulah's gnomes.

They looked like chubby concrete stand-ins for *Carrie*. Streaks of red ran down their little demonic smiles.

Honestly, it's an improvement. Feeling better, she rushed upstairs to get ready for her wedding server gig.

Ten minutes later, after several raging screams underneath the cool water of the shower, she felt better.

Twenty-seven year olds are supposed to have their shit figured out. Not be mortal enemies with the old bat next door.

People in their late twenties host dinner parties for their friends. She snorted. *They probably* had *friends.*

I'd need that first.

A crash sounded outside the bathroom door.

"Hello?" She poked her head out of the shower curtain.

Goddamnit. Did Beulah break in?

More crashing, like things tumbling to the ground.

Joke's on her, we don't have any shit worth taking. She turned off the shower and reached for her towel...

That I fucking forgot.

The towels were in the closet *outside* the tiny, shitty bathroom.

She poked her head out the bathroom door. "Hello?"

Silence answered.

She strained her ears, listening for any other sounds, peeking right and left, making sure no one was in the house.

Stark naked and dripping, water running into her eyes, she gingerly walked to the hall closet.

She was about to reach the closet when a flash of bare skin, black shorts, and neon orange headphones dashed out of Luca's bedroom.

She screamed in fright as a man slammed into her, and she started to topple backward toward the staircase.

"Faaaakk—"

She grabbed anything on the wall to save herself, but a hand grabbed her wrist and yanked her back to avoid sudden death. Arms wrapped tightly around her from behind.

"Sonofa—" She smacked back into a chest. Their arms and legs grappled for purchase as his damp skin slipped on hers. They slammed against a wall.

It registered that the naked man was Reed as they hit the floor on their sides. His arms were wrapped around her, one hand squarely on her left tit.

They both screamed.

"Get off of me!" she yelled, and his hands sprung free, only to give him a perfect view of her tits over her shoulder. "Oh my god, that's worse."

"Sorry." He slapped his hands to his eyes as she army-rolled onto her belly.

She scrambled to the hall closet. "Didn't you hear me calling?" She grabbed a towel from the closet and wrapped it around herself with a vengeance. Her entire thigh and hip were still uncovered.

"Headphones," he yelled, pulling them off. "Running."

The Dead Kennedys blared out of his headphones. She would've appreciated his selection if she hadn't just been wet, naked, and pressed against his body.

His breathing was ragged. "Was only coming in for a second. Knocked over some books and then some other stuff. Didn't know you were"—he panted—"very naked."

She ran into her room and slammed the door. She stood against it, gathering her breath.

The scent of his sweat was all around her.

He smelled so. Fucking. Good.

Cedar and sex and rich cologne curled around her clit and tugged on it like a fucking leash.

That was gross, right? She shouldn't want some dude's sweat on her.

Maybe I could go back and roll around on him again...for science.

"Pearl," he called from the other side of the door. "I'm so sorry."

"So you just *happened* to run out as I came out of the bathroom naked?"

"Why were you coming out of the bathroom *naked?*"

Touché. "Because I'm a fucking feminist, Reed." Did that make any sense? No. She was still gonna stand by it, though. "If you have a problem with a woman's body, you know...go pluck out your eyes or whatever that saying is."

A huff of laughter on the other side of the door made her lips twitch into a smile.

"Look, I'm going to get some food, and then I'll be in my room for the rest of the day playing D&D with my cousins on a video call."

How is somebody that nerdy that hot? It doesn't make sense.

"You gonna do Mathletes this evening, too?" she called, wandering to her lingerie drawer.

He laughed. It was deep and easy, and she decided to ignore the goosebumps running down her arm,

"No, they had a conflict with the chess club. But my barbarian D&D figurine and I will stay out of your way, okay?"

What a fucking delight to start working for him tomorrow morning.

"If you feel a tingling tonight, it's me burning your likeness in effigy," she called.

Heavy steps sounded from the stairs. "Anything for you," he called back.

She paused.

An eerie feeling settled over her, like deja vu.

He had squeezed her like a vise to him, saving her from falling down the stairs. That would have been a bad time for everybody, specifically her spinal cord.

She rubbed her cheek where it had smashed into his warm, firm shoulder. The searing heat of his arms still tingled around her middle, lingered on her breasts.

She should've said thank you, but it got trapped in her throat with embarrassment and...

Oh god. Oh no. Is this attraction? she thought with genuine curiosity. *Couldn't be.*

This was Reed fucking Berry, the dorkiest kid in eighth grade.

The guy who she'd had to save from being beat up in high school multiple times because he was an easy, small target.

The guy who did things like play D&D on a Sunday afternoon *on the internet.*

A goblin, demonic part of her swiped a finger where his arms had been, searching for a taste he might have left behind.

She licked it.

"Oof," she whispered, savoring it. She closed her eyes. "Goddamn."

She'd take this secret to her grave, that she wanted another taste of Reed Berry.

~

IMPOSSIBLYBOOKISH

so

today i was at a wedding

it was going great

until

some old groomsman grabbed my ass

so i turned around and yelled at him

then his WIFE yelled at ME

i guess for having an ass worth grabbing?

in her anger, she tossed my platter of sloppy joe sliders

…which landed alllll over the maid of honor

so i shoved her cake in her face

(the wife, not the maid of honor)

and THEN i took one of the sliders on the floor and pelted her shitty husband with it

the wife slipped on the sliders on the floor

guess they're appropriately named

and she knocked the flower girl INTO the chocolate fountain

so i yanked her back

(the flower girl, not the wife)

cause fuck that bitch in particular

but i lost my balance grabbing the flower girl and fell toward the table

and grabbed the chocolate fountain as it tipped over on ME

but then *I* SLIPPED ON THE SLIDERS

AND YEETED THE CHOCOLATE FOUNTAIN *AT* THE MOTHERFUCKING BRIDE

i just wanted to you to know you're one of the only men i don't hate and it's a very small list because jesus fucking christ do i hate men

and today can go suck a giant bag of moldy dicks

HEMINGWAY_CANSUCKIT

…Why did you have a whole platter of sliders?

IMPOSSIBLYBOOKISH

THAT'S your takeaway????

nevermind, you're off the list

HEMINGWAY_CANSUCKIT

I mean, a platter is like a lot, right? Like maybe 30?

Sorry, got caught up playing a game with some friends

I'm so sorry a man grabbed you. That part is not even a little funny and it makes my blood seethe just thinking about it.

I'd happily fly to Colorado and attempt to flatten him if you wanted me to.

But my body is having a hard time understanding if I'm angry or if I'm happy because I can't stop thinking about you pelting a lecher with a small sloppy joe and the joy it brings me.

Did you actually hit him with it?

IMPOSSIBLYBOOKISH

square in the face.

HEMINGWAY_CANSUCKIT

That's my girl.

IMPOSSIBLYBOOKISH

you'd flatten him, huh?

you could…do that?

HEMINGWAY_CANSUCKIT

I mean, I'd try. I'm 6'2, work out a bunch.

I guess if he was a lineman for the Broncos we'd
need to get creative

IMPOSSIBLYBOOKISH

he was short and old

HEMINGWAY_CANSUCKIT

Then I'd happily punch his face and/or grab his
ass.

Whichever you'd think would be a fair payback.

IMPOSSIBLYBOOKISH

throw in a little balls action and you're back on
the list.

HEMINGWAY_CANSUCKIT

Anything for you, Bookish

Chapter Eight

PEARL

Pearl started her job the next morning with the most professional five words she could think of.

"So, you saw my tits."

"Um, f—" Reed cleared his throat. "F-felt is more accurate." He straightened his glasses and finally met her eyes. He gulped. "But, yes. Yes, I did."

And I liked it, she thought.

She pushed her sunglasses up, and her thick bangs flopped down. She'd worn her best *bookshop assistant* outfit—a black loose crop top, tight black shorts, and fishnets because when you had thighs like hers, they tended to rub together and the fishnets helped.

She liked her body. She liked the size of it, the safety of feeling sturdy, the roundness, and the feminine curves. She thought women who looked like her were really fucking hot, but there were some downsides, like raw thighs in the summertime.

In contrast, Reed was wearing a tight button-up white shirt with a sweater vest and linen slacks. The sleeves rolled up to his elbows made him look like the hottest accountant in Martha's Vineyard.

She sighed. *I am such a slut for forearms.*

He stood back from the circular card catalog, and five iced teas sat waiting. "I got you iced tea to say sorry and happy first day, but I wasn't sure which one you wanted. So I got them all."

Her fingers itched for Fox & Forrest's pink passion fruit that she normally saved as a special treat.

"We can also forget this job thing," he said suddenly, scratching the back of his head. "I don't want to make you uncomfortable."

A "no" rushed out as she darted to grab the pink tea. She sipped and almost moaned when the sweet, tropical flavors hit her tongue.

She couldn't lose this opportunity. She'd already made a list of all the baking supplies she'd buy once she'd made enough to buy AB's EpiPen.

"I think we just need house rules," she said sensibly. "Towels go in the bathroom now, for example. And headphones off so you can hear me calling you."

He nodded. "Those are good ideas."

A little rush hit her spine.

God, why am I such a little praise bitch? There was nothing fucking better in this world than someone smart thinking that your ideas were good.

She cocked her head. "And why do you always leave the room when I eat? Do I gross you out or something?"

She was hypersensitive to people being weird when she was eating. She was plus-size, and yeah, she liked to eat. Who fucking didn't? She'd told off multiple assholes after they'd hassled her when she'd dared to enjoy a hot dog.

"Oh god, no." He looked concerned. He cleared his throat and straightened his shoulders. "Definitely not. I, um, I have this thing. It's called misophonia. Certain sounds feel overwhelming, even painful to me. Eating is the main one."

There was a vulnerable challenge in his eyes, waiting for her to say something. His jaw clenched.

"But sounds like this don't drive you nuts?" She pointed to the cacophony of hammering nail guns and guys yelling at each other across the building.

His shoulders relaxed for some reason. "This? Oh, no. But a fork scraping on a plate? *Awful.* The sound of somebody crunching makes me irrationally angry and I don't like who I become. I feel it all over my body so much that it's...it's painful. So, I just leave the room."

A whole life eating by yourself?

Sounds kind of lonely.

"Is it...curable?" She hoped it was okay to ask that.

His smile was sad. "I wish. I've tried exposure therapy, regular therapy, those earplugs to dull the sound. Most people with misophonia can handle some sounds without a meltdown, but mine's always been particularly bad. I learned I'm autistic last year, actually, thanks to a great therapist. Turns out, I'm a lot more sensitive to sounds and touch than other people. It explained all the weirdness I've had with coworkers and class-mates when I was younger."

Autistic. She rolled the idea around.

He'd been a nice kid, but hadn't had many friends. He'd been smart, but had struggled in the things that'd felt obvious to her, like how to be cool.

Like their first kiss, when she'd dared him to do it. They'd been twelve and thirteen in his treehouse, waiting for Luca to come back with snacks. It had been raining outside, and she'd dared him to kiss her.

Sometimes she still thought about it during a summer rainstorm.

Maybe he'd taken it at face value. That it was just a silly dare.

He'd kissed her and then gone back to reading comics as if it was nothing.

She'd been devastated.

When she'd asked, "Don't you want to kiss me again?" maybe he'd answered honestly ("You didn't dare me to kiss you twice.").

Maybe he hadn't gotten the game she'd obviously been playing.

"Is that why you always look like a substitute teacher?" She tugged on the bottom of his sweater vest.

His smile warmed, and it *did* something to her.

"Yeah, I like the pressure it gives on my chest. It helps me feel more calm. I hate fabric lightly brushing my body." He shuddered.

That explains the tight biker shorts yesterday.

"So, I eat in my room, towels go in the bathroom, no crazy loud headphones in the house, and maybe," he said with a nervous smile, "no death threats during business hours?"

She rolled her eyes. "Fine."

"Great, so your first day on the job." His sunny smile that she was so familiar with was pasted back on. It looked a little strained, though. "I need your help filling in the space. Luca said you decorated the house with secondhand items. It looks great, so I trust you."

A shower of dopamine shot straight down her spine again. *Fuck, my nipples are actually hard.*

She crossed her arms over her chest, lest Reed notice them about to cut through her shirt.

He pulled up his phone, scrolling through inspiration. "I'm thinking of this sort of vibe."

A collection of images looked like a big Victorian home that had expanded into a full-blown library. Floral patterns in the upholstery, burnished gold and brass. "I want the store to feel inviting and wondrous, like you stumbled into a magical old bookshop. Your first mission"—he handed her ten one-hundred-dollar bills—"is to thrift two chairs to sit opposite the reading nook."

"Pfft," she scoffed. She gave him back five hundred dollars. "If I get two nice chairs, can I keep the rest of what's left here?"

"Sure." He shrugged, eager to please.

She rolled her eyes. "You should have said no," she said, poking his chest and finding the muscle underneath.

He stared at the nail digging into his sweater vest. "Why? I was going to spend a thousand dollars."

She face-palmed. "That's not how this works. You're running a business. You gotta toughen up."

"Haven't you always said fuck the man?" He gave her a little attitude back.

She kind of liked it.

"Well, now *I'm* the man, and you can fuck...me...oh." His face drained of color as he realized his mistake. "Oh no. I'm so sorry, that's not what I meant."

She rolled her lips together to keep from laughing and gathered all the iced tea cups in her arms. "I should fuck you. Noted, boss."

She smirked and sauntered out of the bookshop without another word. She looked over her shoulder to find he still had his head in his hands, muttering to himself.

In her car, she pulled up her phone for directions to her favorite thrift store, but a message popped up.

HEMINGWAY_CANSUCKIT

Please tell me your day has been as shitty as mine.

Warmth squeezed her cold, dead heart.

IMPOSSIBLYBOOKISH

sorry to tell you…my day's been fucking amazing

but tell me about it

HEMINGWAY_CANSUCKIT

Did you finally get that promotion you wanted?

In some ways, Hemingway knew the truest version of herself. But she'd never let it slip that she'd never had a real job, didn't know what a 401k was, and probably wouldn't last one day in a real office with her mouth and bad attitude.

So she'd called her new job a promotion.

IMPOSSIBLYBOOKISH

yeah, i started today

HEMINGWAY_CANSUCKIT

pumps fists Hell yeah, you did.

Proud of you 🤍

IMPOSSIBLYBOOKISH

hemingway...

HEMINGWAY_CANSUCKIT

Bookish...

IMPOSSIBLYBOOKISH

stop stalling

HEMINGWAY_CANSUCKIT

Nah, I don't want to bother.

Go celebrate taking over the…printer sales?… world!

IMPOSSIBLYBOOKISH

i swear to god i'll dm janice and tell her you want to be her new mod bff

HEMINGWAY_CANSUCKIT

Diabolical woman

IMPOSSIBLYBOOKISH

😈 you love it

HEMINGWAY_CANSUCKIT

God I really fucking do.

Okay fine.

Why is it that when I'm on the precipice of being
not an awkward fuck-up...I fuck it all up.

IMPOSSIBLYBOOKISH

aha. a topic i'm an expert in.

i'm an elder in the fuck up club.

a fuckups-pert, if you will

look, i fuck up constantly. my car is 1000 years
old because i'd rather save for a new tattoo than
a carburetor

i'm a regular at a dive bar instead of like, eating
spinach and shit

i've learned there's always tomorrow and it
probably wasn't that bad

most people only think about themselves and
not the 17 dumb things i fucked up that day

they can keep whatever judgements they have
of me. it's none of my business.

HEMINGWAY_CANSUCKIT

Sage advice.

Also spinach is overrated.

Have you ever felt like no one knows the REAL
you?

The *you* that you want to be?

IMPOSSIBLYBOOKISH

constantly.

i'm worried that this is it.

it's too late to make any sort of change in my
life.

i'm at the starting line when everybody else has
already lapped me.

and even if I tried to run with them, it would be a
waste because i wouldn't belong anyway.

She typed it all out and hit send quickly, her heart clutching in her chest.

HEMINGWAY_CANSUCKIT

There's no such thing as too late.

You're exactly where you're supposed to be. I
just know it.

Emotion caught her by surprise and stung her eyes.

IMPOSSIBLYBOOKISH

sometimes it feels like you're the only one who
knows me

HEMINGWAY_CANSUCKIT

I'm honored to be the one who knows you,
Bookish.

So what is your professional advice, Madame
Fuckups-pert, for handling the pain of fucking it
all up?

IMPOSSIBLYBOOKISH

::strokes long beard in thought::

i prescribe 200 grams of sweet carbs

chocolate chip if it was especially bad

and a sexting session with a trusted companion this evening

HEMINGWAY_CANSUCKIT

Omg I should fuck up all the TIME

What have I been DOING

Let me see if Janice is available tonight

IMPOSSIBLYBOOKISH

you're hilarious

HEMINGWAY_CANSUCKIT

You love it.

IMPOSSIBLYBOOKISH

🖤

I really fucking do

REED

S creams of The Dead Kennedys echoed in the empty bookstore as Reed pushed a roller up and down with white primer. Bookish had recommended their music months ago and he was now obsessed.

He'd been painting all evening, only breaking for a few minutes to inhale a sandwich he'd brought from home. His phone dinged and a picture popped up of Luca and AB with a superhero at a Florida theme park.

LUCA

Found our hero IRL

They had pored over endless hours of Colossal Man's comics in Reed's treehouse growing up.

REED

Behold! The holder of the ore of understanding is in Orlando

You guys having a good time?

LUCA

Annabelle is zonked

I'm about to pass out, too.

Walking in the sun for 2 days is exhausting, even
w/ her grandparents' help

Reed had been devastated when Luca's partner Lydia had been killed in a car crash a few years ago. He'd always felt bad he couldn't be there for Luca more, living far across the state.

But now he could make up for lost time. Be the Uncle Reed that spoiled AB and helped Luca put together dollhouses on Christmas Eve.

LUCA

Is Pearl behaving?

REED

Only three animal sacrifices on the lawn since
you left.

LUCA

Honestly, that's a record.

REED

She agreed to be my assistant to get the
bookstore running

LUCA

Well, she takes no shit AND no prisoners

And she's read every book under the sun.

REED

It's going to be great

Maybe in a couple weeks, I'll finally convince her
to get matching t-shirts.

LUCA

Lord help you

Reed laughed as he grabbed the paint roller for round two with the ugly yellow walls.

A different sound pinged his phone, his favorite sound—a high-pitched *zuzsh*.

It was supposed to mimic the sound of a page flip, but he'd started associating it with heart emojis and his favorite parts of every day.

He hadn't felt like this with anybody since his girlfriend in college. Grad school had been so intense he'd barely been able to eat and sleep. Then he'd been so stressed finding a new rhythm in his first job out of school. He'd had a few casual dates, but women usually fell off the radar when he told them about his issues.

His inability to go on a dinner date. Have brunch with their parents. A picnic in the park.

His lack of experience.

He was still thinking about her texts from earlier that day. He'd felt hot as fuck when he'd bought her a vibrator and he wondered if she'd use it tonight if they'd fool around.

Digitally, that is.

They'd never made any promises to each other. They were basically just friends with some added benefits. He didn't want to spook her by telling her how hard he was falling for her.

His blood thrummed in his chest as he opened Bookish's message.

IMPOSSIBLYBOOKISH

been thinking about you

HEMINGWAY_CANSUCKIT

Yeah?

IMPOSSIBLYBOOKISH

and staring at your hot as fuck cock

Oh, it *was* going to be one of those chats today.

Heat hit his cheeks. Sending her that photo had been the craziest thing he'd ever done. She'd only seen his cock against his stomach, but he'd felt reckless doing it.

Other men probably were nonchalant about a little dirty texting, but it wasn't a *whatever* thing for him. He cared about her, cared about her pleasure. Felt connected to her when they fooled around.

He'd never asked if she did this with other people, but he also didn't really care. He was just happy to have found someone special. He loved what they had together right now as it was.

HEMINGWAY_CANSUCKIT

You don't know how many times I've looked at the photo of you.

He gulped.

Do I get another one tonight?

IMPOSSIBLYBOOKISH

nah, too comfy.

but my roommate is out

and i have this sad lonely purple friend who is begging me to play with him

HEMINGWAY_CANSUCKIT

Then you should play until you tire him out.

IMPOSSIBLYBOOKISH

i need you

Oof, that did something to him. It always did.

He wanted to be needed. To be thought of and included.

HEMINGWAY_CANSUCKIT

I love to be needed.

How can I help, my darling Bookish?

IMPOSSIBLYBOOKISH

tell me what you'd do to me right now if you
were here.

i want to read and watch.

They'd done this a few times. One of them would read the other's fantasy and get off to it.

HEMINGWAY_CANSUCKIT

Personalized smut coming (ha) right up

What would I do with a bored Bookish who's
been looking at a dirty picture all evening….

Hmmm....

I had a light dinner.

I think I'd like to spend time eating tonight

IMPOSSIBLYBOOKISH

yesssss

HEMINGWAY_CANSUCKIT

I'd find the perfect surface to bend you over.

Maybe a couch arm, a chair, a desk. Something
where your ass is in the air, thighs spread

And just high enough so you have to stand on
your tiptoes.

IMPOSSIBLYBOOKISH

mean

HEMINGWAY_CANSUCKIT

But you like feeling a little vulnerable, don't you,
gorgeous?

> Just a little off balance. At my mercy.

IMPOSSIBLYBOOKISH

yesss

HEMINGWAY_CANSUCKIT

> And I'd bend you over the back of the couch.

> Spread your thighs.

> You said they were thick. My personal favorite.

> I'd take my time, staring at the gorgeous picture of your ass in the air, breasts hanging over.

> I'd spread your pussy so I can see all of it, framed by your thighs. And would tease you.

> Sliding just the tip of one finger in. Taunting you

> I'd want you so wet. Teasing you until you'd drip down my hand

His cock was already thick in his gym shorts. He was tucked in a corner away from the windows facing out to Main Street. The head of his cock pressed against his shorts, and he squeezed it for relief.

HEMINGWAY_CANSUCKIT

> I'd kiss your thighs, nipping along them. Running my nose up and down you.

> I bet you smell so good, Bookish.

> And on my knees for you, I don't think I could wait.

> I'd want to tease you but I'd only be teasing myself.

> I'd bury my face in your pussy, lapping you up.

> I'd lick every inch, catching every drop.

I hope my face would be soaked, burying it in
your pussy.

I'd swirl your tight nub, teasing it. And then
plunge my tongue deep.

I'd tell you to clench around my tongue, and I'd
lick as far in as I could get, wanting to taste
every bit of you.

My hands couldn't help but grab your ass,
pinching it, squeezing it.

Worshipping it.

I'd suck on your clit, my nose buried deep in
your pussy so I never won't smell you on me.

Suck on it like I wanted to consume it. Like I
wanted every drop of you in me. It'd be swollen
and tender and your legs would tremble.

You'd say it was too much but beg for more.

And when you were begging me.

And begging me.

I'd stand up, take off my belt, let it hang loose.

Pull out my cock and shove inside you. I'd sink
hilt-deep into your pussy

Hard.

IMPOSSIBLYBOOKISH

{audio file loading}

what you're doing to me.

He gulped. They'd never shared audio before. With trembling
fingers, he hit the play button.

A woman groaned, husky with a needy voice. It came in
waves, rising and falling. The low hum of a vibrator was a

constant. Wet sounds squelched, sounding like she was moving it in and out.

Her moans were higher, and louder. Incoherent words wrenched out of her, sounding like she fought them every way.

Savoring them.

Her moans got higher and higher. A soft *yes* was a plea as the wet sounds and the hum grew louder, like she'd put the mic by her pussy.

Her cries and moans were louder, faster, higher.

Holy fucking hell.

He ripped his cock out of his shorts and gave himself two quick, hard strokes, wanting to listen again and again.

HEMINGWAY_CANSUCKIT

Fuck B

You using my vibrator, screaming.

Best sound in the whole goddamn world

Did you come yet?

IMPOSSIBLYBOOKISH

not yet.

trying to last

HEMINGWAY_CANSUCKIT

I won't be able to last long either.

Not after hearing you moan

I'm rubbing my cock and wishing I could pound into you, hard, grabbing your hips and making you mine.

Reach my arm down and tug on your hair. Arching your back so your tits lift up

And fuck you against the couch.

You clenching around me

When I'm about to come

I pull out and with one hand on your clit, rub you to climax

While I come all over your ass

Painting it so it's mine

Watching it drop down your cheeks, into your pussy

IMPOSSIBLYBOOKISH

{audio loading}

The hum of a vibrator was loud and wet, squishing and moving faster and faster. In the distance, a woman screamed, "Yes, yes, yes. Fuck me, Hemingway" were screamed in a high, constrained pitch as she crested over the edge of her climax, the liquid sounds getting faster and faster until she screamed a release for a solid five seconds.

He tugged on his cock, dizzy with lust.

My turn.

He spit on his palm and rubbed, replaying the audio of her coming, picturing pounding into thick thighs, sinking between them and watching her ass jiggle as he fucked her harder and harder.

The wet sounds were tugging, begging at him to come.

Would sound just like that when I fuck her.

"Fuck," he yelled out as his climax caught him by surprise, spurting hard over his shorts and hand.

HEMINGWAY_CANSUCKIT

Bookish, I just…

You're so sexy

I just came in about five seconds

Fuck

IMPOSSIBLYBOOKISH

hadn't pegged you for a hair pulling guy

but i'm into it

HEMINGWAY_CANSUCKIT

Is yours long or short?

Not that it matters

But for when I picture this all over again later tonight…

I'd like to be accurate.

IMPOSSIBLYBOOKISH

medium short. like a long bob.

dark.

HEMINGWAY_CANSUCKIT

Perfect.

I'm so glad you messaged

I've had an exhausting day and this is just what I needed. Picturing you missing me

Naked

Being fucked with a cock like mine.

Maybe it was the post-nut fuzzy feelings, but he felt so close to Bookish. How many other people in his life could he tease, talk about any of his favorite books, and share fantasies with that were so dirty they'd climax from just text.

He wanted to see her. See what exactly her face and hair looked like. Her thighs and ass.

But she'd been adamant that she wasn't comfortable when

they first started chatting to show her face. He would never push her. He enjoyed what they had and was happy enough to just have her to talk to.

IMPOSSIBLYBOOKISH

i love your dirty fantasies.

whoever you've fucked IRL must leave very satisfied.

His laugh was sad and hollow.
If only she knew.

IMPOSSIBLYBOOKISH

for me though, it's time for an early bedtime.

you sexted me right to sleep.

HEMINGWAY_CANSUCKIT

Goodnight Bookish

IMPOSSIBLYBOOKISH

night h

If only she knew the secret that grew heavier with each passing month, quarter, year.

The one that made him feel more and more self-conscious each time he went on a date.

I'm a twenty-eight-year-old virgin.
Desperate to fuck my online best friend.

PEARL

PEARL's ancient phone came to life with a video call from Luca.

Luca fucking hated video calls, so that meant AB was calling.

Pearl swiped up with a goofy, stupid smile on her face. "Hey, you, nugget!"

AB was holding the phone way too close to her face. "AP, AP! I miss you!"

Pearl blinked through a sudden emotion. "I miss you, too, goober. What are you guys doing?"

"Um, we, um, saw all the people at the parks, and now we're having quiet time." Her voice was a loud whisper. "Because Grammy and Grampy needed naps. So did Daddy." She swung the phone around to show three people resting in a coastal sunroom in Florida.

"What's the best thing you've done?" Pearl asked.

"Ummm, three cartwheels in a row."

Pearl laughed. Take a kid to theme parks and *that's* what they're excited about, figures.

"Dad wants to talk. I love you. Bye!"

"Aww," Pearl said as Luca's face came into frame. "I didn't even get to tell her about the crows."

Luca switched back to audio mode, not even asking. Pearl rolled her eyes and did the same.

"How's it going?" Luca said in a gruff voice. "You okay?"

"Sure?" Pearl said, confused. "Why wouldn't I be?"

"I don't know. We're not there. The man who drives you nuts is your roommate and boss. Seems like a disaster."

"Whoever suggested it must be pretty fucking stupid, huh?" Pearl said with a smile.

Luca chuckled.

"It kind of is a disaster, honestly. He's just so…"

Handsome, she thought. *Kind.*

"…happy," she said with disgust.

"Be nice to him, okay?"

"He's *your* best friend, not mine."

"I know he seems like a lot and like he has it all together, but underneath all of the smiles and the energy"—Luca sighed—"he's kind of lonely, and he needs a friend. Since I can't be there, I need you to step in."

"Friend?" she said, the word feeling disgusting in her mouth.

"Yes. Just, like, don't threaten to murder him each day."

"Only if you bring me back a snake."

"I'm not bringing any reptiles back."

"Okay, fine. Two snakes. Final offer."

He laughed. "Be good."

"Never," she said with a smile and hung up.

She thought back to the sunshiny guy bopping as he walked, excited, multiple ideas, energy rolling off of him.

Lonely?

He'd have to be really good at covering up his feelings if loneliness was hiding underneath all of that.

Chapter Ten

REED

Reed stared at the photo on his phone as he waited in line at the Fox & Forrest Cafe.

His doppelgänger and three young girls stared back at him in the photo.

A pang of guilt hit his stomach. Ralph Berry hadn't been just a stepfather, but the father who'd stepped up.

His father was the man who'd spent endless hours with him practicing soccer skills, preparing for debate club, and giving him advice on his early college architecture projects. Reed had never *wanted* anyone else. He still remembered how lucky he'd felt the day he officially became a Berry.

Having two fathers would feel even more overwhelming to live up to.

But now, his endless curiosity was piqued.

What would having sisters be like? He wanted to get to know these women before he decided anything.

They'd be three more people whose love he'd have to earn again and again for the rest of his life.

He jumped as a tap on his shoulder revealed a familiar face.

Violet, the middle Parker sister, waved with a sweet smile behind him in line.

He took off his headphones and let them hang around his neck. "Hey, nice to see you."

"I see you've become an F&F devotee as well," she said cheerily. This woman was like a sunbeam personified. "Can I buy your coffee or lunch or whatever?"

"It's just iced coffee, thank you," he said. The sounds of dining, scraping, and clattering in the cafe were grating, turning his stomach.

He tried to push it to the back of his mind.

"You've been working nonstop at the bookstore. If we weren't recording content constantly, we would have stopped by," Violet said tiredly.

"I, um." He scratched the back of his head, a little embarrassed. "I looked up your show because Pearl talked about it. It's really good."

Violet and her husband had a TV series about plants. He'd watched an episode, and Violet was sweet and funny. He'd liked her instantly.

Violet's eyes lit up. "She's so sweet. You guys are roomies, right?"

"Yes, her brother and I go way back. Pearl and I go way back too, but she likes to forget about that part. I was the dorky kid in school who she ignored in the hallways."

"Oh my gosh, *I* was the dorky kid, too!" Violet said, slapping his shoulder with excitement.

"No way." Reed relaxed a little. She seemed so confident and at ease on camera.

Violet laughed. "They literally had to put a fainting cot in my speech class because I hated being looked at so much. What are your feelings on plants?" she said, arching an eyebrow as if examining him.

"I can't keep them alive to save my soul, but I love them."

"Hmm," Violet said, narrowing her eyes.

"Does that mean we definitely couldn't be related?" he said jokingly, as if the fact that they'd be related would be ridiculous.

"No, it puts a point in your favor," she muttered. "Our dad was terrible with plants. Famously bad."

"Can I help you?" the man at the register asked Reed.

Violet stepped up. "He's with me, Nick. I'll have my usual and an iced coffee for our new bookshop owner. Would you like to stay and sit with me?" Violet asked Reed.

"Oh. Uh, no," Reed said with as much of a smile as he could muster in the noise of the restaurant. "I need to see if Pearl is at Bloom, actually."

"Let's go see if we can catch her," Violet said with a happy smile.

Okay, I guess this is a group project now.

Violet paid and handed Reed his coffee. "Aaron, can you make mine to-go? I'll come back."

"You got it, babe," a tall Black man called from the prep counter.

He sort of loved that she knew everyone. Would this be his life in a year? Nestled as a part of the little community?

He hoped so.

They stepped outside and the silence felt like cool water to his overstimulated ears. His shoulders dropped as the tension left his body.

Bloom was next door, and the herby, floral scents tickled his nose as they walked in.

Rose, Violet's older sister, was behind the counter with Pearl and another woman.

That must be Allison. Pearl had mentioned her quirky co-worker at Bloom in passing.

"What do you think?" Allison called, turning around to face

them. "Too much?" Her black lips were reminiscent of Pearl's go-to look. It clashed with her peachy pink, fluffy hair and kindergarten-teacher-like dress with llamas on it.

Violet's eyebrows lifted. "Well maybe—"

"It looks great, doesn't it?" Pearl interrupted, making determined eye contact with Violet.

"...It does," Violet said slowly with a smile.

"Pearl is taking me to the biker dive bar on the edge of town. I'm so excited." Allison danced as she walked to the back of the shop.

Pearl smiled at Allison, delighted by her.

The sight hit Reed in the gut like a bowling ball. She was quite literally breathtaking.

He hadn't seen her smile like that since AB and Luca had left.

Note to self: try to make Pearl smile more.

Reed held up Pearl's wallet that she'd left at home, and she jogged over to him. She was wearing a tight black Bloom tee and jeans, and he *willed* his eyes not to stare at her boobs as she jogged.

"Thanks. I thought the endless abyss of my purse ate it."

Their fingers brushed as he handed it to her, and *Christ*, he shouldn't have enjoyed that as much as he did.

"You remember Rose," Pearl continued with aggressive eye contact at Reed again, nudging her head.

"It's so nice to see you." Rose's smile warmed as she looked at Reed. "You know what? We should grab dinner sometime. Get everyone together whenever this one"—she slung an arm around Violet—"isn't filming, and when Lily and I aren't out opening new stores."

"What about dinner tomorrow night? I think we're all in town. I'm happy to host. Pearl, you'd need to come too," Violet said with excitement, clapping.

He glanced at Pearl nervously. "Oh, um. I'm not really a food person."

Ugh, he hated this part—the part where he couldn't just do things like other people.

"Reed loves coffee," Pearl added quickly. "It's practically all he eats. His gut biome probably hates him."

Ah. She's helping.

I knew it. She's such a marshmallow.

He beamed at her, and she rolled her eyes. "I'd love to show you around the bookstore at some point. I'll buy the coffee."

His phone buzzed. It was Bert, his contractor.

Oh no, Bert never calls. "Uh, sorry, one sec. Hey, Bert."

"Got a problem," Bert's flat, nasally voice sounded in his ear. "Somebody from the county is saying we gotta stop construction."

"Uh..."

Rose and Violet both drew their brows together with concern.

"Somebody from the Historical Society," Bert said.

"The *President* of the Historical Society!" a gargling voice sounded in the background.

Shit. He knew that weaselly voice.

Pearl growled. "I'm gonna kill her."

"Something about some permits," Bert added.

He'd filed every permit, he was sure of it. "I'll be right there." He hung up and looked apologetic. "I gotta go."

"We didn't have to fill any paperwork out when we renovate Bloom, right?" Violet asked Rose.

"No, I've never heard of the historical society getting involved with interior renovations," Rose said, scratching her head.

Pearl's eyebrows narrowed in anger. "I have to go make this

delivery, but I can see if Allison can take it. I'd love to grind Beulah's face into the historical pavement."

Reed shook his head. "No, it's fine. Go—"

"Then take them with you." Pearl nodded at Rose and Violet.

Their faces were hopeful, as if they *wanted* to help.

Reed felt skeptical. They didn't even know him. "No, that's okay. I don't want to bother you."

Pearl glared at him pointedly. "Maybe they could help since you have a lot in *common* with them."

Reed gulped. "Would you both...mind?"

Rose sighed with relief. "Happily. It's been too long since I've had a good fight."

"I don't want to impose—" Reed said, glancing back at a smiling Pearl.

"Trust me, she loves this stuff. It's a blood sport for her," Violet said under her breath. "Plus, you can show us the bookstore."

"Oh, it's not finished yet," he said quickly, wanting it to look perfect before anyone important saw it.

"Come on. We've got your back. Violet knows everyone"—Rose pulled him through the door with a gleeful smile—"and I'm *mean*."

They walked across the town square as Rose furiously texted someone named *Mrs. Maroo-Canon.*

Beulah stood in the bookstore's front door, and flanked by men with clipboards.

Rose cracked her neck on his right.

"Be nice," Violet said to Rose from his left.

An angel and a demon on each shoulder. *Better than doing this alone, though.*

"I've told the guys to go home. She's halted all construction." Bert shrugged as he threw a tool belt over his shoulder. "I'll call you tomorrow. Good luck, kid." He patted Reed's back.

"Young man." Beulah's garbage-disposal-like voice echoed in the empty bookshop. Her hair was pulled back in a steel-gray bun, and she wore an oversized dress suit with a big floppy bow at the collar.

"You have violated three town ordinances," she droned happily, "and will be fined an excess of one hundred thousand dollars if the proper approvals and inspections are not completed for this historical site."

She dropped an enormous stack of papers in his hands.

"Who are you?" Rose said, stepping in front of him.

"The President of the Historical Society and the Assistant County Commissioner."

"We don't have one of those," Rose said.

Beulah showed her badge, yanking an elastic cord from her pocket. "Sure do, toots."

Oh my god, this is so embarrassing. Failing in front of new people is a new low. Reed waved her away. "It's fine. I can figure—"

"Just let her do her thing," Violet whispered.

"Why does he need to halt construction?" Rose asked, towering over Beulah. She was easily six feet in her heels, and Beulah had to crane her neck back to see her.

"He didn't fill out Form 4078B-X," Beulah said, pulling out a long paper he'd never seen before from the stack.

"What if he fills it out right now?" Violet asked with a sunny smile. "Then the construction crew can come back. And thank you so much for taking care of the town's historical architecture. It's very important."

Reed was catching on to their good cop, bad cop routine.

A message dinged on Rose's phone. She looked triumphant. "You know, Beulah, I've seen you in Violet's neighborhood. I think you were visiting the *Commissioner's* house which is just two doors down?"

Beulah narrowed her eyes.

Rose's tone was mock sincerity. "Why, you and Violet are practically *neighbors* with how much you're at your boss's house. We've even seen you late at night, I think, right, Violet?"

Violet's sunny smile had humor to it. "Sure have. Sometimes early in the morning too. I love the robes you have. So silky."

Beulah's eyes widened.

She dismissed the two men that had come with her and they walked out.

"What do you want?" Beulah said, sneering at Rose.

"I want you to lower your ridiculous fines," Rose said, towering over the five-foot-nothing woman in orthopedic sneakers. "Extend the deadline for Reed, in good faith, and"—she drilled her finger into Beulah's shoulder—"allow construction to continue."

Beulah slid her gaze to Reed. She huffed. "Or what?"

"Or a few more people in the county courthouse will find out just how close you and your boss are. I believe fraternization is frowned upon, right?" Rose raised a manicured eyebrow.

Did this woman just threaten blackmail for him?

No wonder Pearl likes her.

Beulah's eyes narrowed at Rose. "Game recognizes game. Fine. The fines are the normal amount, but no exterior modifications. Fill out the forms to get a copy of the final permits." She huffed and walked out the door with no further comments.

"Thank you! I'll fill this out today!" Reed stammered.

He was out of his depth in small-town politics.

Rose and Violet laughed.

"I, um." He turned around, flabbergasted. He gulped, shifting his papers in his arms. "Thank you. You don't even know me."

"Eh." Rose wrapped an arm around his shoulders and squeezed him in a side hug. "Pearl said you were okay, and you know she hates everybody, so."

Violet patted his cheek. "I have a vested interest in this book-store. I intend to buy a *lot* of books from you."

"We should get back," Rose said with a nod toward Bloom.

"See you around!" Violet waved. They cackled over some shared inside joke as they walked out.

He pushed his glasses up to the bridge of his nose, still trying to make sense of it all.

Maybe having big sisters wouldn't be a bad thing after all.

IMPOSSIBLYBOOKISH

god i hate summer

my thighs sticking together

boob sweat. i want fall.

HEMINGWAY_CANSUCKIT

That's a hell of a haiku

IMPOSSIBLYBOOKISH

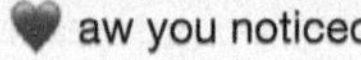 aw you noticed

wanna hear the one about the man from nantucket?

HEMINGWAY_CANSUCKIT

Only if it's very dirty

Is summer in Denver bad? It's so muggy here in Pennsylvania

IMPOSSIBLYBOOKISH

i yearn for fall

much like anne of green gables

also like anne i'm prone to hysterics and getting my friends drunk

HEMINGWAY_CANSUCKIT

Never read it. You recommend?

IMPOSSIBLYBOOKISH

…you've never

read

anne

of

GREEN FUCKING GABLES

hemingway.

HEMINGWAY_CANSUCKIT

Bookish.

IMPOSSIBLYBOOKISH

i'm rethinking every aspect of our friendship.

it is girlhood embodied.

it is feminism.

(not the last five books. those are trash. she
basically gets a lobotomy personality
replacement).

but the first one?? Or the SECOND?!

how dare you not have read it.

HEMINGWAY_CANSUCKIT

I will read your Anne.

If it means a lot to you,

Let's buddy read it.

IMPOSSIBLYBOOKISH

i accept your haiku apology

HEMINGWAY_CANSUCKIT

Now where's my dirty poem?

IMPOSSIBLYBOOKISH

fiiiiine

::ah-hem::

there once was a man from nantucket

whose name was hemingway_cansuckit

his cock was so long

when he stuck out his dong

some bitch out in Denver could fuck it

Chapter Eleven

PEARL

I am gonna choke this motherfucker with his own sweater vests if he doesn't stop moving.

Pearl cradled Reed's laptop as she followed him around the bookstore the next evening. They'd been working all day on inventory.

The air was as thick as her last attempt at dairy and egg-free frosting.

She wiped a bead of sweat from her face. "We need a name for this place. I can't keep calling it *Reed's Bookstore Project* in all these files. What did you put on the county paperwork?"

"Just call it *The Bookshop* for now." Reed whistled as he hammered in the nameplates for the book sections.

How is he so fucking pleasant right now?

"How many shelves were you thinking we'd need for the romance section?" She clicked through the complicated book-ordering catalog system that independent bookstores used.

"I thought maybe six, or maybe two. I'm not sure." He hopped off the ladder and jogged to the toolbox in the front.

"So, uh… four?" she said, scratching her head. God, why

didn't they have AC yet? The doors were flung open, and stingy cross breezes only lazily drifted in.

He jogged across the large open floor where freestanding bookshelves would eventually go. Sometimes she wished she could just tackle him and pin him down as she walked behind him, clicking furiously, trying to get the page to reload.

"Look, do you want me to order your books or not?" she yelled.

"Yes, order me books!" he called with a wide grin over his shoulder.

There was little else that irritated her more than when she was about to lose her goddamn mind and the person she was talking to didn't have a care in the world.

They'd been working for *hours* in the heat, and his smile had never faltered, his hair had never stopped flopping, and he'd barely stopped moving.

He'd worn athletic clothes today, and his compression shirt hugged every single inch of his chest, biceps, and back. He looked like a hot, nerdy rock climber.

It didn't help that he kept adjusting his glasses—it was adorable.

Irritating motherfucker.

How dare he make me attracted to him.

"Will you just sit down?" She gestured to the two chairs she'd thrifted her first day on the job. They were high wingback chairs in a maroon brocade that went perfectly with the dark walnut of the bookstore.

Bert had just finished the small stage by the nook, and the two chairs sat opposite it.

Reed grabbed boxes to unpack. "Sure."

"I need you to decide how many more chairs you want, how many more lamps you want, and what lamps go where," she said, clicking through her to-do list.

"Um," he said, ripping open a package that had more hardware in it. "Oh my gosh, these are going to be so great." He held them up to her so she could see. It was an old-timey looking restroom sign.

"Reed, focus," she snapped.

"You should take a break," he said suddenly, looking at her with concern. "You want me to go get you an iced tea? I know your AC is off in your car. You can cool down in mine."

She growled. "No, I would like to get through this list so that I can go home."

"Come on, why don't we take a break? I'll take you over to, um…" He thought for a minute. "…um, Bloom? They have AC."

She pushed her sweaty bangs back. "It's fine. So, chairs? Lamps?"

"Oh, right. Um, I was thinking a couple more?" He shrugged. She pulled up the layout diagram.

"So you want two more chairs over by the mystery section, and maybe a couple of bean bags for the kids' section?"

"Ooo - what if we had a huge built-in couch in the kids' space instead?" he said, getting excited.

"I. Am going. To kill you," she ground out, tapping her nails on the laptop with every word. "No new ideas. We don't have time to order new things."

"But it has to be perfect. It needs to spark wonder." His eyes sparkled with his new ideas.

"This bookstore"—she stood up and slammed his laptop—"won't spark anything if it doesn't get finished."

He brushed her concerns away as he stood too. "The layout is just a guideline. We can keep moving it until the day we open."

"Ooooh no," she said, tossing the laptop down on the chair. "Because *I'm* the one who has to keep moving everything."

Her hands fisted in his tight compression shirt as she yanked him back and forth. "*Stop—changing—your mind—or I—will toss*

—you out—the skylight," she said with each shake punctuating her words.

His smile was bright and hot as he looked down at her.

Her eyebrows furrowed, and heat hit her cheeks. "What? Stop smiling at me."

He gulped and licked his lips, adjusting his glasses. "May I?"

She froze as he pushed a piece of sweaty hair that had been stuck to her cheek behind her ear. Her hands were still fisted in his shirt.

Better than around his throat.

The side of his mouth quirked into an indulgent, warm smile. "Pearl, you're doing such a great job."

Her heart stuttered in her chest.

What?

"I'm sorry if I don't say it enough. I just want you to know how much I appreciate you. I know this is a lot, and I'm asking a lot of you." His eyes searched her face.

It felt like a caress.

"No, don't do that," she said, releasing her hands and holding them up. "Don't be nice."

"I'll try to stop changing my mind. This place would be a disaster without you," he called as she stomped away, the praise shimmering down her spine like glitter. "Your work ethic is only outpaced by your monumental contributions."

She screamed in frustration as goosebumps flooded her skin. "I'm going home."

"I'm so glad you're my partner in this!" he called across the bookstore.

She swiped her keys off the table, storming out with a vengeance. "Just your assistant! Go away!" she yelled back.

"This just proves you can do anything you want!" he yelled as the door shut behind her.

She'd never had this cocktail of irritation, frustration, and that goddamn praise kink all swirling in the martini glass of her head.

She sped home and slammed the front door open.

She needed to blow off steam.

Maybe a cool shower? Was that it? She rubbed her hand on her chest. *What was this feeling? Oh my god*, she thought, checking in with her body.

Oh my god, I'm horny.

"Why am I such a freak," she moaned.

She rested her head against the cool, cheap Formica countertop. Her phone buzzed with a message from Hemingway.

Yes.

Their flirty banter had been in her head all night. That was what it was. She'd just been revved up and looked at a hot guy in clinging athletic wear.

She could admit that Reed was hot if she didn't think about his brain or his mouth or the smile that she wanted to grind into the asphalt.

She dashed to her room. No telling when Reed would come back home, and she couldn't be caught with her hand down her shorts in the kitchen, even though... fuck, that turned her on. Him walking in and finding her bent over and moaning on her vibrator.

HEMINGWAY_CANSUCKIT

Thinking about you

IMPOSSIBLYBOOKISH

are you alone?

HEMINGWAY_CANSUCKIT

Yes?

IMPOSSIBLYBOOKISH

good. stay that way for 10 min

HEMINGWAY_CANSUCKIT

Can't wait to see what you have planned...

She ran up to her room and ripped off every piece of sweaty clothing except her black thong. She wanted to be reckless tonight—naughty, bad, *wild*.

Wanted Hemingway to come so hard he couldn't stop thinking about her.

Thank god for rechargeable vibrators, she thought as she ripped it away from its charger, sending a silent thanks to Hemingway for getting one that didn't need expensive batteries.

Pearl found a blank space of white wall in her room and backed up to it. She knelt so her back was to the wall.

She leaned over and took a picture of her waist, hips, and ass cheeks in the air against the wall. After about ten tries, she had one that looked pretty good.

She cropped it to avoid including any tattoos. Her tattoo artist always tagged her in endless photos for his site and social posts, so it would be easy to reverse engineer who she was if she shared pictures of them. She didn't have many on her back and hips though, and none on her ass.

She turned on the vibrator and let it dance over her panties as she sent the best photo to Hemingway.

IMPOSSIBLYBOOKISH

was thinking of you too

to help you visualize coming on my ass more realistically.

{photo loading}

HEMINGWAY_CANSUCKIT

SmirGobR $ulifolio

Pearl quirked her head. *Okay not the reaction I had hoped for.*

HEMINGWAY_CANSUCKIT

Sorry

Almost just fell to my death because I got distracted by your ass.

On the ground now.

Bookish…

You…

You are breathtaking.

Your ass is absolute horny fucking perfection. Thick, round. Looks so good in that thong.

Got dizzy because all the blood rushed to my cock.

IMPOSSIBLYBOOKISH

playing with my purple friend too.

if you were here, i'd want to be fucked so hard.

HEMINGWAY_CANSUCKIT

That's exactly how I'd want it.

I can't stop staring at your ass.

It's wide. Gorgeous. My hands are itching for it.

Love those pretty white lines across it.

IMPOSSIBLYBOOKISH

…My stretch marks?

really???

HEMINGWAY_CANSUCKIT

Hell yes. They're real, and raw. Beautiful.

Like how water looks in the sunlight.

Makes me feral. Want to lick it, bite it.

I'd want you just like this. Ass in the air, bending
over for me. Slamming into you so it all jiggles.

Does your ass jiggle, Bookish?

IMPOSSIBLYBOOKISH

you couldn't handle it, hemingway

it shakes.

swings.

wobbles when i'm fucked

HEMINGWAY_CANSUCKIT

Fuccck.

You're perfect

IMPOSSIBLYBOOKISH

i want to be fucked so hard

please

She turned up the vibrator to a higher setting, teasing herself
with it.

HEMINGWAY_CANSUCKIT

I'd slam into you first, hard and rough.

Knowing you could take it

Stretching you.

Pearl moaned, arching her back against the foot of her bed.

HEMINGWAY_CANSUCKIT

I'd sink my hands into your hips, each finger
digging in.

Grasping your softness. Squeezing it.

I might leave bruises I want it so bad

IMPOSSIBLYBOOKISH

yes

HEMINGWAY_CANSUCKIT

I'd punish you with my cock

Slamming in harder and harder.

Faster.

IMPOSSIBLYBOOKISH

fuck yes.

HEMINGWAY_CANSUCKIT

I'd push you down so your face was buried in
the mattress.

Pushing harder, rougher

IMPOSSIBLYBOOKISH

exactly what i want

HEMINGWAY_CANSUCKIT

Tease your ass with the vibrator until I started
sliding it in.

See if you could take both.

Holding it in your ass as I fuck you harder and
harder.

Pearl squealed in ecstasy picturing it.

IMPOSSIBLYBOOKISH

i could

oh my god i want you to fuck me in both holes.

HEMINGWAY_CANSUCKIT

When I've pounded you hard enough, I'd lie
down on the bed and you'd straddle me.

Got a big mirror?

IMPOSSIBLYBOOKISH

yes

HEMINGWAY_CANSUCKIT

We'd face it and you'd ride me so I can watch your ass straddle me, taking the vibrator

I'd watch your tits I can't stop thinking about in the mirror.

You'd take your time riding me while I shoved you down onto my cock, harder.

And harder. You'd slam your hips into me.

IMPOSSIBLYBOOKISH

i'd feel so full.

want to show you something.

She stuck the suction cup end of the vibrator against the mirror mounted to her closet door. Doing the same position as before, bent over on all fours so just her ass cheeks were visible, she held her phone up and hit record.

She fucked the vibrator hard, in and out, rattling the mirror, groaning. She wanted this to haunt Hemingway's dreams.

The mirror showed just how stretched her pussy was around the big vibrator. The smack of her ass as it hit the mirror rattled the door. Her ass moved back and forth, the reflection moving away and then coming back to kiss itself.

She watched the video back. She could only see her waist down, and her ass was so big it took up most of the mirror. The rest of the reflection faced the plain wall next to her closet door.

IMPOSSIBLYBOOKISH

{video loading}

front row seat

She took the vibrator and teased herself with it. She was on edge, trying not to come, and prolonging her pleasure.

HEMINGWAY_CANSUCKIT

Fuck B

I can't

Last

Don't want to stop watching it

You're a wet dream

That pussy stretched so wide for me

Perfect little bud to stick a finger in.

Your ass. Jesus

I want to see it crash into me, jiggling.

Fuck you so hard you can't walk straight.

IMPOSSIBLYBOOKISH

i'm gonna come

feels too good.

HEMINGWAY_CANSUCKIT

Turn up your vibrator

IMPOSSIBLYBOOKISH

yesss

HEMINGWAY_CANSUCKIT

More, Bookish.

So high you can barely take it.

Press it to your pussy and fuck it hard for me

Pearl screamed as she fucked herself, louder, and louder. Rippling cresting waves of need pulled at her as it swirled around her clit, rubbing it up and down, harder and harder. Her hips jerked involuntarily, chasing the pleasure.

Her climax pulled higher and higher screams out of her. She clutched handfuls of her bedsheets, pressing harder to the vibrator, imagining Reed bending her over and fucking her. He'd slam harder, and rougher, pulling her hair back until she couldn't take it.

"Fuck me, Reed," she screamed, until she convulsed again and again on the vibrator, finally climaxing and feeling the burn of the vibrations against her pussy.

She yanked it away, breathless.

Wait…Reed?

She wiped a hand down her sweaty face. *Oh my god, I hope he didn't hear that.*

It's fine. It doesn't count.

It's just a little fantasy to get me over the edge. Only because I don't know what Hemingway looks like.

IMPOSSIBLYBOOKISH

i think you almost broke my pussy.

christ that felt so good.

haven't come so hard in so long.

HEMINGWAY_CANSUCKIT

You've yet again made a mess of me.

Enjoy a picture of your spoils

{photo loading}

Pearl's pussy clenched.

It was Hemingway fisting his cock against his abs. His hand was covered in cum and it had spilled onto his tanned stomach, as if it had spurted hard.

Jesus, he's fit.

His stomach was a nondescript man stomach, but ridges and dips of muscles lined it. It looked white but tanned from the sun, a small trail of light hair from his navel. His hands were large, looking like they had some strength to them. She could see the edge of a watch band, but that was it.

IMPOSSIBLYBOOKISH

too bad i'm not there to lick it all up.

HEMINGWAY_CANSUCKIT

Oh god, don't get me started again.

IMPOSSIBLYBOOKISH

you are genuinely hot, h

like, there's at least 3 of your 6 pack showing

i'm...skeptical you like big girlies IRL

i mean, i think plus size women are goddesses.

a big soft set of round tits? heaven.

HEMINGWAY_CANSUCKIT

On that we definitely agree.

I'm attracted to all sizes, but I'm particularly fond of curvy women.

The softness is inviting, connects to something primal in me.

Like I know I need to mate with someone who looks like that.

Cuddle up and squeeze every bit of softness.

Makes me hungry for it even now.

I just happen to be a guy who works out a lot because it helps me cope with life

And my mom is pretty thin, so the muscles aren't really vanity. Just genetics.

IMPOSSIBLYBOOKISH

slender, easy muscles AND a huge cock?

won the genetic lottery

HEMINGWAY_CANSUCKIT

Don't forget my sparkling conversational skills

IMPOSSIBLYBOOKISH

well sure

but

huge cock!

congrats man.

HEMINGWAY_CANSUCKIT

hahahahahaha

Takes…genetic? bow.

IMPOSSIBLYBOOKISH

and those sexy big dude hands. where they're muscular, like you could easily open a pickle jar, or hang off the ledge of a building.

HEMINGWAY_CANSUCKIT

I'm just glad you have the bubble / peach / shelf ass gene

Cause holy fucking hell. It's perfect

IMPOSSIBLYBOOKISH

thank you for respecting 😇

…in the most disrespectful way possible 😈

HEMINGWAY_CANSUCKIT

I mean this quite literally when I say it…

Any time, any place, Bookish.

Chapter Twelve

REED

IMPOSSIBLYBOOKISH

so, should i save up for nipple rings or an ass
tattoo?

HEMINGWAY_CANSUCKIT

Well

Good morning to you too 

IMPOSSIBLYBOOKISH

good morning h

HEMINGWAY_CANSUCKIT

Hmmm. A tattoo is forever, so seems like a
better investment.

But how often do you look at your own ass?

IMPOSSIBLYBOOKISH

what if the tattoo wasn't for me?

HEMINGWAY_CANSUCKIT

Wait, who's it for??

Who would see it?

Are you…seeing someone?

Are they worth the pain and money of having something on your body forever?

IMPOSSIBLYBOOKISH

look at you being a lil jealous.

it's cute

are YOU seeing anyone?

HEMINGWAY_CANSUCKIT

No, not seeing anyone.

I'm not jealous!

It's your body and your choice.

IMPOSSIBLYBOOKISH

truly the hottest six words a man could type

HEMINGWAY_CANSUCKIT

But I kind of felt like…

Nevermind

IMPOSSIBLYBOOKISH

telllll me

HEMINGWAY_CANSUCKIT

We never talked about what it is we're doing here

And it's fine if it's just having fun.

But, no. I'm not seeing anyone.

Not while we're…IDK, whatever it is we're doing.

Whatever last night was.

And all the other nights.

But I don't expect you to change anything
for me

Please for the love of god say something

Or I'm just going to keep typing and spiraling.

........uhhhh

........Hello???

Bookish!

IMPOSSIBLYBOOKISH

you're so cute when you're flustered.

HEMINGWAY_CANSUCKIT

You're enjoying this, aren't you?

Torturing me.

IMPOSSIBLYBOOKISH

😈

lil bit

....

fiiine

i'm not seeing anyone either.

i was when we first started chatting, but she was
a bust.

HEMINGWAY_CANSUCKIT

I think this is the part where I release a breath I
didn't realize I was holding.

IMPOSSIBLYBOOKISH

fucking hell you're adorable.

what if I told you...

...

...

...

...

HEMINGWAY_CANSUCKIT

Well at least now I know whether you're a masochist or a sadist.

Cause it's pretty obvious what your allegiance is, *sadist.*

IMPOSSIBLYBOOKISH

{gif of 'why not both'}

...

...

HEMINGWAY_CANSUCKIT

IMPOSSIBLY.

MIDDLE SCREENNAME.

BOOKISH.

IMPOSSIBLYBOOKISH

what if I told you the tattoo was

...for you?

HEMINGWAY_CANSUCKIT

Oh

Well now I feel bad for yelling.

Jesus.

That's so...hot.

And...nice?

Nice hot?

I AM flustered.

IMPOSSIBLYBOOKISH

i know you're partial to the peach

HEMINGWAY_CANSUCKIT

But you'd…do that?

For me?

IMPOSSIBLYBOOKISH

anything for you, h

The next day, Reed gestured to the checkout counter in the bookstore, covered in sawdust. "And finally, this checkout section will be a place where we can sell merch," He said with a bright smile.

The Parker sisters had come over for the tour he'd promised. He was starting to understand their unique personalities. Rose was bossy but loving, Violet was as sweet as they came, and he and Lily had a lot in common creatively. They ping-ponged ideas about the store as he walked them through.

"This is amazing!" Violet said, clapping her hands. "You said the romance section is going to be two whole bookcases?"

"Yes. Maybe four."

She bounced with happiness. "I can give you a list of all my favorite authors."

"Here are two referrals, one for painting, and one for on-call plumbing once your contractors are done with the remodel," Rose said, handing him two business cards.

"You said this was the library?" Lily said, hopping on top of the card catalog and dangling her feet.

"In the 20s and 30s," he said, hopping up beside her. "A library, then a fire station, hence the fireman's pole." He pointed over in the corner. "Then I think it was some sort of county office in the '70s, then they sold it to a bank in the 90s."

"Mmm, I remember the bank," Rose said as she typed distractedly on her phone.

Lily unwrapped a crunchy granola bar she'd had in her back pocket and crunched on it as she looked up at the fireman's pole. "What are you gonna do with this?"

The crunch of the bar sounded like a gunshot in the room.

The crackling.

The crunching.

Reed smiled to cover his grimace. "I can't use it unfortunately. It's a liability."

"What about some sort of, like, circular shelf that goes all the way down, surrounding it so it's an artistic display. Ooh, or like book pages shooting out around the pole like they're water," she said between crunching bites of the granola bar.

With every crunch, his skin jolted, and he gulped, trying to push down the irritation growing under his skin.

"That's an amazing idea. No wonder your store is so gorgeous."

"*All* of my stores are gorgeous," Lily said with a jaunty smile, locking her arm through his.

The joy at having friends, maybe even siblings, *just* barely outweighed the scratching irritation in his brain at the loud crunches.

"I think it's time we address the elephant in the room," Rose said, stowing her phone in her back pocket which Reed had already noticed was more like a holster for it.

Rose looked at him expectantly. "Is there a world where we might be related?"

"Um." He scratched the back of his head, wincing. "So, the guy who my mom, you know..."

"Fucked?" Lily supplied.

"Slept with," Violet said, shaking her head at Lily.

"The guy who might be my father—who *is* my biological father," Reed corrected. "H-his name…his name was Frank," he stuttered, finally admitting it out loud to as much to himself as to them.

They gasped.

"It seems astronomically rare for us to meet."

"It's not, really, though," Violet said sweetly. "I looked it up. Apparently, half-siblings meet all the time. Plus, your mom and our dad probably met somewhere in the area."

"I've never had siblings before," he said quickly. "I love people, but they overwhelm me. I'm one of those extroverted introverts." *Or autistics*, he thought privately.

Rose nodded. "Having sisters is a lot—"

"The nicknames." Violet rolled her eyes.

"Nicknames? What about the teasing?" Lily said, pushing at Violet with her foot.

"And the bickering," Rose said with an eye roll. "But it truly is the best, despite all that. Would you be up for doing a DNA test?"

Reed felt like the odd man out with the three of them staring at him. Though, for the first time in his life, he had a chance at being in a club that no one could kick him out of.

He bit his bottom lip. "I'm in," he said, feeling like he'd jumped into the deep end of a pool.

"Great!" Rose reached in her back pocket. "Here's the swab."

"*Rose*." Violet threw her head back in exasperation. "He *just* agreed. Don't scare him off."

Holy fuck. "Is she always this prepared?" he asked Lily.

She nodded. "You'll get used to feeling ambushed with love."

One of the weird side benefits of his amazing pattern recognition (courtesy of the 'tism) was that he almost always had a correct feeling about people. If he liked or disliked them immediately, he found later that there was some reason for it.

He had a bright, sunny warmth in his chest when he looked at the three faces in front of him.

"Let's do it." He followed the complicated swabbing steps, and two minutes later, he handed it back to Rose

Violet smiled hopefully. "Look, whatever happens. Whether we're related or not, we could always just be your friend. We just miss our dad and..."

It all clicked in place, why they'd been hounding him. "And I look just like him?" he realized.

Violet nodded with a small grimace.

What would it be like to see the ghost of his grandpa walking around?

Gutting, he concluded. Their insistence finally made sense.

"And our dad," Violet continued, "though you didn't know him, would want us to take care of you whether or not we're related. Just because you're new to town and everybody needs a friend."

A wash of something hit him.

What was that?

It was an emotion. *Gratitude? Sadness?*

Longing, he realized.

Because whoever the Parkers' dad was, he sounded pretty great.

Rose started toward the door. "We should get going. Lots to do today in the world of flowers."

"Is it weird if I give you a hug?" Violet said, barely keeping her anticipation in check.

"As long as you don't mind a really strong one back," Reed said, feeling emotional.

"Oh my gosh, that's my favorite." Violet laughed. When she wrapped her arms around him in a firm hug, Reed felt like a piece that he hadn't known was missing clicked into place.

"Let me know if you need any more arms twisted for your

construction, okay?" Rose said as she slid her sunglasses back onto her nose.

"That's Rose's version of a hug," Lily said with a wink and a quick hug.

The three of them walked back to Bloom, and Reed rubbed the center of his chest.

This was too many feelings for a Monday. The weight of getting the bookstore exactly right on the first try as he watched his savings dwindle down, paying for all the expenses, for Pearl's time, for ordering the books.

Still lying to my parents.

And now, maybe three new family members he could have for the rest of his life only a stone's throw away.

REED

ours later, a familiar jangling of keys and a silhouette he'd know anywhere appeared in the open doors of the bookstore.

He hadn't talked to Pearl since she'd swirled out in a huff yesterday. He'd stayed late, and they'd missed each other at home. It was Saturday, so he hadn't expected anyone to stop by.

He knew she'd been mad at him, and he'd tried to make her feel better but it had just made everything worse.

I wish I knew how to connect with her.

Her black lipstick was back in place, and the faded and torn band t-shirt she wore was cinched at her waist in a knot. She wore a tight jean skirt, and he had to keep his eyes from lingering on her hips and thighs. She held a large to-go bag in her hand.

"Hey," he called.

"Hey," she answered quietly.

Their eyes connected and the awkwardness of seeing each other after a fight stood between them in the room.

"I remembered what you told me." She inspected her nails, looking bored. "Not being able to eat with anybody sounded kind of lonely, so. I thought we could have lunch together."

She held up the paper bag.

What?

Why didn't people *understand* it wasn't a weird quirk? It was something that ruined his life.

"Pearl, I don't think—"

She pulled out two large green smoothies.

"Lunch," she said with a shy smile. "I also brought a blanket so we could...I don't know, have a picnic. Or whatever."

She looked nervous.

The breath left his body at the surprising sweetness.

A picnic.

Or whatever.

Just for him.

"This would be okay, right?" she said, handing the smoothie to him.

Her eyes looked cautious, and emotion stung in his throat.

No one had ever thought to do anything like that for him. To meet him where he was without pushing him.

"U-um..." His voice was a little shaky.

Embarrassingly shaky.

"Yeah, this would be fine," he said, looking at her warily. "But you don't have to."

She took out the blanket and fanned it over on the curved couch of the reading nook. They both settled in, facing each other a few feet apart.

She took the lid off of hers. "Quieter this way. No straw sound."

She licked the smoothie from the lid and he felt the ground shift under him.

Dizzy with being seen.

And lust, he thought as he watched her tongue trace the edge of the lid, her tongue ring glinting.

"Is this your apology from yesterday?" he asked.

"*My* apology?" she said, outraged.

"I'm sorry, too," he said in a quiet, earnest voice as their eyes connected.

Her lips had pursed over the straw, her cheeks hollowed as she sucked up the dark green smoothie. He was transfixed by the contrast of her dark lips locked around the bright straw.

He shook his head, going back to his own drink.

A mouth like that and a heart of gold?

Careful, Berry.

"What are you smiling at?" she teased, but still, her eyes narrowed.

That was something he would never tell her. "You're very nice."

She scoffed and rolled her eyes.

He raised his hands in honesty. "No one's ever thought to take a creative problem-solving approach to this, including me."

She swirled her straw around her smoothie, and it was blessedly silent. "Didn't you have a girlfriend in college?"

He shrugged. "She'd kind of make me feel bad about it. Like I was a burden. I couldn't keep it together and I'd have to leave her to finish her meal in a restaurant sometimes. I couldn't go with her to family dinners and she hated that."

He sipped the berry-flavored smoothie that tasted like it had kale and protein powder in it.

"Hey." She kicked his foot that was mirroring hers on the bench. "You are not a burden. Annoying as fuck when you won't make up your mind," she said, as they both started laughing. "But not...that."

He nodded. "It wasn't her fault. She was just a college kid. My parents tried their best, but they just wanted a normal kid who could eat at the table. They thought I was just being difficult. They didn't realize it was a physical issue for me."

"People who don't accommodate their loved ones." Pearl shook her head with irritation. "They don't really love them. They love the *idea* of them, not *them*." She pointed at her sternum. "You know? You deserve that. Everybody does."

Reed nodded wordlessly as emotion clogged his throat again.

Maybe he *didn't* know Pearl.

Who was this creature in front of him? It was like a die he'd thought had four sides, but the minute he picked it up, it became a dodecahedron.

"The Parkers were here," he said, wanting to fill the growing tension between them.

"Did you finally man up and tell them they might be your sisters?"

He smacked her foot with his on the bench, and a wicked smile played on her mouth in victory as she sipped her smoothie.

"*Yes*. They seem great."

"They are." She shrugged. "The worst thing that can happen is you have three more people that can give you a kidney."

"And three more people that know where to find a kidney if they need one," he said, raising an eyebrow with a grimace.

"Look at *you*. Thinking on the dark side, I'm so proud of you," she said with a smile.

A laugh rumbled out of him. "I guess you've rubbed off on me."

And...*there* went his mind to the gutter. He went back to the smoothie, swirling it.

"Do you hear that?"

"The sound of the straw against the bottom of the cup? It's fucking terrible, but the blueberries make up for it," he said as he took a sip.

"No, shut up," she said, waving him away.

A faint meowing was coming from somewhere in the building.

"Is that a cat?" he asked.

They crept toward the sound at the back of the building. Their feet made heavy thumping sounds on the wood floor, and Pearl stopped him, a hand on his stomach, so they could listen again.

Another faint meow was a little closer. He looked up.

"Could it be upstairs?" Pearl said, straining to hear. They walked up the spiral staircase to the second floor mezzanine that lined the perimeter.

Construction trash, plywood, and buckets of plaster repair sat along the sides as they weaved along the edge. They both paused again, trying to hear the sound. Insistent meowing was on the other side of a built-in bookshelf.

"It sounds like it's coming from this bookcase," Pearl said, her hand running along an inset bookcase along the back wall.

There was no building on the other side of the wall that Reed knew of.

Reed looked to see if there was a hole somewhere nearby.

"Maybe it got in during construction?" Pearl asked, taking a step back.

"Watch it," Reed said as Pearl caught her foot on a piece of lumber. His hands reached out to catch around her waist, and they both stumbled into the wall edging beside the bookshelf, as Pearl's hand landed on the back of the bookshelf where the back panel moved under her hand.

The bookcase clicked open.

"This was *not* in the blueprints," Reed said with surprise.

"No waaaaay. This is so fucking *cool*," Pearl said as she pulled the bookcase open wider.

A small gray cat darted out and scampered down the steps. "Did you know this was here?" she said with surprise as she turned around in his arms.

A whiff of her vanilla scent crashed over him, and he realized his hand was still on her waist.

He dropped it. "No. There was nothing about a room here in the schematics of the building."

"So cool," she muttered, and they walked inside. It was an oversized deep closet, and the ceiling went all the way up one additional story. Shelves on either side were lined with dusty liquor bottles.

"Oh my god. This must be left over from Prohibition." Pearl looked up in wonder.

Reed was thunderstruck at the surprise of it. His own secret passageway.

Dust on the bottles was an inch thick. No one had been here in decades. He walked deeper into the small room, and the bookcase swung closed, shutting out all the light.

"Great. Now I can't see the cool-ass old liquor," Pearl muttered. "Open the bookcase."

Reed pushed on it.

It didn't budge. He pushed harder.

Reed's heart was in his throat, and he turned in the pitch black to Pearl.

"It won't open."

"What do you mean?" Pearl said, panicked. She slammed on the door.

His eyes adjusted to the dim light, and he felt around the edge of the bookcase. "The latch that locked it must have a release inside."

She shoved her shoulder on the bookcase again.

"Or we're going to die here," Pearl said in a small voice.

"It's fine." Reed put a hand on her shoulder to keep her from throwing herself at the wall again. "We'll just call somebody." He felt for a phone in his pocket, but he'd left it downstairs. "Do you have your phone on you?"

"*No*," Pearl yelled, starting to pace beside him. "Don't you?"

He grasped again, hoping a phone would reappear. "You're not gonna like my answer."

"We're gonna die here," Pearl said, bending over.

"There's probably a lever somewhere." He felt around in the darkness around the wall and shelves of the bookcase.

Ragged breaths came from behind him.

"I'm," she gasped, "claustrophobic. Worst nightmare. Dark small room."

"We're going to be fine. We're going to get out of here," he said with confidence he didn't actually feel.

The construction crew was gone for the weekend.

No one would hear their screams.

"No one knows we're here," she said, her voice wobbling. "They'll find two old husks rotting away when we die from asphyxiation, or malnutrition, or dehydration."

The warm air wrapped around them wasn't helping things as Reed felt a bead of sweat roll down his forehead. He tugged off his sweater vest so he could focus.

Pearl's breathing grew more ragged. "About to have a panic attack. Need something to stop it."

He grasped around blindly on the shelves...Nothing. There was no button, no lever, no handle.

"I need you to slap me," Pearl gasped.

"Absolutely not," he said, horrified.

"Please, I need to do something." Her voice started to fade, and she tugged at her shirt collar.

He'd never seen her like this.

"Can't fucking breathe." She yanked off her shirt. Her luminous skin was barely visible in the dim light and contrasted against her dark bra. She paced in the meager two feet they had in the closet.

He slammed his shoulder against the bookcase again.

"Come on, just do it!" she said, badgering him. Her breaths came in gasps now.

Fuck, this was all going sideways. He grabbed her shoulders. "Pearl, breathe with me." He took a deep inhale, inhaling her perfume.

She wheezed, her hands fisted in his button-up shirt. "Reed, just slap me."

"I will *not*."

She got angry. "Just do it."

"No!" he said firmly.

"Maybe I can slam my head against the wall," she gasped.

He held her arms in place. "*Absolutely* not."

She gasped, staring at him.

"*Fine*. Maybe this'll work." She yanked him down and crashed her lips to his, kissing him hard.

His lips lingered there as his brain registered, *I'm kissing Pearl.*

His hands tightened on her arms.

Fuck, *I'm kissing Pearl.*

Melting into her, he kissed her back. Tentative at first.

Just being helpful.

But she felt so damn good.

Her lips tasted like the berry smoothie she'd brought him, and fuck if that didn't make him want her more.

His hand slid up to cup her jaw, and he savored her pillowy, soft lips as he kissed her.

And kissed her.

And *kissed* her, lingering over every one, heat and urgency growing as he realized he never wanted to stop kissing Pearl Bishop.

He might die if he didn't keep kissing her right now.

Her taste. Her sighs. He needed them like air.

He couldn't get enough of her. He was a man doomed to die of thirst as he gulped water straight from the hose.

Her nails scraped along his chest as she pulled him toward her. She caught his lip between her teeth and he groaned.

Yes. More.

He slid his hand to grip the back of her neck, pressing deeper open-mouthed kisses and taking what he wanted.

Holding her right where he wanted her.

She moaned, pliant and so fucking sexy. He brushed his tongue along her lip, wanting to feel her.

Imagining his tongue in other places.

She opened wider for him, and their tongues brushed for one dizzying moment.

Then again.

Oh fuck. And again.

The ball of her tongue ring brushed against him, and an electric need zipped to his cock, straining in his pants. He could come from just the feeling of her tongue ring against him. He groaned, already at his limit of wanting her, and he pushed her back against the wall.

Fuck, it was so hot. *She* was so hot. The brush of her septum ring against his skin as he deepened the kiss seared him.

Her back hit the wall as he pinned her to it; her nails raked through his hair.

He'd never felt heaven like this. The taste of her, her vanilla and amber scent clouding around him, intoxicating him.

"This helping?" he muttered, his lips never leaving hers.

He didn't want to stop for a second.

"Mmhmm," she moaned into his mouth as he pressed a leg between hers.

"Excellent," he said with a sigh and angled her head to deepen the kiss.

She pressed against him hard, and he wrapped his arms around her tight.

Pearl didn't kiss tenderly.

She was hungry, like him.

And he met her stroke for stroke. Taking whatever she'd give him.

He sucked on the cupid's bow of her top lip, happy to spend the rest of his days lost in this single moment. Memorizing the feeling of kissing her.

Hunger clawed at him, though.

More taste even as he satisfied it, licking into her mouth again.

More feeling as he threaded his hand in her hair, feeling the silky strands in his fingers.

More, more, more.

Her breasts pressed against him, and it was all he could do to keep one hand on her waist. They itched to feel her soft tits again. Had haunted him since that day in the hallway. Wondering what they'd taste like.

He moved to her jaw, raking his teeth there. Wanting to taste her everywhere.

"Don't stop," she panted, pressing his head into her neck.

He nipped her throat and she gasped.

"Don't want to," he muttered, his lips never leaving her skin. He couldn't stop tasting her.

Vanilla would be forever changed for him.

She grasped his arms, his back. Her nails raked hard into his hair, and he moaned as he nipped her neck.

Her tits called to him. He needed to feel them against his tongue.

This was for her, right? Keep her distracted?

A dark part of him wanted something for himself, too.

She panted. "We might be here forever," she said as he kissed down her collarbone.

She pressed his face into her breast, and he decided it would be fine if he died right here, right now. It would never get better than a face full of the top of Pearl's breasts.

"We'll die of dehydration first," she said, panting.

He licked, and kissed, his lips tracing every curve he could. "You wanted to be kissed, right?" he muttered against her other breast.

Her breath was coming in panicked gasps now. "Yes."

He stood, threading their fingers, and pressed her arms above her head, pinning her back against the wall. His nose traced against hers, hovering over her lips. "Then shut up and take it," he murmured. He kissed her hard, squeezing their hands.

She moaned louder, and their kisses grew hungry, sloppy. Claiming.

He'd somehow known it would be like this with her.

Unafraid of her desire—unapologetic.

He punished her with more kisses, moving to hold her head. He'd keep her occupied or they'd die here; he didn't care.

She was the perfect last meal in his opinion.

Her hands raked up along his stomach, her touch hungry, firm.

Her nails scraped under his shirt along his stomach. His cock was a hard brick in his pants, and her palm brushed the top of it.

Perfect. *Harder,* he thought.

She ripped his shirt open and buttons clattered to the ground. She hummed into his mouth with pleasure as she fanned her hands up his chest, gripping him.

She pushed him against the side wall, having her way with him. Fuck, he liked that.

He pulled her to him hard, his hands cupping her ass and squeezing, finding her mouth again.

Fuck, I might come. She was devouring him, their tongues permanently entwined, never leaving each other.

He needed to get a handle on this. He should pull back, but his hands itched for her silky soft stomach.

He raked his teeth hard against her lip and then soothed the bite with his tongue.

This is a perfect way to die, he thought, cupping her jaw.

He pushed her against the opposite wall, pushing her bra strap to the side. His other hand landed on a dusty bottle. It moved back like a lever under his hand, and daylight flooded in the room as the bookcase opened.

Pearl darted out as the bookcase opened, gasping for air. Reed had just enough sense to grab their clothes before he ran out, too.

They stared at each other in the too bright sunlight, their chests heaving.

He held out her shirt and turned away. His cock was on full display, not that she hadn't already felt it.

Her lips were swollen and red. Her black lipstick was a mess around her mouth. He rubbed at his mouth, realizing it was probably all over him. Purple marks came off of his hand after he wiped his face.

He stared at them with an ironic laugh.

The best kiss of his fucking life, and it was from the woman who worked for him, his best friend's little sister, and the one woman who'd never want him.

His cock finally under control, he turned around. "You okay?"

"Yeah," she said, getting her bearings back as she pushed her hair behind her ears.

"Here, you have..." He wiped a thumb under her lip where she'd missed a lipstick smudge.

She didn't move as his thumb moved across her chin, lingering.

No more.

Inappropriate.

His hand fell as he realized that that would be the last time he'd ever get to kiss her.

Chapter Fourteen

PEARL

Maybe it was the lack of oxygen that made her off balance.

Maybe it was the world-tilting kiss.

But Pearl had learned two things in the last five minutes:

1. Reed had a huge cock

2. She reeeeally wanted to fuck him.

"We...uh, shouldn't do that again," Reed said. He wouldn't meet her eyes.

Ouch.

"As if I'd get stuck in there with you again," she said, her defensive spikes coming out.

"Right, no. I meant the..." He gestured to their mouths, wiping his against the back of his hand.

Is he disgusted by me? It poked at a soft underbelly of shame.

"Who said I wanted to?" She tossed a shoulder up with a glower at him, hiding every single one of her feelings.

Her lips still tingled—fucking *tingled*—from where his fingers had caressed them, wiping off her lipstick.

"Pearl." He finally met her eyes with a soft look. "You kissed me."

She scoffed. "You kissed me *back*."

"You were panicking," he said, losing his patience.

"That doesn't mean I want to do it again." She rolled her lips together, trying to get a taste of him.

Liar, liar, black tights on fire.

"I mean, it didn't seem like you were *not* into it." He pushed his glasses up, trying to hide a proud smile.

She'd moaned. She'd moaned a fucking lot; she knew this. She'd been about ten seconds away from begging for more.

"Fine. I pinky promise never to kiss you ever again. It'll be the easiest fucking thing I'll ever do," she said, realizing they were now toe to toe.

"Thank you," he said with a quiet smile.

Obviously, he'd never actually want you. He probably wants some 2.5 kids, white picket fence, cupcake-making princess to plan out his perfect little life.

And what the fuck do I even care about his life?!

"Ugh." She stomped around him.

This was just like when they were kids. He always managed to make her feel like a weird dumbass.

IMPOSSIBLYBOOKISH

so what are your weekend plans

HEMINGWAY_CANSUCKIT

Spending some quality time with my library's audiobook app

Maybe open a bottle of red, put on some candlelight, jazz.

Treat her to a good time.

IMPOSSIBLYBOOKISH

are you trying to make me jealous of a non-sentient data collection?

HEMINGWAY_CANSUCKIT

Is it working?

IMPOSSIBLYBOOKISH

oh honey,

no.

but i love you for trying.

wait

not

i love you.

fuck

i meant 'not i love you'

you know what i mean

it's cute you want to make me jealous.

and i love that

but not LOVE Love

Not that I don't care for you a whole fucking lot

Oh my god I see you reading my messages

for the Love of cheese say something!

....

Hemingway!!!!!!

you're the worst.

HEMINGWAY_CANSUCKIT

...

What's that saying about payback?

IMPOSSIBLYBOOKISH

that people who do it are petty and mean and DON'T have huge penises.

HEMINGWAY_CANSUCKIT

Ah, that's right.

You're so flustered.

Adorable.

Noted, Bookish. You don't LOVE love me.

I care for you a whole fucking lot too.

IMPOSSIBLYBOOKISH

ANYWHO

i started and finished Mr. Penumbra's 24 Hour Bookstore in one sitting last night.

you should read it - so good. whimsical, romantic, edge-of-your-seat mystery.

HEMINGWAY_CANSUCKIT

I dunno.

A book about a bookstore?

Allllll the stories in the universe at a writer's fingertips and it's about the place you buy the book from??

Seems...

...a little navel-gazey

IMPOSSIBLYBOOKISH

i'd personally love to gaze at your navel

HEMINGWAY_CANSUCKIT

LOVE love to gaze at it?

Or just care a whole fucking lot?

AFTER A WEEKEND of very purposefully avoiding Reed, Pearl stood outside the courthouse on the following Monday, a single bead of sweat dripping down the center of her back.

Being a goth girl in the summer was its own cross to bear.

She'd changed her outfit no less than three times, not that she'd ever tell a soul that.

Her only pair of non-ripped tights, a skirt that didn't have any witchcraft symbols or high slits, and a plain black shirt—that was her *serious professional* outfit. Right before she left the house, she'd remembered to take off her earrings that said "Fuck" and "You" on either side of her ears.

This was as presentable as she got.

Reed walked up jauntily looking confident and breezy, but she knew the tic in his eyes. He was stressed.

They were following up on the bullshit permits Beulah had made up. It was probably all her fault that Beulah was even causing them grief, and she had to make it right.

Despite still having hurt feelings over his reaction to the kiss, Pearl wasn't going to let him be thrown into the lion's den of the Fairwick Falls bureaucratic machine. He was too nice.

He *would* take no for an answer.

She, however, wouldn't.

"You look nice," he said with a happy smile.

And like a fucking bird preening, she stood a little taller and forced down a smile. Why did he have to notice things?

"These people are allergic to rips in clothing, so ta-da. Now let's get inside before I melt into a little punk puddle."

"You know, you didn't have to come. I could handle this," he said, shifting the papers in his hand.

His skin was sun-kissed, probably from the runs he went on everyday, and the white button-up shirt clung to his arms and chest. He'd unbuttoned one extra button which gave a tantalizing hint of his chest.

She reached up and buttoned it for him, her long nails scraping his skin. He froze.

"Don't want any of the old bats in there to have an aneurysm from all your muscles," she said, waving a sarcastic hand at his chest and abs as she stepped away. She could still remember what they felt like if she thought hard enough. "Plus, you need me there. I have to scare them into submission."

"I'm not worried," he said with a happy bounce, starting to run up the courthouse steps. "It's just normal paperwork."

Pearl followed him. "I brought fake blood capsules just in case."

"For *what*?" he said in horror.

"In case! I don't know, we need a distraction, or a fake injury, or a man tells me to smile. They always come in handy. You're never gonna say, 'Oh, I'm so sorry I brought the perfect excuse' when shit hits the fan."

He got to the door first and opened it for her, standing back.

She rolled her eyes as he gestured her in. "Patriarchal bullshit," she muttered even as a smile tugged at her lips.

She was a big fat hypocrite, okay? She hated it when a guy was a gentleman and she loved it at the same time.

They wandered the musty, air-conditioned halls of the courthouse. The signs were barely helpful, giving only enough information for someone to find their way through the catacomb of old rooms.

Finally, they stumbled upon the County Commissioner's

office. It was a long hallway of closed, teller-like windows. No sounds gave away that humans even existed.

"Creepy," Reed muttered.

"Pretty sure I just saw a tumbleweed."

One window on the row of teller windows, however, was cracked open two inches. Pearl bent down, saw a human, and knocked hard.

The window raised up and Beulah stood glaring at them. "What?" she said with a flat, croaking voice.

"Hi," Reed said, adjusting his glasses as he set the papers down. "I wanted to check on the permits that we filed to make sure we have final approval."

Beulah stared at them with contempt. "You have to go to the Zoning and Planning Department." She shut the window.

Pearl knocked on the window again. "Open up, you old—"

Reed put a hand over hers, stopping her. "It's fine. We'll just go find the Zoning and Planning Department."

They wandered to the end of the hallway where an old map showed the labyrinth of the courthouse. "I think we have to go back outside, and then go back in the other way."

They walked all the way outside, around the building, and back up three staircases.

Pearl tried very hard not to look at Reed's ass as he jaunted up the stairs in front of her, but it was just so perfect. Muscular, bubble-like.

So, as a special little treat, she stared at it all the way up the third staircase.

That's a motivational ass right there.

A little bit more than out of breath, they went back up and saw what looked to be an identical row of teller-like arches with the windows rolled down and a sign that said "Zoning and Planning."

Pearl knocked hard and the window opened, and Beulah—*fucking Beulah*—was right there.

"Department of Zoning and Planning, how can I help you?" she said, looking bored.

"Jesus fucking Christ." Pearl rolled her eyes. Beulah was in the same office; she'd just turned around to the opposite side.

"So, about that permit?" Reed smiled with what looked like all his charm.

"You have to take this paper"—she tossed up an 8-by-11" sheet with old-style typing on it—"to the Historical Preservation Subcommittee of the Zoning and Planning Department. Do you have Form B with you?"

Reed shuffled through the stack of papers.

"Beulah, cut the fucking crap. Just tell us what we're supposed to do," Pearl said, leaning in.

"No," Beulah said. "No special treatment."

Hot water. She was going to pour hot water all over this woman's flowers tonight.

Was it cruel? Yes, the flowers weren't to blame. Was it a little illegal? Probably.

She didn't fucking care.

"Yes, I have Form B right here." Reed looked victorious.

"Good, you don't need it," Beulah said, starting to slam the window down.

Pearl shot her hand out, holding up the window. "Where is the Historical Preservation Subcommittee?"

"It's around the corner," Beulah said. Pearl yanked her hand back as Beulah continued to slam down the window.

"It's fine," Reed said with a calming look.

Her temper was flaring. "She's doing this because of me. It's my fault and I need to fix it."

"I don't think you were the cause for all these forms," he said, holding up a big stack of papers.

"Yes, I am. Half the shit she made up. She's trying to get back at me for the gnomes."

"The what?" He stared at her. "Never mind, probably better if I don't know. Let's just do it the right way, and then we can get back on schedule."

They wandered around the corner to a door that was closed. A sign that said "Historical Preservation Subcommittee - Zoning and Planning" was falling off the door.

They opened it, and Beulah stood right behind the door.

"This is hell. We're in hell right now," Pearl said.

"Hello, welcome to the Historical Preservation Subcommittee," Beulah droned.

Pearl fisted her hands to keep them in place. "Is there anybody else who works here that we could talk to? Maybe somebody who's not a demon in a sack of skin?"

As if on cue, a man came whistling out from behind Beulah, carrying a cup of coffee and a large donut. His photo matched the one on the wall that said County Commissioner.

Oh my god, it's Pecan Man.

"Hey!" Pearl shouted. The man looked up. "You owe me seven hundred dollars."

The man froze.

"Listen," Reed said, with an edge in his voice as he stared Beulah down. "We just want our permits."

There was a command to his voice that had Pearl staring at his clenched jaw.

"*Shut up and take it*" echoed in her head from their kiss.

So he did have a spine. *Hot.*

"You'll need to come back and schedule a review time with the Historical Society Committee," Beulah droned.

"We're going to schedule it right now," Pearl said. She stepped in front of Reed and pointed to the man behind Beulah. "Or I'm going to tackle this man and take all of his money."

"I don't know what she's talking about," the man said as he started to back away from the door.

She slipped a blood capsule into her mouth.

"We're just trying to do the right thing, so just tell me when. We'll accommodate any time," Reed said.

Beulah looked at them, bored and unmoved. "You'll have to come back. We only schedule appointments on Tuesday from 2:15 to 2:57."

"No," Pearl said. "We're going to schedule it *now*."

Pearl widened her eyes to look crazed and bit down on the fake blood capsule, feeling the liquid fill her mouth. "It would be a shame if there are more pecans on that donut." She smiled as bright as she could muster, staring directly at the man, blood dripping down her chin.

If she wasn't getting her seven hundred dollars back, she could at least fuck with him.

"Um... uh, Beulah, it's fine. You can schedule them now," Pecan Man said as he practically ran out of the room.

Beulah sighed.

Reed glanced over at her and did a double take with a long sigh afterwards.

He put his hands on his hips. "And we can finish up construction, but just not open until the committee's approval?"

"Yes, that's what I said," she said, sliding a piece of paper toward them. "The next available spot is three weeks away."

"We need something sooner," Pearl said. It would be too close to the soft opening.

"Take it or leave it. Maria's on some fancy vacation until then," Beulah said.

"We'll take it," Reed said, resigned.

"Scheduled. Have a nice day. Or don't, I don't give a shit," Beulah slammed the door in their face.

Pearl tossed open the window next to the door, knowing it would peer into the room.

"Eat a bag of soft, gummy dicks!" she said and slammed the window back down.

"Soft?" Reed said with a laugh.

"She's old. I don't want her to, like, break a tooth or something," Pearl said, enjoying the feeling of the fake blood running down her chin.

"You've got a little..." Reed said, pointing to his chin.

She didn't wipe it away as she smiled. "See? Came in handy."

He laughed and she was delighted with herself.

"I'm so glad you came, Pearl. I couldn't do this without you, or the blood capsules. Plus," he said, pushing open the door for her to walk through, "they really complement your smile."

Go away, glitter feelings.

Go away.

Chapter Fifteen

PEARL

"Another round," Allison slurred to Big Dave, the bartender at The Thirsty Beaver.

Pearl's home away from home was a casual, dingy, old dive bar at the edge of Fairwick Falls.

Every once in a while, a Fairwick Falls townie who wanted to jazz up their Friday night would stop in. Pop, the diner owner, and his wife, Mrs. Maroo-Canon, head of the local gossip mill in Fairwick Falls, stopped in sometimes. Pearl counted them among her favorite people now.

The air was thick with a stale, lingering cigarette smell. The sticky floor covered in popcorn, and the scowls of the bikers made Pearl feel perfectly at ease. It was a place for all the misfit sharp edges in this cute-ass town.

Lily sat on the other side of Allison, almost as drunk. She was stuffing her face with red velvet vegan cupcakes Pearl had made for Allison's big night out.

"These are so bucking belicious," Allison said through a mouth stuffed with her third cupcake. "Amb ifs bluben fwee?"

The light pink frosting on each cupcake *almost* matched Allison's hair color. Pearl had nearly gotten it this time. The peachy pink that Allison dyed her hair made her look like a fairy queen come to life.

"Gluten-free and *vegan!*" Lily stood on the lower rail of the bar, pumping her hand in the air wildly in celebration.

Pearl fucking loved Lily—always down for a good time. Another cheap beer and large shot of tequila slid in front of both Allison and Lily. Pearl was the DD tonight.

"Pearl, what's good?" Tom, an old, grizzled man leaned against the bar, signaling for another from Dave.

"Not this weak-ass beer, that's for sure." She lifted the one she'd been nursing for the past two hours.

His hacking laugh was interrupted by the sound of chairs scooting as two guys started a fight in the back corner.

She wiggled down in her seat, enjoying it.

"Isn't this place perfect?" she said to no one in particular, and Allison spun around.

"It is! We should *dance.*" Allison shook Pearl's arms. A table crashed in front of them as one of the guys fell into it.

"Hey fuckwits! Out!" Dave yelled. "Or Tiny will handle the issue for you," he said, pointing to a hulking, large man nursing a long-neck beer in the corner of the bar and crocheting.

"Rats. We coulda been in a bar fight," Allison said, snapping her fingers sadly.

"You wanted a wild and crazy night." Pearl smirked over at her.

She didn't have a lot of friends that were girls. This was the closest she'd gotten to a real girls' night in years, if you didn't count her and AB painting their fingernails while singing "Baby Shark."

Allison and Lily had a lot in common. They loved Taylor Swift. They loved pink. They loved all things girly, including—Pearl shuddered—roses, wildflowers, and weddings.

Pearl was definitely the odd one out. She always had been.

That was why she wanted to do something different: have a bakery that had alternative designs, not to mention alternative ingredients.

"Oh my gosh, are you crocheting?" Allison yelled over at Tiny and threw back the rest of her beer. She spun herself in fast circles on her stool.

Alright, this one is getting out of pocket. Pearl grabbed her shoulders to keep her from spinning.

"Makin' a bandana for my cats," Tiny's echoey, bass voice rumbled. He held it up, showing a camo-like pattern.

"Shut the fuck up," Lily yelled. She leaned over and smushed his enormous face between her hands. "Tiny, you're adorable! Poorly named, but adorable."

Annnnd they're both officially white girl wasted.

"Sorry," Pearl mouthed to Dave, who chuckled.

"Did you try these?" Allison lifted up the Tupperware container to Dave. "Pearl's so good at baking, and it doesn't even have any bad stuff in it like nuts and eggs and milk and gluten, and I don't really know what's in here." Allison swiped her finger along some frosting. "But there's an orgy in my mouth."

Dave raised an eyebrow at Pearl. "These two are fun."

He took a piece of cupcake that had been split into fours— the girl way of cutting—before the alcohol had started. He took a bite. "This is good. You said egg-free? Could you make something for my daughter?"

"Hot damn, she's out of jail already?" Pearl slapped the bar with excitement.

He nodded, grabbing another bit of cupcake. "Good behavior."

"Nice." Pearl toasted him.

"She can't eat eggs, and everything has fuckin' eggs in it. I wanted to do something nice for her, you know? I'm real proud of her." He shrugged, dingy flannel flapping from the motion.

Pearl's heart thumped in her chest. "I don't know if I'm ready for customers. I'll, uh, think about it."

"You know where to find me," he said, throwing a towel over his shoulder.

Pearl's phone lit up in the dark bar.

HEMINGWAY_CANSUCKIT

Have you ever felt like you're failing at every
single thing you're doing?

IMPOSSIBLYBOOKISH

no, because im fucking amazing and perfect at
everything.

which is why it took me three - yes, three full
times - to put on my underwear this morning

first time? backwards

second time? inside out

HEMINGWAY_CANSUCKIT

I mean, you could have left them off. ☺

"Look at that face on her *face*," Allison said with a hiccup, booping Pearl's nose.

"That's a dopey-ass love grin," Lily said, propping her head on Allison's shoulder.

"Who are you texting?" Allison said in a singsong voice.

Pearl slammed the phone face down onto the table. "Nobody. Shut up." Pearl's cheeks started to heat as she grabbed her beer.

"Ah-ah-ah," Allison said, wagging a finger. "That's your tell."

"The rolling of the eyes, right?" Lily added.

"She does it all the time." Allison nodded. "It's the looking up and to the left as she gets mad."

Pearl glared at them over her lukewarm beer. *This is why I don't have friends.*

Then they think they know you or something.

"I wish I had a nobody," Allison sighed, playing with the rest of the shot in her tequila glass. "But I want a baaaaabyyy…" she said slowly.

"Is *that* what this is all about?" Pearl said, finally trying to understand why her normally very put-together, quiet, sweet coworker was behaving like a girl gone wild.

"Wait, you do?" Lily said in surprise.

Allison nodded. "I'm done trying to date here; it's useless. The men are trash. No offense, crochet buddy." She pointed to Tiny.

"I'm married," Tiny said with a shrug.

"I don't want a person in my house who's just some guy." Allison stood up, thunderstruck. "That's all husbands are—just *some guy in your house.*"

Pearl lived with some guy. "Yeah, because sometimes they walk in on you naked," she muttered.

"What?" Lily said, spinning around.

"And I want a family," Allison continued, in her own world. "And you know, I'm about to ticktock according to my doctor," she said, tapping her wrist. "That's why I needed one wild and crazy night," she said, spinning herself around on the bar stool again. "I'm going to the sperm bank next week."

A greasy man Pearl didn't recognize slid up behind Allison. "I can help you make one tonight for free, baby."

Allison burst out laughing as she pushed him away. "Ew!" He slid his hand onto Allison's waist, ignoring her.

Pearl got in his face and pushed him hard until his back hit a high-top table. "Hey, motherfucker. She said you're disgusting. The 'no' was implied."

"Be a bitch about it already," the man muttered, wandering back to his friends.

"I *am* going to be a bitch about it. These are my friends, shriveled dick."

Allison slung a long arm around Pearl's shoulders. "You are a gooey little jelly bean who loves us, I just knew it." She squished Pearl's cheeks together as Lily took a photo, probably to use as blackmail later.

The bar door swung open, and a striking, tall man walked through.

"Husband!" Lily yelled above the loud bar and galloped toward her enormous, hot husband who caught her mid-jump.

Nash was as opposite as someone could get from Pearl, but they'd mutually agreed on protecting Lily from doing stupid shit, like walking home late at night by herself and climbing on top of things one should not climb on.

Pearl gave Nash a nod which he returned, and another tall man walked in behind him.

"Oh fuck," Pearl muttered. "Allison, let's go out the other door."

"I wanna say hi to Nash." Allison turned toward the door, but it was too late. She'd made eye contact with the tall man behind Nash.

Wells Maroo—former resident of Fairwick Falls and Allison's sworn enemy—shook hands with friends as he walked in. He was a bigger guy, both in height and size, with a barrel chest and beefy arms. Honestly, he'd be Pearl's kind of thing if he wasn't Allison's mortal enemy.

"Oh, you, motherf—" Allison launched herself, claws out, at Wells, but Pearl caught her by the waist.

Wells had represented Allison's ex-husband in her painful, long divorce.

Pearl locked her arms around Allison, trying to move her out the bar without further incident.

"Ladies," Wells said, smiling nervously.

"How dare you come here during girls' night? How dare you set foot in the town I live in!" Allison said, pointing over Pearl's shoulder. "Everyone be mean to him!" Allison called as Pearl finally pushed her out the door and it swung shut.

Allison started to cry. "He's the worst, Lily. You don't even *know*."

"I know, sweetie. I got the hint when you smashed a cake in his face during the town Christmas party, but tell me all about it." Lily patted her back as they stumbled to Pearl's car.

"Lily, can you get her in my car? I forgot something at the bar."

Pearl walked back into the bar with her heart pounding.

Allison had big plans. She was going to have a whole baby by herself.

It's punk as fuck to bet on yourself.

Pearl could have big plans too, right?

I'll do it. I'll make a cake.

Before she lost her nerve, she ran up to the bar and locked eyes with Dave.

"How does your daughter feel about edible fake blood?"

REED

The scent of books swirled around Reed as he took in the shelves at the Elliotsville discount used bookstore.

He and Pearl were on the hunt for buried treasures in the stacks. Pearl had gathered a large armful of sci-fi thrillers, poring over shelves with an expert eye.

A worn cover of *1984* called to him. It had scribbles on the cover and marks in the margins. There was charm at finding the remnants of someone else's reading. He grabbed it and moved to the next bookcase.

"I saw Beulah on my run this morning," Reed said, squatting to look at the cookbooks on the bottom shelf. "Pretty sure she flipped me off as she blew through a stop sign."

"She's just a giant curmudgeonly bitch who gets deviant sexual satisfaction from making other people miserable. If I didn't hate her so much," Pearl said, squatting down next to him, "I'd probably want to be her when I grew up."

"Hurt people hurt people," Reed said, echoing one of the lessons he'd learned in one of the many self-help books he'd read.

That was probably his top genre, but he would *never* admit

that to Pearl. She'd roast him. He'd read endless books on how to win friends, how to overcome his anxieties, how to understand all the other humans who seemed to naturally understand how to be normal.

If there even *was* such a thing as normal.

He wished sometimes that neurotypical people would read a book on how to make *his* life easier, rather than the other way around.

"She's giving you shit because I'm helping you, so it's sort of all my fault, really. For some reason she hates me and Luca and AB," she said absentmindedly. Her eyes never left the shelves, scanning title after title.

"It's fine. I want to do things the right way. I'm still an interior architect, and I want to respect the building even if half the forms were basically made up."

"So, why a bookstore? Ooh," she cooed, pulling out a copy of *The Silent Patient*. "You don't seem particularly bookish."

His ears pinged at the word. "I read a lot. I just listen to audiobooks while I run given I've been busy with the store. It's easier for me to get lost in the stories that way."

She squinted over her shoulder, evaluating him. She had on winged eyeliner today and a deep purple, almost black lipstick on. It complemented the deep silver of her septum ring. "I'd peg you for...historical nonfiction. You know, dad literature," she said dismissively.

"*Dad* literature?" he said, horrified. "I read everything." He straightened the cuffs of his rolled-up sleeves, perturbed that he came across as boring.

"Name your favorite literary fiction," she said, shrugging and walking down the shelves.

He pulled *Parable of the Sower* off the shelf and added it to his stack. "I don't have to prove myself to you," he said, feeling cornered. "But just so you know, *The Bell Jar*."

Her mouth dropped open. "Plath? No way. You are a Hemingway slash Fitzgerald slash 'I only like books that don't make me feel things' kind of guy."

He scoffed. "I *hate* Hemingway. Loathe. All that toxic rub-some-dirt on it manliness. Terse writing that feels like rocks grinding between your teeth. He had the gall to call his writing *architectural*. Honestly, it's an insult to every bridge that's ever been built."

Pearl's eyes went wide. "Oooookay, hit a sore spot apparently—"

"*And* one of the best books I've ever read was a middle-grade novel that made me cry like a baby."

"Fine." She pulled four more thrillers off the shelves. "Ten points for knowing what a middle-grade novel is."

"Pearl, I'm opening a bookstore."

She lifted an eyebrow. "I've never seen you even carry a book."

He reached above her on a high shelf, his chest brushing her back, and pulled two biographies that did indeed fall in the genre of "dad literature," but he turned the spines so she wouldn't notice. "It's because you've never seen my bedroom."

She'd turned around, her back against the bookcase, and she was far too close to him. Inches away.

She gulped, and her eyes flitted down to his mouth.

"I've got stacks beside my bed," he said quietly. She licked her lips, and he had to drag his eyes up from staring at them. "There's probably a lot you don't know about me, actually."

Vanilla and amber. Her scent had hooked him by the nose and surrounded him. He fought to keep his eyes from drifting closed as he savored it.

No. No, keep it together.

It's just attraction; it'll pass.

He made himself step back and cleared his throat. "Let's go to the kids' section. We don't have many picture books yet."

"Good idea. I love the Fairwick Falls Library"—Pearl hefted the stack of books in her arms—"but their kids' section is a barren wasteland."

Reed lifted the books from her arms and savored where his fingers brushed her warm, soft skin.

"Oh, AB used to love this one." She crouched down and pulled out a copy of *Harold and the Purple Crayon,* caressing the cover. "I can still get her to sit through it if she's feeling sentimental."

She looked sweetly at the pages, flipping through it. Her smile was incandescent.

Pearl loves hard, he thought. *Whoever she ends up with will be lucky.*

That yearning for her that never quite went away reared its head, hard. "Let me go grab a basket for these," Reed said, wanting to put some distance between them.

You're practically dating Bookish.

But she's also made it clear that we aren't an item, right?

And I can't help who I find attractive, he thought as he walked to the front and grabbed a basket.

His phone buzzed with a message from Bookish, and guilt slunk into his stomach.

IMPOSSIBLYBOOKISH

JANICE GOT BOOTED

!!!

He gasped.

HEMINGWAY_CANSUCKIT

NO!!!

IMPOSSIBLYBOOKISH

so it turns out all of the @everyone
announcements she kept making were rules that
SHE was breaking.

she was harassing people who didn't agree with
her outside of the app.

she even mailed one guy's family.

HEMINGWAY_CANSUCKIT

Holy shit.

Drama drama

IMPOSSIBLYBOOKISH

i guess you never really know people, do you?

The question hung in the air, suspended in his mind.
I know Bookish, right?
...Right?
Doubt crept in for the first time.
She could be a Russian catfisher in a Siberian hut, for all I know.
Maybe catching her off guard would give him an honest
answer.

HEMINGWAY_CANSUCKIT

What's the most popular snack in Denver?

IMPOSSIBLYBOOKISH

uh… probably beef jerky?

Wait. That could be Russia or Colorado.

IMPOSSIBLYBOOKISH

are things better with your project?

He'd admitted the previous night that he was overwhelmed
with it all.

The acre of books in the store taunted him, knowing he'd need this many books for his store someday.

Was this the worst idea he'd ever had?

Worse than bleaching his hair blonde sophomore year? The name 'Snow Berry' had followed him for months.

HEMINGWAY_CANSUCKIT

The paperwork is stressful. Lots of decisions, which is also stressful to me.

I've been working out more than ever to combat it so I can sleep at night, but it's cut into my reading time.

IMPOSSIBLYBOOKISH

i wish i could melt the stress away for you.

i'd get naked, oil up

get my tits nice and wet

HEMINGWAY_CANSUCKIT

Bookish…

He gulped, his cock twitching.

IMPOSSIBLYBOOKISH

i'd make sure you were nice and relaxed,

get down on my knees and spread my thighs

lick my lips, and then…

HEMINGWAY_CANSUCKIT

You are actively killing me right now.

I'm at work.

His eyes darted around, trying to hide the growing problem in his very thin linen pants.

IMPOSSIBLYBOOKISH

have you read this?

i've heard mixed reviews, but also i like murder
and knitting, so it could be a good buddy read.

She pasted a link to a new bestseller with a neon yellow cover.

The wave of lust had passed. He was going to edge her so hard the next time they fooled around.

HEMINGWAY_CANSUCKIT

You'll pay for the visions I'm going to have the
rest of my day.

IMPOSSIBLYBOOKISH

of what? me tying your shoes?

giving you a foot massage?

you're the one with your head in the gutter.

He was still thinking of a clever response when Pearl walked up.

"Have you read this one?" She held up the exact neon yellow book that Bookish had just sent him.

He jolted.

What the fuck?

"Where did you get that?" he said, spooked.

She cocked an eyebrow. "Stop being a weirdo. There's a huge stack of them."

A five-foot tower of yellow books dominated the new releases section. It'd be impossible to miss if he hadn't been staring at his phone.

Right. There are only so many bestsellers in the world.

Weird coincidence.

Twenty minutes later, they were heading back to Fairwick Falls in his car. For some reason, it felt too small for the enormous presence that was Pearl Bishop. Their elbows had brushed seven times on the center armrest.

Not that I've been counting or anything. He'd become hyper aware of her body's proximity to him since their kiss.

"So is it everything you thought it would be?" Pearl said, staring wistfully out the misty car window.

Reed stopped at a stop sign and let his eyes linger on the soft curve of her jaw.

The way it met her pulse point.

The little feathery hairs that wisped down beside her ear. He wanted to tuck them back for her.

He swallowed, thinking about how good her neck had tasted when he'd kissed her. How he'd lost himself working down to the tops of her breasts—

A car honked behind him.

Shit. "What do you mean?"

"Your dream. The bookstore? You're doing it. Buying the books and shit," she asked.

"Yeah, it's pretty great," he said with a slow smile. "It feels good to spend my time making something that matters, to me at least. Especially because I have amazing help."

She scoffed, but it was one of her *you're being nice* scoffs. He liked that one.

"What's your dream, Pearl?"

"Nah, that's rich people shit." She settled back in her seat, propping her knee up on his dashboard.

"Come on," he coaxed. "Dreams are free. Plus, what's more punk than doing whatever you want?"

She sighed wistfully and lowered the window as they sped up onto the highway to hop back to Fairwick Falls. She stuck her hand out and surfed it on the misty breeze.

"I'd save up for a bakery," she said over the wind.

"Wow." He was thunderstruck. Never in a million years would he imagine Pearl as an entrepreneur, but it made sense. She was tough, no-nonsense, smart, and AB's birthday cake had been delicious.

"Like muffins and cookies?"

"Sure. And skull-shaped cakes and bloodbath candles," she said with a wry smile. "But mostly it's so that anybody who has allergies can have something special. It'd be a major-eleven-allergen-free bakery. I'm making a cake for a friend's party tomorrow. My first paying job."

He turned in surprise, genuinely excited for her. "What! Pearl, that's amazing."

She rolled her eyes, looking embarrassed. "It's no big deal. You have a whole store. Luca has a whole body shop. This is just something little."

"You'll start there and build an empire. You've kept me in check and on track. If you can do that, the sky's the limit for you."

He pulled into the bookshop's parking lot.

"Finally, someone appreciates my cat-herding genius." She snorted. "What are you going to do in August without me? Your cats will be all over the place."

Like behind the secret bookshelf where I kissed you back.

"Oh," he said, surprised. "I assumed you'd still work here after we open. I can't be here twenty-four seven."

He turned off the car, but neither of them moved. The rain had picked up and thundered on his car roof.

She shrugged, looking torn. "I get AB from school every day."

Oh fuck. He started to panic. *I don't want her to go. I'll move out of the house soon, and she won't even work at the store in a month.*

"We can work around it."

"Dunno if you've noticed, but I'm not a *people* person. I'd probably cost you sales or something." She picked at her nails, looking embarrassed. "I'm really great at fucking things up when other humans are involved."

"I'd miss not seeing you every day," he admitted.

It would be worth the cost of lost sales.

She smirked and shook her head as if he was joking.

"No, honestly," he said with a smile. "Who else is going to bully county departments for me? Or blare inappropriate music in the shop that makes Bert blush?" He tried to catch her eye. "Or have lunch with me?"

Just the gentle sound of rain on the car roof tapped away as they stared at each other. She chewed on her lip.

"I believe in you, Pearl. You'd be great." His hand itched to cover hers, wanting to reassure her. He adjusted his glasses instead.

That usually helped when he needed to stop himself from reaching for her.

"Welp," she said with a big breath and slapped her thighs hard, making them jiggle. "That's weeks away. I'm sure you'll get tired of seeing me between now and then."

I want to wear those thighs like earmuffs.

He blew out a surprised long, low breath.

What.

The fuck.

Was that?

She lifted herself out of his passenger-side seat. Given the semi-hard-on he was sporting now, he needed a minute.

"I'll meet you inside," he said. "Just going to make a phone call."

He let his eyes linger on the curve of her ass as she ran inside.

Maybe she shouldn't work for me anymore. Who wants their boss lusting after them like a disgusting creep?

He wiped his eyes under his glasses in frustration. He'd *never* had this issue before.

He never dated colleagues. Even if he found them attractive, he could keep his brain in his head instead of in his dick. That was the treatment everyone deserved.

But being with Pearl nearly every day, living with her, talking with her... laughing with her....

Kissing her...

It was torture—pure goddamned torture—to keep this clawing attraction locked down.

The only thing keeping him sane?

Working up the courage to someday ask Bookish to meet in person.

Chapter Seventeen

PEARL

Pearl stared at the bloody creation and proudly wiped sweat away with her forearm.

The cake for Dave's daughter was ready, and it looked fucking magnificent.

She'd made six tall black pillar candles out of cake and inserted a real candle deep within each of the pillars. A drizzle of black royal icing topped each one, making them look like big, realistic melting candles. They sat in a pool of raspberry-flavored fake blood.

It was metal as fuck. She slid it from the kitchen island but stopped when she saw the heavy pillars wobble.

And, unfortunately, heavy as fuck.

Dave needed cake for seventy-five people, and the whole thing weighed almost thirty pounds.

How can I keep it from sliding around?

Fuck.

Panic rose up in her chest.

It was already unstable and she'd have to carry it down the back steps and across the yard.

In the pouring fucking rain.

She'd have a soggy, wet mess of a cake by the time she got it to the bar.

Her stress had decided to manifest in her lower back pain this week, so she wasn't even sure she could carry it, now that she thought about it.

Fuck, I should have assembled it there. I'm such an idiot.

The back door opened, and a sopping molten-hot Reed jogged inside. He was shirtless, his hair was wet, and he wasn't wearing glasses.

It was still a little bit like seeing a hot skunk without its stripes.

He blew out a breath and scooped his hair back. "Had to turn back," he huffed. "The sky turned as black as—oh, well, your cake, actually."

Tantalizing droplets of water ran down his bare chest, mesmerizing her. It took everything in her body not lick them up, chasing the taste of him from their kiss.

She scowled instead. "Yeah, well, the rain's fucking ruined my day, too."

He smiled, all easygoing attitude. "Why? You love the rain. Nothing more metal than the sky screaming out in pain, right?"

Okay, fine. He was right. She fucking *loved* the rain.

It was unsettling having someone that paid so much *attention* to you.

"I just—I can't get the cake to the car without it being wet. And then even if I can do that, it'll be a mess by the time I get to the bar."

He shrugged and started rooting in the coat closet. "I'll help. I'll carry, and you can use my two umbrellas to protect the cake."

She crossed her arms, worried. "But how do I keep the cake dry when I take it out?"

"I'll just go with you," he said, tossing on a shirt that he'd left on the kitchen chair. "I'll be *your* assistant." He slid his glasses on slowly with a smile as he stared at her.

Holy fuck. New kink unlocked.

She'd always had a thing for glasses. She'd take Clark Kent over Superman any day of the week (a nice, corn-fed guy who believed in journalistic integrity and wanted to make the world a better place? Yes, please).

But seeing someone putting them *on* slowly as he stared at her was...

Distracting.

Why yes, Professor No Shirt, I would love for you to be my assistant and do naughty, naughty things to me.

"Come on. I'll hold the cake as you drive. It'll be fine," he said, goading her, his signature sunshine brighter than before.

"Ugh, *fine*." Was as close of a 'thank you' as she could muster.

After much wiggling, trepidation, and panicked teamwork—both to the car and out of the car—the cake was safely inside The Thirsty Beaver at a raucous party fifteen minutes later.

Music blared from the sound system, and everyone oohed and clapped when she brought in the cake, candles lit. Tons of people took photos as Pearl set the cake down.

"That's the coolest fucking thing I've ever seen," Dave's daughter shouted, her eyes bright with excitement. "Can I, like, fucking eat it?"

"Yep, you can like, fucking eat it," Pearl said with a smile. "No eggs, dairy, gluten, or nuts."

An older woman pulled her to the side. "I have a grandkid who'd love this. She's into all that goth shit like Amber is," she said, nodding at the young girl who was gleefully hugging Dave.

"Sure," Pearl said.

"Hey, my wife can't have gluten," another guy said, "and she loves whoopie pie things, but we can't ever find any for her. Could you make those?"

"Um, yeah," Pearl said with a smile.

"Hey," an older leather-clad biker lady at the bar shouted in a husky voice. "My girlfriend's vegan and has a nut allergy—"

"Yeah, she does!" another guy called.

"Shut the fuck up, Tom!" the woman said, giving him the middle finger. "Could you make her somethin' for our anniversary?"

"Sure, I can do that." She was feeling overwhelmed. Having people shout at her from all directions was new.

A heavy hand pulled on Pearl's shoulder, and she turned around, eyes glaring.

"*You* got a nut allergy, gorgeous?" a greasy man who looked old beyond his years slurred in her direction, the smell of whiskey rolling off of him.

"No, but I'm good at de-nutting men who deserve it," she said, shrugging his hand off with a glare and walking to get contact info from her new customers.

She found Dave next, needing to get paid. He handed her a hundred dollar bill.

"Dave, this is too much. I don't have any change." They'd agreed on seventy-five.

"I haven't seen Amber this happy in a real long time," Dave said with a hand on his beard, staring at his daughter. She was probably only twenty. "Take it. You earned it."

"Thanks, man," Pearl said, smiling.

Fuck yes. This was the final hundred dollars she needed to get an EpiPen. It was the first hundred dollars she'd made on her *own* doing something she *loved*.

If she didn't need it to live, she'd probably frame it or some sentimental shit like that.

Maybe she *was* actually good at something. She stashed the hundred in her bra and turned to go.

"You got any more room in there?" the greasy man from before said, walking toward her with his arms out wide.

She saw red. "You know what, motherfucker?" She took off her rings. She didn't want this guy's blood in her jewelry.

As she looked up, Reed was suddenly in between them.

"Hey, buddy," he said with a tense smile, laying a hand on this guy's shoulder. "Trust me when I say: you will not survive if you keep talking. Here's a glass of water"—he shoved a glass into the guy's hand—"and a ten-percent-off coupon for all feminist literature at the bookstore opening in town in a few weeks."

He leaned in close to the guy, whispering in his ear with a friendly smile as his hand tightened on his shoulder. The guy blanched, staring at Pearl in horror.

Reed turned toward Pearl and escorted her toward the door, putting his body in between her and the skeezy guy.

Her head spun. "I could have handled him," she said, her eyes glaring back toward the man who still stood befuddled, drunkenly muttering the word "feminist" as he looked at the card.

"Of course, you could have," Reed said with a shrug. "But then I'd have to bail you out of jail, which means no plant budget for the bookshop."

He shoved open the door for her and let her walk through first.

"I'm used to taking care of myself." She felt defensive as they walked out into the drizzling rain.

"Sure, but now you don't have to." He smiled at her as if what had just happened was normal. As if a man standing up for her was something that had *ever* happened.

He waved. "Looks like it's cleared up. I'm going to run back home. See you there?" He tossed in an earbud as he jogged away.

She waved a hand, utterly confused and yet somehow she was...
Moved?

And fuck, something else.

Oh no.

A little turned on.

THREE DAYS LATER, Reed's voice thundered against the tall ceiling of the bookshop. "Pearl!"

Pearl snickered to herself as she unpacked another box of picture books in the kids area, knowing the source of his irritation.

Construction had finished on the kids' section and it looked great. Reed had designed an interior wall of bookshelves that created a cozy treehouse vibe. Two arches in the wall were entrances—a small one for little kids to walk through and a big one for adults.

It felt like being in the treehouse fort from their childhood and Pearl fucking loved it.

"Why," Reed yelled, walking toward her, "does the horror sign keep getting put on the current events bookshelf?"

"Because I'm hilarious!" she called back.

He peeked through the big arch and leveled an unamused gaze at her. "Really?"

She gestured with a stuffed Curious George to emphasize her point. "It's more accurate. That's all I'm saying."

He ducked under the archway, taking stock of the space. "It's looking pretty good in here."

Bookshelves lined the walls, and picture books had been set out at eye level, their bright covers facing out for display.

"I still think the beanbags are a bad choice. Do you know how *sticky* kids are?" Pearl eyed the bright beanbags in the corner with distrust.

He shrugged. "Eh, it's fine. I'll Scotchgard them within an inch of their life. Every treehouse needs comfy seating."

"Pffft," Pearl said. "As long as you don't kick me out of *this* treehouse."

Reed and Luca had rarely let her in their treehouse when they were kids. They'd insisted she was a *baby*, despite being only 18 months younger than Luca.

Reed's smile was warm and wistful. "Some of my favorite memories are of you in that treehouse."

She gulped, wondering if he was thinking about what she was thinking about.

She avoided his eyes as she unpacked a box and decided no comment was better than reminding him of her first kiss.

He picked up another box of stuffed animals and started pulling them out. Every major kid's book character was represented in stuffed animal form.

"Lily is installing the papier-mâché tree today." He nodded to the mural behind her.

A large mural with an enchanted forest spanned the wall but had a conspicuous blank space for tree branches. Pearl spied Hansel and Gretel, a wolf, Little Red Riding Hood, and endless little nods to children's literature.

"You're really going all out, huh?"

"It's important to get kids hooked on reading early, you know? Plus, parents have a hard time saying no to buying books." He smirked as he unpacked a box of early-reader books. "When I have kids, their room will be wall-to-wall picture books, coloring books, graphic novels, everything."

A little flutter tickled her stomach thinking about him as a dad.

He'd be a perfect dad. Goofy, friendly, happy, and with endless chaotic ideas.

Supportive, she considered. *And helpful, noticing what needs to get done. Inclusive, too.* He'd made sure to order a variety of books featuring all different orientations, races, and abilities, and it was hitting her smack in the face as she glanced across the bookshelves.

"You're having *multiple* kids?" she said, wanting to tease him instead to cover up all the gooey feelings.

He adjusted his glasses with a smile. "Someday, hopefully. You?"

Pearl shook her head. "I don't think I'd be a good mom. I get enough shit from the bitchy kindergarten pickup line."

He leaned against the bookshelf, staring down at her, shaking his head slowly.

Her heart stuttered at the sight. The casual, elegant, masculine confidence, the softness of the care in his eyes.

"Pearl, you're so great with AB. You know she talked about you nonstop when they visited me in Philly? You'd be a great mom," he said, shrugging as if it was obvious. He stacked novels on the middle-grade shelf. "You'd fight for them. That's all kids really need. Someone who'd fight for them."

His voice had shadows of wistfulness in it, like he'd lost something important.

Had someone fought for him?

She hoped so.

She stretched her aching back. "Feels like I'm too behind in life to find someone and pop out some babies."

"Nah." He handed her a stack of picture books. "You're exactly where you're supposed to be. I just know it."

She paused, not taking the books from him.

Deja vu. Hemingway had said that.

"What did you say?"

"I said you're right on time. There's plenty of time to figure out whatever kind of family you want to have, you know?"

"Yeah." She shook it off as a coincidence and grabbed the books. "I *am* a little jealous of your and AB's handshake."

"I *knew* it," he said, clapping his hands triumphantly. "I can teach it to you."

She scoffed. "I don't want your *pity* secondhand handshake."

"Come on," he teased. He tugged her up with both hands, and she came flying up from the floor. She stumbled into him.

Jesus. Wouldn't have thought he could toss me around.

He steadied her, grabbing her waist so she didn't fall into a spinning book display. She grabbed his arms, righting herself.

"You can surprise AB when she's back," he said, his hands still at her waist.

He hadn't dropped his arms, so she took the opportunity to keep her hands on his biceps.

Don't squeeze them even though you want to, you feral tomcat.

They were chest to chest, and she dared to meet his eyes.

They roamed her face. His thumb stroked against her waist, and there was a corresponding pulse in her pussy with each brush.

Fuck, just that little touch feels so good.

He was biting his lower lip in the same way that she wanted to.

How had it only been three weeks since she'd kissed him?

And why hadn't she been able to stop thinking about his *mouth* since then?

His hair artfully hung over his forehead, almost brushing his glasses. His smile looked hungery, wanting.

Or am I just hoping he wants to kiss me?

She licked her lips, wanting to taste him again.

The front door opened. "I'm here!" Lily's bright voice called out.

"Oh, um." He pushed his glasses back up his nose as he

stepped back, clearing his throat. "Be right there!" he called with a loud voice.

"You're good with finishing up?" he said, looking embarrassed.

Her heart sank. "Yeah, go for it."

Reed jogged to the front of the store where Lily brought in heavy papier-mâché pieces. Pearl peeked through the archway opening, her slutty eyes greedily following him.

He had on his normal uniform of a tight, fitted, white button-up shirt rolled up to his elbows, sweater vest layered over it, and loose, professional-looking pants, but that special kind where he could move around easily.

He looks good in his store.

Construction had finished on the first floor, and the wood shone in the afternoon sun. Reed had even installed an honest-to-god rolling ladder on the shelves. She'd taken it for a ride once already today.

Okay, three times, but she wasn't gonna tell him that.

I'm not going to tell him a lot of things.

Like how she'd wanted him to wrap his hand around the back of her neck and kiss her again, holding her in place.

Shut up and take it, she remembered.

She clenched every inner muscle, wanting another glimpse of the untethered, raw man she'd gotten upstairs. It was almost worth being trapped in that nightmare again with him.

But as he and Lily walked back to the kids' space, she tucked all those feelings away and went back to work.

HEMINGWAY_CANSUCKIT

Do you have a minute?

There's something that's been bothering me

IMPOSSIBLYBOOKISH

is it when actors do british accents for norse gods?

cause that irritates the actual shit out of me

why british?? WHY.

and if they're the bad guy, make them be the bad guy in their own accent.

maybe i want thor to sound like the swedish chef muppet.

HEMINGWAY_CANSUCKIT

The cross-over we don't deserve

No, shockingly British accent choice was not top of my list

It's…kind of serious.

But we can talk later.

IMPOSSIBLYBOOKISH

no no, now's fine

everything okay?

HEMINGWAY_CANSUCKIT

Yeah, I just feel weird about something.

IMPOSSIBLYBOOKISH

welcome to every day of my life

bras? i feel weird about 'em

the 'pay for the person behind you' thing? SO WEIRD. just let me buy my own shit in peace

those public bathroom fabric towel things that hang down?

bleeeech

weeeeeird

HEMINGWAY_CANSUCKIT

Bookish

IMPOSSIBLYBOOKISH

sorry. too much caffeine today.

did i do something wrong? i probably did.

probably fucked up something.

i'm sorry.

HEMINGWAY_CANSUCKIT

No no no

Jeez. Just let me get this out.

I…

…kind of kissed someone.

Not kind of.

I did kiss them.

It was an accident.

And I'm not going to do it again. Though…I almost did it again today.

And technically they kissed me, but still. I didn't stop it.

I just feel bad because I told you I wasn't seeing anyone else…

And then…

Well. Anyway.

I'm sorry? I think? Or maybe I'm making a bigger deal out of this.

It was just a kiss right? We're adults.

IMPOSSIBLYBOOKISH

welp.

HEMINGWAY_CANSUCKIT

Oh no.

Please don't be mad.

IMPOSSIBLYBOOKISH

no, not mad

i just realized that i should have told you the same.

i mean, mine was sort of like the kissing version of mouth-to-mouth resuscitation.

and it DID get me kinda hot, but the origin was purely medical.

HEMINGWAY_CANSUCKIT

Are you okay???

IMPOSSIBLYBOOKISH

yes! it was just a weird one-off.

point being, you don't need to feel bad.

you can kiss whoever you want.

but you're adorable for telling me

HEMINGWAY_CANSUCKIT

Thank god.

Finally, I can go to sleep.

IMPOSSIBLYBOOKISH

you were tossing and turning over lil ole me?

i'm blushing

HEMINGWAY_CANSUCKIT

Sweet dreams B

IMPOSSIBLYBOOKISH

only if you're in them, h

Chapter Eighteen

REED

After weeks of incessant banging, shouting, and hammering, the construction crew had *finally* finished up in the bookshop. Now all that was left was to repair his apartment above the store.

Boxes and boxes of books sat in the store waiting to be unpacked.

He tried to ignore the twist of nerves at the dwindling number in his bank account and the date circled on his calendar of the Historical Preservation Subcommittee coming to approve the soft opening.

A grid hung over the stage, and Reed and Pearl had been hard at work for hours on the flying book installation over the stage. He'd imagined a ceiling of open books, their pages fluttering, looking like a wave rolling out into the store.

Pearl screamed in frustration, fighting with a book cover.

He jogged over. "It's late. You should go home."

"It's late. *You* should go home," she said, rolling her eyes. "I'm going to make this grid my bitch. Plus, you pay me by the hour and tapioca flour is expensive." She tucked her lip between her teeth as she fought with the grid.

He stared up at the ceiling, trying really hard not to look at Pearl towering over him on the ladder. She was aggressively shooting a staple gun around the edge of a reference book, her breasts bouncing with each staple.

His eyes wandered down to her hips and thighs, and his hands flexed. What would it feel like to grab those thighs, wrap them around him, sink his fingers in, and squeeze?

He ripped his gaze away as he clenched his jaw. *This is harassment, Berry. Stop wanting her. You just apologized to Bookish for kissing someone and not telling her, and here you are lusting after another woman.*

"Speaking of tapioca flour," he said, pulling over another stack of old books, "how's the Twinkie experimentation going?"

"Ugh," she said, clomping down the stepladder and grabbing another one. "Not quite right, but I found this new substitution that would use powdered sugar instead, and I think that might get the right consistency."

He'd had one of her leftovers this morning, and he'd had to stop himself from eating the entire batch.

"You know, there's a summer festival in a few weeks here. I got a flyer about it for being a vendor. You should do it."

He pulled up another stepladder beside hers. They'd worked their way beside the built-in nook.

Pearl grimaced, her hand going to her lower back.

"You okay?"

"It's fine." She reached toward the edge of the book, trying to staple the cover up of a Hemingway title into the foam. "Come here, you misogynistic son of a bitch."

"Not a Hemingway fan either, I take it," he said with a laugh, stapling another book up.

"Fuck no," she muttered. "*The Sun Also Rises* can eat my ass," she said, pushing into the foam harder as she arched her back.

A cry wrenched out of Pearl and she curled over the stepladder in pain.

Reed immediately hopped off and went to her. "Pearl stop. Let me help you down."

"No, I got it," she said. "It's just my back." She slowly climbed down, but her boot caught on the second ladder rung.

"Oh no. Oh, fuck," she said, tumbling back toward him.

Reed grabbed at her waist as she reached out for him with panic in her eyes. "I got you—oof!"

Her weight landed against his chest and they stumbled backward. Reed's knees hit the bench and they landed flat on the bench with a thud.

Pearl was squarely on top of him, her head on his chest, her body flush with his, and their legs threaded together.

He was discombobulated but they seemed to be okay. "You okay?"

She groaned into his chest slowly. "This is so embarrassing," she said into his shirt. She tried to move and then cried out.

"Hold on," he said, catching his breath. "Just stay here for a minute."

Yes, he'd fallen with someone on top of him but he somehow felt...relaxed?

A serene sense of peace washed over him at the constant pressure of Pearl on top of him.

All the stress—the fast, competing thoughts, the racing around his head of to-do lists, stress, new family, new town, new roommate, new business—it all went silent. Anxiety floated away as he could just be present, thanks to the weighted blanket of Pearl.

"Embarrassing," she muttered.

"Maybe for me," he said, with an embarrassed laugh.

"What?" She lifted her head in confusion.

"I can, um… can you just… keep pressing me?" He grimaced with one eye open, not wanting to look at her.

So embarrassing.

"I don't think I can move anyway. My back will spasm." She'd moved her head to the side so she was no longer talking into his chest.

"It's just, um…" His voice wobbled.

There was silence in his head for the first time in a long time.

The sheer relief of the compression, one that couldn't be met by a weighted blanket or a compression shirt or even a sweater vest, relaxed his entire body.

"Are you okay?" she said, not looking at him, her head still turned to the side.

"Yeah," he said with a self-deprecating laugh. "I, um, I used to have my ex-girlfriend lie on top of me when I was really stressed. Like this."

"*That's* a new kink."

"No," he laughed slowly. "It's not sexual. You know when you want to pop your knuckles or your back and you just need that physical relief? That's what this feels like. Just deep pressure in the most perfect way."

Like a knot unwinding.

He let out a low, slow breath. "Is your back okay?"

"It's all the leaning over I do when I bake. And the work here. It caught up with me. I've always had lower back problems. When the universe giveth big boobs, it also giveth lower back problems," she muttered. "But this feels okay, actually relieves some of the pressure."

They sat there in silence, and he looked up at their handiwork. The ceiling did look pretty magical.

"So, there's a festival?" she muttered.

"You should do it," he said, getting excited for her. "What would you call your business?"

"I was thinking...'Eat Crow.'"

A deep belly laugh rolled out of him. She chuckled.

"Come on," he said, poking her side, trying to catch her eye until she looked up at him.

She put her hands underneath her chin on his chest. "I've thought about...Blackbird Bakery?" she said it with a wince, like it was a bad idea.

He smiled. Of course she would think of something so perfectly her—smart and charming. "It's perfect."

"You still need to name this place."

"I think I've decided." It felt permanent once he told her. He bit his lip and looked at her. "Bookish. What do you think?"

She jolted on top of him.

He leaned up, concerned for her. "Your back okay?"

"Sure, yeah. That's...um...a good name."

"It's a popular phrase so there are a lot of stickers and mugs I could order online. It seems popular but still unique."

It wasn't the only reason, though.

A very important reason sat on his phone. The reason he looked forward to every morning.

"Spoken like a smart business owner," she said.

"Blackbird Bakery is also great. You should do a booth. Oh, we could do one together," he offered.

"I couldn't do something like that." Her sigh was wistful.

How couldn't she see how amazing she was? "I saw how proud you were at Dave's party. Believe in yourself like I believe in you," he said, smiling at her with encouragement.

She twisted her lips, thinking. "I'm not exactly a people person."

"You don't have to be a people person. You have to be a muffin or whoopie pie or cake person. Come on, I dare you."

Her eyes narrowed. "Nope, not taking your bait."

"Double dare," he said, narrowing his eyes.

She rolled her eyes at him.

"Backing down from a dare? Never took you for a giant chicken, Bishop. You've gone *soft*."

She growled as she stared at him. "Oh, *fuck* you. You know I don't bitch out. Fine. I'll think about it."

He chuckled. He loved that he knew how to push her buttons.

She settled her head back down on his chest. It felt nice. He wanted to stroke her hair, run his fingers through it.

"The place is looking pretty good." She pointed up to the flying books. "You know, for people who like whimsical shit."

Bert and his crew had worked hard. So had Pearl.

"Thank you for putting up with all of my...everything the last four weeks. I've had too many ideas and too many changes. I know it's been a lot. I know *I'm* a lot," he said.

That was what his last girlfriend had said. It was always the impression he'd gotten from everyone when he was a kid, too. He laughed too loud, got too excited, bit off too much, expected too much.

He sighed. Carrying the weight of being himself felt a little easier with Pearl pressing into him.

She studied him with concern. Her bangs slid to the side as her eyes traced his face. "You're not too much, Reed. Not for me, at least."

Goosebumps flooded his body. It was like she'd reached into his soul and gently patched a deep crack. "Thanks."

"Now, if only there was a good masseuse somewhere in Fairwick Falls, I could finish the flying book thing," she muttered, trying to rub her lower back.

"Here." He pulled her up a little closer and wrapped his arms around her. "It's my fault. You aggravated it with my over-the-top ideas. Let me."

"I should say no, but fuck it, that's how much it hurts," she mumbled and laid her face against his shirt.

Vanilla and amber surged toward him as her hair scraped his chin. He tried not to be obvious, but he angled his head, needing to smell it again.

"Are you...sniffing me?" she said into his chest in a nonjudgmental tone.

He chuckled. "Sorry. You smell nice."

He pressed his knuckles into her lower back, starting at the bottom of her shirt.

A low moan rumbled out of her, a siren song to his cock.

Fuck me, this is a bad idea. He closed his eyes and stroked his thumbs down her lower back. *She's just a friend, just a friend.*

Her muscles were tight, poor thing, and his hands gripped her hips, rubbing out a stubborn knot. Her shirt rode up, and her skin was soft under his fingers.

"Harder," she moaned into his chest.

Christ.

Pressing harder, he kneaded her waist. His thumbs stroked down her lower back. "This okay?" he murmured.

"Yes," she sighed, pressing her hips into his hands, chasing the touch.

The scent of her shampoo—or was that just her?—was surrounding him. *Something* she wore drove him fucking nuts.

Her low moans grew louder, echoing into his chest. He gulped them down as if they were air, wanting more out of her.

She slid up and down his body as he kneaded her lower back.

His cock twitched and his restraint was slipping. He could *not* get hard right now.

Not with her on top of me. Not with her crotch brushing and brushing mine.

He stopped, needing to get himself under control.

"Mmm," she mumbled into his chest. "Why'd you stop?"

Because I'm going to come in my pants like a teenager if you keep moaning.

He let out a long sigh.

He was the one who'd said they couldn't do anything more after the kiss.

He had been the one to offer the back rub.

He was an idiot.

"Hands got tired," he lied.

I'd never be too tired for that, he thought, *of wringing those moans out of you.*

The silence stretched between them as his heartbeat thundered.

"Please," she whispered into his chest in a small voice.

Oh, fuck me.

The woman who never asked for anything had just whispered, *"Please."*

His hands found her skin again, digging in.

Knots in her back were ruthlessly dug into by all his knuckles. Little sobbing moans still slipped out, and he could tell she was biting back sighs.

Savor each one like chocolate. Remember them.

The little gasp in her voice, the needy pitch in it.

His knuckles drifted inside her shorts, brushing under the waistband's edge to chase out the knots. Her hips dug against his, chasing the feeling with him.

He pushed down on her back so hard, she moved against his body, scraping the material of her shorts against his cock. And then it brushed it again when he released her.

Down and back.

Down and back.

Each time, his hands drifted further into her shorts.

He pushed harder, his breath quickening. *Down* and back.

Feels too good. Want to do this forever. He squeezed his eyes shut at the pleasure.

Fuck, his cock was weeping. He almost didn't care. She wanted more, and he'd do whatever it took to make her happy.

He gulped, not wanting to stop, but knowing this was a terrible idea.

He pushed harder anyway, digging in.

Her forehead was pinned to his chest, the heat of her heavy breathe searing into him.

There was no way she didn't feel the length of his cock between her thighs. He pushed down once more, the zipper of her shorts brushing the sensitive head of it.

Last time, he promised himself, spanning his fingers around her waist.

He gripped her firmly, his thumbs stroking down, feeling the lace edge of her thong.

Aching, dizzy need gripped his cock. *Christ. She wears lacy thongs.*

Swiping his thumbs under its thin band, he stroked down further on the rising curve of her ass.

Wild with need, he did something reckless.

He hooked his thumbs around the top of her thong and stroked again, enjoying the feeling of her panties moving with his thumbs.

She gasped, raising her head.

Her low-cut shirt had tugged down, and her breasts were pillowed onto his chest, pressing against the edge of her bra.

They stared at one another, their chests rising and falling. His thumbs moved slowly back and forth, caressing. Still hooked in her panties.

Back and forth.

Fuck, I want her.

Need *her.*

Her pupils were blown, the thin hazel ring around them looking golden in the dim light. Her pouty mouth with its perfect curves, panting.

He licked his lips, desperate for a taste of her.

It took all of his willpower not to crush her to him, to demolish her, consume her, *devour* her.

"Please," she whispered, barely audible above their breathing.

His hands gripped her hips harder, barely in control. Swiping his thumbs down her ass again, staring at her mouth that would taste so good.

His phone pinged beside them with a text. It was a picture of Luca and AB.

Their eyes met, and Pearl looked panicked.

The spell was broken.

"Uh, you good?" he said, too bright and too loud. He pulled his hands back and tugged her shirt down.

"Yeah, for sure," she said, shaking her head. "Sorry, I, um…" She pushed up, and his treacherous eyes traced the mouthwatering curve of her heavy cleavage.

He sat up quickly, hunching over so she wouldn't see the outline of his dick, hard for her.

She pulled her shirt up. "Sorry, I shouldn't have asked you to keep—"

"No. It's fine. Are you okay? Sorry if I overstepped—"

"No, you're good," she said quickly. "I'm…going to call it a night." She walked to her enormous purse.

"Yeah, you deserve it. You worked hard today," he said, not looking at her. "See you at home."

"Yup," she said with a too bright and cheerful voice that wasn't like her.

He raked a hand down his face. Her perfume lingered on his hands, and he closed his eyes, savoring it.

What was *happening* between them?

She didn't even like him.

...Right?

If only Pearl knew he was a virgin who had lusted after her for years, and now the universe was out to torture him.

TWO HOURS LATER, the art installation was done, and he decided he'd earned a break with Bookish.

IMPOSSIBLYBOOKISH

on a scale of 1-10, how easy do you think it'd be to put my whole brain into a blender, then pour it out, reform it, and start all over again?

HEMINGWAY_CANSUCKIT

Heresy.

I like your brain far too much as it is.

IMPOSSIBLYBOOKISH

but then i could be one of those born-sexy-yesterday characters men always love.

like emma stone in that weird movie or the girl with the white thing on her tits from the 90s.

you know, like frankenstein. kind of dumb but very hot.

you could call me hemingway, after yourself

HEMINGWAY_CANSUCKIT

Technically you'd be Hemingway's Monster since Frankenstein was the doctor.

IMPOSSIBLYBOOKISH

insert eyeroll

you're one of those people

HEMINGWAY_CANSUCKIT

You have a very sexy brain already. I'd rather you keep it as is, if it's all the same.

Having a rough day too?

IMPOSSIBLYBOOKISH

it's like i have all the right decisions lined up

the ones that a responsible adult would make, and then off i fuck, doing the opposite

HEMINGWAY_CANSUCKIT

You're reading my mind.

IMPOSSIBLYBOOKISH

ONLY those are the right decisions for everybody else

and if i did them, i'd fuck up even more somehow

HEMINGWAY_CANSUCKIT

Yes, exactly.

I guess that's why we're perfect for each other

IMPOSSIBLYBOOKISH

i like the idea that i'm not perfect for anybody else but you

His heart thundered in his chest. What was his *life* right now?

He'd practically come in his pants from Pearl on top of him two hours ago. Bookish was his best friend who he sexted into climax sometimes.

A text friend with benefits.

Who you're half in love with.

He shook out his hands, walking on the stage in a circle, trying to get his mind wrapped around what these two women meant to him.

Pearl had clearly indicated she wasn't interested in him. She was gorgeous and so hot, and the way she tugged on her bottom lip when she was thinking made him dizzy with wanting her.

It's just physical attraction. She'd murder me if we ever actually went on a date.

And this woman? Bookish?

She was perfect. They liked each other, cared about each other, made each other laugh.

Romantic yearning stirred in his gut every time Bookish pinged him with a thought, a joke, a complaint, anything.

She could list her groceries, and he'd happily read it.

She was funny, acerbic but he liked that, kind, and smart. She could look like a tortoise for all he cared.

Could you fall in love with somebody you'd never even met?

Would she want the *real* him?

HEMINGWAY_CANSUCKIT

I don't feel like I've been honest with you, though.

There's a lot you don't know about me.

IMPOSSIBLYBOOKISH

then tell me

He debated. *I can't just jump into the deep end.*
Ease her in.

HEMINGWAY_CANSUCKIT

For starters, I wear glasses.

IMPOSSIBLYBOOKISH

hot.

next.

He laughed out loud. *So like her.*

HEMINGWAY_CANSUCKIT

I'm pretty nerdy.

Like play D&D with matching figurines nerdy.

IMPOSSIBLYBOOKISH

ya, i clocked that when you mentioned
Chakotay/Janeway erotic Star Trek fanfic on the
sci-fi discussion, broski.

old news.

also?

hot.

He snuggled back into the nook, delighted.

HEMINGWAY_CANSUCKIT

I also only like to be touched in certain ways.

IMPOSSIBLYBOOKISH

kinky

tell me more.

HEMINGWAY_CANSUCKIT

Soft touches drive me nuts. It gives me anxiety
just thinking about it.

IMPOSSIBLYBOOKISH

so what do you like? whips and chains? shibari?
electric shock to the nipples and/or nuts?

HEMINGWAY_CANSUCKIT

WHOA. I just meant if I'm being touched, I like it
to be intense.

Rough.

Like when we do our thing.

IMPOSSIBLYBOOKISH

fuck. yes.

HEMINGWAY_CANSUCKIT

Even though…

His heart was in his throat.

But this is Bookish. She wouldn't judge him for being a virgin. And what even was virginity? Just a stupid, outdated construct.

IMPOSSIBLYBOOKISH

even though…you have a vestigial tail?

…you're wanted in three states for possession of a pet tiger?

HEMINGWAY_CANSUCKIT

Even though… I don't have a ton of experience.

In person, I mean.

He waited. She didn't respond.

HEMINGWAY_CANSUCKIT

I'm a virgin.

He winced, waiting for her response.

IMPOSSIBLYBOOKISH

oh

Two letters.

Two letters hung in the balance of what felt like their whole relationship.

She knew he was in his late twenties (they'd met in the 'Not Anxious Enough for Millennials, not Cool Enough for Gen Z' book chat group). In his experience, women did *not* think him being a virgin was anything other than weird.

IMPOSSIBLYBOOKISH

is that all?

His heartbeat returned to normal.

Is that all?

How had he found the most perfect woman? And why did she have to live in Colorado?

HEMINGWAY_CANSUCKIT

Yeah. I'm just sensitive about it.

Other women have sort of freaked out when I've told them

IMPOSSIBLYBOOKISH

are you…not…interested? In sex?

HEMINGWAY_CANSUCKIT

Very interested.

It's just one of those things that never happened.

I had a girlfriend in college, but she was terrified of getting pregnant and not interested in penetrative sex.

IMPOSSIBLYBOOKISH

was it because of your huge dick?

HEMINGWAY_CANSUCKIT

Ha, uh, kind of…honestly.

We weren't really compatible in the sex department anyway because of said preferences

^

Then we broke up, life got busy after graduation. I didn't have time to do anything else, including socialize. It kind of just snuck up on me.

And I don't date a lot.

IMPOSSIBLYBOOKISH

ah, so you're a people hater like me

HEMINGWAY_CANSUCKIT

Ironically, I love people. I'm just not very good at dating.

Or at peopling.

It's the flaying yourself open for people again and again to judge all your quirks and eccentricities.

IMPOSSIBLYBOOKISH

the fucking worst.

this girl and I were hooking up for like three weeks

i was starting to get gooey feelings, meanwhile i was just a dare from her boyfriend.

whether she could hook up with a girl.

HEMINGWAY_CANSUCKIT

What the absolute fuck?

IMPOSSIBLYBOOKISH

precisely.

coincidentally, they rolled over a bunch of thumbtacks backing out of the garage after i found out.

HEMINGWAY_CANSUCKIT

Well deserved.

IMPOSSIBLYBOOKISH

well, if your in person instincts are anything like your text instincts...

you have nothing to worry about.

He'd just told his deepest, darkest insecurity, and she'd greeted it like it was no big deal. She accepted him.

That's why I love you, he typed out, but he stopped before hitting send.

Fuck, were they ready for this?

He erased it. Stared at the cursor on his phone.

Would you want to— he typed out.

No, fuck. Too creepy to ask to meet after they'd just talked about sex.

He erased it again.

IMPOSSIBLYBOOKISH

OH MY GOD just say whatever you're gonna say.

She knew him so well.

HEMINGWAY_CANSUCKIT

You can't let me hide from you, can you, Bookish?

IMPOSSIBLYBOOKISH

never, h

HEMINGWAY_CANSUCKIT

I...want it to be with you.

He gulped. What he meant was somebody he cared about, somebody who cared about him, somebody who meant something in his life.

IMPOSSIBLYBOOKISH

best news i've heard all day

it would be my honor to crawl over you, sink down on your giant cock, and be your first.

He let out a shaky breath. It was tempting to type "When."

But he wanted more than sex from her. He wanted it all: love, hopes, dreams.

Trust, too. He still needed to earn that.

HEMINGWAY_CANSUCKIT

And now I know what I'm thinking about as I go to sleep tonight.

Good night, B

IMPOSSIBLYBOOKISH

night, h

Chapter Nineteen

PEARL

A few days later, Pearl kneaded a pile of sticky dough like it was her personal bitch as Reed jaunted in with armfuls of groceries.

They still hadn't talked about The Massage.

The one when she'd almost orgasmed from humping his fucking leg.

Her nipples hardened as she remembered how hot it'd been.

Probably should have worn a bra this morning. Whoops.

They'd just gone about their work, pretending as if nothing out of the ordinary had happened.

"Morning," he called, tossing the bags onto the kitchen island. He was vibrating with excitement. "New recipe?"

"I promised AB I'd make her a classic Wonder Bread sandwich for her first day of school, and the yeast is being a little bitch."

"I went to the health food store in Elliotsville," he said, pulling out bags and containers. "I saw you were low on xanthan gum, tapioca flour, and applesauce, so I picked some up."

He pushed the big containers toward her and started unpacking his groceries.

Her dough-covered hands stopped mid-punch.

"*Why?*"

It had come out like *the fuck?* but only to disguise how much it touched her.

"I noticed you were out." He shrugged, putting milk and gluten-free bread in the fridge.

Shit, did she have enough money to cover it? That store was great but expensive. "Let me get my wallet."

"Pearl, it's no big deal. You don't need to pay me back. Plus, look what I picked up."

He held up a sign. It said "No gluten or nuts inside. Thanks for understanding."

"It's for the store," he said with a bright smile. "I wanted to make sure AB and parents with kids who have nut allergies feel comfortable touching the books. We'll put it in the window just in case. Oh, I also got you this tablecloth, if you decide to do the Firefly Festival. Black, of course." He pulled it out of the bag and shook it out, holding it up.

She stared at him, still processing the firehose of information.

He got a sign to protect AB?

And thought about my table at the festival?

And...noticed shit like being out of weird ingredients?

He tucked his reusable bags into the closet. "They also had pop-up tables on fifty-percent clearance, so I got one in case you needed it for the festival. It's out in my car. I know, I know," he said, putting his hands up in the air as she scowled at him. "I went a little over-board. I'm just excited for you that you might consider doing it. The world needs a Blackbird Bakery, and you've helped me a ton."

"The world doesn't need me," she said, going back to her batter. Her eyebrows furrowed.

Her skin was crawling with embarrassment and gratitude and, oh god, *happiness* maybe?

She didn't like the feeling.

She scowled harder to cover it up. "I mean, Fox and Forrest has gluten-free stuff sometimes."

"Ah, I've never eaten there."

Right, she'd forgotten about his thing. *I figured he would have at least eaten there one time though, kind of a shame.*

He pulled out a bowl and box of cereal. "But that doesn't mean that *your* stuff isn't needed. Didn't you say that the woman cried when you dropped off the whoopie pies?"

He crunched on the first bite of gluten-free granola cereal.

"Yeah." Pearl shrugged as she tipped dough into a loaf pan. "It was probably just the smoke in the bingo hall, though."

The pan wiggled away from her, and he leaned over to hold it in place. "Come on, I believe in you. It's gonna be great." He smiled as he chewed the super crunchy, loud cereal.

How could someone believe in me so much?

"Does the sound of your own eating bother you?" she asked, her eyes narrowed.

He laughed with an embarrassed smile. "Sorry. Is it loud? No, it doesn't bother me."

An idea started brewing in her head.

He started walking out of the room. "I'll get out of your way. Ooh! Wait, let me bring in your table." He dashed in the opposite direction toward his car.

She glanced at the groceries he'd gotten her as she put the dough in the oven.

He'd noticed.

He supported her and he noticed and he did things like make signs to keep her niece safe.

She peeked out the window, watching him wrestle the table out of his car as his muscles flexed.

A distinct gooey feeling hit her heart as she considered the impossible possibility that she just might have feelings for Reed Berry.

~

Two days later, Pearl and Allison unloaded the last of the Cortez/Horowitz wedding flowers into the justice of the peace courthouse room.

"I thought courthouse weddings were supposed to be low-key," Pearl said, stretching her neck.

"As long as they want to buy our flowers, I don't complain." Allison sucked her thumb where a thorn had poked her.

It wasn't that Pearl hated flowers, it was that they were so fragile. You killed them once and there was no going back.

Not a great match for fuck-ups.

They were walking out of the courthouse when Pearl saw a sign saying "Firefly Festival Vendor Applications."

She stopped in her tracks.

"You forget something?" Allison said, dusting leaves from her dress.

"Um..." Pearl weighed her next move. What was the harm in grabbing a piece of paper? "You go ahead. I'll meet you at the van."

"Ugh, no. It still smells like grape hyacinths in there. My least favorite flower," Allison said, shuddering. She matched Pearl's strides. "Where are we going?"

Pearl growled. *Why am I surrounded by nice, cheerful, nosy people?*

"I just need to, um, grab this piece of paper for Reed." She grabbed a copy of the stapled form.

"Hi, there!" A man with a bow tie and a short-sleeve shirt popped up behind the counter. "Interested in being a vendor for the Firefly Festival?"

"Uh..." Pearl stalled. "Why do you care?"

Smart, nice.

Good job.

"We prefer that you fill it out right here, so we get them in time."

Pearl gulped. Her last three baking jobs had been a big success.

Reed was right that the woman had indeed cried when she'd delivered the whoopie pies.

She'd gotten more orders from word of mouth.

She licked her lips, feeling like she was on the precipice of admitting some dark, terrible secret: she might actually want to *do* something with her life.

"Let me just, um, fill this out really quick." Pearl hunkered over the piece of paper, her heart thundering in her throat.

The form asked for optional insurance and a bunch of shit she didn't have yet. "I, um, I don't have all of this yet," she said, pointing to the form. "Can I come back and—"

"Oh, that's okay," the man said with a bright smile. He looked like if Mr. Rogers had a brother. "We're just trying to get a head count. You can fill out the rest of it at the information meeting in a couple weeks."

Pearl shoved the piece of paper at him and stormed off, panicked at having filled it out.

"Ooookay. Guess we're walking back to the van. No need to talk about that super weird thing you just did." Allison jogged behind her.

"Being weird was kind of my thing—" But she rounded the corner and ran into Beulah. *Fuck.*

She clenched her teeth.

"Beulah," Pearl said flatly.

"Hellspawn," Beulah responded. "Move. Belly buttons aren't

allowed to be exposed in the courthouse, especially when there's a tramp stamp on the other side."

Pearl fucking loved her crop tops, and Beulah could go to hell. "You know what?"

Nope, nope.

This woman still held the fate of the bookstore in her liver-spotted hands.

Beulah's eyes sparkled like she was waiting for a fight, just one reason to fuck everything up for them.

"Have a nice day," Pearl said through gritted teeth as she walked around Beulah and out into the thick air of summer.

Allison caught up with her. "Uh, did a full personality transplant happen sometime in the last five minutes?"

"Just trying to keep it together so she doesn't ruin Reed's chances."

"Hmm, that's nice," Allison said as they got into Bloom's delivery van.

Yeah, I guess I'm nice now.

～

HEMINGWAY_CANSUCKIT

Finally finished book 2 of your Anne (of Avonlea)

And a question lingers in my mind

If Gilbert was in love with her, why didn't he just say something?

IMPOSSIBLYBOOKISH

do YOU go around telling everyone you're in love with that you love them?

HEMINGWAY_CANSUCKIT

Such an Anne answer.

Feisty AND defensive.

IMPOSSIBLYBOOKISH

if that's an insult, it didn't work

HEMINGWAY_CANSUCKIT

It was not

He was just so obviously gone for her.

How could she miss it?

IMPOSSIBLYBOOKISH

i think she knew deep down.

but some of us are afraid, okay?

some of us don't make friends easily and would
be terrified to lose the one good thing we can
count on.

anne didn't fit in. she didn't have a good life until
she finally landed in this picture-perfect little
town where she still felt like an odd duck.

and gilbert was this smart, successful guy who
was her friend and believed in her.

encouraged her to go after her crazy dreams.

so she was scared to hope for more

in case she lost what she had.

and, to be fair, she was a teenager and they're
kind of dumb sometimes.

HEMINGWAY_CANSUCKIT

For what it's worth, I promise you'll never lose
my friendship if you admit your undying love
for me

IMPOSSIBLYBOOKISH

such a gilbert response

cute AND irritating.

brb gotta go find a slate to crack over your head.

HEMINGWAY_CANSUCKIT

Promise me I'll never lose you?

IMPOSSIBLYBOOKISH

as if i'd let that happen

Chapter Twenty

REED

Reed stared at the ceiling of Luca's bedroom and willed himself to go to sleep.

It was like if the night before Christmas, the night before the SATs, and the night before buying your first house had all been rolled into one.

His heart was beating out of his chest.

He'd lied to his parents on the phone earlier, saying he was busy with another project at work which was why he hadn't called.

He didn't know how to say, "I wasted the nest egg that Grandpa gave me on maybe a terrible idea, the fate of which currently sits in the hands of the Fairwick Falls Historical Preservation Subcommittee, one of whom actively hates me."

He glanced at the clock, 3:30 in the morning.

He only wanted to talk to one person right now, and she was probably asleep. Denver was, what, two hours behind?

Sometimes she was a night owl.

HEMINGWAY_CANSUCKIT

You up?

> Sorry, probably a dumb question. I hope this didn't wake you up.

He squinted his eyes at the cringey ext. Fuck, was there a way to delete the message?

Miraculously, three dots appeared.

IMPOSSIBLYBOOKISH

did you just send me a 'u up' digital booty call?

HEMINGWAY_CANSUCKIT

Sorry. Did I wake you up?

IMPOSSIBLYBOOKISH

of course i'm up.

somebody texted me at 1:30 in the morning asking if I was up, so here I am.

up.

everything okay?

feeling like someone is about to murder you in the everglades?

They'd talked extensively that afternoon about Harlan Coben's latest thriller. Reed had devoured it on a run where she was only halfway through, preferring the paper version.

HEMINGWAY_CANSUCKIT

Just feeling kind of nervous.

Big presentation tomorrow at work.

He still hadn't told Bookish that he was opening a bookshop. Something about it felt too vulnerable to share, like she might be disappointed if something went wrong. What if he had to close a month afterwards?

It had to be perfect so she'd be wowed when he finally showed it to her.

IMPOSSIBLYBOOKISH

it's fine. i was tossing and turning anyway.

HEMINGWAY_CANSUCKIT

There's something about talking with you that just makes me feel better.

IMPOSSIBLYBOOKISH

i know what you mean.

like, you've never seen my face, and yet you know me somehow better than everybody else.

And I love you, he thought. The yearning ache in his chest had gotten too big to bear.

HEMINGWAY_CANSUCKIT

I know the important things.

I know you're funny and kind. I know you're smarter than you give yourself credit for.

I know you have excellent taste in books and terrible taste in drinks.

IMPOSSIBLYBOOKISH

coffee slut. 

HEMINGWAY_CANSUCKIT

Tea snob. 🤍

When I think about the past five and a half months, you're the best part of it.

IMPOSSIBLYBOOKISH

and you've made me come harder than anybody else in recent memory.

so 10/10 there

The tips of his ears heated from the blush that hit him.

HEMINGWAY_CANSUCKIT

I guess I just wanted you to know I'm so glad that I met you, and you mean so much to me.

IMPOSSIBLYBOOKISH

you're making me feel gooey, and i don't like it.

HEMINGWAY_CANSUCKIT

Don't like it because…it's not wanted?

IMPOSSIBLYBOOKISH

it's…new for me, but very wanted.

i like you a lot, too

like, a lot a lot

He typed out the word "Love." His finger hovered over the keyboard, and he backspaced.

No, you couldn't tell someone that you were in love with them via text.

IMPOSSIBLYBOOKISH

sometimes it feels like i found the other person that speaks my weird little language, you know?

HEMINGWAY_CANSUCKIT

That's exactly how I feel.

His heart was already thundering in his chest as he sat up, feeling as though they were on the precipice of something.

He typed out a message with shaking fingers, gulped, and hit send before he could second-guess himself

HEMINGWAY_CANSUCKIT

Do you think we should…

…meet?

REED PACED BACK and forth on the creaking boards of the bookstore twelve hours later.

Bookish still hadn't responded, the Historical Society Committee was five minutes late, and his brain was running a thousand miles an hour.

Pearl sat on the checkout counter, her feet swaying back and forth, staring at her phone with a scowl. "If you don't stop hitting that creaky board, I'm going to shove your head into this card catalog."

"Sorry, just anxious. Didn't sleep well last night."

She huffed. "Yeah, me neither."

He looked at his watch. "Aren't they supposed to be here already? Maybe they got the address wrong?

"Trust me, Beulah knows where this place is."

Reed's phone dinged, and his heart lurched. *Bookish*. He grabbed his phone from his pocket.

ROSE PARKER

Still no news from the DNA company. Should be any day now. I guess the lab is backed up.

Oh, right. Maybe that was why his heart was still floating somewhere outside of his body.

Everything felt like it was about to blossom. A new family, a new business, meeting a new love of his life.

The door swung open, and the silhouette of Beulah and five other people appeared in the sunlight.

They were a motley crew. Beulah led the way in, followed by an older, elegant-looking woman wearing a Fairwick Falls Credit Union polo, two older retired ladies, and a very large man wearing a denim vest over a black T-shirt.

"Welcome," Reed said, stashing his phone.

"Tiny!" Pearl said with a happy, confused smile as she waved to him. "You're on the Historical Society Committee?"

Tiny waved a large, bear-paw-like hand at Pearl. The large man shook back his long hair, and Reed spied two knitting needles poking out of his ripped jeans pockets. He crossed his beefy arms, revealing a heart-shaped tattoo with a man's name on it.

"I believe in safeguarding historical landmarks and responsible stewardship of local architecture," Tiny said in a slow, rumbling voice.

Reed's stomach was in his throat. He adjusted his glasses. "Is this everybody?"

"Who else'd you expect?" Beulah asked flatly, her frown never moving as she spoke.

"Take a look around. Let us know if you need anything."

"I'm Maria. We're so excited to be here," the older woman said with an encouraging smile as she walked to explore the store.

"Okay," Pearl said, whispering at his side. "That's Maria Lopez. She's in charge of the credit union with Nash. She's no-nonsense, but she's nice. Tiny is a friend from The Thirsty Beaver, totally an in for us."

Pearl reached up and unbuttoned the top button of his shirt. "These old ladies probably haven't gotten any action in a long time." She unbuttoned a second one, pulled his shirt further down, exposing more of his chest. "You should have worn a tighter shirt today." She frowned, looking at his arms.

Goosebumps ran down his skin, his arms tingling at her touch.

"You're going to be pleasant. You're going to charm them," she said, wagging her finger at him. "I'm going to sit here and say nothing so I don't fuck it up for you."

A smile tugged on his lips. *She's being adorable.*

She glared at him. "And they're going to say yes, right?"

"Right," he parroted back.

She got behind him and pushed. "Now go. Charm."

"This is ingenious." Maria pointed at the fireman's pole that had a circular display on it. "My father was the first fire chief in this building. I love that you saved it," she said with a warm smile.

A knot in his chest relaxed. "It's part of the building's history. I couldn't let it go."

"I love that you worked in your own family history." She pointed to the worn picture books on display. He'd put in his favorite books he'd read with his grandpa.

He and his step-grandpa (or Gramps as he'd been told to call him) had bonded over a love of books when Reed had struggled to read as a kid. His stepfather had been very busy, but Gramps had taken time to work patiently through each book with him.

They'd dreamed up the bookshop that they would one day open together, full of ridiculous and whimsical features, like a never-ending candy tube, a nook that was nothing but pillows that you could lie on for as long as you wanted, and a slide to get from one floor to the other. He thought Gramps would approve of the fireman's pole as a worthy replacement.

The committee had spread out. Tiny had wandered upstairs, and Beulah was poking her head in the bathroom, scribbling on a clipboard.

One of the older women pointed to the card catalog. "This was the library when I was a kid. I used to love opening up all these drawers. Oh, it drove old Mrs. Wiggins crazy." She cackled with her friend.

Reed smiled. "It's the thing that made me instantly fall in love with it when I walked in. A couple original drawers were missing, which is why I filled those with plants."

"Oh, and look, they have that new historical fiction that

Martha was talking about," the old woman said, and they started browsing the shelves of the bookstore.

Beulah was writing down copious notes as she wandered through. They'd already passed safety and permit inspections. What could she be noting?

After a nerve-racking thirty minutes, the group reconvened in the center.

"I found seventeen different violations where you did not maintain historical integrity," Beulah said in triumph.

Maria leaned over her shoulder. "Fourteen of those are outlet plates, Beulah."

Reed stepped forward, wanting to smooth everything over. "I'm happy to find more turn-of-the-century style outlet plates if you would prefer."

"I say it's approved," Maria said with a smile, looking at the other two women and Tiny.

Tiny gave a thumbs-up. "Agreed."

The other two women happily nodded. "Yes, and when are you opening?"

Warmth bloomed through him. "Our soft opening is in a few days. The grand opening is in a couple weeks."

"Denied," Beulah said flatly, and Reed's heart seized.

"Beulah," Maria said, shaking her head. "You know you can't flat out deny things. This is a committee, and it's four against one."

"I want it to be on the record that I did not approve this," she said, her eyes sliding over to Pearl. "This trashy future felon is probably rigging this place to sell drugs—"

"Hey," Reed cut in, his voice sharp and loud. "Pearl is an outstanding member of the Bookish staff, and the reason this store looks so amazing. It wouldn't be standing without her. You can leave any comments about the bookstore with me, but I draw the line there."

His jaw clenched, and he hoped he hadn't somehow ruined his chance.

"Yeah, *Barf*lah," Pearl said with narrowed eyes.

"I'm still on the record," Beulah said, storming out.

"Sorry," Maria said, patting his arm.

"We can't wait for the opening," the women said as they waved, walking past them.

"Don't worry," Tiny said in his low, grumbly voice. "You're not the first people she's accused of selling drugs. See you at the Beaver, Pearl."

The door closed behind them, leaving them in stunned silence.

"So...that's it? I was expecting more fanfare," he said with a laugh. "I guess we're okay to open?"

She smirked as she leaned against the checkout counter. "I thought you'd be more excited, given this is your whole dream and shit."

Reed was processing. He laughed, wiping a hand down his face. "Yeah. I think I'm happy. I think I'm excited. It all feels jumbled around with the nerves."

"I think we should slack off the rest of the night"—Pearl grabbed her purse—"and I think you should come with me."

"Where are we going?" Reed said with trepidation.

"It's a surprise."

Chapter Twenty-one

REED

Reed stared up at the Fox & Forrest sign, filled with nerves.

"You said you haven't eaten here, yet. You haven't really experienced Fairwick Falls if you haven't eaten Aaron's tortellini," she said, digging in the enormous endlessness of her purse. "Plus, we need to celebrate because your lifelong dream is coming true and shit."

"That's really nice, Pearl, but you know I can't..." He felt that anxious guilt creep up the back of his neck.

Why couldn't I be like everyone else?

She's trying to do something nice, and I'm going to have to tell her no.

"Hold on," she said, digging again, her whole shoulder in her enormous bag. "I have a solution."

She pulled out two pairs of over-the-ear headphones. "You said the sound of your own eating doesn't bother you, right?"

"Right," he said slowly, trying to understand.

"And you like '70s punk rock, right? The one genre we have in common." She got out her phone and pulled up a playlist on a music app.

He nodded "I mean, I've tried metal. It just sounds like putting a fork in a food processor to me."

She stuck her tongue out. "That's what makes it so great, duh."

She pulled her headphones around her neck. "So, we'll put the headphones on, and we'll listen to music together and have dinner."

He blinked, trying to understand what was happening.

He was awestruck and overwhelmed. She met him where he was at, not where she wanted him to be.

"You'd... do that for me?" he said slowly.

They could have a shared experience together, eating out like other people.

I wouldn't be alone for dinner, for once.

She smirked. "Honestly, it's my preferred way to have dinner. No talking, loud screaming music in your ears, what's not to love?"

He looked with worry at the diners in the candlelit cafe. It was full tonight. "People will stare at us."

She rolled her eyes and smirked. "So? People stare at me all the time. Either because of the tattoos or my fantastic rack. Let 'em stare," she said with a smile. "You're not so shabby to look at either."

She opened the cafe door. "You comin'?"

A burst of excitement split his face into a wide grin. *This could work.*

He grabbed the door above her, holding it open so she could go in first. "Was that a compliment you snuck in there?"

"I'm like a diamond—hard as shit and full of facets," she said, winking over her shoulder.

Butterflies.

Ignore those butterflies from how goddamned cute she is.

The sound of people talking, eating, and forks clinking

against plates was loud as they walked in. It was manageable for a little while, but not for long.

The candlelit cafe was full of tall ferns, white tablecloths, and low candlelight as people talked over dinner. Trendy furnishings and music elevated it beyond just an everyday cafe. It felt chic, and he couldn't wait to finally step past the coffee order counter.

A host seated them along the edge near a window where it was quieter.

"This is so nice," he said, looking around at the gilded mirrors and local artwork.

"I've only eaten here one other time because it's kind of expensive, but their food is *so* good. And they're so good at labeling stuff for allergies," she said, holding up her headphones. "Ready? I found this playlist I thought we could start at the same time."

He slowly smiled, warmth spreading in his chest. She was so sweet. And thoughtful.

And gorgeous, and hot, and stop thinking about this. You're in love with another woman.

"Why are you doing this for me?" he asked, mystified.

She shrugged her shoulders defensively. "I don't know. I kind of *like* being weird in public."

Her mischievous smile tugged at his heart as she slid on her headphones.

He slid his on, and the wash of noise-canceling silence ran over him like a salve.

He could breathe.

Pearl texted him the playlist link, and they hit the play button at the same time. His face was practically broken from his giant, dopey grin.

His text convo with Pearl had been entirely logistical before this. *"Coming home late," "Meet at the store in five."*

The Ramones jammed to their biggest hit in his ears, and their conversation was suddenly filled with deeper things.

REED

This song is such a classic.

PEARL

i know, but i hate that it's been co-opted by
fucking discount shoe commercials

They typed "sellouts" at the same time and laughed, him throwing his head back so hard that he lost his headphones. He scrambled to pick them back up.

Pearl wrote in all lower case, seeming to go out of her way to fix the autocorrects, he noticed.

Bookish did that. *Is it a girl thing?*

Probably just a coincidence.

A waiter came over to take their order, and they paused their playlist long enough for Pearl to order a burger and fries and for him to order a fettuccine alfredo with extra cheese.

Reed was sure people were staring as they put their headphones back on and texted back and forth, but he didn't care.

He was having too much fun.

REED

So, are you and Tiny in the same knitting circle?

PEARL

first of all, it's crocheting, you stooge.

second, he makes the cutest little scarves for his
cats.

Her eyes danced with humor and her perfectly sculpted lips curved upwards in a smirk. *So lovely.*

He hadn't felt this much joy bubbling up inside of him in a long time. He was out—with people—just being himself.

227

REED

Tiny leads a fascinating life.

PEARL

he's a bouncer down at the beave. keeps the big
drunk guys in check, but has a heart of gold.

REED

I thought you were making it up the first time you
said the name of the bar.

Reed shook his head in exasperation. Mirth danced in her eyes across the table.

PEARL

dave knew what he was doing when he
opened it.

there's a reason every woman-who-loves-
women in a three-county radius knows about the
thirsty beaver.

He knew Pearl was bi, but they hadn't talked about her relationships much.

REED

That's how you found out about it?

PEARL

a couple of years ago, some friend-with-benefits
and i went for a laugh before luca, AB, and i
moved here.

REED

So, are you seeing anybody now?

For some reason, he felt anxiety churning in his stomach at her answer. Her chin was lowered, but she flicked her eyes up, staring at him with a quirked eyebrow.

PEARL

are you asking as my boss?

REED

As your friend.

Just trying to learn about your life.

You know, like friends do.

PEARL

it's…complicated.

Reed snorted, feeling that to his very soul.

PEARL

something funny about my relationship status,
berry?

REED

No, I just…feel you.

PEARL

ooh, have you got a
girlfriend/boyfriend/themfriend?

REED

It's complicated. 😊

It's just been a lot on top of the store and the
Parkers.

PEARL

any news?

REED

Look at you, Bishop.

Giving a shit about me.

She stuck her tongue out, and her silver tongue ring glinted
in the candlelight.

Hot.

He instantly flashed back to their very minor, very accidental, (very life-changing) make-out session a few weeks ago. His cock twitched and he clenched his jaw, trying to ignore it.

REED

No news yet.

PEARL

what are the odds your long-lost sisters are here?

Pearl was chatty, he realized, when it didn't come to actually *talking*. A smile tugged on his lips as he stared, enchanted by her. She mouthed, *"What?"*

PEARL

stop looking at me like a doofus.

oh god, do i have something on my face?

REED

You're nice, Bishop.

Like, really nice.

PEARL

take that back

REED

Nope. You showed your cards.

Little ray of sunshine.

She glared at him, fuming, and he bit back a smile.

Adorable. The uneven furrow of her brow as her dark brows arched, the slant of her jaw as she scowled.

Humor she wasn't able to hide in her eyes at his teasing as she tapped away at her phone.

PEARL

i am TEEMING with darkness and hellfire

REED

Sure you are, sweetie.

She burst out laughing, and he wanted to savor her smile forever. Stop this moment, freeze everything where he'd made her smile so big she almost doubled over.

Aaron, the cafe owner, approached their table with two heaping plates and they took off their headphones.

The scratching of forks and crunching of sandwiches, pizza crusts, and salads echoed around him. It was always the forks that got to him.

"Hey, girl." Aaron winked at Pearl with a friendly smile.

"Hey, you," Pearl said with a happy smile back. Reed sighed, enchanted by it. "Are we VIP customers? Is that why the boss is delivering our food?"

"You know it's because I'm nosy as shit. Hi Reed, nice to finally meet you." Aaron set their plates down, and they shook hands. "Any almost-family of the Parkers is almost-family to me."

Reed's interest was piqued. He wanted to know more about his maybe-family. "Really?"

"Oh, we go way back. I practically grew up at the Parkers' house. Vi and I have been besties forever. Two little weirdos in our class."

"Violet was weird?" Pearl said with surprise.

Aaron nodded. "Every middle schooler is weird, but we were 'which Jane Austen hero would win American Idol' weird."

"Henry Tilney, obviously," Pearl said, shrugging as if the answer was obvious.

"No way, it's Frank Churchill," Reed countered, delighted with her.

"Annnd that's my cue. Enjoy," Aaron said with a wave as he buzzed back to the kitchen.

Reed picked up a phone and tapped the screen to unlock it. It had an odd background.

Oh, shit. Wrong phone.

"Sorry, they look so similar when they're face up," he said, switching their phones.

That could have been a disaster. Had Bookish gotten back to him, it would've exposed his whole second life to Pearl.

He'd never hear the end of his anonymous sexting friend from her.

He unlocked his phone and went back to his text to Pearl.

REED

To be continued. This fettuccine deserves my entire attention.

PEARL

i shall prepare my arguments about how wrong you are.

frank churchill, honestly…

Pearl bit off a fry, chewing with a vengeance, eyes narrowed in competition.

His head was already a mess between his deep feelings for Bookish and his attraction to the woman across from him.

He was physically attracted to her. Who wouldn't be?

Her give no shits, take no prisoners, wear whatever the fuck I want and look hot doing it attitude was intoxicating. Her doll-like face, round apple cheeks, and dark lips were easy enough to get lost staring at. Not to mention the ink on her arms, thighs, and her chest. She was badass.

And, he considered, thinking about the touching gesture she'd organized for him, *one of the sweetest, most thoughtful people I've ever known.*

Chapter Twenty-Two

PEARL

Do you think we should…meet?

It had run in a loop in Pearl's head.

For the last forty-eight excruciating hours.

She'd been a scared little nutsack—let's be honest, those were way more fragile than pussies—and she'd ghosted Hemingway.

Straight up abandoned him after he'd asked the thing she'd been too scared to ask him.

"Earth to Pearl." Allison waved to get her attention. "These need four daisies. You've put in eight." Allison pointed to the foam block in front of Pearl.

It was desperate times in Bloom and Allison had called her for help on arrangements. Luckily, though, these were fake flowers.

"Sorry," Pearl said, ripping out the four extra daisies she'd mindlessly put into the foam centerpiece.

She'd been distracted, thinking about how fun dinner with Reed had been last night.

And how it conflicted with the gooey feelings for Hemingway

that were blooming into very dangerous territory. Could she fall for a guy she'd never even met? That she'd never even *seen*?

Was his giant cock really worth getting murdered over?

Maybe Hemingway was an ogre.

Maybe he was one of those guys that wore shoes in the house.

Oh, no, what if it was worse?

What if he owns a Cybertruck?

"Are you a little distracted after your *special dinner?*" Allison said with an overly innocent smile, batting her eyelashes.

"What dinner?" Pearl said, not wanting to give anything away.

"Pearl and Reed, sitting in a tree..."

Pearl shoved her and she laughed, swirling away with a flounce. Allison's summer dress made her look like a '70s milkmaid, with long, billowing sleeves that were just a little short on her long arms.

Allison stood back up and stretched, pressing her lower back. "Ugh, this table was not made for people over five eight."

Pearl pushed a stool toward her with her foot.

"Thanks, friend," Allison said, sitting down.

Maybe she needed a friend's opinion. She and Allison were friends, right? She'd held Allison's hair back when she'd puked outside the Thirsty Beaver. That was prime friend territory.

"Okay, I need to swear you to secrecy."

Allison dropped what she was doing and turned around eagerly. "I *knew* it. You're dating him, right?" Allison said with vindication.

"What, no. Who?"

"Reed."

Pearl waved her away. "That's ridiculous."

Allison gave her a 'come on' look. "You only spend every waking moment together. He makes you laugh—"

"No, he doesn't," Pearl scoffed, lying.

"—and I have it on good authority that you had *fun* at dinner."

Pearl rolled her eyes. Aaron was such a gossip. "This isn't about Reed. I need to swear you to secrecy."

"Alright," Allison said, sobering. "What's wrong?"

Pearl gulped. *This is gonna sound so dumb.* "I met a guy online."

"The dopey love face guy you texted at the bar?" Allison scooted her stool closer, clapping with girlish excitement. "Tell me more."

This was a new feeling, having a friend who liked this shit. Pearl bit her lip. "We've talked for months. He seems great. He's asked to meet and there's like, only a three-percent chance I'll end up a skin suit. But...I don't want him to know where I live in case things go sideways. AB's here."

Allison nodded, understanding. "And you want somebody to report the skin suit faster?" she said, pointing to herself.

"Exactly, you get it," Pearl said, throwing her hands up. "I just need someone to know where I'm going, and it felt weird telling Reed. I would never tell Luca. He's too overprotective."

"Oh my gosh, does this mean we're besties?" Allison said with a smile, pressing her hands to her face and looking like a goddamn Disney princess.

A little knot of sadness relaxed inside of Pearl, turning into a happy, warm glow. Someone wanted to be friends with her? And besties, even? Pearl bit back a smile so she didn't look like a dork. "Sure—"

Before the whole word got out of her mouth, Allison squeezed the life out of her with a "yay!"

Allison went back to the arrangements, wiggling with excitement. "So, where are you meeting him?"

"I was thinking maybe around Lake Erie? I can drive there, and make up a story why I'm in town."

"Why don't we carpool together, and I'll be there in case it goes bad. I'm very tall, and I'm sure I can look menacing enough."

Pearl snorted. Allison was tall but looked as menacing as a plate of strawberry shortcake. Her whimsical outfits full of plaid and lace and patterned cardigans with little fruits and birds didn't scream *intimidating*.

"You'd do that?" Pearl said, finally looking Allison in the eye.

"Of course. We're besties. Plus"—Allison patted Pearl's back—"I don't have time to deliver all the flowers *and* make them if you get murdered."

A little sparkly glimmer shone on her cold, black heart. *I have a bestie.*

Pearl squashed the smile into pursed lips so it didn't overtake her face.

Pearl looked back at her phone, and pulled up the conversation with Hemingway.

HEMINGWAY_CANSUCKIT

Look, there's no pressure. I don't want to weird you out.

I like our…relationship? Friendship?

As it is now.

I would never want to lose that.

She tugged on her lip, fingers shaking as she typed.

IMPOSSIBLYBOOKISH

situationship with benefits is more accurate.

I just…

i don't want you to be disappointed…

She felt very exposed and vulnerable.

And she didn't do vulnerable.

Look, she fucking loved how she looked.

She loved her hips and her ass that looked like a peach and her tattoos and all her piercings. She knew, however, that she wasn't everyone's cup of tea.

Who is, honestly?

She'd lived in a fantasy with him for months where what they looked like was just…mostly irrelevant. He couldn't judge her or fetishize her.

But she didn't want to lose him. What if he didn't like her when they met in person?

Generally, *most* people didn't like her in person.

Her temper got the better of her, she was angry all the time, and her mouth ran off before she could think. She hated most of the world and it hated her right back.

He'd never experienced that side of her.

Could she handle losing the one person who was her refuge from it all?

Three dots indicated he was typing.

HEMINGWAY_CANSUCKIT

You could have one and a half heads, a humpback, and a penchant for eating nickels, and I still wouldn't be disappointed.

IMPOSSIBLYBOOKISH

what about pennies?

HEMINGWAY_CANSUCKIT

Bookish…

IMPOSSIBLYBOOKISH

hemingway…

Fuck it. Let's get murdered and/or fucked.

IMPOSSIBLYBOOKISH

how about 4th of july weekend on lake erie?

i'll be around for a printer conference.

That's probably a thing, right?

HEMINGWAY_CANSUCKIT

It's a date.

This is going to be a ...very cringey question...

But I'm going to worry about it until then

IMPOSSIBLYBOOKISH

don't worry, i'll bring my own pennies to snack on

HEMINGWAY_CANSUCKIT

Oh good, never mind then

IMPOSSIBLYBOOKISH

hemingway, just say it

HEMINGWAY_CANSUCKIT

When I see you for the first time...

...can I kiss you?

This isn't an official agreement. You can revoke consent at any time, obviously

I've just dreamed about kissing you for five months

And again, I don't want to weird you out

I'll overthink it if I don't have a plan.

Actually, never mind

I think I've already over-thunk it.

Let's just play it by ear

IMPOSSIBLYBOOKISH

h, honey

HEMINGWAY_CANSUCKIT

Yes, gorgeous

IMPOSSIBLYBOOKISH

i cannot wait for you to kiss me

DURING THEIR TEXTING OVER DINNER, Reed had ferreted out that Pearl was thinking of doing the Firefly Festival, and so he sat next to her, smugly smiling as the mayor droned on about the festival. It was sweltering in the community room, and Pearl counted water spots on the ceiling to pass the time.

"Now," a reedy voice called out from the front. Bow-tie man was holding up a stack of papers. "Who are all the vendors who need to finish their registration?"

Reed beamed at her, encouraging her to raise her hand.

She rolled her eyes and put up a hand. "God, I hate this. Why can't I just sell muffins out of my trunk?"

"Because trunk muffins are suspicious," Reed said, whispering to her, pulling her arm up higher so she could be seen.

The Parkers sat on the other side of her, and they beamed almost as much as Reed. She got shoulder-nudging from Lily. Bloom would have a large display at the festival, and Lily's husband, Nash, was supplying most of the festival funding as part of his credit union's community outreach.

Reed had offered to split the table fee with her so that he could hand out flyers for the grand opening and sell merch for the shop.

She still had a chill down her spine when she thought about the bookstore being named Bookish. What were the odds?

Though, it wasn't like her name was very creative. Every book girlie under the sun had something in their life that had the word "Bookish" on it.

As bow-tie man droned on about paperwork, and optional paperwork, and paperwork in triplicate, Pearl dreamed about how good a cocktail sounded. Before she knew it, a crack of the gavel meant that the meeting was adjourned.

She threw back her head. "God, I need a drink."

"Oh, same," Lily said. "We should all go." The Parkers' husbands were all in tow tonight.

"Oh, I don't know. Maybe we should get back to Frank," Violet said with a worried look at her husband, Jack.

"You know very well, my love," Jack said, kissing her head, "that he is perfectly happy at my dad and June's house until whenever we want to pick him up."

"Come on," Lily said, bumping Violet's hip. "Pearl keeps promising to take me back to The Beaver," Lily said, waggling her eyebrows.

Pearl's eyes connected with Reed's as she said, "They don't serve food. Is everyone okay with that?"

The relief on his face was palpable. He winked at her with a warm smile. "Thanks," he mouthed.

Her pussy clenched involuntarily in response. Golden, glittery shivers ran down her spine.

"As long as they've got vodka for me and a soda for Gray, I'm there," Rose said, striding toward the exit and leading the charge.

Twenty minutes later, they'd all settled in with cold drinks and sodas. They crowded around a small table, and her knees knocked with Reed's. The Thirsty Beaver was hopping tonight, and loud music played from the old jukebox.

She felt a glimmer of couple-iness with Reed, given the three women and their husbands sat around the table, gossiping about the town and talking about Bloom. Reed, Lily, and Rose were putting their heads together about Bookish's soft opening. Pearl couldn't stop staring at Reed as he talked with the Parkers; the resemblance was uncanny.

She saw their drinks were half-empty, so she decided to buy the next round. She was so damn proud of herself that she could buy eight beers at one time now. The Parkers had been so kind and generous that she was happy to buy them a round.

She told Reed she was going to the bar.

He squinted, not hearing her. He dragged her chair closer until it knocked against his.

Oh my god, that was so fucking hot.

"What?" he called, putting his arm on the back of her chair and leaning down to hear her better.

Cedar and cologne teased her nose as she fought herself from leaning in and mauling him. "I'm going to get another round," she yelled. *And think about this with my vibrator tonight.*

"I'll help you," Reed said, pushing up. As they maneuvered through the busy crowd, she felt his hand at her back. It sent a thrill up and down her spine.

You are such a hypocrite, Pearl. You hate this white knight shit.

But you love it so hard too.

As they got close to the bar, she spotted a handful of women with books on a table and cocktails in hand.

Maria, from the historical committee, waved them down. "Hey, you two!" She was flanked by Mrs. Maroo-Canon and Margie, Pearl's personal hero and sassy waitress at the diner. They all had a copy of a steamy-looking romance novel on the table.

"Book club?" Pearl yelled.

"*Sexy* book club." Mrs. Maroo-Canon waggled her eyebrows.

"Thought we'd get inspired by the ambiance of a biker bar as we talked about *Inked in Ruin: A Motorcycle Club Secret Baby Romance.*"

"Honestly," Margie grumbled, her bright pink lipstick and unlit cigarette between her lips, "it didn't have enough smut for me."

Reed's eyes lit up with humor. "You all should check out the bookstore's soft launch soon. In fact, snacks will be provided by..."

He looked at her expectantly.

They'd talked about this. He wasn't putting her on the spot, but it still felt weird and embarrassing to announce her bakery.

Pearl finally admitted, "Blackbird Bakery?"

Reed beamed.

Shit, she was really doing it. She couldn't back out now.

Maria pulled Reed aside, and Pearl went to the bar and put in her order.

The skeezy guy from Dave's party was sitting at the bar, sipping a beer, and he blanched when he saw her next to him.

He was reading a worn library copy of Roxanne Gay's *Bad Feminist.*

What the fuck alternate timeline did I just step into? "You know, that's a *pro*-feminism book, right?" she called.

"Hey, look, man." The grizzled guy had genuine fear in his eyes. "I'm not comin' near you. Your guy's crazy, man." He moved two stools away.

"What guy?" She looked around.

"The dude you're with." He pointed at Reed talking with the book club. "He said he'd kill me if I ever touched you again." He moved one more stool over just for good measure and went back to his book.

Pearl turned back toward Reed, all smiles and charm as he talked to the ladies about their book.

He glanced up at her with a panty-melting smile and winked as he listened to Maria.

It *did* something to her.

I'm probably in love with Hemingway.

And I'm definitely in something with Reed.

How have I managed to avoid all the gooey feelings for like five years, and then somehow two crash into me at one time?

Chapter Twenty-Three

REED

A sea of deep and light greens surrounded Reed as Violet talked him through the best plant options for Bookish. He and Pearl had stopped by before Bloom opened.

Violet held up a small pot. "Now, you have low light in there, so you'll want these snake plants."

The soft opening was that afternoon. Reed figured the longer he waited to get the plants, the less likely they were to die between now and the opening.

Violet continued, "Now, for this little snake plant, his name is—"

A scream sounded from upstairs, and Lily thundered down the top staircase from her studio.

"Rose is coming over! She got the email from the DNA company!" Lily said, waving her phone.

"Oh, um." Pearl shifted on her feet, looking embarrassed. "I can go. I'll take the first batch of plants over."

"No," Reed said, holding out his hand and grabbing her arm as she turned. "Will you stay?"

He wanted somebody who really knew him, a friend, no matter what happened.

There was a softness in her eyes, a melting in them. Like they were on the same team no matter what. She nodded.

Just a silent conversation between the two of them.

The back door of Bloom flew open, and Rose tossed her bags down as she jogged in.

"Well?" Lily asked, practically running down the spiral staircase.

"I haven't opened it yet," Rose said, taking click-clacking strides across the store.

"No matter what happens, we can always just be friends," Violet said with a smile while rubbing Reed's arm.

"Sure," he shrugged. "I mean, the odds are so unlikely—"

"Oh my god," Rose said, her eyes scanning her phone. "It's— You're... We–we're related."

The three women stared at him in shock.

He smiled with as much excitement as he could muster and gulped.

"Sorry?" He shrugged.

Violet yanked him down in a hug.

"What do you mean, sorry?" Violet said with a watery voice, crushing him. "We get a whole 'nother sibling."

Relief washed over him.

They'd been so insistent, he thought they *might* be happy, but part of him felt like that six-year-old boy all over again, meeting his new stepfather's family.

Hoping he could fit in. Hoping they'd love him despite...being himself.

Lily crashed into his other side, wrapping her arms around his middle and squeezing.

"I'm finally not the youngest!" she said with a smile as he hugged her back.

Rose smiled at her sisters. "You'll get used to the hugging," she said with a slow smile as she squeezed him over Lily's head.

"What did your mom say when you told her about us?" Lily asked.

"Oh. I, um…" He scratched his head. "I didn't want to mention it until we knew. Didn't want to get anybody's hopes up."

Violet walked around to the counter at Bloom and pulled out photo albums. "I brought these over a few weeks ago, just in case."

She flipped open the albums and Reed's eye was magnetically drawn to the man that looked so much like him. Photos of them at Christmas, on boating trips, being silly, around the kitchen table.

"They're all from around the same time period," he said.

"Oh," Violet said with a soft smile. "Our mom died a little after these were taken."

"They were soulmates," Lily said with a wistful sigh, "and losing her just took out all his spark."

"There is a more recent photo at Pop's. You may have seen it when you walked in. His photo's on the wall. They were best friends," Rose said.

"Oh, I, um"—he cleared his throat—"I haven't been in there yet."

"You haven't been into Pop's?" Lily said, aghast. "But the pancakes."

"And biscuits," Violet added.

"They do make a good cup of diner coffee," Rose agreed, leaning over and flipping through the photos.

"Well, we need to have our first official family dinner," Violet said, clapping her hands. "I'm happy to host. The guys can come, too. You'll love Jack; he's also a big reader."

"Yeah, maybe sometime." He tried to give as much enthusiasm as possible. He glanced at Pearl, who nodded encouragingly.

She mouthed, "Tell them."

He looked away.

Violet's face fell. "Oh, sure."

Rose's brows drew together in thought. "I've seen you on runs around town. Do you want to go on a run together at some point?"

Excitement bubbled up in Reed. "I'd love that."

Rose gave Violet a side hug, and a customer knocked on their door, peering in.

He grabbed the plant in front of him. "We should get out of your hair so you can open. I think we'll take the six ferns and two snake plants for now."

"It's a gift," Rose said as Reed pulled out his wallet.

"I can't."

"Trust me," she said, putting her arm around his shoulder and walking him to the ferns in the front. "Our dad loved supporting local businesses. As an *official* member of the Parker family now, we want your soft opening to be amazing. We insist on these being on the house."

"That's so nice." He'd been planning to spend at least three or four hundred dollars here to make the bookstore look as good as possible before the grand opening.

"It's what we do in Fairwick Falls." Rose smiled as she unlocked the door. "We take care of each other."

He and Pearl loaded the plants into his car and drove them over to Bookish.

"You know," she said, pulling the plants out of the back seat of his car, "you could tell them."

He didn't even need to ask what she meant.

But all that work to explain it.

Half the time, people didn't even believe him; the other half, they thought he was being overly dramatic.

"I don't know. It takes me a long time to trust that people

won't judge me for it," he said, hefting two large ferns to take back inside.

"You told me, didn't you?"

"That's different," he said, bringing them inside. "You'd never judge somebody for doing what was best for them."

It was one of the things he loved most about her: the radical acceptance of others' differences. She'd ride at dawn for anybody who needed it. She'd bitch and moan on the way, but she'd be there as sure as the sun would rise every morning.

Wait…loved?

He needed to get his head straight between her and Bookish.

"Hey, I, um…" He set the plants down in their new spots. "I'm going to take off the long weekend for Fourth of July and close the store. I know it's right after we open, but I have something I've got to do."

"Oh." She set down the three large snake plants on the front checkout desk. "Yeah, I was going to let you know that I needed to be gone then, too."

Maybe if he met Bookish in person, he could finally put all the lusty, distracting thoughts of Pearl behind him.

Bookish cared about him. They had chemistry.

He was in love with her.

This thing with Pearl and his attraction, it was probably just unspent lust. And her friendship was so important to him.

It would all resolve itself when he could finally meet Bookish in person and make a decision.

REED'S HEART was vibrating somewhere outside of his body as he saw the clock count down to three.

He turned around in his bookshop. It gleamed in the sun. Plants were on every surface, filling in spaces in the bookshelves.

The nook was finished and books flew over the small stage, hanging on the ceiling. Lily had finished the final installation of the papier-mâché tree in the kids' space two days ago. It was still a little wet to the touch, he hoped it could withstand any kids that stopped by.

They'd invited the business owners around the square. Pretty much anyone that Reed bumped into that he could tell about the bookstore was invited to the soft launch.

He stared at the photo on his phone, his thumb hovering over the send button.

He'd gone outside earlier that day, feeling sentimental, and taken a photo of the sign for the store. In inscribed letters, it said "Bookish, a Fairwick Falls Bookstore."

Sentimental feelings clogged his throat. He wanted to tell ImpossiblyBookish just how much she meant to him, how much she'd inspired him, and how much she'd gotten him through all the times he'd doubted himself.

"Ugh," Pearl grumbled. "The one day I'm running every-fucking-where, and I wear a skirt without any pockets because the patriarchy doesn't want me to be able to find my keys. It would make me too powerful." She slammed her stuff down. "Can I just toss everything under the counter? I need to go back out and bring in the last of the cookies."

"Of course." He stood back from the register so she could dump her phone, keys, and purse on the shelf underneath.

His heart pulled back to his screen.

Was he brave enough? Would she think he was a creepy fool for naming a whole store after her?

Only one way to find out.

HEMINGWAY_CANSUCKIT

My big project launches today, sort of. That's why my head's been everywhere and I've been a little absent.

I hope you're not weirded out by this, but I just need you to know how much you mean to me.

How much all our rambling late-night conversations about nothing have meant to me.

I've honestly never had a lot of friends. I think I can be a bit much in person sometimes.

It's why I'm nervous to meet you, but I'm so excited.

I'm literally counting down the days.

...

Oh god, I sound like such a loser.

I promise I'm not a loser, just...awkward.

Anyway

I didn't want to tell you about the specifics of my big project because... I don't know. I didn't want to get your hopes up in case it failed, but it's coming together.

And I wanted you to know...

He gulped.

you were my muse, so I thought it was only fitting that it would have your name.

He sent the photo of the sign to her.

It's a bookshop.

I'm still in the process of launching it, but I hope it'll end up just like you.

Interesting, kind to all, thought-provoking, and something that feels a lot like my soulmate

So thank you.

Thank you for just being you in this world.

He closed the app immediately. *I can't handle watching her read the message.*

He imagined her deleting her account. *Or blocking me for being fucking weird.*

A light rap sounded on the closed bookstore door. The clock read 3:05. "Shit, we're late."

He tossed all the stuff on the counter, his phone and coffee cup, extra books and papers, under the register.

He opened the door and no less than fifteen people were standing outside in the afternoon sun.

"Welcome to Bookish, Fairwick Falls's first bookstore," Reed said, feeling like he was having an out-of-body experience, waving them in.

The two older ladies he'd seen in the Historical Society Committee beelined it to the mystery section. A couple of bikers Reed recognized from the Thirsty Beaver wandered in with two kids.

"Yinz got any kids' books? The lil' one loves dragons," one of the biker women said, pushing her sunglasses up to the top of her bandana and pointing to a kid with excitement in their eyes.

He practically bounced on his toes. "Tons. Check out the kids' section back there." They wandered in with impressed faces, and Reed felt so proud.

Violet and her husband were walking down the sidewalk, and Reed waved. "Welcome!"

Jack, was wearing their son in a baby carrier, and Violet carried a plant with her. "I hope you got the romance section ready for me." She laughed and gave him a big hug and handed him the plant. "Happy soft opening."

"Violet, you already gave us too much."

"Heard you're part of the family now, mate," Jack said, sticking out a hand with a smile.

"Happy to be here," Reed said. Jack pulled him in for a quick side hug so they didn't squish the baby.

Oh my god, I have a nephew. He was thunderstruck at the idea.

"You don't happen to play football, do you? Er, soccer," Jack corrected himself.

"I do," Reed said with excitement.

"Finally." Jack hit Reed's chest companionably as they walked in. "I've got a pickup game on Sundays. I'll get your number from Vi and text you the details."

Reed stared after them.

Instant family is...crazy.

Rose and her husband, Gray, were walking across the town square, and Reed waved them in.

Rose shooed him. "Go. You have customers. We'll talk later."

Shit, she's right. He wandered through, making sure folks were finding everything they needed. Pearl had been up baking all night, and people swarmed around her cookie table.

Not knowing what else to do so he didn't bother people, he just stood behind the checkout counter, his eyes not fully believing what he was seeing.

People were happy, enjoying perusing the old and new books they'd found. Pearl came up to stand beside him.

"This opening doesn't feel soft at all. It's getting rather hard, actually," she said with a suggestive eyebrow wiggle.

He shook his head at her indulgently. "Your cookies are a hit."

"People love free shit, but yes. They are," she said with a proud smile, drumming her hands on the counter in front of her. Reed heard two *zhush* notifications under the counter.

Bookish responded.

He grabbed his phone from under the counter and swiped up to open it.

It didn't open.

Wait.

What are my messages doing on my lock screen?

A photo preview was on the lock screen with a message from Hemingway_CanSuckIt.

Beside it, a notification said, "Today's your six-month anniversary of connecting with Hemingway_CanSuckIt. Tell them hello!"

Why would his phone show him the preview that *he sent?*

Pearl grabbed her phone from under the counter and muttered, "What the fuck?"

Wait a minute.

He turned the case over, confusion clouding his thoughts. The case was black and spiky.

This was Pearl's case.

Why was Pearl's case on his phone?

"I, um..." Reed muttered.

"Oh my god." Pearl was staring at a phone in her hands, jaw slack and breathing heavy. "This is impossible."

Blood rushed in his ears.

She shoved the phone in her hand at him. "This is yours. You have my phone"

On his screen, there was a similar notification saying, "You and ImpossiblyBookish have been friends for six months."

Reed felt dizzy. Pearl's phone had a message from Hemingway_could suck it. "Then, that would mean..." he faltered

She grabbed her phone, and her eyes scanned the messages on the lock screen.

That would mean...

An image filled her screen—the one he'd taken outside the bookstore.

"Holy. Fuck." Pearl's voice was sharp as she looked at him in panic.

"Uh, this where we check out?" the grizzled woman said as a kid piled three books onto the checkout counter.

That would mean...

...Pearl is ImpossiblyBookish.

Chapter Twenty-four

PEARL

Pearl's mind was full of static as she stared at Reed through uncomprehending eyes.

He was distracted, bagging three picture books for their first customer.

Hemingway sent me a photo of this bookstore.

The store I'm standing in.

The store that Reed owns.

Which could only mean that Reed...

...is Hemingway_CanSuckIt.

What the actual FUCK, universe?

"Okay, you two," Violet said, holding up her phone. "You need a picture."

That was what she'd probably said, at least. All Pearl could hear was a roar in her ears.

Reed is Hemingway.

Hemingway is Reed.

"Oh, come on," Violet said, waving her hands together. "Scootch together. Look happy! You just made your first sale!"

Pearl couldn't look at Reed as she nudged closer.

"You guys," Lily said, exasperated from her spot beside

Violet. "You have to look happy if we're going to post it on Bloom's socials for your launch. Put your arms around each other and smile like friends."

Pearl gulped as Reed's arm wrapped around her back.

Pearl did her best to move her lips in a way that probably mimicked a smile.

It's hard to control your muscles when you're having an out-of-body experience.

"Why do you guys look so weird?" Lily said, grimacing at them.

"Take the fucking picture," Pearl snarled through gritted teeth.

"Say, 'Bookish'!" Violet called.

Can hellfire just swallow me up now?

Please? Pretty please?

"Bookish," they both mumbled quickly.

"Got it, even if it's weird," Lily grumbled.

Pearl and Reed jumped back instantly.

"Could you help me find the religious section, dear?" an older woman said, peering over the counter and leaning on her cane.

"Religion is upstairs." Pearl grimaced as the woman sighed, looking at all the stairs. "I can show you to the elevator in the back, or I can grab it for you."

Please for the love of god get me anywhere away from Reed/Hemingway so I can put my brain back into my head.

"That would be great, dear," the woman said, patting Pearl's arm. "I'm looking for the latest edition of *A Green Witch's Guide to Tantric Sex.*"

"Oh," Pearl said, momentarily shook. "Great, I'll be right back."

She felt Reed's eyes burning into her as she walked away.

She glanced over her shoulder, unable to help herself. When their eyes connected, they both jolted and turned away.

It's gonna be a really long afternoon.

As she came back down with the book, she froze on the staircase and looked out over the beautiful, bustling bookstore.

Her hand came to her throat.

He named the store…for me.

Someone named a whole fucking bookstore…

Just for me.

Reed walked toward the back, showing the family who owned the hardware store where the kids' section was. The kids squealed, running as if they'd found a secret hideout.

Everyone else in the shop faded away, and each puzzle piece clicked into place.

He also hated Hemingway. He'd lived in Philadelphia. He'd been going through a lot of changes. He had a *huge* dick. He had a roommate.

She laughed, realizing it was her.

She was Hemingway's roommate.

He stood, hands in his pockets, as he surveyed the bustling store. His gaze stopped at her on the staircase as she stared at him like a lunatic.

A half-smile tugged on his lips, and he looked as confused as she felt. His hand lifted in a small wave meant just for her. "*Hey, it's me,*" it said.

"Is there a problem?" a guy who stood behind her on the staircase asked.

Oh, Jesus Christ.

She bit her tongue, and instead of saying, "I *can take my sweet fucking time since this bookstore was named after ME, motherfucker,*" she hurried down to give the customer her book.

She warily kept her distance from Reed/apparently Hemingway_Cansuckit during the soft opening, but a few hours in, a man asked for a sci-fi collection on the top shelf. Pearl, excited to use the rolling ladder, unhooked the "Employees

Only" sign and crawled up, pulling out the heavy books one by one.

"People say Scalzi's best work is *Old Man's War*, but I think *Starter Villain* is his best book. It's not sci-fi, but you might like it." She went backwards down the ladder a rung at a time, taking the heavy books with her slowly. The ladder felt sturdier as a hand grabbed it.

"Let me help you," Reed said, his hand coming to her elbow.

She stared down at the strong, large hand on her arm and gulped.

Tan, clear skin was in sharp contrast to her pale arm full of demon faces and sexy ladies.

I've seen this hand with cum all over it as he held his enormous cock.

After he jacked off to me.

Oh my Christ. I've made Reed come.

"Pearl? The books?" Reed said, holding up his other hand.

Reed likes it rough. Reed loves my ass and tits.

Reed wants to kiss me.

"Right," she said, metaphorically thrown off balance. She handed the books to him and avoided his eyes. Her cheeks were on fucking fire.

Her head felt like it was full of bees. Full of buzzing, not able to think straight.

Every single piece of the last five months rolled around like possessed marbles in her head.

It went that way for the next three hours. It was like they were magnetic. They couldn't *stop* finding each other in the crowd.

It was a compulsion. She *had* to keep looking at him—the man who hadn't left her thoughts for months.

As the soft opening wound down, Pearl walked Allison out of the store. She needed some air.

It had started to rain and Pearl welcomed the sound of against the warm pavement as the door closed. The humidity finally released its tension into the air. Street lamps popped on.

"I hope it's okay I took some cookies for the road," Allison said, holding up three lemon sugar cookies as they huddled under the overhang away from the rain. "Thought it would pair well with my new true crime book. Did you have a good turnout?"

Pearl leaned against the brick, out of view from the bookshop window as three people left the bookshop. "Yeah. My personal highlight was Margie buying a pile of smutty books and riding off with a biker from the Thirsty Beaver. Honestly, that woman is goals."

They chuckled, but Pearl's smile didn't meet her eyes.

"Is everything okay?" Allison asked with concern. "You looked a little off in there."

Where would I even begin?

"Just needed some air," Pearl said, waving her away. "Enjoy your murder and lemon cookies."

Allison waved as she dashed to her car.

The last two customers trickled out. *Too bad I didn't grab my purse. I could make a quiet Irish exit and just hole up in my room.*

Forever.

Yes, she was a giant fucking scaredy-cat.

I never said I wasn't a pussy.

This whole time, it had been him.

She'd flirted with him. Made him come.

He'd consoled her, made her laugh, made *her* come.

Her thighs clenched thinking about the purple vibrator. *Reed* had sent it to her.

Reed—straitlaced, buttoned-up, nerdy-as-fuck Reed—was a goddamn savant at dirty-talking.

The brick of the building was still warm from the sunny day

and it soothed her back. The sound of rain pelting the sidewalk mimicked the ping-ponging in her brain.

He wouldn't want me.

The one guy I thought could truly love me...

Who maybe I already love a little...

Who said I could eat nickels if I wanted...

Is not the kind of guy who would want a chubby, crass, alt, stone-cold bitch like me.

She looked at her phone and scanned their chats, reliving her highlights. Mentally, she was already boarding up shop and saying goodbye.

Reed was *hot* hot. He probably wanted a perfect blonde wife with 2.5 children. She had to say goodbye to the dream of someone wanting her the way she was.

Like an idiot, she'd forgotten to appear inactive and jumped when a message came in.

HEMINGWAY_CANSUCKIT

You won't *believe* the day I've had.

She burst out laughing at how ludicrous this all was.

IMPOSSIBLYBOOKISH

bet i can

HEMINGWAY_CANSUCKIT

You done hiding out in the rain?

Want to talk yet?

IMPOSSIBLYBOOKISH

about what?

HEMINGWAY_CANSUCKIT

You're hilarious.

You love it, she wanted to type on instinct as she smirked. A ragged breath pulled on her lungs.

It was all over now. The special thing they'd had. She typed a one letter response.

IMPOSSIBLYBOOKISH

k

The door to Bookish swung open. He was inside, holding it open for her.

He looked shy, confused, maybe a little embarrassed.

We'll just handle this quickly, and I'll go home. Rip the band-aid off.

She walked quickly past him into the store, brushing against him, not looking him in the eye.

But he grabbed her wrist, stopping her.

"Wait," he murmured.

She froze, her heart beating outside of her body. Heat hit her cheeks, and the warmth from his hand radiated up her arm.

He closed the door and locked it. Turned off the lights. Still held her wrist with a firm hand, like he thought she was going to run away.

Which, fair, I was.

Low lights on the bookshelves cast dim, cozy glows throughout the store. The only sound was the patter of rain hitting the skylight over her heart thumping in her throat.

"Pearl, look at me." His thumb swiped on her pulse, and her breath stuttered.

She'd been studying the patterns on the marble floor.

She gulped.

His thumb caressed her wrist again. "Bookish, please." His voice was low and pleading.

Her eyes flashed up to his.

The amber light glowed warm on his face. His brown eyes looked like deep pours of bourbon. He had a five-o'clock shadow, and the little stubble hairs glinted in the low light.

He looked nervous, thoughtful.

"I didn't know, I swear," she whispered earnestly.

He smiled, looking pained. "I know." He nodded. "Me neither. Honestly."

"Are you…" She didn't even want to finish the question, asking if he was disappointed.

Because then he'd answer it.

You should run, her heart told her. It was afraid of getting bruised, poor thing.

Possibly demolished for good.

"How do you feel?" she finally asked. It would be a less direct blow when he answered.

"How do *you* feel?" he said with furrowed brows, looking concerned.

The rain had turned to a thunderous rumble on the ceiling.

"You first," she said, her chin jutting out defensively.

His hand still held her wrist and *fuck,* she hoped he'd never let it go.

His lips twitched with the ghost of a smile and his gaze softened. His head tilted, considering her as his eyes roamed her face.

"Bookish was—is—you are," he stumbled, "special to me."

He moved toward her cautiously, like she might run away. "But I felt bad," he whispered, looking nervous.

"Why?" She breathed, not able to take her eyes off his mouth two inches in front of her.

His hand brushed her cheek tentatively, and the pleasure of it radiated like sunlight to her every nerve ending.

"Because I've been having these feelings…"

His thumb slowly, lazily stroked her jaw, and she thought she might die from how good it felt.

"What feelings," she whispered, leaning into his hand.

"Feelings for my assistant that I shouldn't have. My assistant who hates me."

She felt like she'd been drugged, trying to chase the feeling of his fingers against her cheek.

"I kissed her and I haven't been able to stop thinking about it. About her body. The way I wanted it. I tried not to but I'd picture it every night."

Her breath caught as his thumb lazily traced the bottom edge of her lip.

Every night.

"Spent my nights trying to find what perfume she wears because it haunts me," he said, stroking her chin with a hunger in his words.

She could feel his breath on her lips, that peppermint and cedar cocktail she'd been thinking of for weeks. She tugged on his sweater, needing to feel some part of him.

"She's kind, and funny. Has these gorgeous hazel eyes that look like a nebula. Shocks of gold surrounded by green," he murmured. "Pouty lips that taste sweet. But...my heart had unfortunately already found its perfect match somewhere else. Somewhere in Denver."

Her breathing came in pulls.

She swirled the information together in her head as she fought to keep her eyes open.

Gorgeous.

Pictured every night.

Perfect match.

The rain filled the silence between them.

"Is this too much?" he whispered, his eyebrows knitted together with worry.

Her body buzzed with electricity. "It's never too much," she murmured, leaning into his hand cupping her cheek.

Her eyes searched his. He nodded quietly as his thumb

stroked back and forth, tracing the bottom of her lip. His amber eyes were molten as he clenched his jaw.

She licked her lips. "You...you named the bookshop for me?"

He smiled, tilting his head as he leaned down. "Yes, gorgeous. My Bookish." He barely brushed his lips against hers once, twice.

She chased the feeling but he pulled back, his eyes connecting with hers.

His breathing was ragged as he swallowed, grinding his teeth. "*Anything* for you."

The sound of it in person was too sweet. Too perfect.

Too *him*.

Her heart burst, and she pushed up and captured his mouth.

He kissed her back like a man possessed. Hot, firm. Both hands cupped her face, and her soul melted into him at the feeling of it.

She pressed against him, pulling every inch of his body closer to hers. Swirling desire and pent-up lust had her clawing at him.

His hand ran into her hair as his tongue opened her mouth, and *fuck* if she hadn't dreamt exactly of this for weeks. *Yes.*

A moan floated out of her. *God, he was too good at this.*

Her fingers itched to feel his skin again, and she pulled his shirt out from his pants. The hot muscles of his stomach burned her fingers as he backed her against the card catalog desk.

She was ruthless in grabbing every inch of his stomach.

Letting herself be the feral tomcat she was.

She scratched and grabbed his abs, his chest, pushing a hand up under his shirt. He bit her lip ruthlessly, kissing her like he was trying to consume her.

He moaned, wrapping an arm around her and yanking her tight against to him. She clenched her pussy around nothing. Wanting him.

"I've wanted to do that for fucking *weeks*," he muttered against her lips. "Wanted to kiss you in the kitchen right here"—

his mouth nipped her neck—"when you were making pancakes."

She huffed out a laugh as her nipples hardened and pleasure rained down her spine. She'd been a mess that day. "I wanted to lick raindrops off your chest," she admitted as she pressed his head into her neck, hoping he'd bite harder. "Or your sweat. Fuck, you smell so good." The cedar of his cologne surrounded her, and begged her to open her legs wider.

He bit her neck harder and pulled up her see-through crop top over her tank top to kiss her breasts. "Thought about tracing each"—he placed open-mouthed kisses over her tattoos—"tattoo with my tongue. God, I wanted you so badly," he said as he kissed right where her heart was.

She scraped her tongue along his earlobe, biting there, and he shuddered.

His hand slid down her thighs and grabbed one, firm. Possessive.

Bruising.

"Yes," she sighed, loving it.

"Your thighs have haunted me," he said, kissing her deeply. "Couldn't stop picturing my face between them."

His hand palmed her breast, and she leaned into it. He toyed with her nipple with his thumb, rubbing it around and around. Her clit pulsed and she clenched wanting him inside of her. "Like when?"

"Like when you were on top of me, moaning while I massaged you. The things I wanted to do to you," he said, his voice filled with dark promise.

She could swear she saw the fires of hell in his eyes and she wanted to be consumed by them.

She bit her lip. Wanting him to say it. Hearing it from Reed, not from Hemingway. "Do our thing. Tell me."

A wicked smile transformed his face. His thumb still toyed

with her nipple and he was ruthless, pinching it hard, rolling it. She bit back a loud moan. Wet arousal flooded her panties.

His forehead pressed against hers as he stared into her soul. "I was moments away from rolling your panties down, sliding my finger in your ass, and making you *beg* me to come as I ground you against my cock."

Ho.

Ly.

Fuck.

Ing.

Hell.

Her hands fumbled for the buckle on his belt. He pushed her onto the checkout desk and spread her thighs wide, pushing her skirt up.

"But tonight," he gasped against her mouth, "I have to know, Pearl." His hands clenched her thighs, gripping them, running over her fishnet tights, higher and higher.

"Know what," she said, grasping the outline of his cock as she fumbled with his top button. *Need it.*

He whimpered, his breath stuttering as she gripped him.

"Please." His thumbs rubbed higher and higher on her inner thighs. She thrust her hips toward him until he hit her hot center. "*Fuck me*, you're so wet. I have to know." He grimaced as his muscles bulged and a rip sounded. "I have to know what you taste like."

He'd torn a *pussy hole* in her tights.

He cupped her chin so she looked right at him. "Eyes right here."

She nodded, dumbstruck.

His thumb slowly pressed through the hole and slipped under her panties, connecting directly with her clit. He moaned.

"Fuck," she sobbed. The perfect teasing stroke right where she wanted it.

Their eyes held as he swirled a thumb around her clit, watching her moan, her chin still in his hand. Pleasure snaked up her spine.

She pressed against him, wanting it harder.

"Yes, more," she moaned.

He swirled and swirled his thumb. He captured her mouth, his tongue twisting with hers.

He ducked his thumb deeper, tracing the seam of her. Until he pulled back and sucked it into his mouth. His eyes closed in ecstasy. "Fucking vanilla and...you. That scent I need is just *you*," he muttered, licking every drop.

He hauled her against him as their mouths devoured each other with hot, sloppy kisses. He lifted her up, thighs on his hips. She squealed, throwing her arms around his neck as he walked her back to the sci-fi section away from the windows. Her skirt was up around her waist, and the cool air of the room hit her exposed pussy.

"You can carry me?" she said as he set her on a rung of the book ladder, nestled in a corner out of view.

He held her chin, his voice low and threatening as he gripped her thigh with a punishing need. "If you don't think I haven't been working out for this exact purpose, you have vastly underestimated me, Bookish."

He kissed her as he tugged her tank top and bra down on one side, exposing her breast.

A moan shuddered out of him as his mouth connected with her breast. He sucked her nipple through her netted crop top, and she could have come from the perfect friction on her skin. She could only moan as he pressed his face into her, yanking the other side of her top down so his face was buried in her tits.

"Thought about doing this since the bookcase. Since you sent me that photo," he murmured into her skin. He sucked on the other as he played ruthlessly with her exposed nipple.

"Wanted to fuck you in that bookcase hellhole," she moaned, burying her nose in his hair.

"Was"—he sucked hard and she cried out as he squeezed her breast—"this close to pulling your tits onto my face when I massaged you. Could see the edge of this nipple and I needed it."

She moaned, thinking of how badly she'd wanted him to do just that. "Please, want you."

He thrust her legs apart and knelt, hooking a leg over his shoulder. He stared at her spread legs, licking his lips and pushed them farther apart.

He yanked her panties to the side and stared at her hungrily. "Finally," he groaned.

Jesus.

Moaning, he dove into her pussy.

Fuck this was everything. She could barely breathe from the pleasure of it. Her head rolled in pleasure on the ladder rungs, incoherent pleas sobbing out of her.

She gasped as his tongue slinked around her clit. He ate with abandon, moving his tongue up and down, biting, licking. She held the book ladder with one hand above her and the other shoved his face in deeper.

His tongue lapped every inch of her pussy, leaving nothing to waste. No dip unexplored. He moaned as he sucked her clit, hard.

Her thighs surrounded his face, and he squeezed them tighter around his head.

"Don't stop," she cried.

Loud, wet sounds mixed with his groaning pulled at her desire. "Don't want to," he murmured into her pussy.

He moved his tongue over her clit again and again, up and down and up and down. Then to the side, until he started over again. The same pattern, harder, but always the same.

She fought through the haze of pleasure, trying to make sense of it. "Are you...are you spelling something?"

His chest was ragged as he peered up. His face was wet from her, and his fingers dug into her thighs.

He rubbed his face hard against her thigh reverently as he stared into her soul, the bourbon of his eyes on fire as he nodded.

"M. I. N. E."

Fuuuck. A sob escaped her mouth as she bit her bottom lip, her pussy clenching.

"You like that, gorgeous?" he said with a smirk, his eyes catching the movement under her skirt.

"Only if I get the dirty acrostic poem with it later," she said, laughing.

He spread her pussy wider and buried his face into her with a deep laugh, enjoying himself.

This is crazy. Reed/Hemingway is eating me out like his life depends on it.

Fuck, and he's so good at it.

She fucked his face, grinding against him, using one foot on the armchair next to them for support. He had her at his mercy. Tits exposed and rubbing on the wet fabric where it had been in his mouth. Off-balance and leaning onto him as he destroyed her.

Slippery coils of pleasure rubbed again and again. She needed more, needed this to last forever.

He slid two fingers in, and she clenched around them, crying out.

"Jesus, Pearl," he gasped, pinning his forehead to her soft stomach. He curled his fingers, coaxing her, and she twisted in pleasure. "Can you take three? You feel so tight."

"Fuck," she moaned. "Please. I want to feel full. Spread."

His eyes connected with hers, dark and sultry and challenging. The rolled-up sleeves of his button-up shirt strained against his flexing muscles. He slid another large finger in and she gasped.

"You're doing so good," he muttered and sucked on her clit.

Fucking praise kink. A wave was building, surging inside her. "Going to come," she mumbled, barely able to think straight with a full pussy and Reed biting her clit.

She heard a zipper, and his hand disappeared from her thigh. He jacked himself hard as he stared up at her. "Eyes on me, Pearl."

His eyes connected with hers as he sucked and sucked. She squeezed her nipple. The soft crook of her G spot was teased back and forth as a wicked smile grew on his face, and she ground against his face harder and harder, screaming out his name.

"Fucking gorgeous," he moaned like a man possessed. He came in his hand with a cry.

They gasped for breath, frozen in place. The ragged sounds mixed with the rain still pouring on the roof.

Her legs twitched with the aftershocks, and she curled her spine, savoring the feeling of Reed kissing her thighs reverently. A rumble sounded.

Thunder?

No, wait. Laughter.

She looked down to find Reed chuckling against her thigh.

"What," she said, still out of breath and incredulous, "is so funny about my pussy?"

He stood and kissed her deeply, pressing her whole body against his.

She wrapped her arms around him, still shaking from her climax. She happily tasted herself on his tongue, feeling like he'd been claimed as hers.

"It's just," he murmured against her lips, pulling back. His eyes were warm and full of humor. "When I pictured eating your pussy, like I have countless times, never in one million years did I think you'd scream Ernest Hemingway's name when you came."

Chapter Twenty-five

REED

Reed was in heaven.

Pearl sat on his lap in his bookstore, approximately six inches from where he'd made her come on his tongue.

The lights were low, and the sound of rain on the ceiling made him close his eyes.

This is absolute perfection.

His heart was beating out of his chest, and he knew who the true owner of it was in that moment.

Only her.

Maybe he'd died. Maybe this was all in his head as his brain shut down.

He didn't care.

He'd gathered Pearl on his lap, feeling the glorious weight of her against his chest, his thighs. He could sleep like this every night.

For as long as we both shall live.

His brain had scattered to the wind when he'd realized she was Bookish that afternoon. He'd almost double-charged their first customer because his fingers had been shaking so badly.

He'd been terrified during the entire soft opening that she'd run away. She'd block him. That she'd *hate* that it was him after all.

"Did you ever suspect it?" she asked, nuzzling under his chin.

Goosebumps flooded his arms at the pleasure of her cuddle. She already felt like she belonged in his arms.

"Did I suspect that a Colorado printer salesperson was living one door down the hall?" He laughed at the ludicrousness of it. "No," he said quietly as his lips brushed her head and he inhaled her scent. "How'd you get the vibrator?"

She waved a hand as though it was nothing. "Mail forwarding service."

"There *were* some spooky coincidences now that I think about it, like your taste in books and your way of typing like a serial killer."

She peered up at him, her pretty eyes narrowed. "You said it was endearing."

He kissed her temple. "Endearingly creepy."

"Aw, just like me," she said, cuddling into him.

He pulled her tighter against him. "Did you suspect it?"

"I don't know. There were some things you said to both me and Bookish that made me think I was losing my mind."

"You knew I lived in Pennsylvania—"

"On the other side of the state. You know." She sat up with attitude suddenly, scowling at him. *Adorable.* "I'm a little peeved that you had a crush on another girl when we were so obviously in a serious situationship."

He laughed, exasperated. "Pearl, you told me I could kiss whoever I wanted. Plus, *you* were the other girl."

"*So?*"

He held her chin, knowing she'd want to escape his next question. "You never told me how *you* feel, scaredy-cat."

Her chest rose and fell with slight panic. "I mean, pretty sure I did. You know, when I shoved your face into my panties."

He could smell her on him even now. She'd covered his face and he hadn't wiped a bit of it off. *Pure fucking heaven.*

He kissed her tenderly, brushing his lips against hers. "If I recall, Bookish slash you said you were starting to get gooey feelings."

She nodded, kissing him harder as she reached for his belt.

"Nice try," he said, pulling back and grabbing her hand. He was nervous too, but he had to know.

She bit her lip, her eyebrows furrowed. "I had a crush on two guys, okay? One was hot and sweet and a little broken and a giant fucking nerd. The other one could make me come and laugh and made every day better. He was sort of my best friend," she added, avoiding his eyes.

"So you don't, um..." He swallowed. "...you're not sad that it's me? You don't hate me?"

She considered him for a moment, then relaxed against him, taking her time answering. She played with the hair on the top of his head, and he shivered in pleasure.

"Pearl," he said as his eyes closed. "Please."

"I never hated you," she said finally. "I guess I just pictured you with, I don't know, someone more like Allison. Cute, conventional. Not someone who regularly gets in fights with little old toads."

"Allison's nice," Reed said, his hand rubbing up and down her arm as he tugged her closer to him. "But she's so *happy* all the time."

Pearl burst out laughing. "*You're* happy all the time," she said, sitting up and straddling him, pushing his chest with her hands.

A laugh rumbled out of him. He liked seeing her like this—playful, laughing. Happy.

"Which is why I've always liked people who kept it real, since

I knew exactly where I stood with them." His hands slid up and down her hips. He couldn't stop touching her. "Someone who would make sure to point out the gray cloud coming toward me while I saw all the silver linings."

She smirked.

"And it was a big added benefit if their ass just wouldn't *quit*," he growled, squeezing her butt hard as she laughed and caught his mouth in a kiss.

He savored each one. Couldn't take this miracle for granted. She pulled back with knitted brows.

"But I'm ragey," she said, looking embarrassed.

His fingers threaded through hers as easily as if they'd done it for years.

"I know," he said, grazing her cheek with his knuckles. "I like your rage, and your anger, and your curses. Always have."

Always will.

But she's probably not ready for that yet.

Reed reached over, feeling for Pearl in the bed.

He cracked his eyes open and found himself alone.

He'd offered to sleep in his bedroom last night, but she hadn't let go of his hand since they'd walked in the door of the house.

Such a softy.

And so she'd tugged him into her bedroom. She'd promised him raucous sex, but he'd seen the circles under her eyes and kissed the top of her head, assuring her that he was fine with just sleeping beside her.

She'd fallen asleep before her head hit the pillow with his arms wrapped around her, so they'd done nothing more than cuddle all night.

He'd stayed awake for hours holding her as his brain churned, trying to make sense of how the woman he loved was also the woman he lusted after.

He could still taste her from last night. Smell her on his lips and under his nose and his fingers.

Fuck me. His cock was already hard.

He never wanted to shower ever again.

She normally kept the door closed, so he'd never even peered into her bedroom. He stared at it now, alone in her bed. It was somehow unexpected, but perfectly her.

Stacks and stacks of books filled the room, some occupying old, makeshift shelves, some just pushed against the wall. Taxidermy raccoons and crows sat atop the bookshelves. The art hanging on her walls made him smile. A black cross-stitch with white thread saying "Fuck this shit up" was framed on her nightstand.

Another piece in black watercolor on her wall said "Give no fucks, Take no orders." AB's scribbled drawings featuring an all-black stick figure were tacked up on the wall. A photo of a very drunk Allison in a bar squishing Pearl's cheeks was tacked up beside it. *She's sentimental,* he realized with a happy glow.

He wanted to ask her about all of it. Wanted her right here where she belonged beside him.

A chocolatey scent that meant only one thing drifted through the door, and he followed his nose down to the kitchen.

He rubbed the sleep from his eyes and the pans and bowls on the counter came into focus as he slid his glasses on.

So that's where my shirt went.

Pearl stood braless in her tiny bright underwear. The only other clothing she wore was his shirt—unbuttoned with the sleeves rolled up—as she mixed batter, her headphones probably blaring grind-core in her ears.

His teeth gritted with need at seeing the soft pouch of her

belly curved over her panties. The deep valley of her breasts called to him as they curved under his shirt.

He leaned in the doorway, staring at her. She was makeup-less, and he kind of liked seeing her in her natural state.

Dirty thoughts that he'd pushed to the back of his head for over a month flared up, like pushing her over the counter and sliding into her while he sunk his hands onto her hips.

She jumped when she saw him.

"Morning," his sleep-roughened voice croaked.

"Hi, uh..." She stared at him, her jaw slack and her eyes boring into his chest.

He was shirtless, only wearing the boxer briefs he'd slept in. Her eyes combed up and down his body.

"Uh," she said, blinking quickly. "Morning," she said, seeming shy as she gave him a half-smile. "Couldn't sleep. Festival starts in six hours."

She scooped batter faster onto the sheet.

It was almost like she was nervous to see him. Normally he'd think something was wrong.

But she's wearing my shirt.

And she looks so goddamn good in it.

He slowly walked around the kitchen island, feeling possessive. Craving her.

Need her repeated in his head and his cock grew hard. He didn't even care that she could see it in his boxer briefs.

She stopped as he stood next to her, and he gently tugged on the shirttail, the backs of his fingers stroking her upper thigh. "You look good in my shirt." He kissed her jaw below her ear, and she sighed, leaning into him.

He leaned over her, his arm resting on the top cabinets as he boxed her in, and cupped her jaw to kiss her.

But before he reached her lips, she burst into overwhelmed giggles and slid down to sit on her heels. "Oh my *gooood.*"

"What?" He laughed in surprise, stepping back.

Pearl *giggled?*

She sat with her face in her hands, crouched in a ball. "Jesus fuck you're so hot with the glasses and the naked muscles," she murmured. "And you just, *goddamn.* I can't think when you look like that leaning over me."

She peeked up at him between her fingers.

A smile tugged at his lips. "Pearl. Darling." He crouched in front of her and pulled her hand away from her face. "My face was between your thighs last night. Trust me when I say you're the hot one."

"I'm not used to this. My brain...it hasn't caught up." She bit her bottom lip with worry.

He nodded as his thumb stroked her fingers. "I couldn't sleep last night. It felt like I was already in a dream and I didn't want to wake up. Because I might lose you. Both yous." He brought her fingers to his lips, brushed light kisses there.

She licked her lips.

"Maybe...we should just kiss. Just to make sure it wasn't just a heat of the moment thing yesterday. For science," she added.

He smiled. "For science."

Her normally dark, pouty lips were a dusky rose, and they called to him. He slid a hand up into her hair as he kissed her. She smiled against his lips, and he couldn't take it. He needed more. He fell to his knees as he pulled her toward him.

His tongue traced the seam of her lips, and when she parted them, he dipped in for a taste. Chocolate cookies and lusty flavors hit his tongue. She leaned toward him, chasing his kisses, his shirt slipping off a shoulder.

She moaned and pushed him to his back, her hands clutching his biceps.

She straddled him as he lay on the floor, and his hands slid down to her hips.

He squeezed her against him hard, feeling like his heart would burst from being the luckiest man in the world.

The hot softness of her tits pressed against his chest, and the heat of her core landed directly on his hard cock. He ground her against him, shoving her ass down, and she canted her hips toward him, grinding harder.

"God, I love science," he muttered as he kissed his way down her neck, pushing his shirt off her shoulders.

It got halfway down her arms when a timer went off. She froze, head in the air thinking, but then shook it. "No, that can wait."

He captured her lips and her hips dug against his cock again and again. He rocked her harder, clutching her hips. She was so wet it had seeped through his boxers. The friction was too perfect.

Another timer went off, joining the beeping of the first. Her head hit his shoulder as she sighed in frustration. "Urgh. That one can't."

He kissed her temple, hand sliding over her hair as he tapped her hip to get up. "Come on. I'll put some clothes on, grab your shorts, and come back to help."

She slipped his shirt back on and leapt up to take something out of the oven. "Why? You've seen me pantsless now."

He leaned up on his elbows, his eyes devouring the tattoos running up her muscular, thick thighs, seeing the curving peek of her ass cheek from under his shirt as she moved around the kitchen. "Yeah," he sighed. "But that'll keep happening if I keep staring at your ass."

Chapter Twenty-six

PEARL

"Ohmygod, I think I want to marry you," Lily said, scarfing down a brownie in front of Pearl's table.

"I'm game, but your husband might have a problem with it," Pearl said, feeling giddy.

The Fairwick Falls Firefly Festival had nearly cleaned her out of every single item on her table. Evening had fallen on the town, which meant the main event with fireflies on the town square lawn was about to start and she could finally close up after the longest day ever.

She and Reed had settled on a shared table between her bakery and Bookish, and she sat among non-food vendors like local jewelry and soap-makers.

"Where's your work husband—my *brother*," Lily said, with a little happy dance. "Oh it's so fun I get to say that."

"Oh, he's around here somewhere."

Not a soul knew what had happened between Reed and her in the last twenty-four hours.

"Speaking of husbands." Lily waved Nash over.

"It's looking good, Pearl," he said, picking up a cookie and giving her a ten-dollar bill.

"Let me get you some change."

"Nah." He waved her away and unwrapped the last remaining chocolate chip cookie she'd baked that morning from its cellophane. "You need anything?"

The credit union Nash had founded was sponsoring the festival, and he and his employees were running the event.

"Nah, I'm good."

He probably didn't even hear her though, based on the love-drunk way he gazed down at his wife. Lily had wrapped her arms around Nash's waist, and they smiled at each other.

"Go," Pearl said, shooing them with a smile. "Your gooey love faces are blocking the path to my table."

"Okay, but since Mr. Money Bags is here, I'm just gonna grab these." Lily piled six more whoopie pies in her arms.

Nash shook his head with an indulgent smile, and gave Pearl a fifty-dollar bill.

"Wait, your change!" Pearl shouted as they walked away.

"Keep it, and keep making my wife happy," Nash called back, pulling Lily to him and kissing the top of her head.

Pearl put both bills in her cash box, feeling embarrassingly grateful for him overpaying. This meant she was almost at a thousand dollars for just today.

Even Beulah didn't bother her today as she walked between the tables, scowling at her.

Pearl raised an eyebrow, challenging her to even bother saying anything as she handed two pieces of wrapped confetti cake—or, as she'd called it, firefly cake—to a family stopping by her table.

"Ms. Pearl," a tiny voice shouted. Sophie Hirasaki, one of AB's little friends, waved as she tugged her parents toward Pearl's table. Sophie had a nut allergy, and so she and AB sat together every day at lunch at a special table.

She was wearing a light-up headband with dangling fireflies, with a firefly painted on her cheek.

"Hey, Sophie," Pearl said, giving her a high five. "Love the face tat."

She knew Sophie's parents a little bit from a few park play-dates when Luca hadn't been able to make it. Her mom was a nerdy white woman who Pearl talked to about murder podcasts, and her dad was an effortlessly cool Asian man with throat-to-hand tattoos who did specialty paint work for Luca sometimes.

"Mom, can I have one?" Sophie looked up.

Sophie's mom looked at everything on the table. "Is anything nut-free?"

"Everything is, actually." Pearl winked at Sophie who was practically jumping up and down.

"I want the spider cookie." She pointed to the blue sugar cookie with Pearl's globby attempt at a firefly.

Okay, note taken. Work on my icing skills.

"You got it, kid," Pearl said and bagged one up for her.

"This is awesome, Pearl. Do you have a storefront or some-place we could visit?" Sophie's mom asked.

It's her birthday next week, Sophie's dad mouthed and mimed behind Sophie. The sight of a tatted-up dad miming "birthday" was just too cute.

"Not yet. I'm hoping to rent the place over by the salon on Tenth," Pearl said, handing them a card. "But in the meantime, you can contact me for any...uh, reason." She tried not to mention the b-word as Sophie's dad gave her a thumbs-up.

She waved to Sophie as they walked away.

What is this new feeling? she thought, rubbing her breastbone. Confidence?

Not the *fuck you* confidence she normally had to project to keep herself protected, but excitement for the future.

Wild. Did other people just live like this all the time?

Beulah had been loitering at the next table, and she sneered looking at what was left of her baked goods. "A bakery? Gonna make pot brownies probably."

"Shoo." Pearl waved her hands as if she was an errant pigeon. "Steal someone else's soul, *Barflah.*"

She toddled away, her eyes watching Pearl the whole time.

A welcome sight strode toward her. Reed was talking with a woman who had an official-looking badge on for the festival. His eyes connected with Pearl's as he walked toward them, and butterflies—or, fuck it, maybe fireflies—lit up inside her. It was warm and cozy and romantic.

Definitely fireflies.

"Hey, Pearl," he said with a wink. *Squeeeeeee.* "I want you to meet Jennifer. She's one of the festival committee members."

"The president, actually. Reed and I became fast friends," Jennifer said, shaking Pearl's hand, "waiting in the endless line for the bathroom."

Jennifer's hand rested on Reed's bicep as if they had a shared joke.

Pearl's hands fisted, but she said nothing.

"I told Jennifer," Reed said with a friendly smile at the woman next to him whose *hand was still on his fucking arm,* "that you should be the provider of the gluten-free and vegan shortcake for the Strawberry Shortcake Festival in a few weeks."

"I've heard rave reviews about your brownies," Jennifer said, looking at what was left of her table.

"They're all gone. I'm sorry," Pearl said through gritted teeth, not feeling sorry at all.

This bitch's hand.

Is still.

On his arm.

She looked like the kind of woman Reed should end up with.

Put-together, elegant, confident. Someone who had opinions about wine and contacts at the best schools.

I hate her.

"Here," Reed said, moving behind the table. "We'll get you a card—and do you like lemon cookies?"

"Always," Jennifer said with a flirty little wink at Reed.

Murder. I'm going to go to prison for first-degree, unapologetic murder tonight.

Reed handed her two cookies and a card. "These were a huge hit at the bookshop's soft launch yesterday."

"Can't wait to try them," Jennifer said with a little shoulder wiggle, her eyes still on Reed.

Reed looked at Pearl. "Did you have any questions for her?"

Does she have her next of kin lined up?

"Oh, let's just consider it done," Jennifer said, finally looking at Pearl. "We'll need about a thousand. You can just give me an estimate on cost and we'll talk from there."

Jennifer flashed a breezy smile as she gave a little finger-wave at Reed as she walked away.

"Amazing," Reed said, turning to Pearl.

She growled. "That woman was flirting with you."

"No she wasn't," he said, adjusting his glasses.

"Ah ha," Pearl said, poking. "That's *your* tell."

"What? No, it's not," he said, adjusting his glasses again and rubbing the back of his head.

"You *liked* that she was flirting with you," she said with a deviant laugh, poking his stomach.

"I don't *care* that she was flirting with me," he said, grabbing her hand and squeezing it. "Because if it got *you* what you wanted, that's all that matters."

He leaned down and gave her a quick, firm kiss.

Her eyes darted around. "You are kissing your assistant in *public.* Scandalous," she whispered.

"Honestly, I'd like to do a lot more to you than kissing," he said as his eyes traced her cleavage and traveled back up to her face. "But I'll settle for this."

He kissed her cheek and pulled her into his chest, wrapping his arms around her.

"A thousand strawberry shortcakes," she said, mind boggled as she nuzzled against him. "That's like...a lot of money."

"And it's just the beginning." He smiled down at her. "I'm so proud of you. You are amazing."

God, she wanted to fuck him so bad.

They'd had to stay focused all day getting everything ready for her table.

"I think we should celebrate tonight," she said.

"Mm, what do you have in mind? Some Fox and Forrest '70s punk dinner?"

A smile tugged on her lips. "I was thinking...a game of card."

"Singular?" He squinted and his glasses went askew.

Fuck, he was so cute. She was going to wreck him tonight, especially since she'd worn her special tights just for him.

"Yeah." She shrugged, resting her finger underneath his chin. "The one where I steal your V-card."

PEARL SQUIRMED IN HER SEAT, willing the stoplight to turn green on the way home from the festival.

This is going to be the longest eight-minute drive of my life.

Reed's right hand squeezed her inner thigh as his other clutched the steering wheel. His thumb moved back and forth between squeezes and she thought she might crawl onto the car ceiling if the fucking stoplight didn't turn in the next ten seconds.

They'd packed up from the festival at lightning speed, and

Reed had been quiet since they'd gotten in the car. His jaw was clenched.

"Stupid fucking light," Pearl muttered, adjusting herself in her seat.

"Are your preferences the same in real life as when we texted?" he asked out of nowhere. His voice was strained as he hit the gas.

She glanced over in the dim light and saw the firm, enormous outline of his cock. It was a siren to her as she licked her lips. She wanted her mouth on it so badly, but she settled for just touching right now. *Safety first and all that.*

"Yes, I like it hard," she said, her hand skimming over his cock. "Spanking, face fucking, cum swallowing, being tied up, choking. It's all fair game."

He blew a hard breath out through his nose as she traced the head of his cock lightly with her nails. The skin on his knuckles was white on the steering wheel, and his hand squeezed her thigh hard.

She bit her lip to keep from chuckling. He wanted it *so* bad. His breath was ragged as he turned through the familiar streets.

"I got tested when we planned to meet up, by the way. All clear, also have an IUD," she added.

His eyes went wide. "Shit, do you have condoms? I didn't even think about it."

She shrugged with a mischievous smile, biting her lip. "I do, but..."

Reed stopped at a stop sign.

The millisecond the car stopped moving, Reed turned and kissed her hard. His hand pulled at her, and his tongue traced her lip in his mouth. The peppermint and cedar scent of him was all she could think about. She wanted to lick and eat it up. Bathe in it.

He bit her lip, tugging on it, and she needed to pull him

closer. Her hands were in his thick hair, loving the feel of each strand running against her fingers.

A honk sounded behind them. *Shit.*

"But?" Reed said as he hit the gas, continuing the conversation.

Oh right, condoms.

"I don't really want to use them." Her hands played with his hair.

"If you keep doing that, we're not going to make it home. Either because I crash or because I pull over and fuck you right here on Chestnut Street."

She leaned into his ear, whispering, "I want your cum everywhere. I like getting messy."

It was her kink, okay? She liked being made to take it, have it on her. Nothing was dirtier and better than doing that with someone she could trust. It had been such a long time.

His sigh was ragged. "Haven't been able to stop thinking about last night all day. Dreamt about your pussy."

Pearl used the last red stoplight on the way home to her advantage. She'd finally show the very naughty secret she'd been hiding all day. She'd gotten wet just thinking about it when she got dressed that morning.

"You mean this?" She lifted the black skirt she had on, scraping her nails over her tights, until it was at her waist.

She'd worn her crotchless fishnets.

No panties.

Her bare skin contrasted with the dark tights, and a hint of wetness was visible.

Reed groaned, licking his lips like a predator dreaming about its prey.

"Holy fuck, Pearl," he groaned, his fingers immediately going to it. "That's the hottest thing I've ever seen. Goddamn."

He kissed her, brushing light kisses as his fingers played with her clit. Curls of need wound through her. She'd been on a hair trigger watching him be charming and sexy all day in his rolled up sexy sleeves.

"You are a sorceress intent on destroying me," he said as he dipped in lower, gripping her pussy firmly. "You were bare the whole day?

"Being very naughty," she said, breathless as she licked into a kiss on the side of his mouth. "I wanted you to get a glimpse when I bent over at the table."

He groaned and his fingers swirled in her hot, wet heat. A honk sounded from behind them again, and he ripped his hand away, bringing his fingers to his mouth, licking the taste of her from his fingers as he hit the gas.

She moaned, watching him savor it.

"Christ, you taste so good. Keep your legs spread," he said, glancing at her sternly.

He was coming to a stop sign in the neighborhood. The streets were empty and the houses were dark. Everyone was at the festival. She unzipped his pants and licked her lips.

No one would see.

"Pearl," he warned, slowing down.

She tugged his cock out from the top of his boxers and bent over, licking the head of it.

He slammed to a stop at the stop sign. "Goddamn," he moaned, his hand in her hair. "Never..."

She popped the head of him into her mouth. Fuck, he was huge. She squeezed her thighs together.

"Never did this before," he moaned. "It's too good, Pearl. Can't last."

Holy fuck. She might come before they got home.

She licked the pre-cum dripping off of him. "Good, come down my throat," she said between licks.

"Shouldn't, we're...in public," he groaned, turning onto a side street.

She sucked the first three inches of his cock. "Use me," she murmured. "You'll last longer later."

He stopped at another stop sign. "Bratty sex demon," he muttered, and with a glance around, he fucked his cock into her mouth as he held her head right where he wanted her.

She moaned at how much he wanted it, how firm his hand was in her hair. "Just like that," he said, shoving her head down harder. His cock hit the roof of her mouth, then the back of her throat. Saliva dribbled out of her mouth, down her chin, and he face-fucked her harder.

Yes. Fuck, so hot.

"Oh god, gonna come down your throat."

She hummed as he used her. Her hand wrapped around his cock, and she tugged at him once.

"Pearl," he moaned, shooting salty cum at the back of her tongue. She savored it as she licked him clean.

He kissed her, tongue winding with hers. "So fucking hot, gorgeous."

He threw the gearshift into drive again. His right hand settled onto her pussy, teasing her as he turned onto the next street. "You're going to come at least twice before I fill you up. Still don't think I can last long with how good you smell, and taste. I want you wet, and needy, and spent."

He pinched her clit and a moan wrenched out of her.

He sped down the last street and slammed the car into park behind the house. They both bolted from the car.

"Wait," Reed called. She'd already jogged two steps toward the house. "Your cookies. It's too hot; they'll spoil."

Who thinks about cookies when they're this horny?

"Leave them," she called.

"You worked too hard," he called as he shuffled them into a

large box as fast as he could. She jogged back, annoyed *and* touched.

"Here," she said, taking another box.

He looked at her as she grabbed one, and a guttural growl—a fucking growl—ripped out of him as he kissed her, hard. Nipping, biting.

It was dark outside, and his hands wandered under her skirt. She was so wet her skirt was damp, and it started to spread down her thighs.

He groaned as his fingers found it. "All this just for me. So lucky. I could take you right here in the alley, gorgeous. Fuck you hard in the dark, bent over with your pussy out."

"Yes," she moaned. She liked this entirely unexpected side of him.

Possessive, needy, firm.

She moaned loudly against his mouth. He ripped himself away. "But I want you naked when I eat it," he said with a firm hand on her.

They ran up to the back door with two boxes of cookies. She unlocked the door as he kissed her neck.

"Was torture being with you all day, imagining this, not being able to bend you over the table and fuck you."

She threw open the door and they both tossed the boxes to the floor.

Her lips found his. She was hungry, starving for him.

"Need you. Want your cries," he said between kisses.

He pinned her against the kitchen island, standing behind her. "Pull your skirt up," he whispered in her ear.

Her heart was pounding out of her chest.

She held up the black skirt so her pussy was uncovered, loving the feeling of baring herself for him. His fingers dove in, possessive and hot, finding her swollen clit.

Her knees buckled at the combination of his mouth on her neck, a hand on her tits, and a hand in her pussy.

"Fuck, I'm gonna come," she moaned as he ruthlessly fucked her with his fingers.

"How did it make you feel, Pearl? Being bare for me all day?"

"Like a needy brat. Just wanting to be fucked by you." She sighed against him as he sucked her neck.

"You like that, don't you? Being my bratty fuck toy."

Oh god. Greedy lust made her hips jerk against his hand involuntarily. "Yessss. Want to be used by you," she moaned,

He twisted her nipple as he ruthlessly fingered her clit, rubbing harder and harder. She was pinned between him and the kitchen island and she fucking loved it.

Smoke-like curls of need wrapped around every limb as he decimated her.

She loved how possessive he was. How much he wanted her. How filthy he was.

"So close," she moaned, throwing her head back and panting. Letting her pleasure take over, she let go, screaming and fucking his hand as her climax built.

He pressed her harder into the island, his cock rubbing against the groove of her ass.

"You're going to come all over my hand, gorgeous, right now."

Fuck, she loved it when he told her what to do.

But she loved pushing his buttons. It always made it better.

Her hips moved against his hand, wanting more, bucking into him. "What," she gasped as he flicked her nipple, "do I get if I do?" He teased her clit and she panted, trying not to come.

His hand came to her throat, wrapping around it and squeezing it gently.

Oh god. She felt so possessed, so needed.

So desired.

"Then I'll make a mess of you later, filling you up with my cum."

She broke, convulsing and screaming his name as he drilled her clit, making her scream higher and higher. She chased it, the sparkling glitter crashing through her as she came, savoring it. Letting it wreck her.

She collapsed on the island, panting.

It was always *the nerds who made her come the hardest.*

He kneeled and started unlacing her boots.

"What're...you doing?" she murmured into the island.

He gently took each shoe off, and then his both of his own. She could see how hard his cock was.

"Aftercare matters even if we're not done yet, Bookish."

"A virgin who does aftercare...I...need to go buy a lottery ticket," she mumbled, lazily looking over her shoulder at him with sleepy bedroom eyes.

He was devastatingly handsome as he set their shoes to the side, walking toward her with a possessive clench in his jaw, his forearms flexing.

I am going to fuck the brains out of his gorgeous, nerdy head.

Chapter Twenty-seven

REED

Reed yanked Pearl against him by the waist and claimed her mouth in the kitchen.

It felt like they'd been made for each other, like his body knew its home when she was pressed against him.

How had it only been twenty-four hours since he'd learned she was Bookish?

He'd never get tired of her taste. Of how she felt melted against him, wanting more. He swiped her lip with his tongue, and she moaned.

Her hands were firm on his arms, squeezing him. Burning into him.

"I love how you touch me," he said, breath ragged. *I love you entirely.* "I love that you mean it."

"Because I do," she said as she kissed him, staring up at him. "Because I want you to enjoy every minute."

He crushed her against him, overcome with the feeling of being seen, supported. He held her head against his chest, savoring how precious this perfect woman was.

Alluring, kind, supportive.

His cock throbbed but his heart was about to burst from the sheer joy of it all.

"I cannot believe how lucky—*so lucky*—I am to have found you," he said, burying his face into her hair. "I don't think you can know how good this feels."

His cock throbbed at the sound of her lusty chuckle. "Clearly you've never been choked while getting your clit obliterated. Because that feels pretty fucking great."

If she only knew. "That was for *me*, Pearl. I needed it. I needed to see you come so badly. Unravel for me."

She unzipped her skirt and it fell to the floor.

"How about I unravel you next?" she said, tugging her tight shirt over her head.

All the breath left his lungs.

The fishnets with the exposing hole hadn't just been tights... It was...

An entire bodysuit.

"Surprise." Her lips lifted in a mischievous smirk.

The fishnet material hugged her stomach, breasts, arms, flowing down over her hands. She was completely naked underneath. Every curve and dip was hugged with the material as her skin pressed against it. His cock twitched as his eyes traced every line.

"Holy fucking hell, Pearl," he growled.

He cupped her breast, rubbing the material against her nipple. She closed her eyes, savoring it.

"Feel good?" His voice was raw and needy.

"Yes," she whispered. Her hand slid between her thighs as she rubbed her clit. He grabbed her wrist, and she froze.

"When I *said* I'd make you come at least two times, I meant it. No helping. Now, give it to me," he said, raising her hand to his mouth.

He sucked her pretty, wet fingers, enjoying the sensation of her nails against his tongue.

"What if I can't help it?" she said, her other hand coming to her pussy. She was toying with him. Loved giving him a hard time.

And he loved it right back.

"That's an easy enough problem to solve, you little brat." He bent down, his shoulder hitting her waist, and lifted her over his shoulder.

"What the fuck?" she squealed as he swept her off her feet.

His hand clamped down over her ass as he marched toward the staircase.

"Reed, put me down. I'm too big!"

He walked up the stairs with her over his shoulder.

"I lift this weight all the time," he said, hefting her higher on his shoulder as he heard an adorable "*Oof.*"

"Why do you carry my weight all the time?" she said, incredulous. "That doesn't even make any sense."

"When Bookish said she—you—were plus-size"—he kicked open her bedroom door and kicked it closed—"I did the math on what an average height, plus-size woman might weigh and went from there. You said you liked being tossed around, so I wanted to make sure it was me doing the tossing."

He eyed the vibrator charging on her desk. He'd wanted to use it on her for so long.

"You can put me down now," she said as he stood in her bedroom.

"I kind of like having you exactly where I want you," he said, grabbing the vibrator and turning it on.

Pearl wiggled on his shoulder as he walked to the full-length mirror.

"You know, most men see vibrators as competition," he said,

bringing the head of it to her entrance and teasing her with it, barely letting the buzzing hit her pussy.

He clicked it a notch higher. He brushed it against her clit, barely connecting with her skin. Teasing her back and forth. She gasped, and he dug his fingers into her hip on his shoulder. "But lately, I've been thinking of them as a valued member of the team."

"There's no *vibrator* in team, Reed," she said, biting back her moans.

"There's no *cock* either, gorgeous." He slid it into her, hungrily watching her pussy take it in the mirror. "Fuck, it's going to look so good when I finally slide in here."

Her hips bucked against his shoulder, chasing the sensation as he slid the vibrator out and teased her with it, circling her clit, then brushing it.

"You are so evil," she moaned.

"Evil *and* horny," he said with a chuckle.

He bit his lip, enjoying the view as he slowly, slowly slid the vibrator into her. "I had no idea, Pearl."

He watched her pussy expand, taking it all. Just how she'd take him. "I had no idea how gorgeous you'd look. Taking it so well."

His willpower was fading as she clutched the back of his shirt, crying out as he slid the buzzing vibrator all the way in.

He shifted his weight and turned…but his eye caught on something in the mirror.

A tattoo was bright on the top of her butt cheek.

He hadn't seen it before; it would have been in the video she'd sent him.

He stopped, vibrator in his hand.

A bright red bubble-like heart, like a heart emoji, was perfectly placed on the center of her ass cheek.

It had a lowercase h on it.

His finger shook as he traced the tattoo on her ass. He sucked in a breath as it all clashed in his head.

"Pearl, what is this?"

He lowered her to her feet and tossed the vibrator onto the bed.

She leaned against him, getting her bearings. "For you," was all she muttered as she leaned her head onto his chest.

He held her cheek, turning her sweet, pretty face up to him. She looked nervous staring up at him with those big hazel eyes. "For me?"

She gulped, licking her lips.

"Anything for you," she whispered.

A pull in his heart radiated to his gut, knowing simply in that moment that he was gone for her.

She'd ruined him.

Obliterated.

Wrecked.

She was the end. The absolute finish line that he'd meet when he took his last breath.

His love for Pearl fucking Bishop was all-consuming, and he'd run at full speed for the rest of his life toward her, never looking back.

No other person would ever do.

He captured her mouth and consumed her with needy, hungry kisses. He'd deliver on his promise and make her come again, but fuck, he needed her now.

Yesterday.

Always.

He shoved the bodysuit down, past her breasts, her stomach, down her legs. "Want just you. Only you," he said as they tumbled onto her bed.

He grabbed the vibrator as he fell to his knees. He buried his face in her pussy, sucking hard as he slid the vibrator all the way in. She arched off the bed, bowing her back as she shoved his head down harder.

Fuck yes, he loved it when she made him take everything she had, was as hungry as he was.

"Wanted to have you on me," she moaned, "forever."

Her tits bounced as she rode against his face, and he had to screw his eyes closed so he didn't come from the sight of her heavy breasts bouncing. Perfect teardrop tits with nipples pointing up in pleasure.

Fuck, he needed her now. *I'm being selfish*—he clicked the vibrator up to the highest setting so she'd finish faster—*but I don't fucking care.*

He sucked harder and harder until she sat up, tugging his hair and grinding his face into her pussy as she screamed out his name again and again. She thrashed back onto the bed as he stayed right where he'd been, sucking even harder. He could feel her pussy convulsing on the vibrator as it pulsed in his hand.

He yanked it out, sat up, and undid his belt.

Her hair was a mess as she sat up. He loved seeing her messy. She captured his mouth with hers. "Love it when you taste like me," she murmured as their tongues danced. "Like you're mine."

She pulled at his zipper, shoving his boxer briefs down until his cock sprang free. Her hand wrapped around it, and a low hiss escaped him as velvet pleasure rolled over him.

"Reed," she said in awe as she squeezed it.

"Too big?" He looked at her nervously.

She rubbed the pre-cum on the head of his cock, and hot pleasure shuddered down his spine. He was going to die from the pleasure of it.

She shook her head. "Perfect." She shoved his boxer briefs down further so they hit his thighs, but then she froze.

Fuck, she sees it.

He held his breath.

"I...I got it done a while ago," he said, knowing what she was staring at.

Her fingers traced the simple black heart tattooed on his upper thigh.

"Why is it upside down?" she asked in a quiet voice, still staring at it.

"So I could see it when I thought of you. When I jacked off to Bookish, or, fuck"—*might as well be honest*—"or to you. I stared at it."

She looked up, mouth open in a shocked *O* shape.

"I only thought of you," he said, his thumb brushing her lip and pulling it down, wanting her even messier. His heart beat only for her. "I wanted her to look like you, Pearl. Every curve, every scowl, every tattoo. The way your thighs jiggle in this sexy way when you walk. Your tits," he said, grabbing a handful of her. She stroked his cock. "The way you smell, taste. I never thought I'd be lucky enough for it to actually *be you*."

She pressed a kiss to the heart on his upper thigh, her tongue tracing it. Every stroke felt like a benediction.

She nuzzled her face there, letting his cock fall against her cheek. "The hottest man I've ever met got his first tattoo—"

"My only one, Pearl. Just for you."

The last bit of doubt he'd had—all the bad past experiences from college and dating—melted away under Pearl's hungry gaze.

She was willing—eager, even—for him to be inside of her. He leaned them both back onto the bed.

He cupped her cheek, needing her to feel precious, treasured. His eyes burned into her so he didn't miss a moment.

"You are all the best parts of the universe combined," he whispered, kissing her reverently, "and I am the luckiest man in it right now."

Her arms wrapped around him hard, a fierce perfect pressure

grasping him. He brushed his lips against hers, not even blinking, as he slid his cock slowly, *so slowly*, into her.

In that moment, he knew.

He had always been meant for her.

This moment with her was *destined* to be.

"I'm yours, Pearl. All of me. Always was," he whispered raggedly as sensations flooded through him.

A single tear slipped slowly down her temple. He caught it with a kiss.

"Mine," she sighed, holding him tighter.

He slid further into the hot, wet heaven of her and felt like he was finally, *finally* home.

A wash of sensations rolled over him—pleasure, slaking need, adoration.

The beat of his heart had taken up a strange, three-beat rhythm.

I love you.

I love you.

I love you.

Again and again, it was screaming at him.

His hungry eyes scanned her face as he memorized this moment. The lusty need in her gaze, her teeth peeking out as she bit her dark bottom lip. The little moans as he pushed so slowly into her.

Every perfect thing in the world couldn't compare to this—being in her, with her, *for* her.

She clenched her muscles around him, and he gasped. His vision blurred as he threw his head on her shoulder. A wicked grin stretched her lips when he looked up.

A beast-like craving made his hips retreat and slide close again. A feral need overtook his muscles, enjoying giving in and taking what he wanted.

Sinking into the long-awaited heat was like every good thing at once—winning the lottery, a cool glass of water on a hot afternoon, crawling into bed after the longest day.

She clenched around him again and he rested on a forearm, one hand cupping her cheek, thumb swiping there as he gasped. "Don't know…how long," he muttered. "You feel…too good," he groaned as he slid out slowly and thrust his cock back in.

"Reed," she gasped, her hands pulling him against her, clawing at him. "More. *More.*"

A tense coil within him released, and his hips moved faster. Faster. Fucking her harder. The wet slap of it, the jangle of his belt, her moans—a perfect soundtrack to his lust.

He finally letting himself revel in her tits. He pulled her nipple into his mouth. It was big and he couldn't think too hard about it as he ran his tongue over it or he'd come.

He pressed his face in, knowing that this was what his heaven would be.

His climax tugged on his spine. Fuck, it was too good. *Can't keep doing this or I'll come.*

He pulled back, tugging her so he could stand at the edge of the bed. He'd read that changing positions could keep his stamina going. He wanted this to be so good for her.

She grabbed her huge tits, her thumbs playing with her nipples, and his knees almost buckled at the sight.

"You don't like sucking them?" she said, a teasing smile on her lips.

He huffed out a laugh as he lifted her leg against his chest. "Opposite," he groaned, roughly grasping one in a bruising grip. "Too good."

He slid his cock back in, hard. She was angled so he'd slide in deeper, and she gasped, clutching the bedsheets.

"I want to see all of you when I fuck you hard, gorgeous," he growled. "Dreamed of this for too long. *Years*, Pearl."

He slammed his hips into her as he rubbed her clit mercilessly with his thumb, strumming it hard.

"Fucking years I've thought about this," he gasped, fucking her harder and harder. "Those tits of yours, these hips." He grasped her flank and loved the juicy squeeze of it in his hands.

"This belly," he said, his hand leaving her clit and coming to the sizable pooch below her belly button ring. He grasped it hard, wanting to slake his hunger with it. "Fucking gorgeous. Something in me wants to claim it," he said, squeezing it.

She gasped, looking surprised. She bit back a smile as her eyes fought to stay open. "Yeah?"

He stopped, leaning over to pull her head up toward him, claiming her mouth. "Gorgeous"—he thrust hard and slow, still holding her head—"if I could fuck it, I would."

She moaned into his mouth as her pussy clenched hard around him. He laid her head on the bed, repositioned them and grasped her headboard hard for leverage to fuck her harder.

He strummed her clit faster, mercilessly digging in as he thrust his hips.

"Want your cum in me," she moaned, clawing at his back. "More. Come in me," she moaned again and again, arching her back so her tits bounced in the air.

"Say you're mine," he growled. A crack of wood ripped out in the room, and his grasp faltered as the headboard broke.

"Yours," she sobbed, throwing her head back as a climax ripped through her and her pussy sucked his cock down.

"Christ," he groaned.

The beast took over and he slammed his hips into hers, faster and faster, chasing the release that tugged at him until every atom flushed out of him into her, spurting as his lips found hers.

His hips slowed, savoring one—then two—last pumps as he emptied into her.

His forehead rested against hers as they panted. They were sweaty messes, and still, his tongue searched for a taste of her.

He licked up the salt of her with open- mouthed kisses, savoring the connection between them. She clenched her muscles around him again and he moaned.

"You're no longer a virgin," she murmured as he pulled back.

"But I am now ruined for anyone else." His hands pushed at her bangs, the hair clinging to her face, needing her to understand how much he loved her.

Because he was in head-over-heels, all-abiding, soul-crushing love with her.

Yes, she was his first.

But, by god…

…she's going to be my last.

"Is there a bathroom?"

"Could you tell me where the romance section is?"

"I'm ready to check out."

Questions flew around Reed and he couldn't have been happier.

The grand opening of Bookish was officially a success.

The store was teeming with customers for their official opening. Bloom had posted on their social accounts, which had a crazy large following.

Happy faces walked through the bookstore. People browsed on the second floor, wandering through the shelves. Families of all shapes and sizes came through. Couples, older people—everyone looked excited. The Bookish mugs were almost gone from the side swag table.

He was proud of what he had to offer, but he noticed a single sour-looking face in a big, overstuffed, comfy chair in the middle of it all.

Beulah sat holding her large gray purse on her lap, her face missing its usual scowl.

Instead, she just looked sad.

Her gaze traveled the space around and above them, up to the rafters, like she'd lost something.

Why did she even care?

Yes, they lived next door. Yes, she hated Pearl, but what was her attachment to all of this?

"Do you have a second, Reed?" Rose said with a warm smile. "I wanted to make sure you'd met Pop and Mrs. Maroo-Canon."

A balding, elderly, bowlegged man waddled over with a hitch in his step and shook his hand with a surprisingly firm grip.

"They were good friends of my—our dad," Rose said, correcting herself.

"Now, I'm not one to gossip," the older woman said. The bright orange rhinestones of her glasses sparkled, matching her flowing summer dress. She clutched his other hand in her two tiny, cold ones. "But I heard through the grapevine you are *officially* a Parker, which means you are basically family to us, which is why I told every single person in my phone to come to your opening today."

Reed blinked, trying to process this information.

"You sure do look like Frank," Pop said, patting him on the shoulder.

"That's, uh, what they tell me," Reed said, adjusting his glasses. He waved at Maria from the Historical Society Committee as she wandered in with her family.

He felt like he'd been dropped into a whole new premade family and community.

"Thank you for your help," Reed said with a bright smile to Mrs. Maroo-Canon.

"We should let you get back. You have customers," Rose said, shooing him. "Do you need any help?"

"No, I'm good." He started to wave her away, but on impulse, he wrapped her in a crushing hug. "Thank you," he whispered. "For everything."

For making sure he became a Parker.

For supporting him even though she barely knew him.

She pulled back, a little misty-eyed.

"Sorry, I know you're not a hugger," he said with a guilty smile.

"Eh, I've gotten used to it with the other two," she said, wiping what looked like a tear from her eye. "Let's go on that run soon, okay?"

"You got it."

But you still haven't told your parents, a guilty voice nagged at him. *You've been ignoring them. You're a bad son. They're gonna hate this. They're gonna hate that you've gone out on a ledge again, and you've ruined your family legacy forever.*

"Shut up," he muttered to himself as he turned back, walking toward the back room.

"We need more tote bags!" Pearl called from the register.

"On it." He jogged to the back. He rummaged through boxes until he found extras.

Pearl walked in. "We're almost out of t-shirts, too," she said, looking through the boxes for more stock. He darted a glance out into the bookstore.

He closed the door, and as she stood up with a handful of t-shirts, he pressed her against the shelf with a hot, hard kiss. She kissed him back instantly, pulling at his shirt, her teeth raking against his lip.

"Whoa," she said, pulling away. "What was that for?"

"Because you look so goddamn hot today, and"—he grabbed another quick kiss from her—"you're doing a great job."

She rolled her eyes, wiping at her lipstick on his mouth. She'd let it slip that she had a praise kink and he'd used it mercilessly.

He kissed her neck. "You're so good at customer book recs. I couldn't have done this without you."

She laughed, shuddering as he nibbled her ear.

He whispered through clenched teeth, "And your ideas have already made a huge impact."

"Oh my god, stop"—she ducked under his arms—"or I'm gonna lock the door and ride you right here."

He chuckled as he pulled the door open for her. He kissed her cheek as she walked by. "And I bet you'd be amazing at that too."

"Evil," she muttered with affection as she kissed him quickly back, running away into the store.

This had been the best week of his whole life. *My dream come true, and the gorgeous woman I love in it.* He'd tell her soon, even though it might weird her out.

She has to know, he thought, seeing her pretty, wide smile as she talked with Margie in the romance section. *She needs to know how hopelessly in love with her I am.*

Chapter Twenty-eight

PEARL

HEMINGWAYCANSUCKIT

Hey.

I miss you.

Pearl's cheeks hurt from smiling too much the last few days.

Not to mention other parts of me are sore, too, she thought, rubbing her thighs together.

That man was an all-American, all-natural, no fillers, no preservatives, grade-A horndog now. They'd fucked constantly since the festival. She'd delighted in seeing his joy and pleasure at each new position they tried.

She'd woken up every morning with his body wrapped around hers or his face between her legs.

He made her feel cared for, precious, and somehow at the same time like a slutty little fuck toy.

He really was the perfect man.

IMPOSSIBLYBOOKISH

you saw me one hour ago

HEMINGWAYCANSUCKIT

And you were naked.

10/10 way to start the morning.

I have something to show you when you get
back to the store.

A surprise.

IMPOSSIBLYBOOKISH

is it your penis?

please say yes.

Her thighs clenched, remembering how hard he'd fucked her in the storage closet after their grand opening.

"I'm still bummed you canceled our bestie road trip," Allison said, shutting the Bloom van doors. "I need a break."

Pearl had been a teeny bit offended no one had even bothered to act surprised when it came out that she and Reed were a thing. The general consensus among the Bloom employees had been "Oh, yeah, that tracks," and then they all just moved on to the next topic of conversation.

"How'd your trip to the jizz bank go?" Pearl said.

"Ew," Allison said, laughing as she shuddered.

"The spank bank? The spunk bunk? The *meat juice* factory?"

"*Argh.*" Allison covered her ears, a disgusted look on her face as she laughed. "Too far."

Pearl laughed. It was like a cloud had lifted from her over the last week.

"No, that place was a bust," Allison said, still shuddering after Pearl's last phrase. "They seemed kind of sketchy, so I'm gonna keep looking around." Allison handed her the receipts. "Here are the addresses you're driving to."

Pearl tossed on her sunglasses. "Let me know if you want to

go search for some free-range meat juice the old-fashioned way this weekend."

"Barf," Allison said, laughing as she walked back inside Bloom.

Pearl input the delivery addresses on her phone's GPS. She was going to deliver flowers to the hair salon next door to her dream bakery.

IMPOSSIBLYBOOKISH

i'm driving past the bakery today.

HEMINGWAYCANSUCKIT

You should talk to them again. See if they'll
lower the price.

Bet on yourself.

IMPOSSIBLYBOOKISH

but that'll be years from now.

HEMINGWAYCANSUCKIT

Or maybe not!

I believe in you.

There's no one I'd rather bet on than Pearl
"ImpossiblyBookish" Bishop.

IMPOSSIBLYBOOKISH

my cheeks fucking HURT

stop being so ADORABLE

She smushed her cheeks together to stop smiling and thunked her head on the headrest.

Was it normal to want to barf from joy when she thought about him?

And couldn't *stop* thinking about him?

I'm obsessed.

And I can't wait to see him when I'm done with these deliveries.

309

She'd spent every waking moment with him for the past six weeks for chrissakes, and she wanted more.

She gasped, sitting up.

Oooooh fuck.

Oooooh no.

She thunked her head back on the steering wheel repeatedly, moaning.

"Fucking shit. I think I'm in love with him."

PEARL PSYCHED herself up to talk to the owner of the bakery building as she stood outside of it holding the flower delivery. Courtney Forrest, Aaron's older sister, owned both buildings.

You can do this. Maybe you'll be extra lucky because it's your birthday.

No one other than Luca knew when her birthday was. She'd had too many traumatizing years expecting something special as a kid and instead receiving "Were you expecting cake or some shit?" from her mom. So, she'd learned to treat it like any other day. Take it all in stride.

But maybe today she could hope for just a little bit of birthday magic.

Pearl brought in the bouquets to Tress, the only salon in Fairwick Falls. She waved down a hairdresser. "Is Courtney here?"

"She's next door," the hairstylist said, gesturing with scissors. "Showing somebody the space."

Pearl walked next door with her stomach in knots. *Fuck it, I can fight.*

She peered into the dusty window of the vacant bakery and saw Courtney's bright purple and turquoise locs. She was talking to somebody as they walked toward the front door, and when Pearl saw who it was, her stomach dropped.

A human toad stared at her smugly as she opened the door.

"What the fuck?" Pearl yelled. "Why?"

"I thought about getting into baking," Beulah said flatly.

"Bullshit," Pearl spat.

Courtney's eyes went wide. She was tall and thin, like Aaron, and as sweet as could be.

"Sorry, Courtney. Hi," Pearl added as an afterthought.

Beulah smiled up at her. She had one of her stupid suits on with a big floppy bow at the neck. "You mentioned this was a great spot, and I thought I'd check it out. I've always wanted an investment property. Something I can hold onto until I *die*," Beulah said with a malicious gleam in her eye.

Hopefully soon.

Pearl's fists clenched, her nails digging into her hands. "Why do you insist on ruining my life?"

"Don't be so self-centered," Beulah said, pushing past her. "They want to sell and I might buy." She slid into her gray, boat-sized car and slammed the door

"That woman is the devil incarnate," Pearl said to Courtney, glaring at Beulah. "And not like a cool devil, like this one." She pointed to her inner arm. "Like if a paper cut was a human."

Courtney locked the door and grimaced at Pearl. "I know you love this space. We thought it would be a good opportunity to offload the bakery since no one seems interested or…able"—she winced—"to rent from us."

Beulah rolled down the car window as she drove away. "I'm gonna fill it with concrete gnomes!"

Pearl pointed to the car, as if proving her point.

Courtney grimaced. "Very much like a paper cut."

The gray town car floated down the road and Pearl imagined it taking flight, ending-of-*Grease* style, and just never seeing Beulah again.

"Look," Courtney said with care. "I love your vision for what you want to do. And I'd love to rent it to you, but I have to at least bring her offer to my business partner. Unless you could rent it in the next few weeks?"

Pearl sighed. "No. Don't wait on me." She'd never want to put Courtney in an uncomfortable situation. "It'll be a lot longer than that."

Maybe years.

Maybe never.

Pearl waved goodbye and trudged to finish the rest of her deliveries, trying not to cry over her already lost dream.

AN HOUR LATER, Pearl pushed open the door to Bookish just as Reed flipped off the lights.

It was the day before Fourth of July, and Reed had already planned on closing the bookstore early for the long weekend, so they had a few blissful days to just sleep and rest.

And fuck.

She felt fucking *giddy* looking at him. Whatever was shifting between them was shifting fast.

He bent down for a long, slow kiss. The sweetness of it radiated through her.

Normally, she'd be seething with rage at a run-in with Beulah, but something about this whole situation just made her feel defeated. She'd kept the hurt to herself.

"Hey." He pulled back, his eyes searching hers. "What's wrong?"

She leaned into his hand and shook her head, afraid she'd burst into tears.

She didn't cry, as a rule, and she definitely didn't cry in front of other people.

"Pearl, sweetheart. Let's talk about it," he said, bending down so he was eye level in front of her.

"Stop being so nice," she said as she stepped away.

He grabbed her hand, stopping her. "Is everything okay? Luca? AB?"

She loved him for that.

Christ, you fucking love *him, you dweeb.*

"No, they're fine," she said, turning away so he couldn't see her wipe away a tear.

His fingers stroked the back of her arm gently, his touch supportive as she stared off into the bookshop and tried not to cry.

"I'm not afraid of emotions. Not even yours. You feel things deeply; that is a gift. The world needs your rage."

She huffed out a laugh at the ridiculous sentiment. "No, it doesn't."

"It's made me f—" He cleared his throat. "Uh, it's made Fairwick Falls a better place. So you can rage or cry or, I don't know, do cartwheels. Whatever. I'll be right here to support you."

"I, um..." Her voice wobbled as she looked anywhere but at him. "I went to talk to the bakery owner." Her voice cracked. "Somebody else might buy the building. Fucking Beulah."

Reed wiped a hand down his face in shared frustration. "I don't know what that woman's problem is with you."

"It's just..." Her voice was cracking and wobbling now as a stupid fucking tear escaped, and she shoved at it with her hand. "It's like the universe or whatever wants me to know that I'm never good enough. I'm too stupid. I'm impulsive. I get close to what I want and it yanks it away."

Ugly, snotty tears fell as she lost control and cried.

Reed swiped away tear after tear.

"I just want more from this life than existing, and I don't like having hope that things could be better. I've never been good at anything in my whole life," she sobbed, barely able to get the words out. "Now I finally found it...and...and a big toad takes it away from me."

Reed slid his hand around the back of her neck and pulled her into him, and she sobbed into his chest, overwhelmed.

Tired.

She was so tired of trying and failing of making something of herself.

Of trying to be someone worth loving.

She clutched his shirt, glad he was wearing a black compression shirt since her mascara was all over it now.

This would be so embarrassing if it didn't feel so good.

He held her tight, his hand on her head, stroking her hair as she let it all out.

They stayed that way until his shirt was soaked, him ever patient with her.

The unending hopelessness lifted a little as her tears ran out of steam.

"Well, now I'm mortified," she said with a sniffle into his chest.

He traced her hairline with light kisses, placing each one longer and firmer as he made his way down to her cheek, kissing away a few tears.

"Ugh, don't look at me," she said, putting her hand up over her eyes.

He grabbed her hand, kissing it. "You are more beautiful than ever."

She laughed at the ridiculousness of it. "That's a weird kink, man," she said, sniffling. "I'm a mess."

Reed grabbed a tissue from the counter and handed it to her. She blew her nose.

"Yeah," he said, hand gently holding her head. "But you're my mess."

He took another tissue and wiped off the river of mascara on her cheeks. "Thank you for trusting me with it." he said with a quick kiss on her lips.

He wrapped his arms around her and pulled her close. "You have every right to feel frustrated. I'm frustrated for you."

She sighed, getting gooey again. He wasn't one of those "Stop crying" guys like she'd had so many times in her life.

He rested his head on top of hers, and she loved the feeling of it. "We are gonna have an amazing weekend full of food and very loud sex. And for two days, we're not gonna think about how much Beulah needs to take a short trip down a long flight of stairs."

Pearl laughed.

"Because you are amazing," he said, shaking her until she looked up at him. "You're the hardest-working person I know. You're tough. You're loyal. You're smart."

She scoffed. "Lies."

"I mean, I *guess* I did order and organize all the books in the bookstore by myself..."

"*What*," she said, playfully pushing his shoulder.

His smile was instant. Shit, she'd fallen into his trap.

He kissed her temple. "Of course I didn't. *You* did. Organized the 'whole fucking bookstore,' as you like to remind me."

She smiled.

He adjusted his glasses. "And as for whether you're lovable, well..."

Their gazes locked. She stopped breathing.

Reed tugged Pearl toward the back staircase. "I want to show you something. Bert finally finished all the apartment fixes."

Oh. Right. Of course. What, did you think he fucking loved you or something, idiot? They'd only been together for barely two weeks. That would be ridiculous.

They walked to the apartment that overlooked the store. Reed unlocked the door.

Pearl sniffled. "Maybe you can order a bed next. AB and Luca will be back any day now and I won't be able to scream your…"

Her voice fell as she looked at the scene in front of her.

A single candle sat on a chocolate birthday cake that was covered in sprinkles, accompanied by three wrapped presents and a vase of cream flowers.

"Happy birthday," he said, placing a slow kiss on her cheek.

Her mouth dropped open in outrage. "That motherf—"

"Don't blame Luca," Reed said, placating her and fighting a smile. "I bribed him. Said I'd build an *amazing* treehouse for AB this fall in exchange for the date of your birthday. Joke's on him, though; I would've done it anyway."

His eyes were hopeful but a little nervous. "I thought about doing a surprise party but then I thought how much you would absolutely hate that, and I really enjoy you not hating me. You deserve every special thing today, and I'm sorry you had a bad day instead."

She melted against his chest, cheeks burning in embarrassment. "This is so *nice.*"

"Luca said birthdays were hard as a kid—"

"Castration. That's the only logical punishment for him—"

He tugged her ponytail back and captured her lips, laughing. She smiled against him, licking into his mouth.

"Come on," he murmured against her lips, but she moaned in protest, keeping him right where she wanted him.

"Preeeeesents," he taunted.

"Oh, right," she said, bounding over to the pile next to the cake. The flowers turned out to be old book pages twisted into blooms.

Her *favorite* kind of flower.

Reed handed her the first present. It was big and heavy.

"I know you got frustrating news today, but this can go anywhere. Whatever your journey is, it can follow you there, okay?"

"Okay," she said, utterly confused. They were going on a journey?

She pulled at the pretty wrapping paper, and her jaw dropped.

It was a sign with the name "Blackbird Bakery" hand-carved in a Gothic font. It was square with a rounded bump in the middle, like a sign someone would hang in a store window or on a front door.

"I hope it's okay. We can get another one if you don't like it. I know you might have feelings about the font," he said, worrying his lip as he looked at it.

"It's perfect," she said with a shocked laugh.

"It could go wherever. Maybe at your next booth or the front door of your bakery someday."

She traced the letters with her fingers, still surprised to see her crazy idea brought to life.

"I just wanted you to know that I really believe in you, and wherever it is, it's already real."

"Thank you. I…" She shook her head, unable to think of what to say, setting it down on the counter.

"C'mon, next present." He scooted the next package toward her with an excited wiggle.

"Pushy," she reprimanded. "I like it. I wonder what it could be… A sex toy?" she said, shaking the package even though it was so obviously a book.

"You're hilarious," Reed said.

"You love it." She popped onto her tiptoes and kissed his nose.

He smiled at her indulgently. "I really fucking do."

She ripped off the paper with glee but stopped in confusion. "Anne of Avonlea?"

Maybe he didn't know she already had a well-worn copy?

"Open it," he said, nodding to the book.

She flipped through the pages and saw his neat handwriting in the margins. Sentences were highlighted, notes and reactions scattered throughout the pages. She gasped and clutched it to her chest. "Buddy-read notes?"

"Sorry if it's silly—"

"No, I love it." She ran her hands over it, caressing it. "I like it when books have some wear on them. I like seeing what other people thought. There's charm to it," she said, gently setting it on top of her sign.

He held the final present in his hands, looking reluctant. "I put this together for Bookish for our weekend, and, well, it's the weekend and you're Bookish." He shrugged, holding what looked like a book and not looking her in the eye. "I, um... I'm deeply embarrassed to give this to you."

"Ooh," she said, making grabby hands at it. "Is it—"

"Nope, it's not dirty. It's worse," he said, pulling her close to him by the belt loop of her shorts. "It's genuine," he said with an apologetic look, "and gooey."

"Mm," she groaned with a pained smile, loving it. "*And gooey?*"

"Very."

He handed it to her and wrapped his arms around her from behind, squeezing her to him. She could feel the fast beat of his heart against her back.

She ripped the paper off. It was a simple, black notebook.

The first page, in his handwriting, said "Bookish Quotes." She peered over her shoulder at him, and he grimaced.

"Sorry, this is gonna be nerdy."

She leaned back and kissed him quickly. "You know I love a nerd."

She flipped to the next page. A Douglas Adams quote they'd talked about a long time ago was written by hand on the page. Beside it was a note.

I knew you were special when you likened The Hitchhiker's Guide to the Galaxy *to a very long Monty Python and Star Wars love child.*

Next to it was a quote from *The Princess Bride*, the novel, their first buddy read, because she had woefully never read it.

When you admitted you didn't get the whole love-for-Buttercup thing, it was then I knew I had feelings for you. Specifically, "Why is this dude falling all over himself for some blonde? If she won't have you at your poorest, she doesn't deserve you at your richest, bruh." You fight for what's right, even if it besmirches the name of a worldwide, beloved romantic heroine. Damn the consequences, do what's right. That's who I wanted.

Page after page was filled with handwritten quotes from their favorite books and notes about how special she was to him.

"I started it, I don't know, a few months ago."

She rubbed at a spot between her breasts, feeling an ache there.

Months?

"It felt like we'd lived our...whatever we were, in books," he said with a shy smile, adjusting his glasses.

Agatha Christie, Dr. Seuss, a Dan Brown quote (because they weren't snobs)—each cherry-picked as she remembered them talking about the books and what they loved about them. Several *Anne of Avonlea* quotes, specifically ones from Gilbert to Anne, were included.

She was overwhelmed. Nobody had ever done anything like this for her. She flipped to the last page.

"I don't recognize this one," she said, staring at it. It was formatted like a poem.

"I, um… It's, oh god." he said, rubbing a hand across his eyes under his glasses, not looking at her. "I wrote it."

"For me?"

He bit his lip. "Yes." He looked mortified. "You know what? It's fine, you can forget it. Never mind."

He grabbed for the notebook.

"No," she whined playfully, holding it close to her chest. "I want my poem."

"Pearl, it's really bad."

"I don't care. It's mine," she said, twisting away so he couldn't grab it. "Plus, it could be *dirty*."

He smiled wistfully, leaning against the countertop, the tops of his ears turning pink. "I'm sorry to say there's not even one Nantucket in it."

His eyes held uncertainty, and hope.

"Well, we can always add it in later." She smoothed out the page, giving it her full attention.

> ### *My Purpose*
> *After years of wandering*
> *endlessly in the pitch, my way lit by starlight*
> *I've found my calling*
> *in your bright heart,*
> *tending its burning flames.*
> *Your smiles are my most treasured spoils,*
> *your tears, my greatest enemy.*
> *I will toil, recklessly, happily, loving you*
> *until the stars burn out one by one.*
> *For I do not need them.*
> *Your fiery heart will always*
> *be enough*

Her hungry eyes read it again and again.

I will toil, recklessly, happily, loving you

recklessly, happily, loving you

happily, loving you

loving you loving you loving you

"Pearl." Reed's voice was ragged. "Please say something. I'm sorry if it's corny. Or if it's too much."

She shook her head slowly as she ran her finger over the paper, feeling the indentations of his pen against the paper.

The bumps and patterns of someone who loved her enough to inspire creation.

He *loved* her?

She wasn't sure if she was ready to say it back. She had to be absolutely sure.

It felt too big. Too scary.

Too not-for-her. Like an invite to a black-tie event when she'd only ever worn jeans.

"You...love me?" she said finally, looking up at him.

A tortured smile framed his face. He reached a hand out, running his hand up through her hair as he held her head, his thumb swiping her cheek.

"I have been in love with you, Pearl Bishop, since you dared me to kiss you during a summer rainstorm."

Chapter Twenty-nine

PEARL

Pearl was having an out-of-body experience.

Reed—her best friend, her hate-to-love crush, the boy who had captured her first kiss—loved her.

She didn't know what to do with this information.

This is what happens to other people; this isn't what happens to me.

"You don't have to say it back," he said quickly as she just stared at him in panic. "I fell in love with Bookish—with you. I was going to tell her, uh, you...in Eerie. I'm sorry, I couldn't wait anymore. Everyone deserves to know when they're loved, and...I love you. If you never want me to say it again, that's fine. I understand."

"Keep saying it," she said quickly, the words escaping her mouth without her consent.

Damn brain.

"Yeah?" He looked shy.

She nodded like a woman possessed.

He kissed her. His lips were soft and loving. "I love your loyalty. I love how you take care of everyone around you without them even knowing it, because you care so deeply."

Those glittery feelings were back, dancing along her spine. *He noticed.*

He kissed a spot on her jaw that always made her sigh. "I love that your backbone is as strong as that godawful tea you drink every morning." She chuckled. "And you don't take any shit. I love that you're feisty and sassy, and you have a gooey caramel center underneath." He cradled her head in his hands. "I love that you protected me when I couldn't protect myself when I was younger. And I remember thinking in those moments—when you'd call off the guys who wanted to shove me in a locker, or in the janitor's closet, or in the auditorium attic—"

"Don't forget the girls' locker room," she said with a smirk.

He chuckled. "I loved you in those moments, because you stood up for somebody who could do nothing for you. Your heart is made of valor and loyalty and strength. And though its color is black," he said with a bright smile, "it is pure."

Tell him, she thought as her mouth crashed to his, overwhelmed at his words.

But I can't. Too scary. Like being on the top of a high dive but afraid to jump, just standing there shivering.

But I want to. She pushed him toward the couch in the living room.

She pulled his shirt off and buried her face in the center of his chest, licking, kissing.

What if I change my mind? What if I get his hopes up? I can't be counted on to not fuck something up.

But you loooove him, taunted her heart.

Shut up, shut up, he's doing that thing with his hands.

"You seem...distracted," Reed said as he kissed down to her collarbone. He undid the button of her shorts but lingered there.

She shook her head to clear it. "I'm back, sorry. Sex away, Hemingway."

He sat on the couch and adjusted his glasses as he looked up at her with a boyish smile. "I like it when you're bossy, Bookish."

Uuuungh, I love him.

He tugged the zipper on her shorts down and pushed them to the ground. He kissed the tops of her thighs and turned her hips, placing a kiss right on her ass tattoo.

"But I like it better"—he pulled her hips toward him until she straddled him on the couch—"when you're right here." He bit her shoulder, and she ground her clit over his cock.

His hands pulled at her back as she straddled him, crushing her to him in a hot kiss.

Yes.

He tossed off her shirt as she pulled his cock out, greedy for it.

She slid down onto him, feeling so full.

He buried his face in her tits, inhaling like she was his last breath on earth. She pulled his head in, crushing her cheek against his hair.

I never knew it was possible to feel cherished while being motorboated.

Love is fucking wild.

A catch in her throat burned as she tried to swallow. He *loved* her.

Back.

He loves me back.

Just don't say it. Don't get dick drunk and let your mouth run wild.

She sighed. *But the dick is so* good.

She slid up and down lazily on his cock, and he pulled away to look at her. She ran a thumb over his cheek, wanting to tell him how much she cared without saying the words.

Kisses anchored her palm to his mouth, and he kissed each finger, brushing his face against her hand.

"Tell me something," he murmured as he stared up at her riding him.

Yeah, tell him something, her stupid fucking heart shouted from the cheap seats in her brain.

She kissed his temple, bit his ear playfully. "Like what?" she whispered, trying to keep herself in check.

He grabbed her ass, revved up, and pushed her down on his cock harder. "Anything. I love everything about your brain." He moaned the word, like her brain was the sexiest thing about her.

"I love you," burst out of her.

They froze, but she felt his cock pulse inside her.

"Wait! No," she yelled, trying to pull the words back in.

Shiiiit fuck. You're on my shit list, heart. She could hear it cackling as it threw popcorn around, enjoying the chaos.

His eyebrows drew together as he tried to understand. "No? You just got caught up in the moment? Didn't mean it?"

"Right," she said, panicked. *Shit, I've just royally fucked it all up.*

He ran his hands down her back, looking concerned. "Okay. What's important is that you know I love you." Cool as a mother-fucking cucumber.

No judgement, no pushing away. Just gentle kisses on her cheeks, her forehead.

The last gentle kiss on her nose was what broke her.

She needed him. Needed this 6'2, glasses-wearing, mushy-tattoo-having salve against the world. She kissed him with lust and love, claiming his mouth. Wanting him to be hers.

"I love you," she whispered through trembling lips. Couldn't look at him. Couldn't handle stepping off the high dive *and* watching at the same time.

He paused, head cocked and thoroughly confused. "You don't…mean it, though?"

"I love you," she said and finally looked up as she fell through the air, waiting for the splash to hit. The shocking cold reality.

Wonder danced across his face as he registered her words. "You love me?"

Still falling, stomach still swooping.

"It's fucking terrifying," she whispered. She felt too skittish to say it all at full volume.

His chest heaved up and down as he nodded. He understood how scary this was for her.

Because of course he does.

That's why I love him.

"It is scary. But I'm right here." He pressed her hand to his heart. "I'm right here with you."

She breathed with him, still falling but getting used to the feeling. She needed his ruddy, perfect lips on her or the universe would simply cease to exist. "I love you," she murmured into his mouth as he crushed her to him.

"I know, B." He whispered back between kisses on her cheek and throat, "I love you, too."

She rode him harder, needing to show him just how much she loved him. "I love you," she said, again and again. Lost count of the number of times as she stroked every part of his body—his shoulder, bicep, Adam's apple, chest.

He pushed her hips down harder as she ground against him, again and again. Riding him faster. He sucked a nipple into his mouth and she chased that glittery shower of joy and acceptance.

He loves me.

He slammed her hips down, grinding against him as he stroked her clit in just the perfect rhythm.

"I love you," she yelled into his shoulder as she came, finally splashing into the cool, glittery waters.

He thrust again and again until he groaned, squeezing her tits and cradling her against him hard, like she was precious.

"*Fuck*, my love," he gasped, squeezing her tighter.

His *love*.

Warmth radiated through her as she let herself revel in the cedar and peppermint surrounding her.

She nuzzled in, wanting to rub her face into his neck for the next three to five business days.

His mouth lingered on her neck and shoulder as they caught their breath.

"I think," she panted, tracing his nose with hers, "I'll like birthdays from now on."

REED

REED STOOD behind the checkout counter, watching his first bookstore event with glee. He'd invited a local children's book author who raised puppies before they went to therapy-dog school. She stood on the stage surrounded by fifteen kids as she read her book aloud.

The star of the show, however, was a large golden retriever named Bailey who sat beside her. Bailey did all the right commands as the author/trainer read them from the book.

The trainer's book featured a brave little puppy going to puppy school for the first time and was a great parallel story for young kids going to kindergarten.

Parents stood around, all smiling at the adorable, gangly teenage dog with the working vest on. Traffic had picked up for that Saturday, and he checked customers out happily as the story corner continued in the background.

This is working.

His phone lit up with a call from his mom, and he saw he'd had three missed calls from her already.

He flagged down Pearl. "Can you take over?" he said, nodding at the register.

"Hey, Mom," he said, answering her call as he walked to the back.

"You're alive."

"I'm sorry," he said guiltily. It had been over a month since they'd talked.

"We were getting worried when you didn't answer your doorbell."

Reed stopped in his tracks. "What do you mean?"

"We've pushed the button to be buzzed up to your apartment. We're in Philly, surprising you." His dad murmured to his mom. "Yes, your father wants you to know we brought you the cookies you like."

The kids in the story hour laughed at something the trainer said. He gulped. His heart was thundering.

"Are you not at home?" his mom said. "Where are you?"

He jogged to the back of the store, closing the door to the stockroom. "I'm, um, not in Philly. I'm visiting Luca again," Reed said, panicking.

"Will you be back Sunday evening?" his mom asked. "We can extend our trip and take you out to dinner. Your dad would love to show you some pictures that he took on our stave church architectural tour in Norway."

"I'm gonna be here for a week. Luca needed help and I took off from work."

"Oh," his mother said with surprise. "Well, that was very nice."

"Look, I'm sorry you came all this way."

Tell them, he thought. *Tell them you're finally happy for the first time, maybe ever.*

Tell them you're in love.

Tell them your crazy idea just happened to work out.

"Your dad wants to talk to you."

"Now, Reed," his dad said in a serious voice. "Is it a good idea to take off a whole week when you're in the middle of that big project?"

"The project's going well, actually. I, um—"

"You know," his dad interrupted, "When I was your age, my boss gave me my career-defining moment after I showed how hard I pushed myself on a project."

The Punxsutawney Bridge, he thought, knowing where this was going.

"The Punxsutawney Bridge," his dad said, reliving his highlights.

He felt that nagging need to be perfect for his dad. "That's a good point, Dad," Reed said, wanting to be agreeable. "I'll see when I can wrap things up with Luca."

He was digging a deeper hole for himself. He just needed time to talk to them in person and explain it all.

Maybe over Christmas.

"All right, good to hear it," his dad said. "Here's your mom."

Reed sighed. He heard another round of clapping in the store as story hour finished up. "Hey, Mom, I gotta go." All the story hour families would hopefully line up to purchase some books. "Sorry again. I'll let you know when I'm back in Philly, and maybe we can do something then."

He jogged back out into the store that his parents still knew nothing about.

To make up for all the other parts of me.

Chapter Thirty

REED

"So they still don't know?" Pearl said, lounging on him on the couch.

They'd both collapsed when they got home. He was still staying at Pearl's since his stuff hadn't been delivered yet. Their legs were tangled together, and Reed loved the feeling of it.

Craved it.

He knew he should be racked with guilt, but he just couldn't seem to be bothered as he tucked Pearl's head under his chin and tugged her closer.

She was lying on him, and the pressure was heaven, releasing his anxiety.

His hands traced over the soft, bubble curve of her ass and up her back. This would never get old.

"No," he sighed. "They have high expectations. My grandpa founded his own firm, my dad expanded it, and it was acquired by a large corporation. I think they were hoping that I'd become even bigger. I was given every introduction to the right internships"—he ran his fingers through her silky hair to calm himself—"the best education, but all I ever really wanted was to make them happy. I just happened to be good at math and drawing."

She pushed up to look at him in surprise. "You architected your whole life to make *other* people happy?"

"I'm not as brave as you." His thumb stroked her cheek, and she kissed his palm.

"It's not brave to be allergic to responsibility like me."

"It's brave to do what you want, even if it doesn't make other people happy."

She settled back onto his chest. "My parents couldn't be bothered to care. You know that."

Pearl's dad had pretty much disappeared in middle school, and Reed could count on one hand the number of times he'd seen her mom.

"I just put them through a lot," he said, remembering the endless meltdowns every night at dinner. Him not knowing how to articulate that he was overwhelmed by crowds when they would go to expensive amusement parks. He'd been told countless times he was a difficult but smart child, even though he tried his best to not be difficult at all. "I just don't want to let them down."

"Reed." She pushed herself up again. "You built an amazing bookstore. There are, like, people in it," she said with a wave of her hand. "Practically an army of rugrats today. And if your parents aren't as proud of you as I am," she said, straightening her arms, giving him a tantalizing view of her cleavage in front of his face. She leaned over him, her pretty face above his. "Then I will happily fight them. I've never lost an arm wrestle, and I'm not afraid to bite," she said, planting a sweet kiss on his nose.

"Oh, I remember," he said, suddenly grabbing her by the waist.

He pulled her to him, tickling her sides as they rolled off the couch, laughing. He landed on top of her, his thigh between her legs, arms wrapped around her.

He kissed her solidly, wanting to chase away all his anxiety and worries with a taste of her. She hooked her leg around his, twining them together even harder, and his tongue danced with hers as he deepened the kiss. His hands slid up into her shirt, wanting to feel her skin.

He wrapped his hand on the softness under her breast and squeezed. She moaned, and as he angled his head to kiss her deeper, the front door swung open.

"AP, AP, AP! We're back!" They ripped their heads away from each other, and a shocked Luca stood in the doorway staring at them.

Reed pushed off of Pearl as AB ran across the living room and launched herself into Pearl's arms.

Reed sat with his back against the couch, his arms up around his knees to hide his hard cock. Luca just stared at both of them silently, holding seven bags.

"We were gonna stop," AB said, hanging on Pearl, "but we missed you so much."

"Oh, nugget," Pearl said, wrapping her arms around AB and squeezing her tight. "I missed you too."

"I miss my room," AB said, pulling Pearl along. "And you have to come so I can show you your present."

Luca's eyes silently followed his sister as AB pulled her upstairs.

Reed ran a hand down his face. He'd sort of forgotten to tell Luca what had happened the last three weeks.

Okay, he'd avoided it.

"Uh...the fuck...?" Luca said in utter confusion as he tossed the bags, backpacks, and shopping bags on the ground.

Reed finally looked him in the eyes. "You mad?"

"Mad?" Luca said with surprise. "No, I thought I was delirious after ten hours of driving." He wiped a hand over his tired eyes. "Help me with the bags and clue me in?"

"I will," Reed said, blowing out a breath. "I just need a

minute." *Think about taxes, endangered wildlife. Anything to get this motherfucker flaccid again.*

"Why?" Luca said.

Reed leveled a gaze at him. "I can't stand up right now."

"*Euch*," Luca groaned with disgust. "That's my sister, man." He pushed open the screen door, going back outside.

Sufficiently deflated, Reed threw on shoes and went to help Luca with the bags.

Fuck, fuck, fuck. He'd been hiding a lot from a lot of people. Luca and AB weren't supposed to be back for another three days.

"How was the trip?" Reed asked.

Luca tossed him bags from the backseat. "Amazing. Exhausting. Life-changing."

"Good, I'm glad you guys had a good time," Reed said, trying to make things less awkward.

Luca gathered the rest of the bags and turned around on the walkway back up to the house. "So, you and Pearl...?"

Reed's ears turned pink. He was glad for the darkness outside. "Um." He hefted the bags in his arms. "Yeah. For a little while."

Luca scowled. "What about that girl that you were texting? You dating both?"

"Oh, god no. That sort of...resolved itself. You're not mad?"

"No, you're a great guy." Luca shrugged as if it was the dumbest question. "Why would I be lifelong friends with somebody I wouldn't want my sister to date? That'd be fucked up, man."

Luca's face twisted through a series of expressions as he thought. "I'm pretty happy about it, to be honest," he said with a laugh. "She's done a lot worse. Is it serious?"

His best friend wouldn't judge him; he never had.

A shit-eating, I-just-won-the-lottery smile broke Reed's face in two. "I'm in love with her."

"Fuck," Luca whispered as he walked back to the front door. "Pearl takes no prisoners and no shit either. If she's with you, it's because she's all in. I can sleep on the couch tonight and we'll wash my sheets in the morning."

"Oh, no need." Reed put the bags down in the front room, scratched his head with embarrassment. "I've been sleeping in Pearl's room, and there are fresh sheets on your bed. We didn't want to, you know, get...uh...everything...on yours."

Luca shuddered. "I'm not mad, but it's still weird. That's my *sister*, man."

REED HAULED the last heavy box from his car through the door of Bookish as Pearl held the door open for him.

It was Monday, so they were taking advantage of the closed store and moving him into his apartment.

He'd hate not being at home with Pearl, but four people in a single bathroom was a bad idea.

Now that he'd have his own space, they could resume their X-rated activities.

Pearl stood talking to Violet as she held the door. "And then AB asked if she could *also* have a sleepover in my room with me and Uncle Reed," Pearl said, her hand smacking her face in embarrassment. "So we decided, no more sleepovers in the house."

"Oh, no." Violet laughed with her hand over her mouth. "I should be grateful baby Frank can't ask any uncomfortable questions yet."

Reed's ears tinged pink, happy he wouldn't have to relive the discomfort again.

"You're welcome to stay over at our house if your bachelor pad isn't ready yet. You will have to put up with middle-of-the-night cries, though," Violet offered with warmth in her eyes.

"You're so nice, but I'm really looking forward to settling into, uh…" Reed's voice faltered as he saw two familiar faces.

"Looking forward to…?" Violet asked.

Reed's head was spinning as the impossible walked toward him.

"Mom?" Reed called.

His mom gave a big, exuberant wave. "There you are!" she yelled. His dad was beside her. "We wanted to look around za town before we called. This is cute," she said as they walked up.

His heart was in his throat. He looked at Pearl briefly.

"Oh, fuck," she muttered.

"Hi." He gathered his mom and then his dad in a hug. "What are you guys doing here?"

"We were worried about you." His mom pushed his hair out of his eyes. She'd never liked that he kept it a little long.

"We couldn't come all this way, hop over the pond," his dad said with a smile, "and not see you, so we road-tripped across Pennsylvania. We stopped by the old house, and then your mother looked up where Luca lived and thought we'd surprise you."

"I am sufficiently surprised," Reed said, clearing his throat and adjusting his glasses.

"You were going into za bookshop?" His mom pointed.

"Um, yeah, this is actually the project that I was telling you about," he said.

He was on the verge of admitting everything. Everything that would unravel his whole life with his parents. The lie he'd started in fourth grade that he hadn't seemed to figure out how to back out of. "Uh, you remember Pearl, Luca's sister."

"Ah, yes. The angry one," his mom said with a smile as she waved.

"Hi, Mrs. B," Pearl said with a tight polite smile.

"Haven't seen you since we caught you smoking pot outside our garage in high school," his dad said with a chuckle.

"And you confiscated it," Pearl said, narrowing her eyes.

"That was a good weekend," his dad said with a smirk at his mom.

"This is Pearl's bookshop," Reed said in a panic. "I've been helping her redo the interior. It's a historical building, and she wanted to do it right."

Pearl's mouth dropped open.

Oh fuck. It had just tumbled out.

His dad looked pleased. "Well, that's great. I'm glad to hear it. Not that you're taking off work, but it's for a good cause. Gems like these are few and far between nowadays."

Violet stood beside Pearl, looking at Reed with a hopeful smile.

He gulped. "And this is, um, this is my...friend, Violet," he said, pausing on the word friend far too long.

Not my sister.

His mom narrowed her eyes, trying to place Violet. "You look so familiar."

Violet smiled, though it didn't reach her eyes. "I'm on a TV show with my husband, if you like plants."

"That's where!" his dad said, excited. "We watched you on the plane."

"You were very good," his mother said matter-of-factly.

"That's high praise from Alice Berry," Reed said, feeling bad he might have hurt Violet's feelings. She'd been nothing but sweet and kind, even before she'd known they were related.

"I should get going," Violet said with a pained smile. "I'll see you later, Reed. Bye, Pearl." He looked over to find Pearl glowering at him.

"Violet, wait," Reed said.

"It's fine. I'll talk to you later." She waved and jogged across the street

"Wow, you're friends with a celebrity," his mother said, impressed. "Well, we've got to check in at our B&B down the road, but let's plan on doing breakfast tomorrow morning. Your father and I have big plans at a fancy Italian place this evening."

"Sounds good." He waved them away as they walked to their rental car.

He felt hollow. Disappointed in himself.

You just kicked the can further down the road and hit your sister with it in the process.

"What the fuck was that?" Pearl said.

He locked the door of the bookshop. "It's just for a little while. I can't tell them everything at one time. New siblings, me leaving my job, a new business, a new girlfriend. It was a lot to say all at one time."

She stared at him, probably seeing through his half-truths.

"You could have at least picked one. You hurt Violet's feelings. I would storm off, but you are my ride home and it's time to go watch AB while Luca goes to the shop." She stomped to his car, looking disappointed in him.

He'd chickened out. He'd had the perfect opportunity.

He just didn't want to lose that feeling he had when his parents were happy with him. It had always felt so fleeting.

But he'd tell them soon. *I have to*, he promised himself.

Chapter Thirty-one

PEARL

"Luca, I'm home. You can go," Pearl called as she shoved open the front door.

"Thanks," Luca said, already heading out the back door.

AB cartwheeled through the living room. "AP, I'm gonna watch cartoons in my bedroom."

"Watch the ones that rot your brain, okay?" Pearl called, shuffling through the mail she'd grabbed on her way in.

"Pearl," Reed said, pushing through the door behind her. "Let's talk about this."

She'd been kind of a bitch on the ride over—*okay, a huge bitch*—but he'd made Violet sad and he'd lied to his parents.

And he hadn't even introduced me as...whatever we are. I was just Luca's little fuck-up sister.

It wasn't the first time she'd been hidden from someone's parents, but she hoped it would be the last.

"Since you're so creative with the truth, is there anything you've forgotten to tell *me*?" she said, spinning to face him.

He looked hurt. "Of course not. You'd never judge me for what I needed."

338

She rolled her eyes.

"Pearl—"

She put a hand up to silence him as a pink envelope caught her eye. It was addressed to Blackbird Bakery from the Department of Public Health.

It had a red "Due" mark on it. She tore it open.

She was being *fined?*

"'Due to the risk posed to the public health at the Firefly Festival, please pay the following Public Health Department fines.' Those motherfuckers want five thousand dollars," she gasped.

Three various fines were listed for offenses Pearl didn't even understand. A lack of license, not properly handling food as a food vendor, lack of secondary insurance.

She was gonna pass out, vomit, and then scream, in that order.

"But they said I didn't need a license. We were a goods booth, not a food vendor," she mumbled, flipping through the pages. They and the organizers had decided that at the final registration.

"I'm sure it'll be fine. This sounds like a mistake," Reed said, placating her, as he read the letter.

She pulled at her shirt, not able to breathe.

"Hey," Reed said, concerned. "You okay?"

"No, it's not a mistake," she said, snatching the letter from him. "Because when you're a fuck-up, bad things happen to you. The organizer said I wasn't technically a food vendor, but clearly I shouldn't have relied on a bow-tied man who didn't know what he was talking about. My credit card doesn't even have a five-thousand-dollar limit." The nest egg she'd built to try to actually do something with her life? Fucking gone.

Opening my own bakery was a terrible fucking idea. I should have never even tried.

"It'll be fine," Reed said, his voice still calm. "It's only five thousand. I can pay it for you."

"I need to handle this. It's my mess," she said, getting mad.

And defensive. And embarrassed.

"But I can fix it for you." He looked bewildered at her anger.

"I don't want to owe you anything. I'll find the money for it somewhere."

He shrugged as if she was being ridiculous. "We're partners. It's a gift. It's no big deal."

She seethed with rage. "It's a *big* deal to me," she finally yelled. "Why can't you be mad with me? I don't want to fight my battles alone for the rest of my life."

"I am literally offering to fix it," he said, pointing at the paper in frustration. "Is this really about the fine? Or are you still mad about Violet?"

I'm just Luca's pot-smoking little sister, a secret, clingy part of her whispered. *He's ashamed of you.*

He didn't even say anything to his parents about me.

This whole thing poked a giant sharp stick on the purple bruise of her ego.

"You're embarrassed about your life here. Like we're some place where a big-city failure goes. Where all the fuck-ups live."

"Pearl, I don't think that. Wait." His hands came to her upper arms, his fingers stroking her skin. "You're upset because I didn't say you were my...girlfriend? Aren't you?" Reed said, hitting the nail on the unspoken head.

His eyes could see right into her soul. "I wasn't sure what to call you. We haven't talked about it. I didn't want to assume."

But you told me you loved me.

Pearl shrugged, feeling caught.

And petty. And clingy. And mad.

She stormed into the kitchen. "What about when we have kids? You can stand up to random drunks in bars, but not your dad? I want someone who will fight for *me* when it matters. And I don't think you can."

She hoped she'd hurt his feelings like he'd hurt hers.

He gulped. "I've been fighting my whole life"—his voice wavered and tears shimmered in his eyes—"just to figure out how to live it like everybody else. It's like everyone else got this handbook on how to be 'normal'"—his fingers came up for air quotes—"but they skipped me. You, however, push people away and it's this quirk everyone loves. *Oh, that's just Pearl*, they say as they flock to you."

She scoffed.

"They do," he said, getting mad. "You think it's a coincidence people couldn't *wait* to order from you? To invite you for drinks? People don't *like* me enough, Pearl. Even my own parents, I have to be careful to be perfect so they'll love me. I can't lose the few relationships I have. They're too precious. So, no, I don't rock the boat when I don't have to."

She wanted to push him away, wanted to prove to herself he didn't actually love her, like poking a bruise to see if it would hurt. *Like an idiot.*

"I fuck up constantly. I have a hard life. No rich relatives to make *my* dreams happen," she added with venom, knowing it would be hurtful. "You're better off without me. No point in loving someone who fucks up so much."

She wanted to protect herself one last time.

"Pearl, I know you're upset. Let me just pay this fine for now and we can talk about it later."

"You're asking too much. This has all just been too much. You're being too…"

She stopped, but the verbal punch had landed right where she'd wanted it to.

He took a step back, rubbing his chest.

With a sad, longing look, he walked out the door without another word.

Good job.

Bruise? Pushed. Heart? Broken. Dreams?

Well, they were never for me anyway, were they?

She wanted to scream, cry, throw something.

Pearl clutched the kitchen island with shaking hands. Everything had gone to shit.

"AP?"

"Hey, nugget," Pearl said, trying to get her emotions in check as she turned around to AB. "Brain rotted ye—"

But Pearl stopped as she registered a broken unicorn piggy bank in AB's hands.

"You can have my money," AB whispered, wide-eyed. She held out the two broken halves of the unicorn that had inspired her obsession—a chunky purple piggy bank—as pennies and quarters spilled to the tile.

Pearl's heart shattered into a thousand tiny blackened pennies as she took the sharp porcelain from her.

A small trickle of blood ran down AB's fingers. She'd cut herself breaking it open.

Oh no oh no. "Oh sweetie, don't move."

Pearl's heart was in her throat, and her fingers shook as she grabbed band-aids and antiseptic.

I literally hurt AB by not keeping my shit together.

"Were you eavesdropping?" Pearl asked gently as she cleaned AB's fingers.

AB nodded her head, pouting. "You need money."

Pearl put two band-aids on AB's fingers and pulled AB into her lap. "Annabelle, you don't *ever* have to worry about that, okay? I will always figure it out, and your dad will always take care of you."

She pushed AB's hair back as a tear fell down her little cheek.

"I broke my unicorn." AB's face melted into a sob. "I mess't-up." Her cracked voice crushed all the breath out of Pearl's body.

Pearl fought back tears.

She tucked AB's head under her chin and rocked her. "Sweetie, we all mess up. I do it all the time."

"But you—won't—love me," AB hiccuped.

"What?" Pearl looked at her in utter confusion.

"You messed up and Uncle Reed can't love you."

Well, fuck. Why did little ears have to hear so well?

"Hey, I promise you, best-friend-pink-ring promise"—Pearl held up her pink rubber ring to the matching one on AB's hand—"you can make a bajillion mistakes and I will still love you. Promise."

AB sniffed and nodded. "You can do a bajillion, too?"

She saw a lot of herself in AB. She was a weird, smart little girl who liked creepy doll heads, had obsessive interests, and a larger frame with a cute little belly like Pearl had had at her age.

She would never lie to her.

She'd never want AB to think that she shouldn't believe in herself just because she made a few mistakes. Or a lot.

She wanted AB to *love* herself. Wanted her to know she was perfect and to reach for anything she wanted in life.

Who won when you didn't like yourself? The patriarchy? The benefactors of a capitalist hellscape?

Maybe even if I'm the only one who loves me, maybe that's enough. Maybe that's more important than anybody else, actually.

Being your number one fan does seem like sort of a punk move.

"Yeah. I guess I can make mistakes. You're pretty smart, huh, kid?" She squeezed AB to her, bouncing her until she giggled. She kissed her forehead.

She could make a thousand more mistakes and people would still like her. The important people, like AB, and Luca.

And maybe Reed.

But she had to figure out how to fix her own mistakes. *If I'm good at making them, I gotta be good at fixing them.*

The Parkers were smart, and they'd always encouraged her.

Bloom carried all sorts of chocolates and locally made things. They could carry her stuff too, right? That would help make a dent in the fine if the Health Department wouldn't waive it.

She sighed as she held a still sniffling AB, plotting out how she could make all her fuck-ups right.

Chapter Thirty-Two

REED

Reed sat in his car outside of Bookish, numb. He'd driven back on autopilot.

The one person who he thought could love him just as he was…

Thought he was too much.

And her name is on the goddamn door.

He hadn't been brave enough to tell his parents the truth and had lost the one person who mattered. On top of that, he'd loved too hard and pushed too much.

First thing was first, he had to apologize to Violet. She'd been nothing but supportive and sweet since he'd moved to Fairwick Falls. His gut churned as he walked to Bloom.

As he reached for the antique knob, Rose pushed open the door with a cold look.

"Hey," he said with a smile.

"Hi," she said. Her response was curt.

"Is Violet in there? I need to talk to her."

"Why don't you talk to me first?" She locked her arm through his and spun him around back toward Main Street. "Violet needs some time."

"My parents surprised me and she was there. I panicked and didn't say anything about you all, and I think I hurt her feelings. I feel so awful."

Rose patted his arm. "It's my job to protect her—all of you—and you *did* hurt her feelings. So." Her smile was cold. "Now you get to deal with me."

"Fuck," he muttered, hating the thought of hurting Violet.

You never should have agreed to this. You knew you'd screw it up.

You knew you'd disappoint somebody, make them feel weird, be weird. This is why you didn't want sisters.

"Let's take a walk," Rose said, nodding her head in the direction of a small park outside the town square.

It was a pretty summer day. A nice breeze cut through the humidity, families were out eating ice cream cones, people were jogging.

The day was perfect, except he'd somehow managed to fuck everything up.

They walked in silence for a while. Reed wasn't sure what to even say.

"So, you gonna tell me what the deal is with eating now?" Rose said, not looking at him as they walked.

God, she was a ballbuster.

He ran his hands through his hair. "I didn't want to make anyone uncomfortable or feel sorry for me, so I figured it would be easier not to mention it."

She raised an eyebrow at him.

Reluctantly, he explained the gist of his misophonia.

"Hmm." She nodded. "I have a little bit of that, but it's not as bad. I love my husband dearly, but every time he eats chips, it's like his head is one of those satellite dishes that blasts a laser up into space." She mimed a huge dish and the cacophony of an explosion.

He chuckled. "Something like that, but a lot more intense. I thought Lily was going to make me crazy when she ate a granola bar in Bookish before we opened."

"Why didn't you tell us? We thought you didn't want to spend time with us." She looked a little hurt, if he was reading her right.

He gulped, trying his best to be honest. "I just didn't want to feel like a burden. It's why I tend to shove stuff away. I just go along and usually people like me better."

She hummed in understanding. "Come on, I want to show you something."

They crossed the road into a small cemetery and walked until they reached the top of a small hill. Rose walked to a plot with lots of flowers on it.

He recognized the name instantly. Frank Parker.

"I didn't realize he was...here," Reed said awkwardly. He'd never thought to ask. He'd been too overwhelmed with everything else in his life.

"We come and visit sometimes," Rose said with a sad smile. "I never thought to show you. Is this weird?" She grimaced.

"It's fine."

She raised an eyebrow. "The truth, please."

"Okay, it's a little weird." He laughed. "But...nice."

"Our dad spent a lot of his time running from issues. He just avoided talking or thinking about them. From his heart problems that killed him to his issues with me where we didn't speak for years. The depression when our mom died, and the issues he had with his business." She sighed, looking sad as she dusted off the headstone. "He'd spend his days with friends, but never asked for help with his problems. Never dealt with them. I was really mad because a lot of those issues landed on me after he died."

The parallels were unsettling to Reed. Would this pattern continue until he died?

Would it be *why* he died?

The thought was harrowing. "That sounds really hard."

"When something's important, you suffer through the uncomfortable so you can make everything even better. I wish he just would have had a few uncomfortable conversations. He might still be here if he had," Rose said, pausing over the idea.

Rose swiped leaves and twigs off his headstone. "I feel bad for him. He had a good life, but it could've been great if he'd just dealt with his issues rather than brushing them away."

Reed nodded, processing it all. "I've never been good at being uncomfortable. Most of my life is uncomfortable already and so, I don't know. I don't want somebody to be upset with me. I never know what the final thing is that will make them say, 'Enough, go away forever.'"

Like offering to help the woman you love and making her hate you.

"Everything you want is on the other side of discomfort. So, how bad do you want it?" Rose said.

Reed's life had been a dream for the last few weeks.

He wanted the amazing life that he'd barely tasted.

It was worth everything.

Pearl was worth everything.

The one thing he really didn't want to do was exactly what he needed to do.

"Hey, Margie." Reed waved her in as he flipped his sign to "Open."

She still had her Canon's Diner uniform on as she booked it back to the romance section. "You got that new *Motorcycle Club* series I asked for?"

"It's on the shelf," he called, waving at her as she sped away.

After tossing and turning all night, he'd asked his parents to meet him here in the morning.

Finally time to come clean.

But—he waved at two more customers coming in—*it doesn't hurt to have a few customers to show them I know what I'm doing.*

The door opened, and his mom and dad walked through in breezy outfits.

"Hey, welcome," he said as they met him in the front of the store.

"Oh." His mother slid her sunglasses off as she looked around the bookshop. "This is lovely. Is Pearl here? We thought we could treat you both to breakfast."

He gulped.

"Well, you couldn't eat, but we could treat her," his mother said with a smile.

Ah yes, this is why I rarely visit them.

"Pearl isn't here." He cleared his throat. "Actually, this isn't Pearl's bookstore. She's been a big part of it, but actually, it's, um..." He had trouble meeting their eyes. "It's mine."

"It's *your* bookstore?" his dad said, confused.

"I quit my job, took the money from Grandpa"—his dad sucked in a breath—"and found this amazing space."

That was shockingly easier than I thought it would be.

His smile was proud. He wouldn't let them make him feel bad about it. The morning sun hit the polished woodwork just right. The gentle murmuring over the low jazz he played in the store was cozy and perfect.

"But your career," his dad said, utterly confused.

"It was killing me," Reed finally admitted, a boulder rolling off of his shoulders. "I was overstimulated, miserable, doing work I hated. I couldn't sleep. The only joy I found was reading. Grandpa and I used to talk about opening our own bookstore one day, and it feels like he's still here when I'm in the store."

"Why didn't you tell us?" his mom said, looking aghast.

"I've never wanted to disappoint you. I was a lot as a kid, and me being an architect made you so happy. I've"—he took a deep breath—"I've hated architecture since my first camp in sixth grade."

His mom's hand came to her mouth. His dad was silent, staring at him.

"I never wanted to disappoint you, so I modeled my whole life after you, Dad. I wanted to belong and be a Berry. You saved us."

His dad scoffed, but Reed knew the truth. They'd gone hungry sometimes before his mom had fallen in love with his dad. She'd tried to make ends meet as a single mom, but she'd also had a difficult relationship with her parents and had been on her own.

His dad shook his head in disbelief. "You don't know the first thing about running your own business. How long can you stay open? Do you have a proper P&L? Is there even a demand for books in a town with, what, a thousand people? The last time, we had to bail you out."

"That was when I was barely out of school," Reed said, getting frustrated. "Since I started working, I've done everything I could to get ready. Courses on entrepreneurship, reading every book I could find on running a business."

"Why didn't you tell us?" His mom repeated, looking mystified.

"You haven't really believed in me, Mom. Look how you just reacted after you found out the 'lovely store' was mine? I couldn't let you down again, so I had to wait to tell you until I was absolutely sure it would be a success."

"You have so much potential," his dad said, still aghast. "All those introductions I made to my old coworkers. The internships..."

"You'd said this was a gem of a building yesterday. I saved every architectural detail I could. All the education was worth it to find and save my perfect place." He described the original floors, the card catalog, the curved walls that were original, the skylight.

He stood a little straighter as he waved at a family coming into the bookstore. "Kids love the treehouse corner I designed. People bond over books, cozied up in the chairs in the nook I added."

His dad still looked angry. "But that money was to continue the Berry legacy. Open your own firm when you were ready, not waste it on something that's already an endangered species," his dad said, waving his hands at a stack of books.

"Let me show you something." They followed him to the fireman's pole display. "This was a fire station after it was a library, but I kept it to pay homage to the history of the building and to showcase our personal stories."

A worn copy of an old picture book from the '60s sat on the shelf. It had been the one his grandpa had read over and over to his dad, and then to Reed.

His dad went quiet. A picture of his grandfather sat next to it with a handwritten note about why the bookstore was so important to Reed.

"I wanted to honor his legacy in a way that goes beyond designing cubicles and office spaces and parking garages. He was so much more than a man who made some buildings."

His dad teared up.

"The legacy I'll create is one where I'm *happy*. I've never wanted to disappoint you, but if my happiness disappoints you, then I'm okay with that. Thank you for everything you've done for me—the camps and lessons, therapy, introductions, internships, but I'm going to live my own life now."

"And you're happy?" his mom asked through a shocked hand on her mouth.

He'd make things right for Pearl next.

Reed's face split in two as he thought about Pearl. "There's not a big enough word for it. Elated? Ecstatic? I'm in love with Pearl. I think I always have been. She and I launched this store together. It's as much hers as it is mine."

His mom raised an eyebrow at his dad. "Told him," she said, looking victorious. "You were half in love with her in high school. Poor boy." She chuckled. "She's angry. I like that."

He saw Violet out of the corner of his eye.

"I also have something else to tell you," he said to his mom.

He'd apologized to Violet last night after Rose had put him through his paces. They'd hugged, and she'd understood where he was coming from. She'd even gone so far as to brainstorm with him on how to convince Pearl that she was perfect for him.

He grabbed Violet in a quick hug as he brought her over. "I'm sorry again."

"No problem," she said with a sunny smile. "We have our whole lives for me to give you crap about it."

"Mom, Dad, Violet isn't my friend," he said with a nervous smile. "She's my half-sister."

His mother's eyebrows shot to her hairline.

"Nice to see you again, Mr. and Mrs. Berry," Violet said with a friendly wave.

"There are two others," Reed added.

"Our sisters, Rose and Lily," Violet said, emphasizing the *our*.

His mom's mouth was open. "I don't know if I can take much more. So your dad was Frank?"

Violet nodded.

"Is he…?"

"He passed away," Violet said, smiling sadly.

"I looked for years. I swear." His mom shook her head in disbelief. "But then I fell in love and it all seemed to have worked out okay."

"Holy clover, I'm just so excited to officially meet you," Violet said happily. "Can I give you a hug?"

His mom blinked in surprise as she was enveloped by Violet's crushing hug.

"You'll get used to the hugging," Reed said with a warm laugh.

Violet was beaming. "I heard you love plants."

"Uh, yes," his mom said.

"Excellent. I can't wait to talk to you about it over the Berry-Parker family breakfast," Violet said with excitement. They'd brainstormed last night on how to make it possible for him to go to Canon's Diner with the rest of the family.

"You're not mad?" he said finally to his parents.

"You pretended that whole time to like architecture for me?" his dad said softly.

"It's just how much I loved you," Reed said, adjusting his glasses and feeling embarrassed.

"Oh." His dad pulled him into a hug. "I'm sorry you felt like you had to pretend."

He wanted to replay that again and again in his head.

"Want to give me a tour of the building?" his dad said with a tentative smile.

"Can I take a rain check? I have someplace I have to go. In fact, everyone needs to check out in the next five minutes," he called to the whole store.

"Here, I got it," Violet said. "I can close up."

"You sure?"

"I'm always sure when a grand romantic gesture is involved." She caught the keys to the store as he tossed them.

"Thanks. Having a sister's pretty great."

"It's just so I can butter you up for a kidney later!" she yelled with a smile.

It was time to go be a better man.

354

Chapter Thirty-Three

PEARL

Pearl chewed on the inside of her cheek as she waited... and waited.

Annnd waited.

Damn, Rose takes a long time to eat a fucking cookie.

"So, what do you think?" Pearl said nervously.

Rose's taste was impeccable. She, Lily, and Violet had started an empire, taking rundown flower shops and rebranding them, making a larger franchise. Bloom had local chocolates, lotions, crafts, and gifts interspersed with all their plants and flowers. Pearl hoped she could be one of their vendors.

She respected the hell out of them for doing what they wanted on their own terms and improving communities along the way.

I should probably tell them that, but that's really hard.

"I think...I'm shocked this doesn't have regular cookie ingredients in it. It's great," Rose said, licking spiced chai frosting off her thumb.

"So you think I make good cookies," Pearl said, stumbling through her pitch.

I can do this. That's what Reed would say if he was here. She kind of wished he was here, even though things were still weird between them.

It had been odd not seeing him for over twenty-four hours. They'd spent practically every minute together the last seven weeks.

Rose angled her head in confusion. "Is there something you wanted to talk about? Like selling these in the store?"

"I want to sell in the store," Pearl said at the same time Rose did.

Wait, what?

Rose considered it for a split second. "Sure," she said with a casual shrug.

"They'd need to be refrigerated." Pearl winced.

"Eh." Rose waved her away. "Lily can find some cute baskets. We'll label them and put them in the refrigerator. It'll be great," Rose said, snagging another cookie for the road as she took off through the store.

"Oh, well, thanks," Pearl said. "Um, there's one other thing I wanted to talk about, though."

"Is it the fact that you need to stop working for us because you're gonna be full-time with Reed and your own bakery?" Rose said, smiling over her shoulder as she tapped away at her phone.

Holy shit.

"Are you a witch?" Pearl said, totally taken aback.

Rose laughed. "Nah." She holstered her phone. "The writing's been on the wall for a while. Obviously, we'd love for you to stay as a part-time driver, but something tells me your heart's in other places."

Pearl sighed. She didn't know where her heart was these days. "You deserve to have somebody who actually *likes* flowers working at your flower shop. Can I let you know when my last few weeks will be?"

"Sure," Rose said as she grabbed her stuff to leave.

"You're not mad?" Pearl asked. She'd been the first employee the Parkers had hired, and they'd taken a chance on her—the girl with an attitude and no references.

"No. Plus, now we have a brother we can draft to help," Rose said with a wicked smile.

Pearl was so jealous that Reed had this woman as a sister. She was cool, tough as balls, successful, and though she had a tough exterior like Pearl did, she was *actually* nice underneath.

Allison was lovely but still had a bad taste in her mouth about men from her divorce. None of Pearl's other friends at the Thirsty Beaver could give any solid relationship advice. Maybe Rose, being the married, bad bitch she was, could help.

"Can I ask you a personal question?" Pearl asked.

"As long as you don't mind walking me out to my car." Rose was constantly in motion, like one of those swinging ball things rich lawyers had on their desks.

"How did you know Gray was the one?" Pearl asked.

"Oh, god," Rose stopped, thinking, looking like she was trying to remember. "He loved all the bad things about me, appreciated all the good things. Ultimately, I was a better person after being with him. I knew I wanted that for the rest of my life."

He loved all the bad things about her. Reed's "I love your anger" echoed in Pearl's head.

"He kind of helped me get through my shit, you know?" Rose said, sliding into her sleek sports car.

Pearl nodded. She'd always liked Gray, Rose's husband.

"I'm sworn to secrecy, but...I'm sure whoever you're thinking about"—Rose peered over her sunglasses with a pointed look—"probably feels the same way about you." She winked at Pearl as she started the car.

"You're pretty good at this advice shit," Pearl said over the roar of the sports car's engine.

"It comes with the territory of big sister. And, big sister-in-law...in case you were curious." A teasing smile tugged on Rose's lips as she backed out of the spot.

"Hey," Pearl called, feeling overwhelmed with gratitude. "Thanks. For taking a chance on me." That was all her emotions would let her get out before her eyes blurred with tears and her throat caught.

She swallowed them, trying not to let it show.

"I bet on smart people with good hearts," Rose called back. "And you're one of 'em." She waved and took off.

A glow lit inside Pearl's chest. Hot damn. She was going to sell her stuff in a fancy-ass store.

Pearl hefted the heavy bag on her shoulder. It held the stupid fucking piece of paper she needed to deal with next.

Step one on becoming a self-loving badass? Crushed it.

Step two? Find old Mr. Bow Tie Guy and drag him to the Public Health Department to contest these stupid-ass fines.

Eight flights of stairs later, wandering through the courthouse, Pearl huffed up to the Public Health Department by herself.

Honestly, why was the fucking County Commissioner in charge of everything? Ugh, small-town living.

Bow Tie Guy was nowhere to be found, and threatening government employees with blackmail and baked goods hadn't produced any results.

She'd just have to handle this herself.

And me, fresh out of fake blood capsules.

She paused in the stairwell, trying to catch her breath, when she heard a familiar voice.

"I'm not leaving until you waive the discriminatory fine for my business partner," Reed's voice echoed.

His business partner? Pearl peeked around the corner in confusion.

A motley crew surrounded Reed, and they stared at Pecan Man who looked pink-faced with anger. Aaron, Nash, Mrs. Maroo-Canon, and Tiny all flanked Reed who stood in the middle.

"My business partner was targeted with unfair fines at the Firefly Festival despite no one else having to meet those requirements. Citation 24.0.1, 1B-1.4, and 57 Form A," Reed said in a clear, firm voice.

"We were a food vendor at the festival," Aaron piped in, "and Fox and Forrest didn't have to fill out any of those forms."

"Well," Pecan Man scoffed. "We know you; you've passed all other inspections in your restaurant just fine."

"I didn't have to either," Pop jumped in from behind Tiny.

Pop is here for me? Pearl thought, getting mushy.

"Now, Pop," Pecan Man said, "You're an institution."

"So." Nash leaned up into the counter. His imposing six-and-a-half-foot height towered over the weaselly Pecan Man. "As the sponsor of the upcoming Strawberry Shortcake Festival, the Fairwick Falls Credit Union will need to rethink sponsorships if you admit to openly discriminating against some businesses. I'm also happy to personally donate a *disgustingly* large sum of money to whoever runs against you in the next election."

Pecan Man's face drained.

Nash had a *lot* of money.

"Ooh, maybe *you* should run, Nash," Aaron said with a wicked grin.

"Hm," Nash said, smiling, "maybe I should."

Pecan Man looked rather nervous at that comment.

Mrs. Maroo-Canon leaned against the counter. Her rhinestone glasses were a bright red today, only outshone by her bright red lips. "I'm prepared to represent both Reed and his business partner as their legal counsel in a discrimination suit. If half the things he's told me are true, you wouldn't be allowed to plunge a toilet in the courthouse when I'm through with you. *And*, Bobby Snodgrass"—she pointed a finger at Pecan Man—"I will happily call your mother and tell her what a little ass you are."

Bobby/Pecan Man gulped.

"Yeah." A large bark of a sound came from Tiny, who had stood in the back with his arms crossed. "Pearl didn't do nothin' wrong."

Bobby flinched when Tiny stepped closer.

Pearl's heart swelled. Reed was standing up for her, and he'd somehow found a bunch of people that believed in her, too.

"We'll investigate and get back to you," Bobby said, reaching for the rolling window.

Reed slammed his hand against it, stopping him.

"I'm not leaving until you waive the fines. I will happily wait all day, and the next day, and the next day until I am your worst nightmare. And did I mention that your boss, the mayor, is my biggest customer? I'd happily call in whatever favor is needed to make sure you won't do this again to anyone else."

Reed wasn't taking no for an answer.

Pearl's jaw dropped, and to be honest, her pussy clenched, too.

Bobby looked at Reed for a long moment. Pearl couldn't see his face, but Reed stood a little straighter.

"Beulah," Bobby called. Beulah walked in around the corner and jumped at the crowd. "We misfiled the issues for the Blackbird Bakery. You can just delete those from the system. Must have been a mistake. All right, I hope you fine folks have a great rest of your day." He tried to pull down the window cover, but Reed didn't budge.

"*And* you'll remove Beulah from public-facing duties. This

isn't the first time she's used her power to pick on people she doesn't like."

Mrs. Maroo-Canon tapped her nails lazily on the counter. "I have plenty of time to happily subpoena every single document to prove fraudulent activity in this department, and then you can kiss that reelection goodbye, can't you, Bobby?"

"Fine," Bobby said. "She'll be put on a leave of absence." Reed moved and Bobby slammed the window down.

"Wow," Reed said, turning around, looking relieved. "Thank you all so much."

Mrs. Maroo-Canon had already started for the staircase. "Oh, I was happy to give that used Swiffer mop a piece of my mind, honestly. The shit he used to pull as a boy…"

They were all walking toward her. *Oh shit, oh shit.* She looked over the railing. The only place to go was down four flights of stairs. *I can't go down them because then they'll know I heard them.*

"Hey, girl!" Aaron said from the corner, catching her panicking on all fours and peeking around the corner. "We were just talking about you."

"There's our woman of the hour," Mrs. Maroo-Canon said, pinching Pearl's cheek. "I am so proud of you."

Pearl wanted to die of embarrassment, even though she kind of loved it.

"You were all here for me?" Pearl winced, expecting the inevitable guilt trip. Her eyes connected with Reed's in the back, his smile warm and apologetic.

"Well, we just want to help," Mrs. Maroo-Canon said as she and Pop started walking down the stairs.

"Reed said you want to expand. Maybe you could sell some of your stuff at the cafe. You know, like a grab-and-go thing," Aaron said as they ambled down the flights of stairs together.

"That's a good idea," Pops said over his shoulder. "Maybe you could make some gluten-free pancakes and we could freeze 'em. I always feel bad that I don't have anything for folks, but I've never been able to figure out a good batter." Pops shrugged, going down the stairs nimbly for somebody who was easily in his eighties.

"We could talk to Dave about adding some snacks at the Beaver," Tiny said behind her. "Sometimes you just want something a little sweet to go with your light beer, you know?" Heads nodded back in agreement.

Ideas kept ping-ponging past her as they walked down the steps, her issues now having miraculously vanished.

Her bag felt lighter for some reason; the pink envelope no longer had any power over her.

Neither does Beulah.

She hung back, waiting for Reed once they'd gotten outside the courthouse.

As Nash walked by her, he gave her a nod. "He's a keeper," he whispered and thwacked her arm with a friendly smile.

"Did he tell you to say that?" Pearl said over her shoulder.

"Nope," Nash said, rolling a toothpick lazily in his mouth as he walked toward the Fairwick Falls Credit Union office. "I just know how busy my day was today and how much arm-twisting it took to get me out of my office," he called as he walked away.

"Now, you two get inside before it starts raining. My left knee is never wrong," Pop added as he walked back to the diner.

Pearl could feel Reed next to her before she knew he was there.

"Hi," he said, his voice low and intimate. He looked nervous.

I'm gonna crumple like an old dollar bill. How could she ever stay mad at that face? The one who looked so nervous to make her happy?

"Hi," she said back, lost in his eyes.

"I don't know how much you heard, but, um..." He scratched

the back of his head. "The fines are gone. They basically all but admitted to targeting you, and me to some extent."

She bit her lip, nodding. The weight lifting off her shoulders made her feel giddy. "I heard everything. It was very sexy," she admitted with a laugh.

"Thank you," he said, the word coming out almost as a sob. He looked torn and grateful and so handsome. "Thank you for pushing me to be who I really am. I'm so sorry I let you down, that I let Violet down. I was so used to hanging onto scraps of the relationships I could get my whole life that I never thought that would ruin the few good things that have ever happened to me. I told my parents everything."

She sucked in a breath. "And..."

He bit his lip as it wobbled. "Pearl, they *apologized*. For making me feel like I couldn't be myself. That's the best gift you could ever give me." He shook his head in disbelief. "And I told them I'm in love with you. My mom really likes that you're angry, too."

She laughed, wiping away a tear that had dropped onto her cheek.

He took her hand. "I will fight for you. I'll fight City Hall, I will fight Beulah, I'll even fight you as long as you want me, if that's what it takes to convince you that you are perfect for me. I came alive when I met the *real* you. I will spend every day for the rest of my life convincing you that you deserve every good thing in this world." He pushed her hair behind her ear, his fingers lingering over it. "You are worth the risk of losing everything else, including the bookstore–"

"But it's your dream," she interrupted, not understanding.

"You are my dream. A life with you? *You* are my purpose."

My purpose. It echoed down into the bottom of her spine as she remembered the poem he'd written.

"I want you to have a spot in the bookstore until you have

your own bakery. You're also getting a percentage of the store's sales. It's our store, not just mine. When I told my parents everything, I realized how much of you surrounded me in that bookstore. If you're not with me, I don't want it."

This was more than she ever thought was possible.

He held her hands, gently rubbing his thumbs over her knuckles. She loved that he always needed to feel her, brush his thumb or his hands against her, as if reassuring himself she was real.

"Can you ever forgive me?" he said, even as she leaned into his touch.

She closed her eyes, savoring it.

"You were right. I am soft," she sighed, admitting the terrible truth. "The world is really hard for soft people, and I couldn't take it. I had to put up this spiky shell. So, I started playing this game." Her lip trembled as she finally looked him in the eye. "If I beat the world to the punch and said I wasn't lovable, no one could have the upper hand. If I said I was a bitch, then I won. No one pulled one over on me."

He looked at her with such love. No judgment. It was an overwhelming wave of warmth washing over her.

"But then I met this guy online, and he spoke my weird little language and broke down every argument I had that no one could love the real me. And then this guy I worked for—he was so annoying, you wouldn't even believe it." Reed chuckled, pulling her hips toward him, and she wrapped her arms around his waist. "He kept saying these things about me. Yelling that I was amazing and smart and it made me feel fucking *glittery*," she said the word with disgust.

"The audacity," he murmured as he kissed her hairline.

She nuzzled in. "Truly the worst. He was smart, hot, and successful. The real trouble was, I started believing him."

He sighed with satisfaction, and she finally looked up from her favorite spot against his chest.

"Being hopelessly in love with you made me realize just how far I'd fooled myself. I mean, you make me fucking giggle. It's disgusting." They laughed as he kissed her temple. "And I still like death metal, and I definitely want to fuck the patriarchy straight off a cliff—"

"You name the time and place, and I'm there," he murmured. His lips hadn't left her skin for a moment.

She hugged his waist tight, like he liked. "But I think I like this new version. Where maybe I can love myself some."

"A lot," he countered.

"Okay, fine," she said with a smile.

He tipped her chin up. "And even if you have a hard life, I will be there in every way in the hardness with you—"

"Dirty," she interrupted.

"—But moving forward, it's my job as the person who loves you to make your life as soft as possible."

She stared at him in wonder. How was this her life?

He kissed her sweetly as a few errant rain drops landed on her cheeks.

So, they'd had their first fight.

And here he still was, loving her.

He'd come back even after she'd pushed him away. It boggled her mind.

"So, now that we've made up, you get to experience the wonders of make-up sex—"

"Hey!" Reed yelled at someone in the distance.

Pearl jolted and looked over her shoulder.

Beulah walked out of the courthouse holding a cardboard box, looking dejected. They turned to stare at her as she shuffled past them to her car. The air was thick with an oncoming summer storm.

"Why?" Reed said, breaking away from Pearl. "*Why* have you tormented her? And me? What did we *ever* do to you?"

Oh shit. She'd thought this 'fighting for her" thing was going to be more theoretical, not something ongoing.

Fuck if it didn't make her just a little horny.

"This woman"—Reed pointed to Pearl—"is the most loyal, kindest, loveliest person I have ever known. And yeah, she's a little ragey," he said, straightening his shoulders, "but she would never go out of her way to hurt someone. So *why*?"

Beulah stared at Pearl in defeat. Her floppy bow was crushed against her ugly old suit. The lines on her face had deepened, and she looked miserable.

Why aren't I happier right now? This is my wildest fantasy come true.

"I just..." Beulah whined. "...I missed my husband, okay? He died, and I liked when the neighborhood was quiet. I didn't have to think about what I was missing. Then you moved next door with the little devil spawn and her big father, and I just wanted you to move away. I wanted to forget what it felt like to live life. But you were so *happy*," she said the last word with disgust. "Laughter and yelling and dancing. I couldn't forget when I saw it every day."

She shifted the box full of photo frames, a plant, and a gnome in her hands. "We met at the bank, Curtis and I," she said finally, as if giving away her final hand at cards as she nodded to the bookstore. "If it was still like it was, then a part of him was still there. When you're my age, there aren't many things left from your past." She shook her head, fighting back emotion, but turned with a resigned sigh back to her car. "I don't like to lose, and it got out of hand. But you won. I'm on administrative leave and I'll be home by myself. Listening to your disgusting happiness." She toddled to the car with her heavy box.

Reed looked at Pearl.

The ball was in her court.

She saw the ghost of her future in Beulah, a grumpy old woman who had no one and had doubled down on misery.

Who's to say I wouldn't be just like her?

Pearl's heart clutched. A phrase echoed in her head that Reed had said a long time ago. *Hurt people hurt people.*

"You know how you get rid of a bully?" Pearl yelled. Beulah stopped. "You *love* them," Pearl said, emphasizing the last two words.

Pearl gulped, standing in front of Beulah with her hands on her hips.

Love *was* punk as fuck. No one could tell her otherwise.

"Beulah fucking Spurgeon, I am going to love you so hard it's going to annoy the absolute shit out of you."

"Why?" Beulah asked with wide eyes, looking scared at the notion.

"Because hurt people hurt people, so I am going to treat you like I'm the grandchild you never wanted," Pearl said, getting in her face, pointing a finger at her. "Every Sunday? We're having breakfast. Christmas? Your ass better be in our living room eating gluten-free cookies. And on your birthday? I'm getting you the ugliest fucking gnome I can find."

The prospect sounded pretty fun, actually.

Beulah's toad-like eyes stared in wary vulnerability. "That sounds terrible." She looked darkly delighted at the prospect.

Pearl narrowed her eyes. "It *will* be. I promise," she said with a threat in her voice.

Beulah sighed, as if giving up. "Fine, but you're fixing breakfast. And I hate coffee, so you'd better shill out for some decent tea. I'll bring the bourbon." She toddled off to her car.

Pearl's body was vibrating.

Had it been that simple all along?

A hand rubbed her back, and Reed pulled her into his side. "I'm proud of you," he said, kissing the top of her head.

Distant thunder rumbled.

A fat raindrop spattered onto his shirt and another one hit her arm.

Pearl turned around to see Reed staring at her with a warm, proud smile as the sky opened up and rain poured down. "Now, what was that about make-up sex?"

Chapter Thirty-four

REED

The soundtrack of Pearl's laughter and rain slapping the pavement was one Reed would remember on his deathbed.

Pure, incandescent joy radiated from him as he pulled her to the bookshop in the rain.

They were absolutely soaked, and Reed couldn't wish for a better summer afternoon.

"Wait," she gasped, pulling to a stop. "My shoes are hurting because they're wet."

"No problem." He leaned down and tossed her over his shoulder, clamping a hand over her skirt. She squealed, predictably.

Fuck, I love that sound. Note to self: toss Pearl around more.

People walking with their umbrellas stopped and stared as he leisurely walked with her on his shoulder, soaked through and laughing.

"This is ridiculous," she called over the rain.

"It's how I love you," he called over his shoulder, fishing for keys in his pocket as he walked toward the bookstore.

He unlocked it and set Pearl down as he turned the knob, but a gust of wind blew open both doors the minute the lock unlatched.

Wind swirled in the entryway as the rain pelted them, and the stack of permits Reed had left inside Bookish fluttered in a vortex around them.

Reed barely noticed the papers swirling in the doorway, however, as they each stared at the unexpected, thrilling, perfect person in front of them.

Water dripped down Pearl's bangs and he brushed them away from her eyes. He leaned down, kissing her again as the rain pelted through the door. The water drops on her lips were cool. The taste of vanilla drifted on his tongue as he traced her bottom lip.

"What is *wrong* with you two?" Aaron called as he walked by under an umbrella against the wind. "Get inside!"

They burst out laughing and shut the doors, pushing against the wind of the storm on the slippery wet marble.

"We should clean this up," Pearl said as she walked toward him, looking as hungry as he felt.

The bookshop was dark from the thunderstorm, but Reed still turned off the lights.

"Later," he said, locking the door. His hands were already on her waist as he tugged her toward him.

His hand was in her hair as he kissed her, sucking her pouty lip into his mouth. Biting it, craving it.

He walked her backward toward the nook. He'd wanted to see her unravel there on his cock since her massage. He pulled the curtain closed on the nook window.

His jaw clenched with the cutting need inside. "Say it again," he moaned as his hand cupped her soaked breast, squeezing it.

"What?" she murmured, groaning and pressing into his hands.

"You said you were hopelessly in love with me." He captured her lips again, needing them like air. "I need to hear you say it again."

"I love you, Reed. More than you can know. More than I can show you," she gasped as they kissed. He moaned into her neck, savoring the words.

Never again. Never again will I spend an entire day without her.

He pushed her soaked shirt over her head, revealing the knee-buckling sight of her tits in a lacy black bra. "I'd really, really like you to try and show me," he said with a smile, sitting on the bench in the nook and pulling her between his legs.

He dove his face between her breasts, licking between the soft curves. The tops of her breasts were wet and slippery from the storm, and he lapped up every drop. He grabbed her ass for leverage, and Pearl raked her long nails through his hair, pushing his face in harder.

This is heaven.

Fucking heaven.

His tongue swiped under the cup of her bra. He growled, yanking it down like he'd wanted to when they were trapped.

"I've wanted to do this to you"—he sucked a wide nipple in his mouth and his cock twitched with the need to come—"right here for months." He breathed through his nose as he sucked hard, pushing against her so her tits covered his face.

"I wanted to ride your cock so hard when you gave me that massage."

"Gorgeous," he moaned, moving to the other one, wanting it in his mouth. "You could have robbed me and I'd still probably come from how much I wanted you." He sucked the other pointed nipple into his mouth, wanting to consume her.

A pulse of need tugged at his cock, begging him to come.

She moaned as he swiped his tongue back and forth, back and forth in his mouth. A hand snaked under her skirt, and his hands landed on a bare upper thigh.

He pulled back, momentarily shocked.

But she has on tights today?

His confusion must have registered on his face because she held up her skirt to show him.

"Wore my come-fuck-me garters today. For confidence." Pearl bit her lip with a mischievous smile, and her eyes were half-lidded in desire.

His heart fully stopped for two seconds.

A hand came to his mouth as he looked at the impossibly sexy, unexpectedly erotic view of Pearl's bare tits, wet from his mouth and the rain, thigh-high tights with black garters, and silky black transparent panties.

"Just...stay. Just like that." He sat back, hand clutching his chest. He closed his eyes for a moment just to be able to breathe.

He opened them again and a *"Fuuuuck me"* escaped him. Her laugh was lusty and somehow got him even harder.

"No one on earth deserves you," he said as his fingers snapped the leather garters around her thighs. "Least of all me. But I'm too selfish to stop."

He brushed his palms against her bare skin, swiping his thumbs under the garters. He'd memorize this. Would picture it every night.

"I can take them off." She shrugged with mock innocence.

"No." His eyes shot to hers like fire and she laughed again, enjoying torturing him. "Never, you little brat." He kissed the tops of her thighs, pressing his face into her.

"Please," he murmured against her skin, looking up at her devastatingly gorgeous face. Those big eyes fanned with dark lashes, button nose and pouty lips. "Please turn around so I can worship you properly."

She bent down and kissed him, pressing him back against the wall of the nook. Her lips were hungry, possessive, and her hands raked against his chest.

Her forehead pinned to his. "Are you okay, though? Aren't the wet clothes overstimulating for you?" She bit her lip with need, but her eyes held genuine concern.

Tears tugged at his eyes at how overwhelmingly sweet she was.

He'd just ordered her to turn around and have her pussy eaten, but she cared about his needs first.

"Hold these, please." He handed her his glasses, staring at her hungrily, and a little sob melted out of her.

He yanked his sweater vest over his head, never breaking eye contact. Then, one by one, he undid the buttons on his shirt.

"If we ever need money for the store, I'll just film thirst traps of you doing this," she said, squeezing her thighs together and pinching her nipple.

He huffed out a laugh and peeled the wet shirt off his shoulders. *Ah.* Static he hadn't even heard in the back of his brain went away.

"Better." He nodded and put his glasses back on, not taking his eyes from hers for a moment.

He dragged his lips against her palm, kissing it. "Thank you, my love."

He grabbed her thighs and spun her around. "Now, gorgeous. Spread your thighs and bend over."

Tossing her skirt over her ass, he sighed over the view.

Two thick, biteable, peachy cheeks with garter straps digging across them to her thighs. A black thong down the middle.

He bit her ass cheek, unable to help himself, and she squealed.

"Your next tattoo idea," he murmured, and she laughed as he bit the other side, hard enough to leave a mark.

Mine.

He spared a quick kiss for her heart tattoo before pulling her panties to the side.

Ravaging hunger drove his face into her, and he moaned as her taste hit his tongue.

So wet. She was soaked and he lapped every drop up with wide, firm strokes. Her clit was begging for attention, so he flicked it with his tongue. A high squeal squeezed out of her, and her moans built and built as he devastated her clit.

"Yes, yes," she panted, clutching the armchair. "Fuck me, please. Reed, I need you." Her ass pushing back against his face as he sucked and licked was almost too much for him. The view was too good.

Hard strokes on his cock over his soaked pants were an appetizer. He wanted to fuck her so hard. But he wanted more squealing.

He continued, flicking his tongue over her as fast as he could, wanting to torture her. Her face wrenched with pleasure as she fought her orgasm, even as she pushed against his face for more.

Her cries were higher and breathier. "Please," was the long plea that broke his resolve.

He stood and wrenched open his belt, sliding his cock into her, hard. She gasped as he yanked her hips against him and held them there, breathing through his nose to last longer than one pump.

"Goddamn, it's too good," he murmured, looking at the ass he squeezed in his fingers, balls-deep in her. "This perfect ass jiggling as I fuck you is too good."

"Harder," she moaned, clenching around him. His vision went starry as he threw his head back. Water from his hair rained down his cheeks, a cold contrast to the hot, tight perfection around his cock.

He smiled as he dug his fingers in tighter, pulled back, and fucked her harder, enjoying the view of her ass smacking against him. "Wanted to do this for months. Just like this."

In a trance, he could only think of the white-hot pleasure of her pussy as he mercilessly pounded into her, letting the beast inside take control. "There's nothing—better—than this."

She pinched her nipple as guttural moans wrenched out of her. *Need them.* He licked his lips with feral hunger.

He pulled out and sat on the nook, tugging her around so she'd straddle him. She sank onto his cock, kneeling on either side of him, and his lips crashed into hers. "I love you," he muttered as one hand clenched her ass, slamming her harder into him.

His love for her was protective, heart-wrenching. This combination of lustful claiming and deep, soulful connection was entirely unexpected.

Entirely perfect, like her.

Long fingers combed through his hair as she held his face, staring into his soul as she rode him. She ground her hips into him with every stroke, little sobs slipping through with each push. "Not a word"—a moan cut through—"strong enough."

She panted, wrapping her arms tight around him.

He buried his face into her neck as he pressed her against his chest. This was his heart outside of his body.

His person. His truest love.

He squeezed her tight with each thrust. *Need to taste her.*

He pulled back, wrapping his hand around the back of her neck, swiping a thumb along the tight cord of her neck. He pressed every feeling into his kiss as he claimed her mouth. Every hope and dream with the press of her soft lips. His tongue spelling unspoken promises against hers. Of their future, how much he loved her, how he'd do anything for her.

"You," he said, pulling back. Her pretty face was flushed, smiling and perfectly framed by his bookstore.

Their bookstore.

Every inch dripped with their love and fights and laughter. He never wanted to be anywhere else than right here with her, forever.

His purpose and his dream in one heartbreakingly beautiful frame.

He kissed her right over her heart, his lips a supplication to the universe to protect her always. "A thousand love stories across a thousand lifetimes could never compare to you."

Starry hazel eyes shimmered at him until a tear slid down her pretty cheek and she planted her forehead against his. "I need you for the rest of forever," she whispered.

It was too much. *Mine*, his hips said as they thrust again and again up into her.

He needed her, craved her more.

He ground her against him harder and harder. Their cries grew louder into each other's mouths, feral and beautiful and raw. Nothing hidden, nothing held back as they fucked and moaned and took and gave with a ferocity only known to true love and trust.

Harder and harder they ground, sweat pouring down their cheeks until finally, with gasping breaths, Pearl screamed out her climax into his mouth and he finally let go, releasing the tight hold on his need and filling her, making her *his*.

TWO DAYS LATER, a cacophony of overlapping conversations surrounded Reed, and Pearl squeezed his hand.

He was practically levitating, he was so happy.

"Could you pass the creamer?" Jack said with his hand held out to Reed. "I'm gonna need seven more cups because this little wanker was up all night." Frank, Reed's nephew, was bright-eyed and awake, despite the early hour of 4:30 in the morning, and was strapped to Jack's chest.

The entire Parker family—Rose, Gray, and Gray's son, who was visiting before his school started, Violet and Jack and baby Frank, Lily and Nash, Reed's parents, Luca, Pearl, and a very sleepy AB—all sat around the table of Pop's Diner at the crack of dawn.

Pop had made a special exception to open early just for them. Reed had felt only a little bit embarrassed asking for the accommodation, but Pop had been happy to oblige.

Reed could see Frank's photo staring at him from behind the register at the diner, and his throat caught.

How special a man would he have been to have his picture still up two years after he'd passed?

He still didn't know much about him, but he felt close to him here, somehow. He hoped Frank was a little proud of him for working through his issues and said a silent thanks to him for maybe having a hand in Reed meeting his three sisters.

A gust of wind blew open the door. The thunderstorm had continued overnight and Gray jogged to the front to close it.

"Okay, so you need a game plan," Lily said to Reed's parents, opening up the menu. "The apple pie pancakes are legend." She pointed out the local highlights to Reed's dad.

Violet was trapped in a conversation with his mother who was monologuing about her garden. Reed mouthed, "Sorry" to her, but she smiled and waved him away.

Jack pushed his seat back to get up, took baby Frank from the carrier, and handed him to Nash.

"I need to go wash my hands. Calling for backup, Uncle Nash," Jack said as Nash took the wiggling, happy baby.

"You still up for a game of two-on-one with this guy tomorrow?" Gray said, nudging Reed.

"I'm really bad at basketball."

"Don't worry," Nash offered with a teasing smile as he patted the baby's back. "Gray is, too. I'll take it easy on you guys."

Pop came out to say hello and took their orders.

"What's up with the B-team this morning?" Gray teased Pop, who chuckled. "We like Margie better."

"I'll try to flirt just as good as she does," Pop said in his gravelly voice. "It's nice to see all you kids together." Pop winked at Reed. "Frank would be real proud. And you're my first customers today, so you're the first to know the news."

Pop wiped a hand down his face. The table came to a standstill. "Somebody finally took me up on my offer and bought the place."

"No," Violet said with a sad sigh.

"Oh, it's not sad, sweetie. I finally get to go hang out with my lovely wife and retire off into the sunset."

"Who bought it?" Gray asked.

Reed's eyes scanned the table, registering the sadness. *This place must mean a lot to them.*

For some reason, Nash wouldn't meet Reed's eyes, and he instead fussed with his nephew in his arms.

Well, that's interesting.

"Some big company." Pop shrugged. "But it's been on the market for seven months and it was time. I've laid out some stipulations, so I'm hoping we'll keep all the good stuff and get rid of all the bad stuff."

"Like the pickled fish," Lily said, shuddering and glaring at Violet.

"That was *one* time and I was *pregnant*," Violet said, throwing her hands up.

They talked over coffee, Reed's hand never leaving Pearl's back or thigh or hand. Pearl had brought pancakes for AB so she could have her own since they hadn't quite worked out the perfect recipe yet for her gluten-free pancakes at Pops's.

"You happy?" she said with a smile as she kissed his cheek. She still wore the black lipstick, even at 4:30 in the morning. He'd decided to accept his fate as a man who would permanently have some black lipstick stain on him for the rest of his life.

"Indescribably. You are a genius, my love. Thanks for this moment."

She kissed him again soundly. "That was a lovely haiku."

He whispered into her ear, "I'll save the dirty one for after breakfast."

A sleepy AB crawled into Pearl's lap, and she tugged her close as Pop and Gray brought out dishes.

"Does everyone have the group chat? And their headphones?" Rose said, raising her phone with the air of a four-star general. "Ralph, Alice, you can't let us down," she said, staring daggers at Reed's parents.

Like admonished schoolchildren, they held up their phones and earbuds.

One by one, the Parker, Bishop, and Berry families all put on their headphones and started talking in their group chat as they ate their breakfast.

GRAY (BRO IN LAW)

So, no pickles on your eggs this morning, Vi?

VIOLET (SISTER)

ONE time. ONE TIME and I was SO pregnant!!!!!

DAD

These pancakes.

Thx for the rec Lily

LILY (SISTER)

Any time Ralphy boy. Next time, try the vegan
egg casserole

DAD

Oh, are you vegan?

ROSE (SISTER)

Tell them about the time you wreaked havoc on
the diner, Lily.

LILY (SISTER)

One time I wreaked havoc on the diner.

ROSE (SISTER)

😏 Such a smarts.

Violet (Sister)

Pop said he had nightmares about live chickens
running through here for weeks!!!

LILY (SISTER)

Coincidentally, I had vegan options on the menu
soon after

MY IMPOSSIBLY BOOKISH LOVE 🖤

i didn't know you were so punk, lily. respect.

Jack joined them back at the table and put on his headphones. He reached for the baby, and Nash waved him away.

NASH (BRO IN LAW)

Eat. Someone as athletically inclined as me can
do both.

JACK (BRO IN LAW)

You lose ONE game of two-on-one basketball
and you never hear the end of it.

ROSE (SISTER)

Did I ever tell you how Nash got the scar on his
cheek? Because he was a loooooser.

NASH (BRO IN LAW)

Pro-tip: never play Rose in anything sharp she
can throw at you.

VIOLET (SISTER)

This is so fun!!! We should do this all the time!!!!

REED

Based on my new love affair with these biscuits and gravy, it will need to be a regular thing.

MOM

Luca, how's your business going?

And so it went, the conversation weaving in and out of topics on the text thread, everyone joking and laughing as they ate.

He and Pearl had paired their playlists as he tried to remember this amazing feeling: being surrounded by everyone he loved and people accommodating him without question, without guilt, all because he'd just asked.

And because the woman beside him gave him the courage to do it.

Chapter Thirty-five

Frank had watched all his children walk out of Pop's diner in the early morning rain, fighting the gusty breezes he'd sent their way. Hoping maybe they'd remember him one last time.

People dashed, unseeing, past him on their Saturday morning errands and holding bright umbrellas. A squirrel even darted through him to escape, but he didn't mind.

He was so proud of the young man he hadn't even known about. Proud of his girls for choosing to do the hard, right things.

For living their one precious life while they had it.

"They'll do well together, I think," he said, feeling sentimental. "All of them."

A pretty brunette sat next to him under the gazebo, unaffected by the thunderous rain like him. She didn't even need to ask what he'd meant.

"Of course they will, dear. They just needed a nudge."

He was finally done.

All his unfinished business was handled after what felt like both an eternity and a blink of an eye.

Some he'd expected, some he hadn't.

"It's time to go," Ivy said, fingers threaded through his, and he pulled her up so they walked hand in hand. "There will be a lot less wind in this little town, though."

Frank smiled at his love. "You always did say I was long-winded." He waggled his eyebrows, and she chuckled lazily, at ease with him.

He took one last look at the little town he'd called home, looking lush and bright and alive.

The preciousness of life hummed in every blade of grass.

He hoped they'd never take it for granted. The smell of a summer rainstorm, the brush of a hand of someone that loved you, the gorgeous, gentle weight of your chest breathing up and down from love or laughter or tears.

He'd miss it all.

He smiled despite the ache in his heart.

He'd always hated goodbyes.

They walked by Bloom one last time, lingering as they saw all three girls jogging back and forth through the store, preparing for something special as they laughed raucously.

Love. He hoped that was his legacy.

Just love.

It's all anyone could ever need in this wild world.

And the shops on the little town square stood unmoved in a summer rainstorm as two unseen souls disappeared into the mist.

Chapter Thirty-six

REED

Reed dozed, drifting off into sleep as gentle rain pattered on the roof of his apartment overlooking the bookstore. It was a lazy rainy Monday morning, and he couldn't imagine a better way to start the week.

His legs were intertwined with Pearl's on the couch, and she had an arm around him. She lay half on him and he was in actual heaven.

It had only been a few weeks since her birthday but he knew he wanted this for the rest of his life. Lazy rainy mornings, the scent of her newest concoction in his oven, her things beside his on the nightstand and bathroom counter. Her smelling like his soap.

She stayed over most nights but not all, as she still loved her girls nights with AB. He hadn't wanted to spook or rush her. He was just happy that the miracle of Bookish/Pearl even existed, and thanked the universe every day for it.

He kissed the top of her head, nuzzling in as her hair caught on his stubble.

He'd never thought that the kiss had meant anything beyond a dare to her when they were kids. But he'd carried a small flickering hopeful memory that he'd savored. It had been happily replaced by kissing her in a thunderous summer rainstorm, drenched to the bone and cemented in a perfect love.

He squeezed her to him, sighing over the memory of it even now.

"I knew you were a cuddler," she murmured into his chest, nuzzling in.

He pulled the blanket over Pearl as she dozed on him.

He played with her hair, running his fingers through the silky strands. He inhaled deeply, pressing his face into the top of her head. He reveled in her vanilla and amber scent as he realized he'd never need to be away from it if he didn't want to be.

How soon? he wondered. *How soon would be just long enough not to weird her out?*

He needed to marry her as soon as she was ready. He wanted this every day for the rest of his life. Someone who was gorgeous, was his soulmate, and made him want to be the best version of himself.

"I thought," Pearl murmured, her eyes closed against his chest as she nuzzled in, "black belt cuddling included Walden being read aloud."

He chuckled, remembering their conversation from so long ago. He looked at the stack of books on his side table.

"Sorry, only Agatha Christie is available."

"Mmmm," she hummed happily, squeezing him tighter. "*Murder*, even better."

He reached over and grabbed a copy of *Murder on the Orient Express.* He flipped it open to the first page.

Her voice cut in. "So, when we talked in the kids' section before we opened...you said you wanted kids, as in multiple..." She cracked open one eye, looking up at him. "How *many* multiple?"

His gut clenched, and his heart beat faster.

Honesty.

Ask for what you want.

"I've recently learned that having siblings is pretty great. So, maybe two? Or three?" he asked, wincing at the last number.

It was hard not worrying about being too much, but he was getting better at it.

He'd loved the chaos of breakfast with three sisters, three brothers-in-law, a baby nephew and an older nephew (because they didn't do steps in the Parker family either, apparently).

Pearl sighed with a noncommittal hum.

"I was thinking four," she finally murmured against his chest. "Unless you think that's too much."

He smiled into her hair, elated. "It's never too much. I want as much of you in this world as possible." His heart was in his throat as he mapped out endless plans and timelines.

He pulled back so he could read her pretty face. "Did you, uh...have a timeline?"

She smiled as she kissed the side of his mouth and nuzzled back down into his chest. "We've got plenty of time. I feel like I'm right where I'm supposed to be." She sighed.

"With you," she whispered.

REED BERRY WAS IN LOVE.

And it wasn't with a bookshop, or a building, or a best-selling thriller, or even the idea of being a success.

He was in heartbreaking, gooey, lightning-bound love with the woman in his arms who loved all the broken pieces of him. Who smelled of seductive dreams and soulmates and his future.

As long as they both shall live.

Epilogue

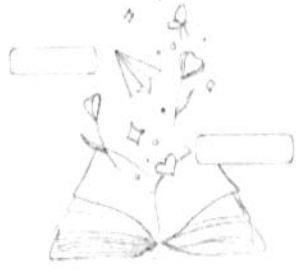

PEARL

3 Months Later

"Can I get a Murder of Crows chocolate muffin and a skull cake pop?" A bundled up young woman peered over the jet-black counter at Pearl.

Pearl glanced to see what she had in stock. "What flavor? We have bone-ash vanilla or bloodfire cinnamon spice left."

"Bloodfire, please."

Pearl handed two treats through the window of her tiny, jet black Blackbird Bakery camper.

Luca had rehabbed a little camper for her to take to festivals and she was in a prime spot at the 49th annual Fairwick Falls Fall of Fairwick Festivities Festival.

"You can pay the cute man with the glasses." She pointed to Reed who stood at the end of the camper by the checkout machine.

He winked at Pearl as their eyes connected, and it still gave her gooey, glittery feelings.

The last three months had been full of laughter, love, copious amounts of books and sex, and only a few tears.

Pearl had been a blubbering mess when she'd moved out of

Luca and AB's house and into the apartment with Reed last month. Luckily though, she still picked AB up from school most days, and they hung out at the bookstore, which AB considered her own personal playground. Pearl was happy to note that AB seemed to take after her aunt and loved books.

"Come visit our new location next month," Reed said, handing the woman a flyer.

Pearl's stomach flip-flopped with nerves and excitement. They were only a few weeks away from opening Blackbird Bakery's first official location. She couldn't wait to finally have her own goddamn bakery.

Pearl rubbed her hands together to keep herself warm as Allison stepped up.

"Could I get a Coffin cake?" Allison asked with excitement, clapping her hands.

"Sorry." Pearl grimaced. "Sold out. Plus, I don't trust you not to throw it since Wells is right over there."

Allison sighed. "That was *one* time. Fine, I guess I'll get a slice of the Witch of the Black Forest cake."

Pearl smirked as she loaded the cake onto a plate. "For eating only," she said as she handed it over. "I work too hard on this shit. Use mud like everyone else for your vendetta, okay?" Allison laughed as she went to pay Reed.

A man stepped up to the window next. "You know, I tried to get a cake from the Shop & Save but this little old woman practically slapped the cake out of my hand and told me to order one from you instead. Could I place an order?"

Tiny little demon, Pearl thought with affection, knowing exactly who the little old woman was.

Beulah had indeed bought the bakery building, but since Pearl had forced her into their lives (they regularly had boozy bourbon Sunday breakfasts now; it was pretty fucking great), Beulah had become her fiercest advocate. It was

Beulah's birthday next week, and she couldn't wait to make her the ugliest, raspberry-blood-covered gnome cake in existence.

Her line thinned out as dusk settled over the festival, and it was time for the pumpkin-chucking contest. She finally had a chance to check her phone as Reed checked out a customer. A giggle burst out as she saw his messages, sent over the last two busy hours.

HEMINGWAY_CANSUCKIT

I've been staring at your thick ass leaning over the window for

Three

Fucking

Eternities

My hands are itching to squeeze it, lick it, bite it. Something. Anything.

Oh god, now you're smiling.

Did you know that's my favorite thing about you?

You have these gorgeous, beautiful lips that curl and curve like a 1940s movie star.

Your tits are heaven, your ass makes me fall to my knees, but your smile?

It's unbeatable.

And now you're being so sweet with an older couple who need help.

My soft, sweet, gorgeous Bookish.

Gah, I love you so much and you are just smiling away, unaware I'm blowing up your phone

I'm so proud of you.

You are in your element, and thriving and I
KNEW you could do it.

"Did you know some crazy man texted me like twenty times about how much he loves me?" Pearl said with a glittery laugh as Reed wrapped his arms around her, squeezing her against him.

"Tell you he loves *you*? Sounds perfectly sane to me. Any man would be obsessed," Reed said, biting her earlobe and kissing her neck.

"AP, AP!" AB sprinted toward the camper in a full-body leaf costume, tights, and sneakers. "I did all my pirouettes perfect!" she said, peeking over the ledge.

Unicorns were now dead to AB, and everything was now dance-themed in her life. Ballet shoes on her folders, tutu bedspread, tap-shoe-themed t-shirts, decorations in her room, the whole nine yards.

"Did you crush it?" Pearl asked as she and Reed poked their heads out the window.

"I *murdered* it," AB said with dark delight. "'Livia said I'm the best back right leaf in the whole class."

Luca and Olivia, AB's dance teacher/Luca's new "We're not putting labels on it" walked up behind AB.

"She did, indeed, murder it," Olivia said with a warm smile at AB. "Just one more festival performance to get through." Her tired smile connected with Luca's, and he looked downright love-drunk.

Yeah, "We're not putting labels on it" my ass, bruh.

"Hey, you three," Reed said. "We haven't gotten your RSVP to the Halloween party at Bookish. It'll be a costume party," he added in a sing-song voice.

"I have trick-or-treating with Sophie," AB said importantly.

"We'll be there," Olivia said, staring with lusty eyes at Luca.

Barfffff, that's my brother.

Pearl liked Olivia, though. She was spunky, driven, and she adored AB for all her perfect weirdness.

"Just no animals this time?" Luca said, leveling a look at Reed.

The bookstore had thrived for the past three months. Reed still had crazy ideas, like a murder mystery party where Allison had accidentally gotten trapped in the bookshelf, or when a zookeeper came for story hour that did *not* go as planned (they'd had a missing monkey for fifteen minutes and AB still talked about how amazing it had been).

Reed tossed his hand in the air as he slid an arm around Pearl. "Promise. But you *do* get a gift bag if the costume is based on a book character."

AB pulled at Luca and Olivia's hands to go see the pumpkin-chucking contest, and Pearl waved them away. She and Reed rolled down the windows on the camper, shutting up shop for the night.

She flipped off the camper's outside lights, and two strong arms wrapped around her.

Goosebumps fluttered down her arms.

"I'm so proud of you," Reed murmured as he kissed her neck. She leaned back against him, savoring his warmth. She turned around and wrapped her arms tight around his waist. The comfort of his cedar scent and firm chest on her cheek relaxed all her frustrations of dealing with the public away. She was still getting used to it and only had one tense interaction.

But Jennifer winked at him so she can go straight to hell.

Or Ohio. Same thing.

She blew out a long breath.

"Thank you for being here all day with me. I know it could have been a big day for Bookish to be open."

He slowly placed a lingering kiss on her forehead, her nose, each eyelid, each cheek.

Each one lingered longer than the last.

Her smile was so wide it hurt her fucking cheeks. *I am such a dweeb for this man.*

Can't wait to have his nerdy, bookish babies.

He kissed her wide smile and pressed her back against the counter. *Yes.* She loved when he invaded her space and made her take all of what he wanted to give her.

Would never get tired of it.

He kissed down her neck, lingering on her ear.

That gooey glitter wobbled again all over her body as he towered over her, brushing his lips against hers.

She'd take this view for the rest of her life, please and thank you.

"You should know by now, my love."

He caressed her cheek, smiling down at her with the promise of forever.

"Anything for you."

THE END

Thank you for reading Unexpectedly Bookish!

Not ready to leave Pearl & Reed's cozy little bubble yet? To read a free bonus epilogue for this story and other stories, sign up for my newsletter at elisekbooks.com

AUTHOR'S NOTE

I'm so proud to show autistic representation in *Unexpectedly Bookish* from the perspective of a late-diagnosed autistic person like myself.

The mystery of feeling like an 'other' my entire life has been hard to explain, but I hope I did it justice with Reed's story. It's also worth noting that I wrote Reed as someone who likely has ADHD but wasn't diagnosed for that.

If you've read other stories by me, you've likely read ADHD characters (Lily in *Conveniently in Bloom*, Sophia in *Falling in Vermont*, Peri in *Hot Cocoa and Mistletoe*), and autistic characters (Rose in *Accidentally in Bloom*, Iris in *Fall Inn Love*), as I tried to channel my experience of both conditions into those stories.

Autism, however, is not a monolith. For every late diagnosed person who has sound and texture sensitivities, there is another whose autism manifests in a myriad of other ways. It's part of the beauty of neurodivergence, in my opinion. The strengths and unique thinking we bring to the world add color, depth, and innovation. And yes, sometimes the world is overwhelming for us (much like a blaring siren might be for neurotypical people). I thank the universe every day for noise cancelling headphones, weighted blankets, and soft, non-scratchy clothes.

I hope every neurodivergent person can find someone like Pearl who is thoughtful and nonjudgemental in accommodating whatever needs they may have. She is deeply inspired by Mr. Kennedy. 🤍

For other own-voice stories featuring neurodivergent love, I recommend Helen Hoang's *The Kiss Quotient* or *The Heart Principle*, Talia Hibbert's *Act Your Age, Evie Brown,* and Mazey Edding's *Tillie in Technicolor.*

CONTENT WARNINGS

Off Page

Bi-phobia, Fatphobia, CPS called.

On Page

Allergic reaction (EpiPen), minor injury of a child (brief), claustrophobia, panic attack, fatphobia (brief), bullying, autistic sensory overwhelm, parental dismissal of feelings, addition of new family members, scenes featuring kids, mention of wanting kids, alcohol use, cursing, sexting, oral and penetrative sex, rough sex, light choking, sex toy play, cum play, road head.

Acknowledgments

Thank you as always to my fantastic beta readers, my editors, and dictation transcriptionist!

Special shout out to the team of lovely humans who guided me through the process of getting a formal diagnosis of autism and ADHD this fall, and support in getting my needs met. It is entirely the reason this book is able to exist. Their patience and perseverance mean that I am back at a place mentally and can put books out into the world again. I'm itching to write the next two Fairwick Falls books! Everyone give them a mental high five!

Thank you as always to my amazing ARC team!

Kristina Holmes, Reed Towne, Sara Rawson, Persephone Hawker, Meagan Vogus, Amanda Brown, Kaylee Holland, Jennifer Gibson, Alexus Smith, Kailey Huber, Rachel Kent, Kelsie Wheeler, Terryn Winfield, Stephanie Toot, Katie Anne Ranney, Jenna Rhiannon, Melanie Granata Egan, Nicole Scarborough, Tiffany Amber Schwartz, Laura Jones, Kelly King, Bianca Sevidal, Rania Laham, Alizae Cratch, Grace Casteel, Laura Lee, Amanda-Jane Savage, Kaylene Ledger, Božena Stojanovič, Nicola Butler, Allison Thommen, Sarah Gwerder, Janina Majeran, Mary McCabe, Melinda Mauro, Thuy Cu, Chloe Simpson, Lisa Christensen, Oasis Donnelly, Jenny Ellis, Jen Williams, Jenna Baker, Shaafia Kasmani, Kailyn Glassmacher, Eva Bower, Caitlin Timm, Trish Meade, Cristie Lynn, Lottie Sheppard, Caitie Parker, Marianne Kay, Ashley Babineaux Medina, Susan Dara, Heather Kelley, Rachelle Leblanc, Cynthia Cabrera, Lyna Nguyen Stanley, Riley

Collins, Jennifer Castillo, Celeste Velocci, Chelsea Higley, Sam Nelson, Melissa Letts, Kimber Kennedy Alexander, Sasha M Fountain, Ashley Marie Vaccaro, Karli Jordan, Jane Litherland, Amanda Preece, Sarah Elyse, Julie, Jenna Coulson, Christine Fass, Lauren Giacalone, and many others!

About the Author

Elise Kennedy is an author of cozy, spicy, heartfelt small-town romances. She lives in the midwest with her (very) patient husband and two perfect pups.

Join Elise's private Facebook reader group to chat, vote on future books, and make general romantic merriment the small town romantics